NEW MASSES
PROSE, 1926-1933

NEW MASSES
PROSE, 1926-1933

A MODERN TIMES ANTHOLOGY

EGMONT ARENS, JOSEPH FREEMAN,
MICHAEL GOLD, JAMES RORTY (EDITORS)

MODERN
TIMES

TABLE OF CONTENTS

EDITORIAL PREFACE

When the *New Masses* launched in May 1926, *Time* described it as "a smoky vessel, ungainly but powerful, with daubs of red on her lunging bows and red marks here and there on her somewhat disorderly running gear." Created to replace two defunct leftist magazines, *The Masses* (1912-1917) and *The Liberator* (1918-1924)—both headed by writer and activist Max Eastman—the monthly *New Masses* aimed to breathe life into America's social and intellectual debates. Focused equally on artistic quality and social progress, the editors included veterans from *The Masses,* who had been writing and publishing since before the United States entered WWII, and new voices from a generation of writers, poets, artists, and activists coming of age during the post-WWI period known as the Roaring Twenties. Unlike the speakeasy party-goers of the Prohibition Era, whose interests lay primarily in earthly delights, these cultural producers were mainly concerned with one overarching question: Where is the world heading?

The fact is that no one knew—which is why the *New Masses* is best understood when we admit about the past something that we feel more tangibly about the present: the unknown. It is easy from today's perspective, when we know the history of the twentieth century and the trauma unleashed by the Soviet regime, to dismiss writers on account of their political beliefs. This is even more tempting when we can retroactively point to news reports available in their day and ask how they supported ideologies that oppressed the people they claimed to liberate. All kinds of excuses are given and many accusations are made—from willful blindness to moral deafness and even unforgivable ignorance. But trying either to condemn or to exonerate historical figures sometimes misses the nuanced parts of their efforts—the playfulness, the openness, the unfinality—all of the ambiguities that are part and parcel of creative expression.

The interwar period of the twentieth century was filled with more frightful contingency than we can fathom in our time. The political, social, and economic world order that emerged with the fall of the Soviet Union in 1991 rested on innumerable conflicts and horrors stretching back at least to the early 1900s. That the Holocaust was only the heinous climax of a century from hell should give us a measure of humility when it comes to judging the past. That today's world order—itself a fraught amalgam of technology and illiberalism—lies on shaky fault lines that are now moving under our feet should also give us pause when judging the present. But one way we can gain wisdom for the coming years and decades is to examine how earlier generations struggled with the unknowns of their times. Engaging with both their vision and their blindness, we may be able to gain some necessary perspective on our own blind spots.

The team that envisioned and produced *New Masses* included a mixed group of activists and fellow travelers, among them publisher and industrial designer Egmont Arens, writer and editor Joseph Freeman, illustrator and muralist Hugo Gellert, novelist and critic Michael Gold, cartoonist and muralist William Gropper, writer and poet James Rorty, and painter and etcher John Sloan. This group worked on the magazine for the first two years of its run, but tensions between progressive leftists and Soviet loyalists led to a split within the team. Those who were open to internal debate and critique increasingly received pushback from those who were active members of the Communist Party—in particular Joseph Freeman, Hugo Gellert, and Michael Gold. By June 1928, Gold was listed as editor and Gellert as art editor. This remained the case until July 1931, when only an editorial board was listed. By late 1933, as the Great Depression overtook most other immediate concerns, another shift took place: the magazine was repurposed from a monthly to a weekly, changing its mission from a politically committed publication of arts and culture to a magazine answering a growing demand for political news, agitation, and critique.

The Modern Times anthology of the *New Masses* covers its publication as a monthly with an intellectually open focus, ending with "An Editorial Announcement"—an explanation offered by the magazine's editors for its shift to a weekly. As the announcement notes, "The weekly *New Masses* will positively NOT be edited for a limited audience of intellectuals." With this, the editors revealed their past commitment to intellectual inquiry while also exposing their view of "workers and professionals" as non-intellectuals. This points, in some ways, to their limited view of their own readers. By singling out a need for a "swifter tempo of reporting, interpretation, and comment," they harmed the type of slower reflection that is necessary precisely at times of rapid change—making it harder for their readers to ponder the realities unfolding before their eyes.

Despite its editors words, *New Masses* had never been a venue for unengaged intellectual probing. It was always a magazine whose debate centered on a redistribution of opportunities—financial, social, political. Yet its very name admitted that masses change, that group dynamics shift, that no mass remains static. *New Masses* was always intended for those who wanted to examine how social structures undermined the security and freedom of underprivileged groups. It always looked toward a future that its writers hoped would improve living and employment conditions for the working class in the shortest time possible. But the complexities of WWII and the global Soviet threat to individual freedom made the fight for justice difficult to frame as a struggle for communism.

In 1948, *New Masses* stopped publishing altogether. But it can help us today in our efforts to develop a reflective perspective our own complex times. If we can see where activists of the past succeeded when speculating on their own times—and also where they failed—perhaps we can look upon our own times with more critically astute eyes.

—*David Stromberg*

A DIALOGUE IN LIMBO

BABETTE DEUTSCH

PLACE. *A shady bower in the Spirit-World.*

TIME. *The present.*

ANATOLE FRANCE *(very much at ease in his monkish red dressing-gown, with a scarlet Florentine cap on his head, and slippers lined with episcopal purple on his feet,—leaning forward to place his fine long hand on his companion s knee):* You have no idea, my dear Vladimir Ilyich, what a relief it is for me to be out from under the thumb of the good Josephine. That most excellent of servants had an incorrigible habit of editing all my contacts with my fellow-men.

LENIN: Of course! I didn't lose my *need of pressing,—restlessly turning his cap around in his stubby fingers):* Really!

FRANCE *(with a sly smile):* You seem somewhat abstracted, my friend. Is it that you do not relish the freedom which is the portion of those who put off, in the curious Christian phrase, the burden of the flesh? Or are you perhaps subject to that ache which a man believes himself to suffer in an amputated limb?

LENIN: You know Homer,—didn't Achilles say he'd rather be a peasant's hired man than ruler over all the dead?

FRANCE: Yes,—no doubt,—after all.... For myself, however, after eighty years I found my capacity for pleasure somewhat warped. There was even a sense of luxury in this laying aside so poor an instrument as this aged body. But you, like Achilles, were not trained in the difficult art of leisure. What annoys you really is your immortal soul.

LENIN: Immortal tommyrot!

FRANCE: This is one of those cases when it is not the noun, but the adjective that is important. We would have done better, we two, had we followed Pascal's advice. You will recall that he said that it is better to have faith, because if there should be a Hereafter, you have the next world to gain, and if not, you have nothing to lose.

LENIN: There your Pascal talks like a shop-keeper. *(With a short laugh):* As a matter of fact, all these religious fellows have merchants' minds. Come to think of it, what was religion in the beginning but barter in kind: I'll give You an offering of roast meat, corn and wine, and in return You prosper my crops. By the time you get to Christianity, as understood by brokers and stockholders, you have in operation a credit-system, involving the practice of certain middle-class virtues, and an I. O. U. of a portion in Heaven.

FRANCE *(gently):* The ghost is still an economic materialist.

LENIN: Of course! I didn't lose my mind when I lost my body. *(His irritation suddenly breaking through):* "Ghost" indeed! You will be talking to me of demons and angels next, like a Russian monk.

FRANCE *(with unruffled urbanity):* Why not? The older residents here tell me that this choler of yours is, if I may misquote Shakespeare, a malady most incident to shades. Who are we but ghosts?

LENIN: My dear France, now I know that I am in Hell. Nowhere else would I be compelled to do nothing but engage in metaphysical arguments.

FRANCE: One is in Hell as soon as one grows old: then even love becomes metaphysical. But on occasion, I have found philosophers entertaining. It is the thinkers who have been most fertile in giving a fresh complexion to the face of the world. The thinkers, and of course, the artists, too.

LENIN: I knew that sooner or later you'd put in a word for your fellow-craftsmen. You gentlemen believe that the universe is nothing but mud for you to make pies with. Of course, I don't know anything about art—

FRANCE (*interrupting obligingly*): But you know what you like.

LENIN (*sharply*): No. I haven't had time to think about that. What I do know is what we need. And that's more important. We need good reporters,—men who will throw a searchlight into the dark corners of our life. We need satirists, to laugh at our stupidities. But what we need most, right now, is a brass band to hearten up the soldiers, so that they'll do a good job of fighting.

FRANCE: You forget yourself, *mon cher*. This is not a speakers' platform in Moscow: this is a retired bench in Limbo.

LENIN (*sighing*): And so I talk as I used to do in exile.

FRANCE (*maliciously*): Since they embalmed you like a Pharaoh, you dream, possibly, of resurrection? Happily, I was treated differently. Do you know, I was scarcely cold, when the young iconoclasts published a sheet about me, entitled, *Un Cadavre!* Confess,—that is the fate you would have preferred. You are consumed with envy of me!

LENIN: Much more sensible. However, it's all of no consequence.

FRANCE: That is how you deceive yourself. Me, they will safely bury in the text-books of literature. They will talk eloquently about my master, Renan, from whose hands I accepted the torch without a flicker of the flame,—about my style, so pure; my spirit, so tolerant; my mind, so Latin, so acute. They will forget completely everything that made me human: my cupidity, my egotism, my adorable little weaknesses—I do not refer to Madame—but to *helas,* I forget their names, I remember only their little ankles, their caresses—Unless Brousson speaks. He was my secretary: the valet to my books. I was not exactly a hero to Brousson. But yes, I am certain of oblivion: I shall become a classic. You, however, will have no rest. Your dead hand will weigh like iron upon the generation that is growing up even within sight of your mausoleum. Your name will be taken in vain very time an orator opens his mouth, and my God, how you Russians can talk! You will be responsible for every crime committed against freedom of thought and of conscience. You will be helpless, because you will be canonized. You will be the father of your country, and of every taboo that is begotten by such a parent. Sublime paradox! *(Sinking into despondency):* What a subject for me, who can never use it!

LENIN: If I had blood, it would run cold listening to you. *(Comforting himself):* But after all, skepticism didn't die with you. And they can't take my word for Scripture, because I was not always consistent.

FRANCE: The Gospels are not always consistent. Yes, yes, I may become a bore, but you—you will become a bond!

LENIN *(facing France with a twinkle):* Why are you so anxious to make me uncomfortable? What do you have against me? You were a Communist, weren't you?

FRANCE: True. But I was also, as you have just reminded me, a sceptic. Both my Communism and my scepticism were rooted in pity for the race of men, those ridiculous and pathetic creatures, who, of all the animals, are the only ones to prey upon their kind, and who, being endowed with reason, employ it to torment each other and themselves. And pity, I take it, is not a virtue with you.

LENIN: A relic of bourgeois psychology. The young must be instructed not in sympathy, but in impatience, not in meekness, but in harshness, not in piety, but in courage, not in liberty, but in iron discipline. You know it yourself. The growing generation has a cruel, dirty, bloody job ahead of it, and must be fitted to perform its historic task.

FRANCE (*stroking his chin*): Ah, my dear Vladimir Ilyich, it is all very well for the young to be ruthless. They can tear down with impunity the bleak walls they had no hand in erecting. But when one has lived in the shadow of the Bastille of custom and tradition as I have lived,—even if one has spent one's days in lighting candles to disperse that darkness, one comes to feel that if the prison were down, one would miss the chiaroscuro that it made. Even I, who labored for enfranchisement with all the strength and skill that was in me, with how much expenditure of ink and excellent paper, and at what a sad loss of hours that should have been more pleasurably employed,—even I tremble at the thought of what liberation would actually involve. A man might raise his voice a thousand times to call down fire from heaven upon the Sodom in which he passed his miserable days, but if it were his native city, he could not hear it crash behind him without pain.

LENIN (*who has been listening with his left eye screwed up, and his right eyebrow raised*): If everyone who felt as you do were to turn into a pillar of salt, like Madam Lot, you would at least be of some use in the world.

FRANCE: The notion of being the salt of the earth is not a little alluring. But come now, have you never felt compunction about throwing the whole past into the discard?

LENIN: Have you never felt compunction about preaching water and drinking wine?

FRANCE: Now that is unkind. You know I never spared myself when it came to working for the Cause. How many pretty women I have disappointed in order to keep my promise to speak in some dismal hall to a crowd of illsmelling comrades! (*He sniffs reminiscently*). How many tender susceptibilities—housed in such charming frames, too,—have I not shocked, how many learned colleagues have I not alienated, how many exquisite moments have I not lost forever, simply to carry on the fight against privilege and to play the oculist a little to poor suffering astigmatic justice! I may have lived too elaborately for your taste, but for me, it was reasonable. I chose always the proper conditions for the creation of what the critics call my masterpieces. And you must admit that my writing was not calculated to please those in high places.

LENIN: I must admit I don't, to any degree, know your writing. Again, I had so little time for that sort of thing. But I'll tell you frankly that if you had come to me, while we were both alive, and asked for a job, I would have sent you away with empty hands. You're not one of us. You can't be. You belong to a decaying culture, and that smells worse in my nostrils than any unwashed proletarian ever did in yours.

FRANCE: Comrade, you are right. You think I talk like a philistine. And so I do. It is this vice of pity that is in me. I am sorry for everyone: I am even sorry for myself. After all, the bourgeois, as well as the workman, must suffer the aches and infirmities of life, of old age,—he too must become incapable of inspiring affection, and at last, for one grows colder with the years, even of feeling the divine passion. The bourgeois, like the workman, must change from a pretty, wicked, clever infant to an ugly, dull, good old man. The bourgeois, like the workman, like you, like me, must die and make an end. The class as a class is evil, but the individual is only pathetic. And I am still enough of an anarchist to be thoughtful of the individual.

LENIN: My dear France, you are neither a Communist nor an anarchist. You are an eloquent chameleon.

FRANCE: That is not true, for then I should be taking my color from you, which I do not.

LENIN (*glancing at France's clerical-looking garments*): You seem to be taking your colors from the Church.

FRANCE: You mean that I show such ecclesiastical tastes? It has been considered a pity that the devil should have all the good things. I feel the same way about the Church. I have ever been devoted to its gorgeous pomp. I always feasted upon the splendor of its ritual. My library was like a chapel, stained with the light from rich glass windows, crowded with religious objects. You cannot conceive the pleasure I took in sitting in that room, dressed in this monkish garb, dictating to some clever young man heresies as round as a priest's paunch.

LENIN: Yes, I can imagine that it amused you. It tickled me, occasionally, to sit in the Romanoff throne-room in the Kremlin, presiding over a meeting of farmers and factory-hands. But more often it just made me uncomfortable. Still *(reflectively)*, it was no worse than most of the lodging-houses I had to live in, one time and another. But that's irrelevant. The point is, for whom did you write your beautiful heresies?

FRANCE: For whom is literature created? For women.

LENIN: You wrote for the kept classes.

FRANCE: I wrote for the middle class. The aristocracy, like the peasantry, is largely illiterate. After all, a man does not make pots for savages who eat their meat raw. I wrote for those who would buy my books: the ladies of the bourgeoisie. And, unfortunately, for plain and aging ladies. The lovely ones, like the the stronger sex, have no leisure and patience for vicarious pleasure.

LENIN *(with a twinkle)*: And that is how you played—what was the phrase?—the oculist to justice? FRANCE *(with a shrug)*: With me, writing was a necessity—a painful necessity. What could I do? At least, I wrote as wisely, as wittily, and as beautifully as lay within my power.

LENIN: My dear France, you are a scholar. Tell me for how many centuries now have wisdom, wit, and beauty been cultivated by men of letters, by artists, by moralists and statesmen, by the whole tribe of those who were born with golden spoons in their mouths? And of what use has it been? Do you suppose the slaves in the silver mines of Laurium led more beautiful lives because Aeschylus was writing his plays in their neighborhood? Do you think that all the books in the British Museum, all the miles of canvases in the Louvre, have taken a jot of the burden from the men who got lead-poisoning making the paints, or from the rag-pickers who brought stuff for pulp to the rag-merchants supplying the paper factories? Do you find it possible to be finicky about the structure of your sentences, and anxious about the charm of your peroration, when you know that for an overwhelming proportion of the human race your efforts are worse than wasted? Is beauty a luxury reserved for the Villa Said, to hang about your chapel-like library, among your precious trinkets and historic curios, your wooden Madonnas and Tanagra dancers? Or is it a royal carcass to be buried in Westminster Abbey or in the tombs of the Medicis, for tourists to gape at, while ugliness and ignorance batten on the tenements and the canneries, the cotton-mills and the wheat-fields, wherever cities rise and earth is under the plow? We have had enough of wisdom in libraries and beauty in museums. If we cannot have beauty and wisdom in life itself, in the existence of those who do the work of the world, then civilization is as rotten as Aristotle and as mean as the worm that eats him.

France *(to himself):* Still harping on bodily death! How his embalming irks him!

Lenin *(who has overheard):* Yes, I'm a plain man, and I like plain facts. It's an equivocal business, this being a mummy. *(With a rueful smile):* And you do rub it in, you know!

France: The irony is too exquisite.

Lenin *(cheerfully):* But it is only a question of time. If only they make me tyrannize over them sufficiently, there'll surely be a generation of rebels to throw the idol down.

FRANCE: *Exoriet aliquis nostris ab ossibus ultor!* And so you still hope for death?

LENIN: If I may borrow some of your irony, it is, in more senses than one, the hope of mankind.

Curtain

THE FIVE DOLLAR GUY :: A STORY

WILLIAM CARLOS WILLIAMS

ALL the forenoon I had been thinking, returning to it and having it submerged again as more pressing matters were thrown over it by the tide: To put down, to find and to put down some small, primary thing, to begin low down so that all the color and the smell should be in it—plainly seen and sensed,—solidly stated—with this we should begin to have a literature; but we must begin low. It is not to write intriguingly, to fabricate a fascinating tissue of words (so I had been thinking) but to get down to one word where that is fastened upon the object, and so to begin to write—some plain phase: that would be story enough. But I did not then know how strange the common object seems when it is stripped naked before eyes freed from that artifice of seeing which concern for a clever literature enforces. ...

She was washing clothes in the sink. It was the second floor of one of these quick up, back street places, a home. There was a big middle room outside of which the stairs ran down to the street door. From this bare-floored center containing a coal range and a small oil stove for quick service, there branched out two bedrooms, a small laundry place containing tubs and the sink—before which the blond haired woman had stood—and a front parlor, closed in winter—where they had kept the fern for me one night. My goodness, is that you? she said. You always come at the wrong time. She wiped her hands on her apron. The baby has just had his bath and has gone to sleep. I suppose you want to look at his belly button.

Her elder daughter, three, who looked exactly like the husband with his half closed docile eyes, was standing at her side. The second daughter, clownish, always grinning like a half wit, but clever as a clown, was probably asleep in the closed bed room. We walked into the other bed-room—the scene of the confinement a week before. There she fished up the baby from the bundle it was in in the dark corner of the bed and began talking as she undid it. How are you getting on? I said. Oh, I'm all right except I get a little dizzy sometimes. But the old man is out of work again and Ma had to go home. I'm all right if I keep on working, but if I stop I get dizzy. Then breaking off, she said, I wish that sister of mine would have another. I hate to see only one kid in a family. It isn't right. She says if she could have them as easy as I do she wouldn't mind. The second one is usu-ally easier, I told her. Sure it is, you don't have two the same. Well, maybe she'll have one whether she wants it or not, I interposed. You're right, she may,—if she keeps on fooling with those boarders they have in the house the way she does. The way she carries on with those two fellows, making up to them, makes me sick at my stomach. Good for her, I said. Yea?

Say, I'm going sporting myself pretty soon, she continued. What are you going to do with the kids? I asked her. Oh, I'll get Ma to come down here some day and mind them. She knows I got a fella but she thinks I'm only fooling. I'm going out for a joy ride on one of those Mex Pet trucks. Say, you'd laugh yourself sick to see him. The house in which she lived was on a blind street near the railroad with a filling station for the Mex Pet Gas and Oil Co. at the end of it. There were several large tanks flanked by a row of old willows with a soccer field adjacent where the employees of the nearby Standard Bleachery Company—mostly Scotch—played foot-ball on Sundays and holidays. All the gas trucks passed her window—shaking the house heavily as they did so. Well, I said, it's a good thing to have a load of gas behind you when you go for a joy ride. What d'ye mean? she laughed raising her voice shrilly. You can take that two ways, she said. All right, I answered her, I mean it that way.

He's too old, she concluded, turning up her nose jokingly. (Clown is right, for that second youngster, from the mother's side.) How old is he? Thirty-two. *Old!* I said. Why he's not even ripe yet. Wait till he gets to forty. You're older than that, she corrected. Forty-two, I said. And your birthday is September 17, ain't that right? I smiled and assented, pleased. She had given me a palm once on my birthday. Thirty-two is just a young man. She shook her head. No.

You should see him, she added laughing and doubling herself over in mockery, he's big, a big German fella. He's married—and she looked at me a moment—he's got a wife older than himself. She weighs 165 pounds: they haven't got any kids. He's the half brother, or something of the sort, to the Boss down there. I don't know what—they both have the same mother but different fathers. Henwood, that's the boss. But this guy. He's so bashful he blushes every time I talk to him. I sure will have to give him a good bringing up before I take him out. But he's nice though. So you think he's too old, I reverted pensively. But she was tricky. Try and find out if she means it.

I was standing looking out of the side window down on the yard below. It thrilled me to see it. Nothing seemed more common or more bizarre. It flashed across my mind, what I had been thinking all morning.

It flashed across my mind that here it was, the inexplicable, exquisite, vulgar thing—rarest of the rare in the imagination, the trodden and defeated atmosphere of perfection. All while she continued to talk and to laugh and to blush with clownish pleasure and excitement, in her after-maternity-exaltation and release-to-enjoyment, I stood with overcoat and hat on in that uncarpeted room watching that yard unfold its grave and comical secrets: On a long slat-back yellow bench—exhalation of what atmosphere I could not guess—not even a nigger church—a bench fifteen feet long standing before a heap of weather-beaten boards, a bench of most exquisitely worn yellow in that colorless yard—upon this bench lay sleeping a large white mongrel covered with that curly, silky hair of a little poodle so prized by the poor. I say there lay upon this bench a large dog of that luxuriously long, silky hair loved by the poor, coat of their favorite dog since nowhere else in their experience is there to be found such another soft, delicate texture of richness—but a dog pure white only once or twice yearly, when washed. Upon this bench, leashed and sleeping was a large, soiled, silky-haired dog, mongrel breed of some waddling poodle and whatever he had found not too big for him in some field or alley nearby: the narrow yard of the ramshackle house next door.

SMILE :: A STORY

D. H. LAWRENCE

H E had decided to sit up all night, as a kind of penance. The telegram had simply said: *Ophelia's condition critical.* He felt, under the circumstances, that to go to bed in the *Wagon-lit* would be frivolous. So he sat wearily in the first-class compartment, as night fell over France.

He ought, of course, to be sitting by Ophelia's bedside. But Ophelia didn't want him. So he sat up in the train.

Deep inside him was a black and ponderous weight: like some tumor filled with sheer gloom, weighing down his vitals. He had always taken life seriously. Seriousness now overwhelmed him. His dark, handsome, clean-shaven face would have done for Christ on the Cross, with the thick black eyebrows tilted in the dazed agony.

The night in the train was like an inferno: nothing was real. Two elderly Englishwomen opposite him had died long ago, perhaps even before he had. Because, of course, he was dead himself.

Slow, grey dawn came in the mountains of the frontier, and he watched it with unseeing eyes. But his mind repeated:

> *"And when the dawn came, slow and sad And chill with early showers,*
> *They softly closed her eyes: she had Another world than ours."*

And his monk's changeless, tormented face showed no trace of the contempt he felt, even self-contempt, for this pathos, as his critical mind judged it.

He was in Italy: he looked at the country with faint aversion. Not capable of much feeling any more, he had only a tinge of aversion as he saw the olives and the sea. A sort of poetic swindle.

It was night again when he reached the home of the Blue Sisters, where Ophelia had chosen to retreat. He was ushered into the Mother Superior's room, in the palace. She rose and gave him her hand, in silence, looking at him along her nose. The she said in French:

"It pains me to tell you. She died this afternoon."

He stood stupefied, not feeling much, anyhow, but gazing at nothingness from his handsome, strong-featured monk's face.

The Mother Superior softly put her white, handsome hand on his arm and gazed up into his face, leaning to him.

"Courage!" she said softly. "Courage, no?"

He stepped back. He was always scared when a woman leaned at him like that. In her voluminous skirts, the Mother Superior was very womanly.

"Quite!" he replied in English. "Can I see her?"

The Mother Superior rang a bell, and a young sister appeared. She was rather pale, but there was something naive and mischievous in her hazel eyes. The elder woman murmured an introduction, the young woman demurely made a slight reverence. But Matthew held out his hand, like a man reaching for the last straw. The young nun unfolded her white hands and shyly slid one into his, passive as a sleeping bird.

And out of the fathomless Hades of his gloom, he thought: What a nice hand!

They went along a handsome but cold corridor, and tapped at a door. Matthew, walking in far-off Hades, still was aware of the soft, fine voluminousness of the women's black skirts, moving with soft, fluttered haste in front of him.

He was terrified when the door opened, and he saw the candles burning round the white bed, in the lofty, noble room. A sister sat beside the candles, her face dark and primitive, in the white coif, as she looked up from her breviary. Then she rose, a sturdy woman, and made a little bow, and Matthew was aware of creamy-dusky hands twisting a black rosary, against the rich, blue silk on her bosom.

The three sisters flocked silent, yet fluttered and very feminine, in their volumes of silky black skirts, to the bed-head. The Mother Superior leaned, and with utmost delicacy lifted the veil of white lawn from the dead face.

Matthew saw the dead, beautiful composure of his wife's face, and instantly, something leaped like laughter in the depths of him, he gave a little grunt, and an extraordinary smile came over his face.

The three nuns, in the candle glow that quivered warm and quick like a Christmas tree, were looking at him with heavily compassionate eyes, from under their coif-bands. They were like a mirror. Six eyes suddenly started with a little fear, then changed, puzzled, into wonder. And over the three nuns' faces, helplessly facing him in the candle-glow, a strange, involuntary smile began to come. In the three faces, the same smile growing so differently, like three subtle flowers opening. In the pale young nun, it was almost pain, with a touch of mischievous ecstasy. But the dark Ligurian face of the watching sister, a mature, level-browed woman, curled with a pagan smile, slow, infinitely subtle in its archaic humour. It was the Etruscan smile, subtle and unabashed, and unanswerable.

The Mother Superior, who had a large-featured face something like Matthew's own, tried hard not to smile. But he kept his humorous, malevolent chin uplifted at her, and she lowered her face as the smile grew, grew and grew over her face.

The young, pale sister suddenly covered her face with her sleeve, her body shaking. The Mother Superior put her arm over the girl's shoulder, murmuring with Italian emotion: "Poor little thing! Weep then, poor little thing!" But the chuckle was still there, under the emotion. The sturdy dark sister stood unchanging, clutching the black beads, but the noiseless smile immovable.

Matthew suddenly turned to the bed, to see if his dead wife had observed him. It was a movement of fear.

Ophelia lay so pretty and so touching, with her peaked, dead little nose sticking up, and her face of an obstinate child fixed in the final obstinacy. The smile went away from Matthew, and the look of super-martyrdom took its place. He did not weep: he just gazed without meaning. Only, on his face deepened the look: I knew this martyrdom was in store for me!

She was so pretty, so childlike, so clever, so obstinate, so worn—and so dead! He felt so blank about it all.

They had been married ten years. He himself had not been perfect— no, no, not by any means. But Ophelia had always wanted her own will. She had loved him, and grown obstinate, and left him, and grown wistful, or contemptuous, or angry, a dozen times, and a dozen times come back to him.

They had no children. And he, sentimentally, had always wanted children. He felt very largely sad.

Now she would never come back to him. This was the thirteenth time, and she was gone for ever.

But was she? Even as he thought it, he felt her nudging him some-where in the ribs, to make him smile. He writhed a little, and an angry frown came on his brow. He was not *going* to smile! He set his square, naked jaw, and bared his big teeth, as he looked down at the infinitely provoking dead woman. "At it again!"—he wanted to say to her, like the man in Dickens.

He himself had not been perfect. He was going to dwell on his own imperfections.

He turned suddenly to the three women, who had faded backwards beyond the candles, and now hovered, in the white frames of their coifs, between him and nowhere. His eyes glared, and he bared his teeth.

"Mea culpa! Mea culpa!" he snarled.

"Macche!" exclaimed the daunted Mother Superior, and her two hands flew apart, then together again, in the density of the sleeves, like birds nesting in couples.

Matthew ducked his head and peered round, prepared to bolt. The Mother Superior, in the background, softly intoned a Pater Noster, and her beads dangled. The pale young sister faded further back. But the black eyes of the sturdy, black-avised sister twinkled like eternally humorous stars upon him, and he felt the smile digging him in the ribs again.

"Look here!" he said to the women, in expostulation. "I'm awfully upset. I'd better go."

They hovered in fascinating bewilderment. He ducked for the door. But even as he went, the smile began to come on his face, caught by the tail of the sturdy sister's black eye, with its everlasting twinkle. And he was secretly thinking, he wished he could hold both her creamy-dusky hands, that were folded like mating birds, voluptuously.

But he insisted on dwelling upon his own imperfections. *Mea culpa!* he howled at himself. And even as he howled it, he felt something nudge him in the ribs, saying to him: *Smile!*

The three women left behind in the lofty room looked at one another, and their hands flew up for a moment, like six birds flying suddenly out of the foliage, then settling again.

"Poor thing!" said the Mother Superior, compassionately.

"Yes! Yes! Poor thing!" cried the young sister, with naive, shrill impulsiveness.

"Gia!" said the dark-avised sister.

The Mother Superior noiselessly moved to the bed, and leaned over the dead face.

"She seems to know, poor soul!" she murmured. "Don't you think so?"

The three coifed heads leaned together. And for the first time, they saw the faint ironical curl at the corners of Ophelia's mouth. They looked in fluttering wonder.

"She has seen him!" whispered the thrilling young sister.

The Mother Superior delicately laid the fine-worked veil over the cold face. Then they murmured a prayer for the anima, fingering their beads. Then the Mother Superior set two of the candles straight upon their spikes, clenching the thick candle with firm, soft grip, and pressing it down.

The dark-faced, sturdy sister sat down again with her little holy book. The other two rustled softly to the door, and out into the great white corridor. There, softly, noiselessly sailing in all their dark drapery, like dark swans down a river, they suddenly hesitated. Together they had seen a forlorn man's figure, in a melancholy overcoat, loitering in the cold distance at the corridor's end. The Mother Superior suddenly pressed her pace into an appearance of speed.

Matthew saw them bearing down on him, these voluminous figures with framed faces and lost hands. The young sister trailed a little behind.

"Pardon, ma Mere!" he said, as if in the street. "I left my hat somewhere——"

He made a desperate, moving sweep with his arm, and never was man more utterly smileless.

TWO FACES

WALDO FRANK

N the literary office of a certain magazine there is a vast table piled with books. "Mostly junk," the editor will explain. "Newly manufactured stuff too dull for mention." My hand feathers the outskirts and picks a volume with title: *Calvin Coolidge, His First Biography.* I am not permitted to speak of it here. Nor shall I linger wistfully over the so symbolic circumstance that a book about a living President should be a thing void of ideas, vile in composition, rancid and false in spirit. Within its covers, I found the portraits of two faces: one of the President and one of the President's mother. Thereby hangs my tale.

She was beautiful. She looks out at you in a black dress of satin, stern-cuffed in white, high collared, with a cameo at the throat. The hands lie demure in the lap. The hair is drawn tight and sideways to the ears. She looks out at you, not so much from the frontispiece of a book as from New England.

She is impressive. The sharp small chin is firm. The mouth is pursed, its prim lips faintly flexed into a downward frown. The nose is straight. It has delicacy; its nostrils seem to quiver not from emotion but from restraint of emotion. Under the plastered hair is a forehead high and ample: a square forehead which is the feminine form of the stern unsubtlety of pioneers. It holds a mind serene through exclusions, right through lack of doubts. The eyebrows are straight as a whip lash. Above them the flesh puckers like a girl's, ere the forehead's rigor claims it. But the eyes are deep-set as in some dark seclusion.

They glower. Their gaze is reproof. And their sight is a shadow. Pain lurks in them, muted and proud, and constant. There speaks a virtue assumed, a mastery willed: almost a habitude of judgment. The eyes dominate all. Under the girlish brows with their faint fleshliness, above the exquisite nose, within the contour both fragile and brittle which the folded hands whitely enhance, these eyes are paramount. Tenderness turns hard; frailty assigns itself master; weakness wills itself mighty. The result is a transformation. This face, so gracious in its elements, gives for its final word inhospitality and shutness. The result, in more personal terms, is Calvin Coolidge.

His face is the response to his mother's. She was the obscure farmer's wife in the Connecticut River Valley. There, as with countless other women, her loveliness had its begrudging bloom. Winters long as a siege, summers of swift fever, the inclement lordship of Puritan ideals made her astringent. Weather attuned to will hardened this flesh and drew the spirit down to the sure rigor of material affairs. Virtue became a saying of Nay and an economic cunning. Poetry took property for symbol. And so at last, on a certain Fourth of July, this daughter of New England gave birth to Calvin Coolidge. Not she alone. A whole decadent Puritan tradition gave birth to him; fathered his spirit; moulded his memorable face.

The little man waxed great. And as he grew, his face became the caricature of his mother's fairness. It is a caricature horrible in its significance, superb in its logic.

Chin, mouth, nose, brow, eyes of Calvin Coolidge are children of the splendors fading in his mother. Her face already is this twilight, is a recession of splendors. Her features speak but greyly an ancestral greatness. Moral and spiritual power, will, devotion, chastity, singleness of vision bore this woman. But the essence of their means to life made the mind intense to the exclusion of content; made the beauty neurotic; made the virtue shut. Made, inevitably, their own culminant death whose Person now presides the American lands.

The chin of Calvin Coolidge has grown pointed out of all proportion: it is a shallow, contentless thrusting. The lips have almost disappeared. The mouth is a crease of shrewd, complacent purpose. The fold of resolution beneath his mother's nose becomes a dug-out of meanness. The nose itself is bulbous, perhaps with too much half-baked nutriment: it is a proboscis of forwardness unchallenged along the path which the canny eyes select from all the paths of the world. The forehead is blown into a windy conch, unruffled and unfilled save with the echoes of dead covenants. It crowns the face like a sea-shell; and the face itself becomes, beneath it, a pucker of soft parts like some naked creature peering forth for food. The head indeed is the Rhetoric of absence. The face is the expression of an immaculate instinct for sure and mean details.

Again, as with his mother, the man's eyes give the key. They have lost the tragedy of hers. They have flattened, hardened and come out to the surface. They do not, from a secret depth, glower upon a hostile world: but have pressed, with a twist and a leer, to Victory. They twinkle. They have the lasciviousness of cold possession. They are the logical eyes of the battener on nullities: the eyes of the democratic politician.

So, as Calvin Coolidge, professional legislator might declare: The Nays have it. Here is a face at last, ultimate and stripped to the model of a will like a machine. A face where no dream lingers beyond the dreams approved by a smug world: a face which no thought troubles that has no answer in the current coinage: a face that knows not passion, unless it be charted and chartered in the Statutes. The mother's frown is gone with the conflict it expressed. Here, in lieu, is a smirk. All the realms of spiritual risk which her men, good pioneers, to such good purpose barred, have here stayed out indeed. A race's turning of its ideal power into the body of Success becomes this face and body, stripped to cunning, instinct with the spirit of acquisition. The symbol becomes a man; the man becomes a symbol. He crawls up the greased ladder of public honors. He becomes a leader and an idol, in whom the mob can worship its own miseries.

So this is the fate of our inherited virtues? It was written: On the Fourth of July 1776 these virtues shall give birth to the United States, and on the Fourth of July 1872, these virtues shall give birth to Calvin Coolidge?

There is no reason for repining. To be reborn, America must die: yea! her most immemorial virtues must rot and die. The face of our President should hearten us with knowledge, that we are well on the way.

PICNIC DAY :: A STORY

MARGARET LATIMER

NONE of us church people mistrusted Louise Markle when she began using red on her mouth. There were some that talked, of course, but heaven sakes, we thought we knew that girl through and through. She'd been raised in our church and her mother before her. She was brought up with all the fine things of religion around her and she sang in the choir from the time she was fourteen. But when her mother died and she began to do typing at the court house I noticed that she started to act kind of free and easy. No, that wasn't until the Horace McConkles came to town.

They were an elegant couple. Mr. sold insurance and Mrs. was one of the sweetest little bodies in our town with her three children and another on the way. They went to our church, of course. All the big business men go there. Our minister, Dr. White, says it's a constant inspiration to him to have most of the splendid men of the town in his congregation. But they always tell him that he's the inspiration.

First thing we knew Louise was thick with Mrs. McConkle and always talked with her after service. And on the days Louise sang in the choir Mr. used to come and we all laughed and joked Mrs. and Louise in front of him. But he was good natured, kind of big and hearty, and he wore his hat tilted and walked important. Then Louise began going to their house to do special typing for Mr. McConkle, she said, and after Mrs. was back from the hospital she went there to see the baby. She was there so much that we all joked her about it and told her that next thing she'd be living there. But nobody could get a word out of her then and I noticed she was getting thinner and paler all the time. All of a sudden the McConkles moved away.

I guess it was a month later that Louise came to see me. I was real pleased because she hadn't been to my house since her mother died and when she was little she'd always been such a one to come. It was awkward the way we sat there in the parlor, me asking her all kinds of questions about her work, the McConkles, her clothes that she always made herself, anything I could think of to ask her. But she looked so stiff and white that I wondered if she was out collecting money for something.

"Well," I said, "Louise," I said, "it's good to have you here even though I do see you every Sunday in church."

"I hate church!" she said. "I don't think I'll go any more."

I couldn't imagine what had come over her to say such a thing, a girl like her, twenty years in the church. Her mother carried her in before she was a year old.

"I guess you aren't feeling well, Louise," I said.

She shook her head and I suggested that the weather had been trying and that she had to work pretty hard but she ought to take all her troubles to the church, she ought to go there and pray, I told her, and tell our minister, do all those things that I'd done all my life. "Try that," I said, but she shook her head again.

Then I told her that maybe her friends, the McConkles, going away had affected her and she began talking about something way off the subject just as if she hadn't made that blasphemous remark about our church. And she stared at a picture of her taken when she was about four with her hair up on top of her head and a little locket around her neck. I always thought that was the dearest picture that ever was even though she did look kind of peaked and scared.

"Well, Louise," I said and pointed to the picture, "when you were that little girl you used to like church."

"I liked it until the McConkles came," she said.

"They're gone now," I said. "Can't you like it again?"

"No."

"We all get our spells, I suppose," I told her.

"But I'm glad it happened," she said.

I looked at her eyes and her thin neck and arms. She looked burned out, as if her whole life was done. "Louise," I said, "are you eating right?

Are you sure you get enough sleep? You know I feel responsible for you, Louise," I said, "since your mother's gone."

Then she told me. She was in love with Horace McConkle. (Just think that nice girl, as nice a girl as we have in our church!) "But what difference does it make," he told her, "when we love each other. What difference does anything make? This is ours. My wife has nothing to do with it."

One night his wife was taken to the hospital and Louise staid there in the house with him. They put his children to bed and laughed and joked with them and Louise staid. In the morning they took flowers to the hospital.

"I'll never regret it," she said, real defiant, "but I can't keep it in any longer. I have to tell it. Imagine me there and nobody knowing. She didn't even know. And I wanted every one to know. But he kept saying, 'This is between us. Just us. It would be common to tell.' "

When Mrs. McConkle came home she and Louise went every where together, to church, to the movies, and when Mr. was away Louise sometimes staid with her to keep her company. Other times she went to the country with him to a meadow to lie in the sun and then under the moon. But on Sundays she had to be back to sing in the choir and to teach her Sunday school class and anyway, they didn't dare to stay away for long.

All of a sudden she couldn't endure singing her hymns any more. She wanted to sing about her own life right there in the church in front of all of us instead of her special solos or Praise God from Whom All Blessings Flow or Count Your Many Blessings. She said she wanted to sing about her hatred for his wife and children, especially the little baby that McConkle liked to watch while it nursed. And nights she would go home in the dark and wonder what she would do if she had a child, imagining herself standing there in the choir before all her mother's friends, and then she would shake with fear, picture death, long for it, but something would make her love him all the more.

One day she got up her courage, he was so awfully grand acting, and said, "What if I have a child?" and he answered, "Well, then, we'll run away to the moon. How's that?"

After that she was afraid to live or die but he always told her, "Life is wonderful when you know the secret."

"I'm not afraid when I'm with you," she said. "Oh, how can you stay there with her?"

"Can't you two be good friends?"

"I can't stand her not knowing!"

"Be reasonable, Louise. It's no concern of hers what we do. That concerns ourselves."

"How about me?" she cried. "What do I get out of this? I'm left out!"

"Aren't you satisfied to be giving me everything?"

Then she would hate herself for not understanding his love and she would go with him to his table and talk with his wife and kiss his children and she would invite them to the movies even if she didn't have much money. "I used to think I'd die or scratch her to death," she said. "And when I had time I'd go down in our cellar and practise my new solo for church with the words I wanted to sing to it."

One day he told Louise they were going to move to Glendale. I can imagine how she stared at him and when she begged him to take her off somewhere far away from his wife and children he said, "Funny little Louise, be reasonable! You shall come to us for a long visit, I promise you that. Do you think that anything can take away what we have had? Why, no!" And when she looked at the branches of warm apples almost touching the ground and felt the wind on her face she screamed and threw herself against him. All he said was, "Louise, have I ever given you reason to suppose I was an ordinary man?"

So the McConkles made their plans for moving and Mrs. said she would miss Louise because she had been such a good friend to her and added that the children would miss their "second mother" as they called her. And McConkle, too, he would miss her, she always said, laughing at him roguishly and shaking her finger; he would miss Louise.

The first time Mrs. McConkle said that Louise cried, "Oh, but I'm afraid he won't!" and Mr. looked sober and said, "We'll have to see about that," while his wife just beamed at him and stroked his cheek. After that Louise never said anything to Mrs. McConkle's jokes.

"Dearest," said Mrs. McConkle just a week before they went. "I want to do something for Louise. She has been so lovely to me. Can't we have a party or something? Don't you think so, darling? Don't you think so, Louise? Of course. A picnic's the thing!"

They went on a bright, cool day in September and McConkle who knew only one meadow in the country that was quiet enough for a picnic took his wife, Louise, and his four children there. They stepped out of the car and he went on ahead to the only safe place in the meadow that he knew. Behind him came his wife with her baby at her breast and the three little boys begging for pickles. That reminded McConkle that he had promised his three little boys a good spanking if they teased Mama for pickles. But he led them on to the lovely spot and Mrs. McConkle, spreading out the robe, cried, "Oh, look! Apples and everything. Why, even the grass has been prepared for us. *See!* Oh, darling, you know all about picnics and lovely meadows and things!"

He agreed that he did and wished that they had brought sunshades for the sun, offered a newspaper to Louise for fear she might spoil her dress on the weeds, and asked Mrs. how soon the baby could go on prepared food. "Oh, not for six months yet," she said blushing. "Do forgive us for being so domestic and intimate," she begged Louise who didn't know where to look. "But we always consider you one of the family, you know." And then Mr. went off to the woods in that grand way of his with his three little boys hopping behind him.

Louise looked at the branch of warm apples that almost touched the ground but she didn't speak. And even when they stopped a few days later on their way to the station she didn't say anything. She only looked at them and shut her eyes when Mrs. kissed her and made the little boys do the same. But when she held the baby up for her to kiss Louise kind of groaned and put her hands over her stomach and McConkle said real quick that he had to telephone and took her back to the house.

Then he put his arm around her and shook his head. "I'm disappointed in you, Louise," he said, and patted her on the back. "But you're as reasonable as a woman can be, I guess."

She leaned against him with her arms hanging straight, her head down and her tears falling. But she didn't make a sound. Then the little boys began shouting for Papa and Mrs. started calling and the baby began to cry so McConkle brushed off his coat and went. Louise watched the car go down the street with the little boys hanging out the sides waving their straw hats and when she heard the train pull in she sat down by the window. And then it pulled out.

"Never mind, Louise," I said. But I couldn't look at her long, she looked so white and stiff and finished. "You keep on with your solos and don't give up church. You'll forget about it sometime, Louise."

TERMINAL :: A STORY

LOUISE TOWNSEND NICOLL

"**M**ama must be still alive. 'You *better* come', the telegram said. If mama was dead, they woulda said, 'Come at once', wouldn't they, Hat?"

"Yes, maybe," Hat said.

Their voices were slow, drab monotonous. They sat side by side on a bench in the Grand Central Station, in the rush between five and six o'clock at night. They were middle-aged, poor, workers very likely in a factory. Hat was tiny, scrawny, shrunk. She held in her clawlike hands a bunch of withered garden flowers with a paper around their stems. The one who was going away was unwholesomely large. Her straw hat, untimely for the Fall night, sat high above her round, bewildered face and careless hair. Her hands, fingering her pocketbook nervously, rested on her high stomach.

They did not look at each other as they talked, but straight ahead unseeingly or into their laps. Their voices went on as if detached from them—strange flat voices in the din of the big waiting-room, voices speaking in a monotone of death and the frailty of human life. Around them life was at top speed. Commuters rushed by them, grabbing news-papers from the stand. Girls powdered their faces, reddened their lips, leaning against the ends of the benches, waiting for boy friends.

"Mama won't last long now. 'Mama unconscious,' the telegram said. They always get unconscious before they go, don't they, Hat?"

"My sister didn't," Hat said. "She wanted to live."

"She knew everything? Did she say anything—about the Hereafter? About those who had gone before?"

"No. My sister didn't say anything like that. But she wanted to live. She woulda lasted longer, but the priest he told her she was going to die. After that she just wilted down and died. Only two weeks she lasted after that. We wouldn't a told her. The doctor he wouldn't a told her, either. But the priest he told her. She cried awful."

"What a thing for a priest to do, Hat! Did you tell him what you thought."

"No."

"What did she die of, Hat—the T.B.?"

"No, the cancer."

"Oh, well, then, everybody knew she had to die."

"Everybody but her. She didn't have to aknown."

"I'd feel bad if I thought I had to die now, wouldn't you, Hat?" the gray question came. The bulging ankles of the big woman, in cotton stockings, were crossed heavily in front of her. In them there seemed no joy of life.

"Yes," said Hat.

They were silent awhile.

"I guess I better get the ticket out, don't you think so, Hat?"

"Yes, I guess so."

"It's a fine thing to have the money to go with when you have to," said the big woman, speaking as if from a distance, slowly, dispassionately. "It's a fine thing to have a job. I'd be foolish to give up this good job I got, wouldn't I, Hat?"

"Well, if you're goin' to be sick, you'll have to," came Hat's reply, like the reply of fate.

"I ain't goin' to be sick, Hat. All I got's a cold. I feel better'n I did this morning. And the change will do me good. It's dry there—not damp. And the long rest on the train, sittin' still so long."

Hat said nothing. It seemed, in the replies of Hat, in her silences, as if she were the old associate of Death. The other one had chosen unerringly from among her fellow-workers which one was to come and see her off—Hat, whose sister had died—whose sister had wanted to live, and who might have lived a little longer than she did. She knew restlessness, bitterness and its futility, the small chance life has of flickering on.

"Mama won't last long now, Hat." It came again.

"No," said Hat.

"I'd feel awful if I knew I had to die, Hat."

"Yes."

They stayed silent then, the one clinging to her pocketbook, the other to her withering bouquet. Life was dear to them. The one had fear, the other a grim resignation. The one needed reassurance, the other knew there was no reassurance in the world. And life was dear to them, because they knew so starkly about fear and death and the feeble chance of human life. Living, the putting off of death, the chance to earn a living, the luxury of having carfare with which to go home for funerals, the chance of a rest sometimes on a train, a change of air when someone died—these things were precious. These women had a profound, a fearful, thankfulness for them. The one most fearful named these blessings again and again in her flat, dead voice—placating Death. They sat clinging tightly to their money, their flowers, to their lives.

A porter came through, calling a train.

The large woman bent forward toward him painfully.

"Is that my train?" she asked, holding out to him artlessly the long envelope containing her tickets. She looked at him as awed, as sure of his finality and power, as if he were a black Charon come to ferry her across.

"Yes,'m, that's your train," he said, not unkindly, and went off shrugging a careless shoulder at the way she held her suitcase back from him. He could not know it was her life she held.

"I better go, Hat. I mustn't miss the train."

"No," said Hat.

They were gone, in a kind of terror, Hat half-shoving the other's bulk along. They knew so well that life and death and trains brook no delay.

BERTIE :: A STORY

IVAN BEEDE

I T was a sad summer evening, and Bertie was susceptible to sadness. He was standing in front of Merrick's restaurant, watching the red sky, feeling lonely and blue.

There was a quality of eternal sorrow about the earth, exhausted after the long siege of the sun, waiting for night. As yet there was no trace of night even on the far edge of the prairie, but he could feel it, he could hear it, murmuring in the distance like a sea. When it came it would be overwhelming.

Bertie had just eaten supper in the restaurant, alone. He usually ate by himself; people, for some unspecified reason, felt uncomfortable when seen in the company of Bertie. There had been nothing else to do after supper, and he had stopped in front of the store to stare at the sky.

He placed himself at the curb, so that he would not see those passing behind him. If he were looking at them they would glance at his lilylike form with a wise smile and say, "Hello there Bertie."

They made Bertie tired. The more they grinned through the years, the more he prinked and preened. He swore he despised them and tried to be as different from them as he could. He lived alone in a pink house with lace curtains where he had his own world: his dairy, his flowers, his maltese cat and his dreams. Only one person in Greeley he cared for; as for the others, the Germans could blow up the town; he wouldn't mind.

Although he did not look at the passersby he could hear them talking as they sauntered along. The voices had a sad sound, even in laughter, and seemed to possess lives of their own. People walked on and left voices lingering there.

One he distinguished from the rest, the voice he would have known anywhere—in Madagascar, or China. Paul Moon was passing, somebody had stopped to talk to him in the street. "What's this I hear, you're going to war?"

Bertie didn't know who was speaking to Paul, he didn't even turn round to see. He kept looking at the red sky while the words hung there outside his ears.

A minute later, on the other side of the square, he could see Paul swinging along in his shirtsleeves, a cap far back on his head. So Paul was going to war. The news fell on his mood like an angelus, making him feel more than ever fateful and sad.

Paul was no more Bertie's friend than anyone else, but Bertie had the habit of dreaming he was. It was the way Bertie found compensation. In spite of the loneliness of his life he could afford to look down on the rest of the town, because of his dreams about Paul.

He took it for granted that they would one day be friends, and often pictured how it would happen. It would begin with a misty confession to Paul, in which he would twist his mouth up in a pained smile and tell Paul what a funny fellow he was. Paul would listen with a compassionate light in his eyes, a regard like that of Jesus, and then he would say something or other like this: "I understand. We are different, as different as the sun is from clouds, but we can be friends."

Whenever people got snotty, or he felt particularly useless, Bertie would decide the time had come to make some advance. He would plan to invite Paul out to see his pictures, or set a Sunday afternoon to drive up to the Moons. But when the moment arrived, he always held back.

Now as he stood there he saw Paul returning, walking into his mood. The sad evening, the sad news, were too much for Bertie. It was like the clicking of fate; and he could not stifle the impulse to speak.

"Hello, Paul."

"Hello there Bertie."

"I hear you're leaving us, Paul. When?"

"A couple of days I guess, Bertie. I got a chance to go direct to flying school."

"A couple of days. Then maybe I won't see you again?"

"I guess I'll be around: I don't know."

"Listen Paul."

"Yes?"

"I got my Brown Betsy here. Suppose we hop on and ride. Get out and find a breath of fresh air."

Paul was surveying him coolly. "Now what is Bertie up to, I wonder?" he seemed to be saying.

He looked sublimely secure, like a knight in shining armour, and let his hands rest lightly on his hips a moment, as if testing his strength.

"Oh, all right," he said.

Bertie did not lose any time. He opened the door of his Ford truck for Paul to enter, than ran around and jumped in at the steering wheel.

They cleared the town and got on a wide stretch of road that led to the valley. Grasshoppers and crickets and bullfrogs were singing, and in the west, where there was still an afterglow, a great star shone like a Christmas candle.

Bertie placed his straw hat primly between them, and let the breeze stir his sparse hair.

"Paul, do you know the poem,

As beautiful as any star

When only one is in the sky?"

"No. Who wrote it?"

"I'm mortally ashamed to say I don't know. I'm not much of a reader, and didn't get beyond the tenth grade: papa died, you know, and I had to go to work. But it's nice, don't you think?"

"Yes, I like it."

"Somebody said it to me once."

"Was she good-looking?"

"Yes," said Bertie, and blushed.

He turned his head to look across the open fields to the west, over miles and miles of corn. The stalks were breast high; they seemed happy and alert, whispering to one another. All around night was rolling in like a sea.

Bertie sighed happily.

"When you go away, Paul, you'll learn a lot of things."

"About what, exactly?"

"Oh, lots of things. Somewhere, in the army or out, you'll meet people who know something about life. That's what these farmers don't seem to realize, Paul, that everybody isn't alike. It takes all kinds of people to make up a world, you know."

"I know," grinned Paul. " 'Everybody to his own taste,' said the old lady as she kissed the cow."

A red Harvest moon began to lumber over the fringe of trees to the east.

"Look Paul."

"It's only the moon."

"I know, but how wonderful it looks. There is something great about tonight, and sad. Do you know why? Because you're going away—you and everybody else." He giggled. "Doesn't the moon look sad to you, or am I a nannygoat?"

Paul made sure where the moon was, and turned in the opposite direction.

"I'm only joking," laughed Bertie. "But I like to say things like that. I like to talk sometimes, and let go." He breathed deeply, and looked around. "And I guess this is one of the times. I'm only an old woman, and have to talk or go crazy, so please don't mind."

Paul was silent.

"I don't believe you do mind, Paul. Somehow I feel I can talk to you. You're not like the rest of the folk in this town. You're different."

"I'm different?" Paul demanded sharply. "What do you mean?"

"Oh, you got some sense," Bertie answered, discouraged. "You weren't meant to be one of these small-town men. I suppose you won't believe it, but it's true. I've been watching you, Paul. You've got brains, and things. The good Lord meant you to be bigger than these people."

He waited for Paul to say something, but Paul remained silent. He felt the situation slipping out of his hands, and became desperate all of a sudden.

"I know what you think, Paul. I know what everybody thinks, that I'm ... well, I'm not."

He clutched the wheel tightly with his white hands. He had expected to tell Paul the truth, and was lying. Why? Usually fear made him lie; he didn't want anybody to have anything on him; but in this case it was not that. It was because he wanted Paul to like him, no matter what. Paul simply had to like him, even if he lied until he was black in the face.

Perhaps he had better lie some more.

"Listen. I'll tell you something, Paul, something I've never told anybody. I'll tell you what's the matter with me. Do you remember Bill Marvin and Hank Garhan?"

"I've heard of them."

"They were a good deal older than me, but I went to Omaha with them once. They got drunk and took me down to Capitol Avenue, to a place full of negroes. Blue women in pink kimonos. They were all fat, and insisted on hugging me. They smelled—awful."

He waited. There was not even a grunt out of Paul.

"Then something else happened. When we were going home one of the women got sick. She was so sick she turned white, I'm not joking. It was my woman. When I asked her what was the matter, she said we were going to have a baby."

Paul eased out his legs and laughed.

"You didn't believe her?"

"Of course not. That is, I knew she wasn't, right then. But I didn't know what to believe; I was only a kid."

Paul looked at Bertie curiously.

"Well, it was a tough break, I admit. But I wouldn't let it bother me now. I know it would never phase me." town and approached the square. "You can let me out at Merrick's," Paul said, and Bertie obeyed. Paul got out of the car without a word and went in.

Bertie started the car up again. He did not know where to go, or what to do. He drove around the square, round and round. As he passed Merrick's he could see Paul standing at the cigar counter, talking and laughing. What were they laughing about?

If Paul told ... but Paul would not tell. Not Paul.

He drove around some more, and passed Paul headed for home. He was walking jauntily along, humming to himself, and took no notice of Bertie. Why didn't he speak? Did that mean he had told?

Bertie drove around again and reconnoitered at Merrick's. He struggled awhile, then stopped the car and went in. He had to find out.

There were farmers inside, making purchases: tobacco, fruit and ice cream. They seemed healthy and whole, their voices rang in the air. They all stared at Bertie. Old Man Merrick, behind the cigar stand, had a broad grin on his face.

If they knew anything, they would say something, make some wise crack.

He looked down in the case and ordered some cigars. One, two, three. He could think of nothing more masculine. Lighting one, he leaned against the counter and waited. He gave them plenty of time, but nobody said anything.

At last he went out, bobbing up and down like a girl. Just because he didn't want to, he had to walk that way. He couldn't help it.

People in the street, families going home from the movies, the watchman in front of the bank, all stared at Bertie. The whole world was staring at him.

The moon was high now, flooding the night, and it cast strange flat shadows of Bertie driving home in his truck. The Ford bounced crazily over the road; he drove faster and faster, and his fear grew to panic. He abandoned control of himself as a washwoman might scatter her apron of clothespins. He loathed himself, he called himself unspeakable names. Paul should have killed him, or somebody should. Or else he should commit suicide, and leave a note for Paul, saying, "What you were too good and kind to do, I have done with my own hand ... my friend."

Everybody would be glad, and nobody sorry, not even Paul. Why should Paul be sorry? He was right, the world is always right, and Bertie was wrong. He praised Paul; he could not find words fine enough. How he wished he could have been in Paul's place and hit himself as Paul hit him!

But Paul would not tell ... now. Later, when he came home from camp in his flyer's uniform, and the home town looked new to him, he would ask, "How's our friend Bertie?" And then, "Say, do you know ... "

There would be no stopping it then. It would spread, he would never escape it. He had a vision of himself running wildly from something: from a prairie fire, stamping and running.

Once when he was a small boy he had made a bonfire on a windy day, against his father's orders. The dry grass caught on the edge of the pile and swept out of his reach. It spread in three directions, and approached the house and barn. It was not really a bad fire, but seemed so to him. He watched it with terror, utter terror, believing if only he could wipe this sight from his eyes, he would be safe and same. Then, while he struggled helplessly with the flames, his father stalked grimly out of the house.

That is the way he felt now, only now he was older, and his abasement was more pitiful and complete. There was nothing left of him save a desire to conform, to put a stop to the fire. Whatever there had been of soul in him died, and a piece of the world took its place.

He abandoned his truck in the yard and stumbled into the kitchen. When he turned on the lights the maltese cat rubbed at his heels. He screamed, and kicked at it like a girl.

In the bedroom the picture of Paul met his eyes. He snatched it down and tore it to pieces and stood swaying there.

They would get nothing on him: he would show them. He would be a man like the rest.

He would think and feel as they did. He would chew tobacco and swear and chase whores, and marry the first woman who'd have him.

He dropped to his knees at the dainty pink counterpane, and raised his falsetto voice to Heaven, praying God to help him to be a man.

DO THE CHURCHES CORRUPT YOUTH?

SAMUEL ORNITZ

NE day's Feature News; three columns in the *Times*, two in the *World*. Repeat the dose several thousand times and you get an idea of the education in lust which our daily press is industriously administering to the American "mind in the making"—and all this news is "Fit to Print!"

A Justice of the United States Supreme Court addresses the Red Cardinals (Roman, not Russian Red) and the vast Catholic Conclave at the Eucharist orgy. (See Frazer's *Golden Bough* on the subject of the sublimation of barbarous, cannabilistic rites.)

Three *catch-as-can-catch-cash* Presidents of Universities also make speeches that day at solemnly sweet Commencement exercises. ...

A nation's press reports their speeches. No one reads them, so the copy writers put the hot stuff into the headlines and the opening paragraphs. What say the bold faces? They are always gayly grim.

DEBAUCHERY!
LAWLESSNESS NATIONWIDE!

Save Youth by Religious Education!

For four years now the newspaper copy experts, recognizing the unbridled sex appeal in the orations of the crusaders for religious training, have given daily prominence to the speeches at religious conventions; special sermons by assorted bishops; the Sunday night "sacred concerts" by clerical specialists in smut; ambitious district attorneys;

thousands of office seekers; the odd panhandlers and notoriety hounds of the Anti-Saloon League, the Security League, Federations of Women's Clubs, Daughters of the Revolution (and Tories?); the percentage pressure salesmen of the Seminaries, Yeshivas and Sunday Schools; the publicity-spirited bankers, brokers, Chairmen of Chambers of Commerce; the pep secretaries of the Y. M. C. A., Y. M. H. A. and K. C.; the convert-catchers in fraternities, sororities and slum settlements; the cheer leaders of the Rotary and Kiwanis kiyoodles; Christian Socialists; repentant radicals; and any one else able to provide First Class Dignified Dirt.

For it all makes swell, *safe* sex stuff.

For it all gives the reader a nice hypocritical kick, provides howling headlines that sell newspapers. ('Tis the Tale of the Tabloid Terror, the *World* and *Times* will tell you.)

The speeches are good copy, that is, their high spots. Such as: *Menace of Modern Radical Literature. It is the Cause of Debutantes' Demoralization. Love Tots Thrown In Sewer. Cocktail-crazed Collegiates. Necking, Petting This Side of Paradise. Irreverence for Elders and Tradition. Obscenity. Rank Irreligion. Drunkenness. Daylight Robberies. Blasphemy. Bobbed Hair Bandits. Every Spit Curl in the Crime Wave.*

There is a single antidote. Religious Training for the Young! This has been yelled one billion times from platform and press. The pandemonium of propaganda has so filled the air with din and dust that the voice of right reason no longer guides the mauve liberal and the prosperity-tired radical. ... They have even come to make a plea for "good taste and ordinary decency" to the editors of the NEW MASSES. ... Let up. Radical Literature, ere the youth of the Nation corrupts. ...

$$* * *$$

I have examined the effect of religious education upon growing children and herewith I make my report. You will observe that I use only the infallible methods of the Anti-Saloon League's statistical logicians and of the Catholic agitators famous for "irrefutable" facts.

And my findings, I regret to say, seem to indicate most alarmingly, that religious training tends to increase criminality.

First, let me qualify as an expert. I offer in evidence the actual case experience of my own career. I spent twelve years as an expert for the Prison Association and the Brooklyn Children's Society.

I have had first-hand contact with the family history of gunmen, panders, prostitutes, murderers, rapists, grand-scale embezzlers, burglars, baby Borgias, hold-up artists, etc., etc.

It is unusual—because extremely rare—to find a man or woman answering for some heinous crime who has not had some sort of religious training, simple or elaborate.

The Catholic killer wears his scapular about his neck.

The Jewish Kid Dropper murderer has a sacred Palestinian talisman in his vest pocket.

The Protestant clergyman who poisoned his mistress husband refers to the Bible before he replies to the District Attorney.

Gerald Chapman, most famous of recent assassins, had a splendid Catholic training. He showed such promise that his aunt had hoped to make a priest of him.

The Whittemore Gang—Protestant, Jewish and Catholic—had their day of fame by killing ruthlessly, and stealing a million dollars worth of jewlery. They all had religious training.

No one remarks in grave addresses and serious editorials upon the number of men and women to be found in our state prisons, reformatories, workhouses and jails, men and women who have had the ideal start in life with a parochial school education. Or the many others, who have had the assorted benefits of clergy.

In my work in the Children's Society I interviewed hundreds of boys and girls and read thousands of similar interviews and investigated the facts and the family histories. I refer to children under the age of sixteen who had become involved in some sex offense. I discovered that they had command of an obscene vocabulary that was extraordinary and yet they had never read James Joyce! How then did they come by it? Many of these kids, like James Joyce himself, had had a perfect parochial upbringing and I conclude that they had acquired the filth defensively during the time that they were taught most threateningly to shun, fear and abjure it.

Ninety-nine and one-half per cent of these youngsters came from homes in which radical writings were totally unknown. Of course such elevating literatures as catechisms, prayer books, Bibles and Macfadden moral-thwacking magazines were always on hand and in circulation. Messiah Macfadden sees to it that every piece that goes into his periodicals is scrutinized and sanctioned by a Board (on Mac's payroll) of God's Ministers, loophole-agile lawyers and professional moralists. In fact, Bernarr boasts that only the Bible has a larger circulation than *True Stories*.

Slum, middle-class, upper crust, all contributed cases. They were folks who did one thing well—sent their children to church and Sunday school. Particularly the impoverished Catholics did very well by their children. They sent their boys and girls to the parochial schools where they could have the heavenly influences at work upon them for five hours a day. None of these people ever came in contact with the depraving radical readin' and writin' and 'rithmetic of economic interpretation or an oblately obscene NEW MASSES.

Somehow or other, despite church and clean books, these parents and children became involved in sexual atrocities that are supposed to exist only in the literature of erotology. Somehow or other their language of lechery was rich and resplendent.

Backward and best people's children alike suffered from the same outbreak of obscenity, and it seemed as unescapable and inevitable as measles.

Catholic Red Hook young men and girls held orgies in their Social Clubs, Baptist Flatbush youths had scandalous strip-poker parties in their uncontaminated homes, Williamsburg sons and daughters of synagogue members practiced free love surreptitiously in cellars and on roofs. Nordic, Nigger, Semite, Firbolg, Alpine, Mediterranean—none could be controlled in their appetites, not even by religious training; nor could a prayer or a sermon adjust the economic situation which brought them to steal.

But ask the churchmen and they will tell you everyone else is to blame but themselves, and yet *they get the first chance at the child*. Even atheists send their children to church and Sunday school. It is one of the saddest facts I know.

DO THE CHURCHES CORRUPT YOUTH?

The last summer I spent in the Children's Society I was the supervisor of the law enforcement work. I noticed a lush upspringing of incest cases. It made me curious (scientifically, of course). As I pored over the records a certain fact impressed itself upon me. I made a careful analysis and sent in my report. ...

THOSE TERRIBLE AMERICANS

ANN WASHINGTON CRATON

THE Boston train was very late. All the way from New York it had crawled through the snow drifts. A February blizzard gripped all of New England. In frantic haste, I had been ordered to Boston by the President of the Union, although I was busily and happily engaged in organizing shirtmakers in Pennsylvania. "I don't want to go to Boston," I protested vainly. The only answer to all of my objections was the stern command, "Take the next train."

Very weary and cold, I stumbled into South Station to be met by a gloomy set of young Italian organizers, who informed me that they were a reception committee. They carried me off to a spaghetti joint, where they reproached me bitterly for my late arrival. It was not until large and heaping plates of spaghetti had been consumed that they could be cheerful. It seemed that the Boston Union was confronted with a most unusual problem. It had waged a gallant struggle against one of the largest and most important clothing firms in the Boston market for ten weeks. With a 100% strike, the firm was managing to fill almost all of its orders. No one had been able to discover where the scab work was being made. Finally Organizer R. had successfully trailed some packing cases to a small and secluded village on the South Shore, about thirty miles from Boston, where a flourishing shop was turning out coats. He had found a number of skilled Jewish and Italian workers there, but the majority proved to be American women. A meeting had been called and a strike declared. While many of the American women workers had attended the first meetings, only seven had answered the strike call. And these seven New England women were rapidly wavering in their faith in the Union. No one could please these seven strikers. Man after man—Jews and Italians—would be sent out from Boston, only to disgrace himself in some most innocent manner by offending their ideals of religion, patriotism, Americanism.

"Do you expect us to lose the strike because of a lot of stupid Americans?" challenged Comrade C. "Every Italian is out of the shop. It's just those terrible Americans, my God, such terrible Americans…Americans are the worst people in the world. Jesus Christ, why did Christofo Colombo have to discover this country!"

Forthwith I vas presented with the South Shore strike. I was an American, wasn't I? Well, I was expected to organize those terrible Americans and stop the production of coats. "Our Boston strikers are so discouraged," mourned Comrade R. "Every day the firm ships its orders and every day the Union issues a statement that not a coat is being produced in Massachusetts."

Comrade C. escorted me proudly to Quahasset the next afternoon, although it was Sunday. On the train he informed me that I was to live with Miss Lucretia, whom he confided was a "vergine." I refused flatly to live with Miss Lucretia. "She can't help being a "vergine," answered he blandly, "besides there is no place to live. There is no hotel and you are going to have a nice little room. I helped clean it myself. Miss Lucretia has an old mother and they must have your board. They are more destitute than the others."

Quahasset proved to be a charming New England village, peaceful and lovely in its heavy blanket of snow. Loveliest of all was the eighteenth century church to which, much to my amazement, Comrade C. directed my steps. "Bible class will soon be over," he announced casually. "I want them all to see you, the seven strikers and the scabs. They are all here."

"Do they all go to Church?" I asked aghast. "Certainly," he answered. "Church, Sunday School, prayer meeting and Bible class."

We waited near the gate, while the women passed us. Some of them hurried past with evident embarrassment. With Sicilian gestures, Comrade C. indicated in an unmistakable fashion, both the scabs and the strikers. I surveyed them with inward alarm. They were all of old New England stock, gaunt, weather beaten, hard women. Most of them appeared to be between forty-five and fifty. They were poorly but painfully-neatly dressed. They wore funny little hats, trimmed with feathers, perched on top of their heads and as their hair was combed back tightly and severely from their faces they had a pinched expression accentuated by the cold. These women were the native hundred percent Americans in every sense of the word. Their forefathers had been the Pilgrim settlers of this town. They had the same names that one could trace upon the crumbling tomb-stones in the old burying ground at Plymouth nearby. They had worked since childhood, largely in the shoe factories, leading starved, barren lives, making brave efforts to keep up appearances and to pretend to be the equals of the more prosperous citizens.

Down the church yard walk between the walls of piled snow came two middle-aged, archaic ladies.

"This is Miss Craton, our new organizer," said Comrade C., our organizer. Miss Lucretia nodded grimly. Miss Elvira, her companion, invited me to their house for tea. Comrade C. was also included as a special favor.

"No Eyetalian man has ever been inside my house before, and especially on the Lord's Day," she informed him. "I live alone and I am a respectable woman. Until this last week, when I made up my mind to be a Union girl, I ain't never done anything unless I could see some good would come from it. Now I am all mixed up in my mind. Giving you a little bite before you journey back to Boston, don't seem would make things any better or any worse. But don't you go getting any wrong impression."

Miss Lucretia took off her shabby coat. She emerged in a wine colored woolen dress, made in a style popular twenty-five years ago, with huge puffed sleeves, a tight bodice and a long full skirt. She was plainly proud of herself as she guarded herself carefully from stray crumbs. Although Miss Lucretia solicited subscriptions for the Ladies Home Journal to help eke out her expenses from her small wages and read it faithfully from cover to cover every month, changes of style in clothes had never seemed to occur to her. Her dress had once been all that was desirable and as it had never worn out, therefore it must be used.

After tea, she thawed considerably and dropping her refined Sunday manners, she became quite chatty about her new role. "My scabbing days are over," she confided. "I wish I had understood about Unions before. I might be somewhere now in paying off Pa's funeral expenses. It has taken some hard lessons to show me, but the last shoe factory strike opened my eyes. I always thought that Unions were fine for men, but I never understood what good they were for women, until now. Why, I was a great one for working for the Boss. I'd get all of the girls to stick to him, and I'd be that proud when he'd ride me home in his limousine during the strike while the other girls rode in the trucks. Then after the strike was lost he cut our wages again, and his wife, who was the president of the Ladies Aid, would insult and snub me at the socials. She would expect me to stay in the kitchen and wash dishes all the evening, when I wanted to wait on the tables and see all the people."

On the way to Miss Lucretia's little hundred year old house, one of the most beautiful in the village, she pointed out a large and ugly modern house. "Aint it elegant," she said. Its owner was Sis Jenkins, who was now acting as leader of the scabs. "She's got it all paid for, and she's got a telephone and she's got a husband. He's stone deaf and seventy years old, and even with the ear trumpet she bought him, he can't hear, but she gives herself airs because she's got a wedding ring. She's got no need to scab. I'll say for myself I always had the mortgages to worry over, and Ma and Pa, even though we did keep him at the poor farm."

"Why does she scab now?"

"She is trying to get into society. Breaking the strike gives her prominence. She rides home in the Boss' Packard now. She drives to Weymouth with the foreman and gets girls from the shoe factories for our jobs. She even has got her poor old husband pulling bastings. Clothing factories are so clean and refined after you have worked on shoes. Everybody is crazy to work there. I loved my job. If we lose the strike I'll have to go back to cementing shoes."

My first strike meeting was held the next afternoon and every afternoon thereafter in Minnie Thomas' parlor. Minnie was a widow and it seemed more fitting for her house to be used. Halls were completely taboo as far as the women were concerned. No lady could go inside of a public hall. The prejudice against foreigners was still strong. Comrade C. worked hard to get jobs for most of them in Boston, but the others came to the strike meetings. They were not allowed to come in the parlor. Their place was in the kitchen adjoining. They were not even admitted to the kitchen until a committee of girls had supervised the manner in which they used Sister Thomas' doormat. The foreigners had no resentment at their isolation in the kitchen or at any of the treatment accorded them, humorously and kindly regarding it as the peculiarities of "old maids" or perhaps as strange American customs. They would attempt amiable conversation from room to room, while I stationed myself on neutral ground in the doorway. Meanwhile the native aristocrats sat stiffly in their chairs, crocheting or tatting. They were always silent and glum. They never seemed pleased or interested. Would they stick to the strike or not? I could not know. I never could penetrate the masks they hid behind. Yet every afternoon I would find them unresponsive, suspicious and apparently disapproving, but still loyal.

After much house to house visiting, a number of other women joined the strike. Many more stopped work. They refused to come to strike meetings or to associate with foreigners but they accepted strike relief and remained in seclusion at home. When the coat shop was practically crippled, the ice of the New England reserve began to thaw. They brought me little presents of a pie or a glass of jelly or some doughnuts, offered apologetically "to help Miss Lucretia out with my board." In reality it was an indication that I had been accepted.

I took heart and called on the arch enemy, Sis Jenkins. Through a half opened door, while her old husband stood with his ear trumpet to hear as much as possible, Sis was emphatic as to her position. "I aint sunk so low that I'll stand so many foreigners around, running things," she said. "I went to all them meetings, myself, and I know what I saw. Eyetalian and Jewish men, with their hats on, smoking all over the place, and even playing cards, bold like, in front of us. And everybody talking some different foreign language. It aint Christian and it aint decent. It aint no place for a lady in such a foreign Union." Then as I led my delegation away came the shout in which the deaf old man joined in. "The Union will never win, the Union will never win."

As a matter of fact, the strike was almost lost. It was the nightly diversion of Miss Lucretia and her old mother, frankly curious and frankly critical, sitting back against the kitchen wall, in their straight, hard chairs, in disapproving silence to survey their helpless shivering boarder while I undressed. It was bitter cold and the only heat in the house was in the kitchen. "That nightgown is something terrible," Miss Lucretia was moved to comment. "I aint never seen anything like it in my life," giggled Ma nervously, "nothing like it aint ever disgraced my house before. It aint got no modesty and it aint even respectable." Ma made so bold as to cross the room and to take the offending garment from my unhappy hands. She examined it minutely under the lamp. "It ain't got a mite of a sleeve in it and a nice girl like you running around in it in the dead of winter. It is a shame before the Lord." So spake Ma and cast it from her.

That was enough for me. The next morning, with the excuse that I wanted to send a telegram, I hastened to a small general store kept by two maiden ladies, notorious village gossips. On the street I heard a group of women openly discussing me. "It's that Union organizer, they say she aint got a petticoat to her name and that her nightgown is sinful. I'm for Unions, a Union is all right, but I do say that our girls have got to be careful."

I bought the ugliest canton flannel nightgown in the store. It had a high neck and long sleeves, and large china buttons down its front. I wore it that night. At the strike meeting the next day Miss Lucretia told them all about it. The crisis passed, but à new one loomed.

The Boss resorted to violence. The picket line had consisted of a dignified procession of a few oldish women, who reluctantly walked up and down in front of the shop, augmented by some of the younger Italian boys. The minister began to call upon the women and to urge them to give up their unseemly behavior and to return to work, although both factions still attended his prayer meetings. One cold morning only Miss Lucretia, Minnie Thomas and Miss Elvira were on the picket line with three of the boys. Suddenly from out of the shop there appeared the chief of police, an old Civil War veteran, and five husky town toughs. Without warning they jumped upon the boys and beat them unmercifully. From the factory windows Sis Jenkins' crowd howled approval. Gino and Tony were left unconscious in the snow, while Salvatore, in a dazed condition had his cut and bleeding face bandaged by the frightened women, who vainly besought the chief of police for help. His only reply was to advise them to go back to work, while the hired toughs jeered, "Come back again, you damned Wops, and we'll kill you."

Next day the old maids, dressed in their Sunday clothes, went to court as witnesses and heard the Judge dismiss the case as a "boy's fight."

"It just don't seem to me that God could have let that happen," puzzled Miss Lucretia, the devout, when, the following afternoon, my somewhat shaken cohorts assembled once more in Minnie Thomas' kitchen. The flame of battle had burned away all ideas of race or creed. No longer were the Italian boys segregated in the kitchen. Minnie Thomas was worried about the picket line. She could not endure having Sis Jenkins think that they were scared. They weren't. The old maids were full of fight, but they needed help. I telephoned Comrade C. in Boston.

Two days later about a hundred strikers, employed by the same firm in Boston, arrived in two huge motor trucks. In the cold grey, misty morning light they looked a vast industrial army. Miss Lucretia and her 100% American pickets clutched each other. The new pickets were all foreigners. The Revolution had certainly come. The chief of police called out the reserves, trembling, weak old men like himself. He telephoned to all the neighboring villages for reinforcements. Within an hour he had fortified himself with several sheriffs, the fire department, and the shiny, new patrol wagon, the pride of a town twenty miles away, never before used.

Sis Jenkins, herself, was so plainly nervous that she had to be led past the terrible pickets by two shaky old policemen. Jubilantly Miss Lucretia thumbed her nose at her, with almost the entire village, including the minister, watching her in horror. Miss Elvira and the others shouted names that they had never even whispered before. It was a glorious day for the girls.

Intoxicated with the excitement of their new lives, Miss Lucretia and Miss Elvira vied with each other in deeds of desperate daring. No more militant strikers were ever found. If Miss Lucretia threw mud on the snowy wash of Sis Jenkins, left out over night, Minnie Thomas and Miss Elvira made mysterious journeys to nearby villages and bought up all of the stale eggs, which they heated in the oven to further enhance their value. Armed with the eggs and a bag of flour, they grimly waylaid the women they had a particular grudge against. While Minnie Thomas pelted them with eggs, Miss Elvira plastered them with flour. The results exceeded their most hopeful dreams. And still they never missed prayer meeting. It was there that their inspirations came to them.

The Wednesday that saw the victorious settling of the strike, Sis Jenkins was absent from prayer meeting. Strangely Miss Lucretia was also missing. Her anxious friends found her waiting at the Church gate. "I was detained on important business," she explained mysteriously, "I've been arrested. I am out on bail.

THE CZAR BUMS ME FOR A CIGARETTE

HYPERION LE BRESCO

A FIVE-CENT ferry ride from New York brings one to a land of mystery and romance as glamorous and thrilling as any depicted in Graustarkian movies. In Arrapagli. Staten Island, a ferry and a streetcar ride from New York City, Major General Count Cherup Spiridovitch, former right-hand man to the late Czar of Russia, former head of the Russian Secret Service Police, and the "future Czar and Mussolini" of Russia has established royal Muscovite Headquarters. The General has aides-de-camp and a general staff, and their families, and a multigraph machine, and everything but money. He also has at least a million trained men under arms today in Russia, and in two years he is sure he will be Czar of Russia.

The Barrett mansion, where the Royal Russians hold forth, is owned by a Mrs. Beauley, a small, thin, dervish woman. Mrs. Beauley at one time held open house for a group of nature dancers, young art ladies who would cavort nudely on her lawn with the dawn. ... Indian Yogis and "Fourth dimensional artists" have also enjoyed her hospitality. At present she is very busy, what with the tempestuous Russians, and an "International Center of Culture, Art and Beauty" she is forming. As she says, poets from as far as Pittsburgh have come to her meetings.

The house is a huge brown mansion on the top of a hill, dominating its surroundings like a castle. A visitor to the house is struck by the great central hall, and the balcony, which looks like a set from "The

Miracle." There is a somber light filtering through, the particles of dust that come from dying wood and brick. Decayed statuary and paintings line the walls, and broken chairs are placed here and there. It is like an art cemetery.

Col. Bennett, the aide-de-camp, whose real name is something like von Antons-Doerp, greeted me at first. He needed a shave very badly, and his trousers had evidently made up their mind to leave him. He was a tall, officer-looking man, with a clean-cut face that once had been good-looking, but like the house, was now a ruin. He bummed me immediately for a cigarette.

I gave him one, and he accepted it with a courtly gesture, as if doing me a favor. Then he talked about the "life-work," a fanatic gleam in his eye.

"Yes, in two years the General will be Czar of Russia ... When we give the word ... pouf ... A million trained men under arms in Russia alone ... more ready to rise ... Rumania, Jugoslavia, Lithuania, Poland, England all with us ... The others, France, Germany, they will have to come in ... England, America, they will wait ... but they too will come in ... Of course, the great international financiers like Rothschild and the Sassoons are against us, they are really behind the Bolsheviki ... we have proof ... proof ... The Duke of Northumberland is with us ... British royalty with us ... Queen Marie of Rumania, who will be here soon, is with us ... Every week thousands of couriers are in touch with us ... You will see, you will see ... "

He frowned. I gave him another cigarette and he looked happier. "I'll take you to the General ... "

Up a long stairway, around a balcony, into a huge room, filled with a long table piled high with documents and pamphlets. A thin, sparse man with a hawk-like nose, and cruel narrow eyes rose from a chair, and stood stiffly at attention, as if reviewing a regiment. This was the future Czar. He apologized for his shirt-sleeves. He spoke in French. We apologized for our intrusion, but he forgave us and asked for a cigarette.

The walls were decorated with French newspaper clippings, portraits of the General in uniform, of his officer-friends in uniform, orders the General had worn, portraits of the late Czar, of the King of Jugoslavia, of Mussolini, Coolidge and Dawes.

The beautiful marble head of a strong woman weeping was in a corner of the room, next to an Ikon. She was waiting for the release of death. "Ruined Russia," was the name carved on the statue, "Ruined Russia," which these men are so confident they will rule.

They talked. Russia needed strong hands. Their hands. Russia wanted trappings, glitter, a court, gold. They would give it to Russia. Russia wanted to be free from the Mongol domination. They would free it. It was all so simple ... They had millions of men under arms. Millions ready to come over to them when they should beat the drums of war from their ruined brick mansion in Staten Island ... They complained that America was not with them. They could not understand that. Their cause was so obvious, so simple, so just ... Russia, ruined by the Bolsheviks who were not really Bolsheviks, but the Mongol hordes, the Moors, the army of Attilla, in a new guise. Japan plotting against America. Asia rising against America and Europe. They were fighting the White Man's Fight. They would make Russia the advance guard of the Anglo-Saxon, of the Teuton, of the American ... and America would not help them. Pliss give me a cigarette.

Their eyes flashed as they spoke, their tongues lingered on words like *royal, army* and *king*, as if the expression of such words gave sensual delight to the curling red strip of flesh in their mouths that could talk, that could bring armies in the room, could slay millions, while the millions lived.

"The Mongol," "A million men, trained, under arms, waiting for the call," "The next Czar," "The Mussolini of Russia," "international bankers," "British royalty," "Queen Marie of Rumania ... " A cigarette.

Like gilded balls between jugglers, the grandiose phrases were tossed back and forth. Their talk was a purple cloud in which they lived a beautiful romantic dream. The reality of rags and squalor, the smell of burnt beef stew wafted into the royal chamber, the ignoble squalling of noble ragged brats from the rooms upstairs, the babble of excited Russian resounding all over the house like a barroom fight, all faded away. The dream-world of "Army Orders," duly signed and counter-signed, of "International Plotting," of revolution, of "Rulers of the World," of saviors of civilization, this alone was real. Their fingers writhed like restless snakes, as they spoke their eyes gleamed like bayonets, hungry to lunge into the throats of their enemies.

The interview was over. The general bowed. I bowed. The aide-decamp bowed. I bowed. The majordomo, Colonel Doerp, escorted me outside. We sat down and talked again.

The aide-de-camp of the general hurried out after me.

"Major General Count Cherup Spiridovitch wishes to tell you that he is willing to exchange the Queenship of Russia for American millions."

He bowed. I bowed.

The major-domo took some cigarettes and left me, haughtily hitching his pants up as he went.

An "orderly" ran up to me in the hall. He informed me that a mass of "nobility" would come tomorrow for a ball they were holding, sympathizers from New York and New Jersey, Russians. Would I come too? I gave him several cigarettes. He took them, smiled and left.

On the wall I saw an importantlooking document, typed in red in Russian, with the major-domo's imposing title and names, and someone else's counter-signature. I stole it for my newspaper and had it translated, later. It was an order calling on the nobility to throw their garbage out more carefully.

The Colonel ran out after me . . .

"Don't forget," he panted into my ears, "a million men are under arms," and asked for a few more cigarettes. But I hadn't any left. I hope the future Czar had other visitors that day, who were cigarette smokers, too.

Is that it?" I asked. And she said, 'That's it."

And still I questioned her, "Why must a man suffer these doubts and fears? and who is the evil one who has inflicted such disease upon the bodies and minds of men? for death and destruction reign supreme and man and woman are forever worsted."

"Once long ago," said my soul, "when you were a little boy we were walking together through the forest. And I, as your mother, was holding your hand. As we walked along through the speckled shade of the trees where the shadows were chasing the sunspots as the leaves rustled overhead, you pointed to this and to that, asking me why and how this was so. And I told you of the secrets that lay hid in each seed and how a seed unfolded into a tree.

"We came to a great oak spreading its branches far out on every side. At the foot of the oak was a large wooden chest, bound by strong iron bands and locked with two padlocks.

"You asked me what that was and I told you that the chest contained evil.

" 'What is evil?' you asked, and I told you that it was belief in destruction and defeat.

" 'Defeat?' you exclaimed, 'what is defeat?'

" 'So long as the chest is locked,' I said, 'you will never know, for words cannot tell.'

" 'Open it,' you demanded. Then I told you what terrible things fear and hate were and how they turned all things sour. But you could not understand.

" 'Open it,' you demanded a second time.

"But I cautioned you again, telling you how evil would harden your heart and make you blind to beauty and goodness.

" 'Would it really hurt me if you opened the chest?' you asked.

" 'It would surround you by doubts and fears,' I said, 'and you would think yourself lost. You would be alone and lose all love for me. You would fall and rise and fall again until finally you would understand evil and master it.'

" 'Could I master it?' you asked.

" 'You could,' I said, 'but it would take a long, long time—so long that you would believe you could not endure. Again and again you would surrender. You would declare yourself too weak and cower before the strength of deception. Finally you would rise in your strength and master it.'

"After I had told you all this, 'It is for you to decide,' I said, 'the chest is yours to be opened or to stay closed, but think well before you speak.'

" 'I want to master it,' you said, and I unlocked the padlocks."

III

I stopped at a house to inquire the way. Inside I found an old married couple and their grown up daughter. The man told me which road to take. As I was going out I paused on the doorstep. Inside I heard the man say: "He looked like a good man. I wish I had offered him something to eat." The wife said, "I will watch as he goes out to see that he does not steal some of our chickens." And the daughter said, "He looks like the minister's son, who, they say, leads a riotous life." I went in as one. They received me as three.

MR. GOD IS NOT IN :: A FARCE

HARBOR ALLEN

SCENE: *An office with an air of prosperity, conventionality and efficiency. Desks, chairs, a small safe and filing cabinets. A door on the left is marked "Private" A door on the right is half open.*

(Gabriel, who looks like a clerk, is trying to keep a young woman, poorly dressed, from entering the room).

GABRIEL: What do you want to see him for?

MINNIE: That ain't none of your business.

GABRIEL: Then you can't come in.

MINNIE: I gotta see 'im. I tell you, I gotta see 'im. Aw, lemme in. *(She tries to rush fast him).*

GABRIEL: Here, stop it. You can't. It's against the laws—don't you—*(The woman struggles to enter. Meanwhile a dapper fellow enters the room from the office on the left. He is thin-lipped, business-like, the apotheosis of the efficient secretary).*

MINNIE: *(Shrilly)* You can't stop me. Try it once! Lemme in, I tell you! *(She forces her way in, hustles him into the hall, slams the door, and locks him out).*

GABRIEL: *(Outside)* Here, you can't do that. It isn't allowed. You come right out of there, do you hear?

MINNIE: Shut up.

GABRIEL: *(Pounding on the door)* Open the door, you—you slut!

PETER: *(The secretary)* Gabriel! No obscenities, if you please. *(The woman turns. A primitive type, lean and fierce, she is nevertheless half-cowed by the secretary's air of efficiency. He brushes her aside and opens the door).*

GABRIEL: *(Entering)* She's a tough one, sir. She pushed me out and locked the door on me.

PETER: You may go, Gabriel. I'll take care of her. *(Gabriel leaves.)*

PETER: *(To Minnie)* Well? *(She stares. He takes a stef toward her.)* Well?

MINNIE: *(Hesitating)* I—I wanna see—Are you—? *(Suddenly she breaks down and throws herself on her knees.)* O God, help me, help me! Help me!

PETER: Get up!

MINNIE: I ain't got nobody else to go to now.

PETER: My dear woman, will you get up?

MINNIE: Not till you promise me you're gonna help me.

PETER: That sort of thing is not allowed around here. Get up at once! *(He helps her up. With his foot he carefully straightens the rug. Then he brushes himself off.)*

MINNIE: Are you him?

PETER: Who?

MINNIE: The Lord.

PETER: No. Of course, not.

MINNIE: Who are you then? *(He doesn't answer: she isn't worth it.)*

What's the matter? Afraid to tell me who y'are?

PETER: If you must know, I'm his private secretary. My name's Peter. Now, if you tell me what you came for—

MINNIE: Oh, you're Saint Peter, ain't you?

PETER: I suppose that's what they call me. Popular mythology, anthropomorphic deities, and all that sort of bunk.

MINNIE: Ain't that funny? I always kinda thought you was just a fake the preachers kept pumpin' the hot air about. But you ain't, are you? *(Awed.)* Saint Peter! *(She goes down on her knees again.)*

PETER: *(Vexed)* Say! Stop that, can you! *(She scrambles to her feet and he worries with the rug again.)*

PETER: *(Talking to himself more or less)* They all do that, these ignorant people. Wearing a hole right through that priceless Persian rug presented to us by the Borgias. *(To Minnie)* Well, what do you want? Be quick about it. Time's valuable around here.

MINNIE: *(Simply)* I wanna see God.

PETER: What do you want to see him for?

MINNIE: I want to pray to him—

PETER: Yes, yes. What do you want to *get* from him.

MINNIE: Help. He's gotta help me. I'm sick. I'm poor. I got troubles. Terrible troubles.

PETER: We all have those, rich and poor alike.

MINNIE: *(Persistently)* I wanna see God.

PETER: *(Lying)* God's not in.

MINNIE: They told me God's always in for the poor and the sick. They told me God's everywhere.

PETER: Don't be silly. How could he be everywhere at once? It isn't rational. *(There is a loud laugh from the Private Office.)*

MINNIE: That's him. That's him. I know it's him. *(She rushes for the door. Peter goes after her and holds her back.)*

PETER: You can't go in there. That office is private. Where do you think you are, butting in everywhere like that?

MINNIE: *(Fiercely)* I'm in heaven, ain't I?

PETER: Offices in heaven are private like anywhere else.

MINNIE: Private! Private! That don't mean nothin' to me. You lied to me. You said God wasn't in. He *is* in. I wanna see God.

PETER: God's in conference.

MINNIE: *(Desperately)* I tell you, I gotta see him. He'd help me if he knew. My kids are hungry. I'm sick. I'm gonna have another kid. He's gotta help me. There ain't nobody else that can.

PETER: *(Bored)* That may all be very true, but it's old stuff, old stuff. For the last five thousand years people have been trooping in here one after another with sob stories about hungry children. I wish they'd put some of these new fangled Marxian theories in practice down there on earth if only to give us a rest. My God, I'm tired of this job. *(God, a stout man who looks like a comic strip capitalist from his bald head to the diamond stud in his tie and the spats on his pudgy feet, comes out of the office on the left. Laughing, he carries a cheap-looking magazine open in his hand.)*

GOD: Did I hear you use my name, Peter?

PETER: Yes, sir.

GOD: Just don't use it in vain, that's all.

PETER: No, sir.

GOD: And Peter, you might send a note to the heavenly editorial staff complimenting them in my name on the last issue of *Celestial Confessions*. *(He thumbs the magazine.)* It's good. Very good. In fact, you might tell them it's almost as amusing as *Infernal Frolics*, published by the firm in the basement. *(He opens to a page, chuckles, turns over, and chuckles again.)* Listen to this: "He took me in his arms and his wings beat passionately in the air. 'My angel!' I cried, as we floated away gently on a cloud." *(Peter tries to signal to him the presence of Minnie, but he is too absorbed. Chuckling.)* Here's another. This is even better. *(He reads and laughs in a salacious manner.)* Well, well, now who'd have thought that of James? Listen to this: "Then St. James took us to his room and—*(Suddenly he becomes aware of Peter's signals)* Huh? What? Oh—oh, yes. *(He turns and sees Minnie.)*

PETER: *(Taking the magazine suavely from him)* A woman to see you, sir.

GOD: Yes, quite so. *(He assumes an official manner.)* You wish to see me?

MINNIE: Are you God?

GOD: That's me.

MINNIE: *(After an uncertain fause)* You don't look like God. God: Peter?

PETER: You look all right to me, sir.

GOD: The mirror, please. *(Peter hands him a mirror in which he inspects himself.)*

MINNIE: You look just like the boss in the mills I used to work fer.

GOD: Peter. *(He indicates a circle about his head.)*

PETER: Yes, sir. *(From a drawer he gets a wire halo which he fastens to the back of God's collar.)* There you are, sir.

GOD: *(To Minnie)* Now, what can I do for you?

MINNIE: I need help, God. My man,

GOD: Just a minute. What's your name?

MINNIE: Minnie Blunt.

GOD: Do you pray, Minnie?

MINNIE: Well, not very often. You see—

GOD: Just a minute. Peter?

PETER: Yes, sir. *(Peter goes to the filing cabinet in the rear.)* B—B1—Blunt, Blunt. *(Turning.)* There's no record here, sir. There's a Mamie Blunt, but no Minnie.

GOD: You haven't prayed lately, I fear, Minnie. We have no record in the card index system.

MINNIE: *(Defiant)* I ain't had no time to think about prayin'.

GOD: That's bad, Minnie. Very bad.

MINNIE: I gotta work day and night to keep the kids clean and well and going to school. And Charlie—that's my man—last week Charlie—he—he—*(She is about to break down again, her breath coming in gasps.)*

GOD: *(Impatiently)* Yes, that's too bad. Too bad. But—er—I'm rather busy now, Minnie. Peter?

PETER: Yes, sir?

GOD: A blank.

PETER: *(From the drawer of the desk)* Here you are, sir.

GOD: You just sit down in the outer office there, Minnie, and fill out this blank. Name, age, married or single, occupation, husband's occupation, political views—that's very important—church affiliations, education, income tax, petty sins, major sins, and so forth and so on. Hand it to Peter when you're through. I'll have the Board consider it and we'll see what we can do. You take care of her, Peter.

PETER: Yes, sir. *(God sighs in relief and starts toward office.)*

MINNIE: God, I can't tell you this way. You gotta listen to me. It ain't only me. There's thousands like me. You gotta listen to me, God.

GOD: Don't you see how busy I am, Minnie? Fill out the blank. That'll be enough.

MINNIE: No. I won't. It's your business to listen to me.

PETER: Minnie, calm yourself. We can't stop and listen to idle stories. We've got to be efficient. We get thousands of petitions like yours. It will be filed and attended to when we get around to it.

MINNIE: Petitions! Blanks! You'd think I was in a shyster's office. I won't let 'im go till he listens to me. (*She seizes God by the coat tails. He tries, with Peter's help, to escape.*)

GOD: Minnie!

PETER: Woman! That's sacrilege! (*In the midst of the struggle, the door opens to admit Gabriel.*)

GABRIEL: Right this way, gentlemen! (*He goes out. Enter a large, florid, pompous man in a cutaway, and a drab, wizened little fellow with a sour face. All are taken aback. Minnie, nonplussed, releases God. Peter removes her through the right door.*)

ROACH: (*The large man, a glib talker*) Pardon me. I take it I am speaking to God.

GOD: That's me.

ROACH: Permit me to introduce myself, God. I am the Rev. Billy Rolls-Roach, D. D., LL. D., F. R. C. S. E., general secretary of the Christian Fundamentals Society of the World, the Bible Crusaders of the Universe, and the Anti-Evolution League of the Western Hemisphere.

GOD: The pleasure is mine. (*They shake hands.*)

ROACH: This (*Pointing to the little fellow*) is Judge John D. Dispepsy. Judge Dispepsy is owner of two steel mills, three mines, and a string of Florida hotels with a bible in each room. It is he who magnanimously provides the money with which we are enabled to fight for the salvation of the world in Jesus' name.

DISPEPSY: *(Loudly)* Amen!

GOD: *(Sanctimoniously)* Amen!

DISPEPSY: Pleased to meetcha, God. *(They shake.)*

ROACH: When the great prophet Bryan—

DISPEPSY: May his soul rest in peace.

GOD: Amen!

ROACH: *(Rhetorically, with a hand on Dispepsy)* When the great Bryan fell and died leading the gallant charge for the kingdom of heaven on earth, the standard of the pious was caught up by this noble, Godfearing, Christian business man of Clearwater, Florida, and today the flag of Fundamentalism is borne aloft and the heart of every pious American and every soldier of the Cross and every lover of religious liberty is stirred as never before, and every one is nerved for the great battle which will never end until every Evolutionist and every Infidel and every Anti-Christ is driven from the pulpits and the tax-supported schools of America! *(He ends in a burst of soap-box rhetoric.)*

DISPEPSY: A-men!

GOD: Splendid! I am heartily in accord.

ROACH: *(Ecstatic)* God, do you know that the theory of evolution is sweeping the world and is causing the very foundations of liberty, morals, and Christianity to totter?

GOD: Indeed?

ROACH: *(Approaching and shaking his finger in God's face)* Do you know that godless men are teaching young, innocent, and impressionable minds that your own son, the Saviour Jesus Christ, was not immaculately conceived?

GOD: No! How dare they?

ROACH: Do you know that scientists now claim Christ did not come down from heaven, but that he came up from the jungle, from a monkey with a tail?

GOD: This is intolerable!

ROACH: *(Mournfully)* God, my good friend God, do you know that these men are trying to do away with you? Before you know it, God, people won't believe that you exist any more!

GOD: *(Pounding the desk)* I won't stand for it. I won't stand for it. *(Walking up and down.)* But what am I to do? What am I to do?

ROACH: Send down a bolt of lightning or a plague to exterminate these mind-poisoners, these faith-destroyers, these vile, blasphemous, unholy creatures.

DISPEPSY: Amen!

GOD: No…No, I can't do that. The day of the plagues, I fear, is passed.

ROACH: Then at least you can endorse our campaign and sign a statement saying that you yourself wrote the bible and created the world in six days as per Genesis.

GOD: *(Hesitating)* Well—as a matter of fact, you see I really *didn't* write the bible.

ROACH: *(Starting)* What is this you say? You didn't—write—the—

GOD: I don't do detail work like that. I'm a high-priced executive, don't you understand, gentlemen? The bible was written by the celestial editorial staff. *(He rings.)*

PETER: *(Entering)* Did you ring, sir?

GOD: Peter, you read the proofs of the bible, did you not?

PETER: Indeed, I did, sir. And what a time I had with all that queerlooking Hebrew language. I remember it well.

GOD: There, gentlemen. I trust that is satisfactory.

ROACH: Perfectly. Now, if you will affix your signature here, God—

GOD: Hm. . my spectacles, Peter.

ROACH: Ah, let me read it for you. *(Rhetorically)* This is to certify that I, Almighty God, who created all earth and man, as I have heretofore explained in Genesis, believe that the hour has come when evangelical Christians must heed the scriptural injunction to contend earnestly for the faith which was once delivered to the saints, and must organize to establish the rising generation in the orthodox faith of the fathers, to war against modernism, to promote faith in the miracles, the immaculate conception, and all the other doctrines of historical Christianity, and to secure effective legislation in every country in the world against the insidious spread of the un-Christian doctrine of evolution. To the Christian Fundamentals Society of the World, the Bible Crusaders of the Universe, and the Anti-Evolution League of the Western Hemisphere, I give my heartiest personal endorsement. Signed—

GOD: *(Signing)* God!

ROACH: This meeting has been a great pleasure to us, I assure you. *(Patting God on the back.)* God, old chap, remember if you are ever in trouble you can always count on your warm friends, the Rev. Billy Rolls-Roach and the magnanimous Christian gentleman from Florida, Judge John D. Dispepsy.

GOD: That's very kind of you.

ROACH: Good day.

DISPEPSY: Goo' bye.

GOD and PETER: Good day. Goodbye. Come again. *(They leave, Roach pompously, Dispepsy shuffling. Peter dances attendance to them out the door.)*

MINNIE: *(Entering the moment they are out)* Honest, I can't fill this out. I'm all upset, what with worryin and my man—

PETER: *(Returning)* Minnie! I told you not to—

MINNIE: *(Ignoring him)* God, won't you listen to me?

GOD: Why don't you do what you're told to do, Minnie?

GABRIEL: *(Announcing at the door)* Right this way gentlemen. *(He goes out.)*

GOD: There, you see. More conferences, Minnie. What am I to do? *(Two men appear at the door.)* Come in, gentlemen. *(Peter takes Minnie out again. The visitors are business men of the alert type, both dressed in dapper Fifth Avenue fashion, both with long cigars in their mouths, papers in their pockets, fort-folios under their arms, and an air of consuming important.)*

BULL: This is God, I gather?

GOD: That's me.

BULL: Pleased to meetcha, God. My name is Bull. This is my partner, Durham. Bull and Durham. *(Handing God a card.)* Advertising and publicity specialists. *(Shakes God's hand.)* We are both very much interested in selling religion to the common people.

GOD: Is that so?

DURHAM: Yes. We've written a book called *Christ, The Original Go-Getter.* It proves absolutely that your own son, Jesus Christ, was the best salesman in Palestine and the Near East. A remarkable book, God, with a complete analysis of the salesmanship methods by which the young man sold high-pressure Christianity to the world.

GOD: Well, well, who would have thought that of the lad?

BULL: It's a book, sir, no man who calls himself educated can do without. An indispensable book in office, home, school, factory, church, or paradise. *(Draws a thick book from the folio.)* Do you know how many bushels of olives were sold the day after the sermon on the Mount of Olives?

GOD: Why—no—I—

BULL: Do you know how much the tabloid and moving picture rights for Gethsemane were worth?

GOD: Now let's see. Well, to be frank—

BULL: Do you know who syndicated the *True Confessions of Mother Mary* and to how many newspapers?

GOD: Who, I'm afraid—

DURHAM: *(Shaking his head)* Really, God, a man in your high executive position—t-t-t-t-t-!

GOD: *(Shamefaced)* Well, you see I'm a busy man. How much did you say the book costs?

BULL: Five dollars down and a dollar a week until millenium. Sign right here, sir. *(God signs.)* And here's the book. No, wait. *(Magnanimously.)* I'll autograph it for you. There! Five dollars, please. *(God rings. Peter appears.)*

GOD: Make out a check for $5 to this gentleman, Peter.

PETER: How shall I list it?

GOD: Books.

PETER: *(Shaking his head)* You know how the executive board feels about spending money for books, sir. Especially since you never read them.

GOD: *(Irritably)* I'll take care of the board, Peter. *(Peter makes out the check for Bull.)*

DURHAM: *(Offers God a long cigar)* Smoke?

GOD: Thanks. *(Smells)* Hm, Havana. *(He lights up. Both sit down.)*

DURHAM: Now, God, what we really came to talk to you about is a little project we have in mind. You see, the whole world has been made absolutely efficient, thoroughly purified for big business. There isn't a village anywhere that hasn't already been boosted nor an empty lot that hasn't been boomed. So we have been sent here as representatives of the Rokiwanary Clubs of the Solar System to help you launch a campaign for a Bigger and Better Heaven. What are your latest census figures?

GOD: Peter!

PETER: Yes, sir?

GOD: Our latest census figures.

PETER: *(Whipping out his note book)* 22,869,103 to be exact, sir. Of course, that doesn't include the 8,426 in the non-Nordic section or the 31 in the Jim Crow division.

DURHAM: And what is the population of hell?

PETER: They claim over 80 million. But then, hell always cheats. Besides, they accept aliens, radicals, actors, artists and other such riff-raff, whereas we are accessible only to citizens of solid worth and substantial social position.

BULL: Ah, but you are being left behind.

DURHAM: Hell is growing more powerful.

BULL: Hell is doing better advertising.

DURHAM: Hell is making a stronger appeal.

BULL: Smart people have begun to *prefer* to go to hell.

DURHAM: Can you allow that, God?

BULL: Are you willing to sit back and become a back number, a second rate resort?

GOD: But what am I to do? We haven't enough room for more. They are sitting three and four on a single cloud already.

BULL: Then lease more space from the nearest solar system.

DURHAM: That's the idea. Expansion, God, expansion. The whole world, is expanding and you don't want to be left out of it, do you?

BULL: Let me tell you what you need. First, a good brisk advertising campaign. Posters, circulars, car ads, handbills, electric signs on public squares. A few good slogans, such as—

DURHAM: "Heaven Wants You."

BULL: "You Won't Be Lonesome With Us."

DURHAM: "It's Hell Not to Be in Heaven."

BULL: "See Heaven First."

DURHAM: How about a few miracles?

GOD: No. No miracles. I've tried them recently. They don't get across the way they used to.

BULL: Nonsense. You leave it to us. Together with our old friend the Rev. Billy Rolls-Roach, whom we met on the way, *we'll* take care of the miracles.

DURHAM: You'll also need some good road signs on the way up.

BULL: And an electric flash over the Golden Gate. "Welcome to God's Own Country!"

DURHAM: "Free Camping Sites for Tourists."

BULL: "Clouds for Sale Cheap."

DURHAM: I tell you, God, such a campaign would put heaven back on the map.

BULL: And it would cost you only—(*he makes notations on a piece of paper*)—only 499,999 dollars and 98 cents.

DURHAM: And 15 per cent for our services.

BULL: Total: 507,499 dollars and 96 cents.

GOD: Hm. What do you say, Peter?

PETER It seems like a lot of money to me, sir.

BULL: It's a bargain

DURHAM: Dirt cheap!

BULL: As a matter of fact, we usually charge 20 per cent for our services.

DURHAM: It's only because this is such a noble, Christian project, that we have agreed to undertake it at such a personal loss.

BULL: Besides, hell is already "sold" on the idea.

GOD: Oh, are you going to do the same thing for hell?

DURHAM: Yes. The gentleman below was keen about it.

BULL: Fairly ate it up.

DURHAM: God, can you afford to hesitate?

GOD: Are you going to manage both campaigns?

BULL: Why not?

GOD: At the same time?

DURHAM: Of course.

GOD: But I say—

BULL: Oh, you mustn't let sentimentality interfere with business, God.
God: No, but—

DURHAM: Think of the publicity value: Heaven versus Hell. The upper world pitted against the lower in a battle for souls. Think of how the sport writers will eat it up.

DURHAM: That's the idea, God. Friendly rivalry and sportsmanship. *(Clapping God on the back.)* And above all, God's a good sport. Eh, what?

GOD: *(Yielding)* What do you think, Peter?

BULL: *(Shoving a paper under his nose)* The contract's all drawn up. Here's where you sign. *(Forcing a fen in his hand.)*

GOD: Eh, Peter?

PETER: Suit yourself, sir. But you know how the executive board feels about our expenditures.

BULL: *(Moving the fen in God's reluctant hand.)* Yes, sir. That s the way. *(God has signed almost before he knows it.)*

BULL: *(Pocketing the contract)* So! *(Shaking hands with God.)* I'm sure you will have nothing to regret.

DURHAM: We will do our utmost for heaven's sake. Smoke? *(A cigar to God.)* Smoke? *(A cigar to Peter. Both accept with nods.)*

BULL: Good day, gentlemen.

DURHAM: Good day to you.

GOD and PETER: Good day, good day. *(They go out arm in arm, keeping stef.)*

GOD: *(After a fause.)* Well, that's that.

PETER: A lot of money, sir.

GOD: But worth it.

PETER: The intellectuals will say all that advertising is vulgar, sir.

GOD: *(Irritably)* I wish you'd stop throwing the intellectuals up at me all the time. They never did take much stock in me anyway. All they care about is logic, rationalism. I'm not rational.

PETER: *(Losing control)* That s just it, sir.

GOD: *(Angry)* That's just it: you are You're getting entirely too rational to suit me, Peter. I'm beginning to think even *you* don't believe in me any more.

PETER: Have I ever intimated such a thing, sir?

GOD: No, not directly. But if you don't look out, there's going to be another secretary around here, that s all I can say.

PETER: I'm very efficient, sir. shouldn't have any trouble getting another job.

GOD: *(Sneering)* With the resort in the basement, I suppose?

PETER: They pay more than you, sir. Union wages.

GOD: So? No doubt they've already approached you on the subject?

PETER: That's not altogether impossible.

GOD: Indeed? And when are you leaving us, if I may ask?

PETER: At once, if you say so.

GOD: *(Melting)* Now, now, Peter. Don't be a fool. How much have they offered you?

PETER: Double what I get here. God: Hm. A lot of money. I'll have to take it up with the board. You know how the board feels about expenditures! But I'll do my best for you, Peter.

PETER: Thank you, sir.

GOD: *(Yawning)* Well, I hope that's all for today. People don't realize what it means to run a place like this. *(At his watch)* Two o'clock. How about a little golf?

PETER: That was just what I was thinking.

GOD: I'll get the clubs. *(He starts to go. Minnie enters.)*

MINNIE: God!

GOD: Holy Jerusalem! You still here?

MINNIE: I'm still waitin' for you, God.

GOD: I told you I haven't any time.

MINNIE: You had time for them others, all right.

GOD: Those were important religious delegates.

MINNIE: Yeh! I heard what kinda delegates they was.

GOD: You heard? Peter, how did she hear us?

MINNIE: I listened at the door.

PETER: She listened at the door, sir. God: Oh, very well. Go ahead with your spiel. Only make it short. I'm a tired business man. *(He sits down gloomily in a chair.)*

MINNIE: It's about my man, God.

GOD: What about him?

MINNIE: My man—he—he got killed.

GOD: What can I do about it? I can't bring him alive again. The scientists wouldn't stand for it.

MINNIE: But you can help me and the kids. Where else can I go fer help! I went to a preacher, but all he said was I should call on God.

GOD: Were you married to this man, Minnie?

MINNIE: Sure. What you think I am?

GOD: How'd he get killed?

MINNIE: He was excavatin' for one of them skyscrapers and some rock fell down on 'im. Smashed 'im. Smashed 'im flat. God, you shoulda seen the way they brought him home—all smashed and bloody. He was a good-lookin' guy, my man was. Big and strong as a horse. He had blue eyes and yella hair that sorta kept hangin' down over his eyes. And he was good to me, too. He didn t beat me much, 'cept when he got drunk. You can't blame a man for drinkin' a drop when he's gotta work so hard. He was good to the kids, too. Always bringin' 'em somethin' home from the ten cent store: one of them little jumpin' monkeys, or some choc'late drops or a balloon or somethin.' The kids was crazy about 'im. He was kinda spoilin' 'em, I'd always tell 'im. But then he'd always say, "God knows, they am t gonna have life none too easy." He was jist gettin' the new furniture paid off and things was goin' kinda nice and then—one day they brought 'im home smashed. Smashed flat. *(She rocks a little.)* And he was a swell lookin' man, he was. You shoulda seen 'im, God. He was sorta big and clean-lookin, and then—then—they brought him home smashed.

GOD: *(After a fause.)* Hm. That's too bad, too bad. *(Rising.)* Now, you leave your blank with my secretary—*(Minnie starts to object but is silenced by a gesture)*—and—Peter! *(Quietly)* Fix her up, will you?

PETER: How much, sir?

GOD: Oh—one. *(Generously.)* No. make it two. *(He starts out.)*

MINNIE: God—

GOD: Now, now, Minnie. No more. I've just given Peter complete instruction. *(He goes out. Peter goes to a safe and takes two bills. These he flourishes grandly into Minnie's hand.)*

PETER: Here you are, Minnie. One, two.

MINNIE: What's that for?

PETER: *(Patronizing)* Oh, a little contribution from God—and myself. Your blank. *(He removes the paper from her hand as she stands dazed before him.)* Why, you haven't filled it out! It's got to be completely filled out, Minnie. *(He returns it.)*

MINNIE: *(Staring at the money)* Conterbution. Conterbution. Say, what you think I am, a beggar? *(Growing suddenly furious)* Here, take your lousy two dollars. Two dollars. *(She throws the money in his face.)* Blanks! Name, age, married, sins. *(She tears the blank to bits and hurls them at him.)* There! There!

PETER: Then you'd better go. That's all we can do for you.

MINNIE: No. I won't go. I want what's comin' to me.

PETER: I'll have you thrown out.

MINNIE: All right. Throw me out! Throw me out! I'd rather be in hell any day. All my life I been told God'd help me. I struggled and sacrificed, and my man he struggled and sacrificed, and the kids they suffered and hungered. But we didn't mind 'cause we thought God'd help us in the end. Help us? That's funny! *(She laughs.)* That big fat mutt help *us!* *(Turning on him fiercely.)* You're a fake, that's what you are. All heaven's a fake. It's just a big fraud to keep us poor people from gettin' what's comin' to us. "You'll get pie in the sky when you die." Yeah! The hell you will!

PETER: That's blasphemy. Sacrilege! Gabriel!! Gabriel!!

GABRIEL: *(Entering)* Yes, sir. PETER: Put this woman out.

GABRIEL: Yes, sir. *(As he approaches her, she strikes him in the face. He staggers back. She glares at them, a veritable tigress.)*

MINNIE: Touch me. Touch me, why why don'tcha! I dare you to. *(For a long moment the men glare at her, not daring to move. The right door opens. Enter a timid little woman, poorly dressed.)*

WOMAN: *(Timidly)* Please, may I see God? *(A fause. All turn toward her.)*

PETER: *(Sharply)* God's busy.

MINNIE: What you wanna see God for?

PETER: You keep out of this.

MINNIE: You shut up.

WOMAN: My man got killed in a mine and I—I wanna ask God—if he can't help me and the kids.

MINNIE: Help you? Say, that's good. You won't get any help around this joint unless you got something *sell*.

WOMAN: But what can I do??

MINNIE: Go back to earth and *take* what's comin' to you. That's what I'm going to do. Come along. *(She takes the woman by the hand and out they go. The two men stand watching them depart.)*

GABRIEL: My! Isn't she a wild cat!

PETER: There's been entirely too much of this Red stuff lately. A little advertising won't be a bad thing, after all. *(He goes to God's door.)*

PETER: God?

GOD: *(Peevish)* What now?

PETER: She's gone.

GOD: *(Appearing cautiously)* Thank the saints.

PETER: How about that game of golf?

GOD: First rate.

PETER: Gabriel, the clubs. *(They start off.)*

(CURTAIN)

SOME SOUTHERN SNAPSHOTS

GEORGE S. SCHUYLER

SOUTHERN KENTUCKY

B——, a hustling, thriving community in the tobacco country, is conceded by both its black and white citizens to be one of the best towns in the South. Incidentally, this is a belief held by the inhabitants of every Southern town. Well, Johnny S——, a Negro youth of sixteen was employed in a white barber shop as porter and bootblack. He is an affable chap and knows how to get on well with white people. He always has a smile for everyone and doesn't seem to resent having his woolly head rubbed or his pants being kicked occasionally. He was a favorite in the town until several months ago. Then one day the rumor got abroad that he had made or tried to make a date with a white girl over the telephone. One of the white barbers said he heard him. The white girl in question denied that Johnny had said anything out of the way to her; that she had only telephoned about a pair of shoes she had left to be cleaned. However, public opinion was aroused. Johnny's past popularity was of no avail. He was told to get out of town at once. He got.

NORTHERN GEORGIA

Mrs. F. teaches in one of the many Negro colleges in A——. One day, a short while ago she boarded a side-entrance street car and being out of breath sank down in the first seat in the rear half of the car. This section is usually alloted to Negroes. The conductor gruffly ordered her to sit in the rear. "You know where niggers belong," he admonished. Without a word she went back to the rear of the car and opening a book began to read. As she glanced up from time to time, she noticed that the conductor was making frequent trips to the front of the car and conferring with the motorman. Then the car stopped and the conductor got off. When she looked up again there was a policeman standing at her elbow. He grabbed her by the collar and ordered her to get out of the car, at the same time twisting her wrist. All the negroes who were on the car got off and hastened away. She begged the policeman to let go her collar and stop twisting her wrist, but he only tightened his grip, saying: "If you don't want to obey the regulations here, why don't you go up North?"

When the patrol wagon arrived in response to the policeman's summons, she was bundled inside. The only other occupant was an elderly policeman who made repeated advances to her during the trip to the station and mauled her all over. At the station she gave the required data as to age, residence, occupation, etc., and requested the privilege of using the telephone. This was denied. While in the room, several patrolmen who were off beat entertained themselves by making comments concerning her.—feigned to doubt her sex and suggested that the doubt should be removed by examination. She was turned over to the matron who allowed her to telephone to the President of the college where she taught. He immediately came down and arranged bond. A few days later at the trial, she was fined twenty-five dollars.

Northeastern Alabama

In T——, a beautiful hill town, which is the seat of one of the best Negro colleges in the South, a white farmer of considerable means is wont to come into town with either of his two little sons. He likes to take them around to the various stores and ask them in the presence of other white men: "Tell them what your name is?"—*their* name being *his* name. Nothing extraordinary about this, of course, until the fact is mentioned that the boys are mulattoes and their mother a black woman. This happy family lives in a neat bungalow on the outskirts of T——. The Klan, which has considerable strength in the community, has threatened to go out and teach this farmer a lesson, but they have neglected, so far, to do so. The white farmer says he is anxious to have them come. He has an excellent reputation as a rifle shot.

Southeastern Louisiana

B——boasts of possessing the largest sawmill in the world. It also has a huge paper mill that utilizes all the waste from the sawmill. One company owns both, and most of the inhabitants of the community (about ten thousand), make their living by working for this company. It is alleged to be controlled by Northern capital. The company owns most of the houses in B——and operates a large general store, where workingmen may get goods for cash or credit. Negroes constitute one-fourth of the population. Shortly after the late alleged struggle for democracy, the white and black workers got it into their heads to form a union and try to get their pay raised. Poor fellows! A white worker was chosen president and several negroes were made officials. Alarmed, the company immediately shut down the mill for ninety days, surrounded the plant with a high fence, hired a platoon of tough "guards," ousted union men from the company houses and sat down to watch the workers starve. Since there was no other work to be had in the town or vicinity, many of the workers nearly did starve. Others went to work in distant places.

At the end of ninety days the work started up again—with scab labor. Picketing was tried. The "guards" beat, buffeted, and it is alleged, murdered. Certainly some mysterious bodies (black) were found in neighboring swamps and some of the Negro union officials were missing. The company surmised that certain prominent Negroes, who owned much property or operated small businesses, were instrumental in getting Negroes to join the union. Consequently, several of these were administered terrible beatings and given only minutes to get out of town. The town's only Negro doctor was horribly maltreated and banished, but later he was found to be innocent of any offense against the company, so he was written a letter and told he might return. Some of the Negroes never dared to return. One Negro who owned a nice two-story house on the edge of town, was nearly killed by a group of "guards" police and white citizens and told never to return. He never has. Today his house stands deserted, the prey of the elements. Negroes of the town say there is "a standing mob" in the town, ready at all times to riot and murder to uphold white supremacy and the open shop. But then, Negroes are so imaginative, you know.

The Mississippi Delta

In the heart of what is probably the richest cotton producing area in the world, stands G——. Half of its population of fifteen thousand is black. In the surrounding county inent and wealthy white man. One night, after the graduation exercises at the Negro school, this black boy was shot to death by two other Negroes on the steps of the school. It is said the two Negroes were hired for the purpose. This is doubtless a falsehood since it is contrary to the spirit of Southern chivalry. At any rate they were both acquitted very promptly by the court. A few months ago I saw both of them walking the streets in G——. there are six Negroes to every white person. This town is just a supply station for the neighboring plantations. The planters are lords of all they survey. This includes, of course, the Negro women. Negro men bitterly complain that scores of Negro women are "kept"—rather willingly—by white men. Since there are a number of Negro men around town who do no work and yet dress well and eat frequently, the charge is probably true.

Well, a year or two ago a Negro boy of fourteen who was attending the Negro high school, began keeping company with a beautiful brown girl. This girl was "kept" by a very prom

Not so long ago a white man and a young Negro had an argument on a plantation not far from G——. It ended in a fight and the Caucasian came out a bad second. As a measure of precaution, the Negro immediately bundled together his effects and moved to G——. The white man came to town soon after and while walking around the streets came upon the young Negro sitting on the curbing. Pulling out his revolver, the white man walked up behind the Negro and pressing the gun against his wooly pate, said, "Ahm gonna kill you, you black son of a——." He pulled the trigger and the Negro fell dead in the gutter. The white man was not arrested, the white observers informing the coroner that he shot in self defense.

Northeastern Texas

In C——, there is a very pretty little *public* library. There is reason to believe, however, that one-third of its ten thousand inhabitants are not welcome there, being Negroes. At least it is assumed they are not welcome because a Negro doctor said that although he had been born and raised in the town, he had never tried to get a book from the library. Nor had any other Negro. The two races, it seems, "understand each other" in C——.

P——is a town near the Oklahoma border, where about six years ago, two Negroes were barbecued for "the usual crime" by a group of orderly whites on the Fair Ground. The Negroes have boycotted the County Fair ever since. They seem to think that procedure wasn't fair. Time and again the whites have tried to persuade them to attend the County Fair, but to no avail. The Negroes are adamant.

Eastern Alabama

Mrs. X is a Negro cook in the home of a wealthy merchant in O——, a town not far from Tuskagee Institute. Some time ago her husband got into some difficulty that required her presence at the court house. She informed her mistress that she had to go away for a short while, explaining that the midday meal was all prepared and ready to be placed on the table. The mistress, was furious and denied Mrs. X permission to go. Mrs. X went. She had hardly departed when the merchant arrived and his wife told him what had transpired. Very angry, he jumped into his car and overtook Mrs. X right at the door of the court house. With an oath he grabbed her and administered a sound beating. A large number of Negro men were standing around but none interfered. There were a number of white men standing there, too, with hands ever ready to whisk light artillery out of rear pockets. After severely whipping Mrs. X, her assailant saw Mr. X descending the court house steps. Walking over to him, the merchant told him what had taken place and asked him didn't he like it. The husband meekly replied, "Yassuh, Ah likes it."

Western Georgia

Bill Smith is a sturdy brown man, close to fifty years of age. All day he sits on a stool behind the counter in his little restaurant, which is located on a dusty street in the Negro district of L——. It was only after some time that I discovered why he remained so stationary. Two or three years ago he lost both legs above the knees when an old wall collapsed where he was working on a construction job. For many years previously Bill had been a bricklayer and had worked in all parts of the country. As we sat in his little place and watched the clouds of dust plowed up by the passing automobiles, we fell to talking about the town.

I commented on the absence of sewers, sidewalks and trash collection in the Negro section, and the miserable shacks occupied by the majority of the Negroes but owned by the cotton mill and the fertilizer plant. I ventured the opinion that something should be done about it. Bill glanced at me pityingly.

"When I came back here after my accident," he said, "and opened this little place, a lot of fellows used to hang out here, playing checkers and talking. Naturally they would ask me about the places I had seen in other parts of the country and the condition of the colored people living in those parts. Well, of course, I told them the truth just like it is in the North, East, West and South. Well, sir! You know one day a white man came in here and sat right where you're sitting now, and told me that he and some other white folks had heard about what I'd been saying, and advised me to stop talking or get out of town. He said: 'Since these niggers don't know any better, there ain't no use telling them no better. You know better because you've traveled, but they don't. So you better keep your mouth shut hereafter.'

"So," Bill concluded, "that was the first or last time I, or anybody else, ever tried to tell these people around here anything for their own good. It ain't safe in L——." Bill Smith was born and raised there, so he ought to know.

Northeastern Mississippi

T——is a progressive town. Negro men, women and boys sentenced for crimes or misdemeanors are all worked on the city streets together under armed guard. Consequently the white section of the city is very neat and clean.

Central Oklahoma

B——is a town of 2,000 Negroes in the heart of a rich cotton district. For ten miles in every direction everything is owned by Negroes. Everything is controlled by Negroes from the mayor down to the telegraph operator.

There are two banks, each with a quarter million deposits, three cotton gins—one the largest in the state—three blocks of stores housed in substantial brick buildings, and many neat and beautiful homes.

There is no jim-crowing in this town. Many white people visit it on business every day. If they wish to eat they must eat in a Negro restaurant; if they wish to sleep they must sleep in a Negro rooming house, where Negroes sleep on all sides of them. Do the white men and women who frequently visit B——, go without food and shelter because there are no separate provisions for them? Not at all. In my rooming house there was a white man to the left of me and a white woman across the hall. We all ate in the restaurant together. Yet a similar situation ten miles distant might have caused a race conflict.

Eastern Mississippi

O——is a very small town not far from the Alabama border. Here is located a Negro industrial school which has been in operation for a quarter of a century. Two years ago a dog belonging to one of the Negro professors killed one of the domestic animals of a white citizen. On Commencement Day, when the campus was crowded with visitors for the ceremony, this white citizen walked on the grounds and after a brief exchange of words with this Negro professor, shot him dead before the crowd. The murderer was never arrested. Naturally the Negroes were considerably wrought up over the tragedy but feeling has since died down and the community is now pursuing the even tenor of its way.

Central Arkansas

Some time ago Miss G, a pretty Negro school teacher in one of the Negro colleges in L——, was walking home along a dark street. Suddenly a long, low roadster driven by a young white man slowed up alongside the curb and the driver called to her: "Come here, baby." She merely quickened her pace. He continued to keep abreast of her; telling her to "Come on in and go for a ride." Finally, when he saw that she was not heeding him, he stopped the car, jumped out, and grabbing her by the arm, hissed in her ear: "You black bitch! If you don't get in here I'll take this wrench and knock your block off." She pulled away from him, screamed for help and ran up the street. He followed her a few paces, but when a policeman and several Negroes hove into sight he returned to his roadster and sped away. The policeman gruffly inquired of Miss G what the trouble was. When she told him he replied, "Oh, he wasn't gonna hurt yuh, kid. Don't be disturbin' the neighborhood."

THE RED CHAUFFEURS OF PARIS

IDA TREAT

FORTY years a militant. The union, the old socialist party,—I never believed in 'pure syndicalism and no politics'—and now I'm with the communists and the C. G. T. U. Always kept in line. Forty years— that's before you were born, Marcel."

The big restaurant-keeper grinned, patted his uncle affectionately on the shoulder.

"A great old boy, he's got the faith all right," he announced to the group of Paris chauffeurs. "And he's made his way too, in the world——"

"One of the best grocery houses in Corrèze," the old man agreed, with pride. "And before I left Paris, five cabs of my own. But I've always stood by the Revolution. ..."

It was dinner hour at the *Rendezvous des Cochers et Chauffeurs*. Out in the Circle, a close-packed file of taxis lined the curb beneath the agitated hoofs of an equestrian Roi-Soleil. Overhead not a window glowed in the dark facade of 18th Century houses. Concierges' children played *marelle* on the empty sidewalk and an occasional autobus, tracing a noisy semi-circle across the asphalt, furnished the last reminder of the day's traffic.

Within the restaurant, a narrow L-shaped room wedged between the walls of two wholesale houses, not a seat at the three long tables remained empty. Fifty chauffeurs, a constant number, though from time to time individual customers, with a parting *"Bon Soir, tout le monde,"* pushed through the crowded chairs towards the doorway, their departure followed by the cough of a starting motor and the rack and grind of gears. Fifty chauffeurs in compact noisy rows between the zinc bar, its red and green *apéritifs*, its heaped *produits d'Auvergne*—sausages, hams, and goat-cheese—and the tiny kitchen where Big Marcel's wife and his two plump sisters—the restaurant is a family affair—moved in a haze of savory smoke.

At the far end of the room, Big Marcel the proprietor—until six months ago he was a chauffeur like the rest—bent above the table where a stout old man with bristling white mustache in a round red face spoke earnestly to an interested group.

"I learned my lesson back in the eighties," he told his hearers. "You young fellows never drove a horse, but it's all the same. Cochers yesterday and chauffeurs to-day, there's not much we don't know about the rottenness of the class on top."

"You're right we do," agreed one of the younger men. "By the time you've toted drunks, driven senators to bawdy-houses, and other respectable citizens to parties in the Bois... Pah!" he spat noisily over the table rim.

"And the women," remarked his neighbor. "Just now I'm driving a dame from one of those grand apartments up on the Avenue d'Jena. She's afraid her own chauffeur might tell her husband. Every night at a quarter past ten... "

"Rotten crew," nodded a third. "Only it pays." He grinned cynically across the steaming plate of soup.

"Oh, yes; it pays! That's a fine bourgeois point of view! An extra ten *balles* for slipping a drunk past his concierge, or lending a... hand in a *partouze* at the Bois—and the devil take the rest!"

"Look here, I'm no professional night-hawk. Only I don't see why all the profits should line the pockets of a lot of Russians——"

"Careful, you talk like a *chauffeur francais*."

"The hell I do! I'm every bit as good a *unitaire* as you. But I'm not going to let a crowd of princes and White colonels spoil the profession."

"*Mais oui, mais oui*," the old man at the head of the table broke in impatiently. "There are *jaunes* in every trade. And we all have to earn a living. Only stand by the union, boys, and don't lose sight of the Revolution. That's the essential. Look at me; for forty years... "

The "uncle" was off again. This time no one interrupted, for Big Marcel's wife had just set down a steaming plate of *cassoulet* in the middle of the table.

✳ ✳ ✳

One of the most interesting groups of French transport workers is formed by the "red" taxi-drivers of Paris. They represent sixty per cent of the fourteen thousand Paris chauffeurs—sixty percent who are members of the red union, the *Syndicat Unitaire*, C. G. T. U. Of the non-union taxi-drivers, many are "white" Russians, debris of the Wrangel army, recruited by the big taxi companies to offset the influence of the 8,500 revolutionaries. A year ago an attempt was made—at the instigation of the same taxi companies—to create a "patriotic" organization, *les chauffeurs francais*, which was to group the exclusively French elements among the non-union chauffeurs. The attempt proved unsuccessful; within a few weeks every tri-colored badge of the new organization had disappeared as if by magic from the Paris streets.

The red taxi-drivers form one of the best organized and disciplined unions of the C. G. T. U. Often they play an important role in mass-meetings and political demonstrations. Many a clash with the police has been avoided because at the strategic moment, the union chauffeurs interposed a barricade of taxis between the crowd and the charging agents. At the recent funeral of a red driver killed in a collision with a "bourgeois" auto, several thousand taxis took part in the funeral procession, tying up traffic for several hours in one of the busiest quarters of Paris. During the last elections, every night dozens of taxis carried Communist speakers to all districts of the departments of Seine and Seine et Oise. The Communist Party paid for the gas, but the drivers offered their services—from seven o'clock until often two or three in the morning—after their day's work.

For the average Paris chauffeur the eight-hour day does not exist. Generally he spends from ten to fourteen hours in the streets. He pays for his gas at the union rate, ten francs for five litres. The taxi companies generally allow him a rebate of three francs on every five litres after the first ten. His percentage of the receipts varies progressively from 27 to 42 per cent. His day's earnings vary between fifty and a hundred francs. Certain of the smaller companies pay their night drivers a fixed rate, from 35 to 45 francs. A few chauffeurs own their taxis; there is also a co-operative—the *Syndicale Taxis*—with several hundred cabs.

Nearly all taxi-drivers come from the country. They are peasant boys from the mountain regions of the center—Corréze, Creuse, Aveyron, and Lot—a tradition that dates from the days of the horse cabs. These "immigrants" form a transient population who live during their stay in the capital in the suburb of Levallois, a veritable city of chauffeurs. Few of them settle definitively in Paris. Like the postmen from Ariège, the policemen from Corsica, and the coal-and-wine merchants from Auvergne, their ambition is always to return to the *fays* after ten or fifteen years on the "box." In the old days, the excab driver generally passed from the transports into the *alimentation* and put his savings into a country store. But the chauffeur on his return to the village is more inclined to set up shop as a mechanic and spends his days tinkering with farm machinery, bicycles, occasional autos, and more recently, radio apparatus.

To the village and its outlying farms, he represents the city, and what is more important still from a revolutionary point of view, the organized workers of the city. He becomes the hyphen, the connecting link, between the peasant and the factory. He reads *l'Humanité* and his shop is a center for the discussion of radical politics. Generally he is a mortal enemy of the *curé*. In many an instance he and he alone furnishes the initiative for organizing agricultural workers and tenants, or creating a local "cell" of the Communist party.

The red chauffeurs of Paris are propagandists of the, Revolution throughout the region of central France.

* * *

"*Tiens, voila Paul! Bonjour! Bonjour!*"

A familiar figure, the editor of the communist daily, pushed his way between the crowded tables. The chauffeurs greeted him with noisy affection.

"Sit down with us, vieux! And what'll you have?"

"Sorry comrades. No time for dinner. Just a bouillon, Marcel. I've got a meeting at Ivry."

"Ivry? Then comrade, take your time." A big chauffeur leaned across the table towards the newcomer. "Got to go to Ivry myself. I'll take you along."

"On your way home?"

"That's my affair."

"But your evening—your work?"

"*Dis donc, tu veux m'infurier?* There's work—and work. To-night I'm going to work—for the propaganda!"

THE DANTE STATUE :: A STORY

MARIE LUHRS

The pastor of the church near Tenth Avenue where Amelia Mueller first breathed the dust of New York thought of her as a poor, wayward girl, and all the landladies in the neighborhood circulated the rumor that she was "N. G." But a sailor who knew more about women than priests or landladies, even, described her without moral bias. She was a "good-natured slob."

Her father was a waiter in the Hotel Majestic. He was fat and the lower part of his face always had a blue look. Her mother was short and sharp—a skin stretched over bones. She bore six children after Amelia, buried two of them elaborately in coffins banked with flowers, and cooked, washed, ironed, and prayed for the survivors. Amelia, since she was the oldest, was expected to labor for the edification of her brothers and sisters. Her First Communion wreath of white cotton flowers and the red satin hair bow that she wore for her Confirmation were the dream and aspiration of Elsie and Lena. And when Amelia went to work as a packer in a candy factory, Paul and Willie were shamed into part-time work as delivery boys in a grocery store.

No one had ever received First Holy Communion with more ecstasy than Amelia. When she knelt before the altar rail on that solemn occasion her hands trembled and the altar candles lost their individuality and became mist before her eyes. No one ever worked more cheerfully. Like a patient, brown-eyed beast she packed chocolates in the factory and never wasted her employer's time.

Katie Fleming, who sat beside her in the factory, marveled at her.

"Gee, you're a fool working for your boss and your kid sisters and never a blow-out."

Katie had "blow-outs." She was stunted and bony and hard-breasted; her nose was long and sharp, her eyes small and close together, but she had "blow-outs." Every evening when she walked home with two or three of the factory men, Amelia watched her and wondered. Hearing Katie's attractive descriptions of chop suey restaurants and Coney Island, she wanted to be taken out too. Sometimes she talked to the elevator man, who was distinguished-looking in his uniform.

Mr. Mueller, one evening, paused long enough from sucking in his soup to notice the extreme whiteness of his oldest daughter's face.

"Say, wash off the white-wash, Millie. You're getting *ganz* gay these days."

"*Ja.*" agreed Mrs. Mueller, "she come home from work like the beauty doctor up the street."

Now, in the morning, she quickened cheeks and lips with raw rouge and a dust of death-white powder before the mirror of the slot machine in the subway station. She removed the streaked remains of her handiwork on the way home. After her supper she washed the dishes and slipped into the parlor to heat her curling iron over the gas jet. She transformed her hair into a rough, smoking swirl. Her mother would come in and throw up the windows and spatter German.

As soon as possible Amelia slipped out of the house and walked a few blocks east toward the triangle of pale grass surrounding the statue of Dante at Sixty-fourth Street. The taxis and closed cars at that hour were nearly all headed toward the electric signs that burst into bloom at Columbus Circle. In the depths of the vehicles as they buzzed past her, Amelia caught glimpses of life in its flowering aspects: red velvet, a man kissing a woman, a diamond hand holding a cigarette, a woman sitting on a man's lap. Amelia regarded the gestures and trappings of pleasure wistfully and wondered by what trick of birth or fortune these women achieved orchids and earrings and chauffeurs.

She wondered, too, who was this Dante on his pedestal. He appeared to be a monk from his garment. She considered the expression of his face stern, his nose Jewish. She surmised that he must have been a great man, since New York allowed him so much space, and she attributed his great-ness to the book which he carried so carefully: no doubt he had writ-ten one of those books which nobody read, like *Hiawatha* in her school reader. She felt very reverent toward the statue. It made her think of the statues in church and the priest who spoke so beautifully on Sunday of the love of God.

The flashes of silver cloth and the love-making that she saw in the taxis suggested to her an easy, beautiful life beyond the chocolate factory and the gas tanks on Tenth Avenue. She very seldom had money for the movies; such musings at Dante's feet were the only recreation that she ever had. She never stayed long because her mother cautioned her about staying out late; and it was true that after a certain hour men would sit next to a girl on a bench near Broadway and ask her where she was going, girlie.

Amelia began to have "blow-outs." Katie grew very good-natured and introduced restaurants

The neighbors Mrs.

Mrs. in

stopped laughing. His apron had a familiar look; she thought her father was shaking her.

By the time she reached home she was so dazed that she hardly understood what her mother was shouting at her. When her mother used her fists she ran into the bedroom and slept a few hours on the floor, because it was hard to wedge herself in between the thick, sleeping bod-ies of Elsie and Lena. She imagined that the Dante statue would not have approved of her "blow-outs" either. But when Jo looked at her, what could she do? She could still hear his muffled "Aw, come on, Amelia," spoken with his lips on her throat.

When she turned up, shadow-eyed and with trembling fingers, in the factory, Katie would snicker at her:

"Why don't you get some money out of him?"

Amelia hated Katie. She felt that Katie had drawn her into a game without telling her the rules. She would have brooded over Katie's taunts if she had not felt so desperately ill. She fainted once in the factory and had to go home. The doctor told her that she was going to have a baby.

Her mother became hysterical and tried to kill her with the wash stick. Tears came into her father's eyes; he shook his head sadly.

"Milly, Milly," was all that he said. He came home as usual and dropped into bed like a clod immediately after supper.

Mrs. Mueller begged the pastor of the parish to send Amelia away. He remembered having awarded a gold medal for excellence in Christian doctrine to a big-eyed, guileless Amelia. Now she stood before him with still bigger eyes and a smaller face and her trouble. He arranged that she be sent to a convent in the country until her baby was born.

Amelia's baby, carried in so much shame and despair, was a seven months' child and was born dead. Amelia returned to her home silent and thin. The pastor had secured a position for her in a small laundry. It was the best that he could do for an unskilled, uneducated young woman with a bad character in her neighborhood. She stood all day long and ironed boarding-house sheets. There were no bad companions in the laundry; only broken old creatures and consumptive young ones and foreigners who spoke English with their iron and their folded pillow cases.

Night after night Amelia came home and listened to the German lamentations of her mother: Paul was starting to smoke cigarettes, Lena would not study her lessons, Elsie had a cough. Amelia combed Elsie's hair for her and tore it back from her forehead. She wanted Elsie to become a nun. Such a vocation was better than men or jobs. The laundry was worse than a job; it was a steaming purgatory. Even her mother felt sorry for her and bought her an amethyst ring for her birthday—a pale, watered stone, but still an amethyst.

"When we need money very bad we can hock it," said Mrs. Mueller to excuse her softness and extravagance.

Amelia atoned patiently amid the steam and the odors of wash until the spring. With the milder weather she took walks again. The air was healing and quickening and the grass around the Dante statue was covered with frail, green pricks. She felt that her sins were now as white as snow. She curled her hair again, but the laundry took the curl out very quickly. She drew Elsie's hair back less severely. She wondered if she could not find an easier job. During lunch hour, once, she entered a Broadway millinery shop with a placard against its plum velvet window drapery:

WANTED—AN ERRAND GIRL

The work was only part time and paid less than the laundry. This Amelia gathered from the fat, silk creature who was in charge of the shop. Amelia stayed at the laundry. Elsie's cough hung on and required visits to the doctor and tonics. Yet the spring made her feel less tired, less beaten, and she knew that her sins were as white as snow.

She sat watching two sparrows advancing upon a piece of bread in the grass before the Dante statue one evening, when the bench moved violently. A man eyed her boldly when she turned. His hair under his slate colored hat had decisive edges; his tie was Oriental in coloring; his suit was definitely striped. He showed gold and white teeth in friendly greeting.

"Nice evening!"

"Sport class," thought Amelia. Katie had taught her how to catalog men.

"Very nice." The laundry had been as hot as hell that day.

"I know a slick place right near the Circle," he told her.

Amelia took a table at Wilbur's with an air. Wilbur's was just like the Palmette—low, dark, with screens in the rear, from which bull-dog waiters emerged with trays of thick crockery. She knew how to act. She shivered a little with excitement as she used to do when she dined with Jo. She looked at the card again and ordered:

"Ice-cream, steak, fixing', spaghetti, tomato salad, *demitasse*, an' make it snappy."

She ate without regarding "Billy," as he was pleased to call himself, and eyed any man that came in coquettishly.

A kind of frenzy rose in her. She had been a fool once, but that experience had taught her how she might get out of that hole of a laundry. It was all very well for nuns in a convent with trees all around it to talk about chaste bodies and climbing to the stars, but no nun had to work all day in a laundry or sleep all night in a bed with a girl who had a cough. She looked at Billy; he was "class." She wondered how much money she could wheedle out of him. Savagely she ate her salad. Why couldn't she feel happy about doing what she wanted?

"Pretty nice ring you got—did your sweetie give it to you?" He shook the table with his laughter.

"My *sweetie*—? No, my *mother*."

He pushed back his chair so as to have more room to laugh.

"*Chee* what a good line. *Chee*, you're funny."

Amelia clutched the table. He must be crazy—that fat, wobbling, hideous man! Her mother had sewed nights for weeks to buy her that ring.

She pushed her ice-cream and coffee away and stood up.

"I'm goin' to fix my hair."

"Oh, you're goin' to fix your hair." He pinched her shoulder and shoved her back into her seat. "I've had them before what wanted a free meal. You stay where you are! Why—" with a spurt of laughter—"you didn't finish your ice-cream."

Amelia laughed too. There was something fluttering about her laughter. "Billy—look at my hair. I gotta fix it. I'll be right back."

He kept hold of her shoulder.

"Why Billy—!" She took a swallowing breath. "Look! Here's my ring so you'll know I'll be back sure for my ice-cream."

It was a pretty ring—pale and pretty. He shoved it half way down his little finger.

"Aw-right. But hurry back."

Amelia reached the street by a roundabout way and ran. She felt happy and relieved. She was still a good girl, her sins were still as white as snow. Tonight she had met the devil and sent him back to hell. She wanted her life to be a beautiful climb to the stars as the nuns had told her it should be. When she reached the Dante statue she was breathless. There it stood—shadowed, lonely, unchanged. And tomorrow she would go back to the laundry. Well—she lifted her head a little—she had never taken money from a man. She had even paid for her supper tonight. Tomorrow she would go back to the laundry with the summer coming on.

She had scarcely turned the key in the latch when her mother was upon her.

"Say—where you been all this time? You ain't been meetin' this *Gott verdammte* sailor again?"

"No—no! It was warm tonight, mama. I just forgot how late it was gettin'. Really, mama!"

"I've been waitin' for you for over an hour. The doctor has been here again. He says Elsie ought to have a coupla weeks on a farm."

"Yeh—" Listlessly Amelia hung her coat on the hook screwed to the door.

"An' I guess Papa better take your amethyst ring out an' hock it."

WHITE MAN :: A STORY

GRACE LUMPKIN

I WENT to see Alma Lee's mother today. She and her husband and two little boys had a tent in the Red Cross camp for flood refugees. Alma Lee's mother is my half-sister. She was born in a cabin on my father's plantation up in northern Louisiana in Madison county. My father had a large place about fifteen miles along the Mississippi, beginning at Cabin Tiel and stretching down opposite Vicksburg. But it had to be sold to pay the mortgages and I went to Baton Rouge to teach school. Alma Lee's father was a share-cropper on the place, and he stayed on after it was sold. His cabin was not far below Cabin Tiel and close to the river.

After I began teaching school I kept on visiting Alma Lee and her mother. My conscience made me. If I had inherited money I would have given them some of that and it would have ended the matter, as far as my conscience was concerned. Going to see them didn't help any. They wouldn't allow it somehow. I don't know why I kept going. I'd travel up there and sit in the little cabin close by the yellow, sluggish river and talk a little trying to bring things around to tell them why I was there—that I owed them something. But if I tried to get personal Alma Lee's mother would laugh, and they'd talk about the river and the crops and I would get side tracked. They were pleasant enough, even humble with me. But underneath I felt antagonism or maybe a contempt of me. It made me mad sometimes after I had left. But I'd always go back once a year at least. I was interested in Alma Lee and I wanted her to get an education. But they side-tracked me on that. I hadn't much money anyway. A school teacher's salary just does carry her over the three months vacation. Maybe they realized that. But maybe, too, they didn't like half-way measures. Yet what could I do? If I told everybody that these colored people were my relatives people would think I was crazy, and I would lose my position. So I kept on salving my conscience by *going to* see them like that, and trying to do something for them. It didn't do any good. I always came away baffled and often angry at them because they wouldn't understand the position I was in.

Then I decided to do something without letting them know. I had some friends in Vicksburg, and I recommended Alma Lee to them, and asked them to find her a place as a servant girl with some nice people who would let her go to school in the mornings. I knew that Alma Lee's mother was ambitious for her and would persuade her father to drive her into Vicksburg in their wagon every other Monday morning, and go after her when she came home. I made my friends in Vicksburg promise that they would see that Alma Lee would get home every other week, because I knew how fond her mother was of the girl, and I asked them to try to get her a place as nurse maid so she could live in the house and not have the extra expense of lodging. My friends wrote me that it had all been arranged, so I was very well satisfied.

Later I went to see Alma Lee's mother. She was very glad about the arrangement, and I had a triumphant feeling. I felt more satisfied than I ever had after a visit to them. The ice was still there—even under the laughing and joking and agreeing with everything I said I felt it. But I didn't mind so much any more.

Alma Lee went to work in December. I visited her mother in February. Some time in April I got word from her mother that she wanted to see me. I felt good over that. But I felt bad, too, because I thought it must be some trouble that had made them turn to me. I had been planning to go up there again anyway because the first levee had broken on the Arkansas and I wanted to urge them to get away while they could save everything they had.

When I got to the cabin Alma Lee was there by herself. Her mother was in town helping some white people move and her father and brothers were at work piling sandbags on the levee. Alma Lee was sitting in a cane-bottomed rocking chair by the chimney. It was a small cabin, with one big room and a leanto that was Alma Lee's bedroom. They cooked in the fireplace.

Alma Lee sat in the chair and rocked and told me the news. About the work on the levees, and that the river had risen, but not more than in other flood seasons—and that the leanto had caught fire from sparks from the chimney and burnt a hole in the roof, so she had to move her pallet into the big room.

It was raining outside and Alma Lee said, yes, the rain would probably make the flood higher. Outside we could just hear the river moaning along. I was a little afraid. But Alma Lee said they were going to move in plenty of time, maybe in a day or two. She didn't seem concerned at all. Just sat there and rocked and rocked—not fast. She was too relaxed to rock like some women do in nervous little jerks. She made me feel that she never wanted to move again, except that slow motion, backward and forward. Her body seemed to be a part of the rocking chair—spread out sluggishly into every corner of it. She was a nice looking girl. I believe I would call her lovely as she sat there. Her head was flung back and her neck had a beautiful taut curve. Her head rested heavily back on her shoulders. From where I sat her turned up face, dark brown like old wood worn by use to a beautiful even darkness, had a tormented look like it was trying to detach itself from the sluggish body underneath. The head and shoulders went together. The rest of the body that rocked so slowly belonged to the chair.

I said a few things. That they ought to be getting out soon. I had said that before, but it was very difficult to find something to say. The rain had been coming down hard on the roof. It sounded like the chattering of people outside the church at a country funeral. But now it had let up suddenly as conversation does when everybody sees the hearse coming a long way down the road, and just a few drops hit the shingles as if people were saying short, whispered words about the dead person and the sorrowing family.

It was in that quietness Alma Lee began talking. She didn't stop rocking and she kept her neck strained taut all the time. She was looking up at some spot on the ceiling, and kept her eyes fixed on that.

She said she was going to have a baby. I asked her if her mother knew. She said no, and she didn't want her to know. Her mother was worried though because she didn't feel so well, and because she had lost her place in Vicksburg. Her mother had wanted her to get some education. Alma Lee said she had wanted it, too. And she knew she had to get it for herself, because share-croppers never had any money, so her father couldn't help. If crops were good one year, they were usually bad the next. They always owed the good crops. When the chance came to go to Vicksburg Alma Lee said she and her mother were very glad.

She was nurse to Sonny, five-year-old boy of a lawyer in Vicksburg. Miss Eloise, the lawyer's wife, was going to have another baby. At first Alma Lee went to school every day, but so many things turned up to be done around the house she didn't get time for school and had to stop. She didn't tell her mother that though, because school was the one thing they had been counting on, and then by the time she had stopped school there was another reason why Alma Lee wanted to go on.

Alma Lee said Miss Eloise stayed in bed in the mornings. Alma Lee had carried her breakfast up and she had liked looking at Miss Eloise sitting up so comfortable in bed with lots of pillows. The room was so pretty. It had yellow organdy curtains with lavender and yellow ruffles around the edges. And there was a cover for the bed made of yellow silk. Miss Eloise liked frills, and they looked pretty around her. Alma Lee said she would sit up in bed and drink her coffee and talk to Alma Lee about Sonny, or ask her to do something extra around the house, because she was sick and couldn't. Alma Lee was glad to, she said. Miss Eloise was so pretty and asked in such a nice way. I asked Alma Lee why she didn't beg Miss Eloise to let her keep on going to school. She said she did ask her once if they couldn't arrange the work so she could go every day. But Miss Eloise wouldn't let her talk about that. Alma Lee said she sat up straight in bed and looked so excited Alma Lee was afraid she'd be real sick. She said, "Alma Lee, one of the finest women I've ever known, was my old black mammy—and she couldn't read or write a word. I respected her, Alma Lee, but I don't respect these young niggers with their newfangled notions. My husband doesn't either."

I asked Alma Lee if they let her go home. She said yes, that every other week her father brought her back to the cabin. I said it must have been good to get back. She said it was, her mother was so glad to see her. Sometimes she put herself out a lot to make things homey for Alma Lee, but she was too tired to do much. Alma Lee wanted to get some organdy in town and make some frilled curtains, and her mother liked the idea, but they couldn't get enough money. The first time she met him down by the willows, Alma Lee said, he offered her money. She wouldn't take it at first, but then she remembered the curtains and let him give it to her. But she couldn't think of any good reason to give her mother for having that much money so she buried it down there in the Indian mound where they met.

I asked Alma Lee who it was she met. And she said Miss Eloise's husband. She said it had begun when she first went there. Only she didn't realize it was beginning then. He liked to come in some nights and hear Sonny's prayers and tell him stories about King Arthur. He would make Sonny stand up and say "My strength is as the strength of ten because my heart is pure." Alma Lee said Sonny was very earnest about it, and his whole body would shake from trying to make his voice sound deep like his father's. Alma Lee thought her liking him began then because after Sonny had been put to bed, sometimes he would stop and ask her about the little boy and what he had said and done during the day. He was very kind to her. Then one day he brushed against her in the hall, and at another time he pushed her up against the wall and pressed against her. He said excuse me and went ahead. But other things like that happened, and then he told her to meet him at the willows the night she was at home.

Every time she slipped out of the leanto and went down there, Alma Lee said, she was afraid, thinking about what would happen if Miss Eloise or her mother found out. She thought they would surely search her out. She said those willows down the river was their place—the levee was low there and the ground was marshy, but the Indian mound was above the marsh, and covered with soft grass. She had played there when she was little and thought about the old Indian chief being buried along with arrow heads and caly pots. She had tried to tell him, Alma Lee said, about that, but he hadn't wanted to talk much. Once he did tell her that she was like the river, running smooth and easy without hurry or fuss. Alma Lee seemed to like to remember that. Her throat relaxed and her eyelids drooped. She told me she had answered back that sometimes the river gets on a rampage. But he laughed, and said, "But you are not that kind—you are my slow, docile river running to the gulf, and I am the gulf waiting with my arms furrowed through the delta—waiting to receive you and take you to me." Alma Lee must have said that over to herself many times. She repeated the words as if she knew them by heart.

I said something like that to her. She said yes, she did remember his words sometimes, but his voice was the good part about him. Usually his words didn't mean so much to her as the way he said them. She could believe what Miss Eloise had told her, that he had studied to be a preacher. At the house many a time he would talk to company as if he was preaching and she loved to listen to the boom boom that came out of his throat. No matter what he said she could feel that sound and be satisfied.

One time, Alma Lee said, after supper she was out on the lawn letting Sonny play a little before she took him up to bed. Sonny's father was on the porch with Miss Eloise and some people that had come for tea. He was talking and his voice coming across the lawn got into her. He had been talking about white people. She went closer, keeping one eye on Sonny. He said he had just read about a white girl marrying a Jew. Somebody interrupted him and said, "Well, Jews are human beings." And he said, "Yes, and so are niggers, but you don't marry them." That came out rich and full. He had that wonderful voice. Alma Lee said he knew he had it, too. She said he took pleasure in his own voice just like Sonny when he hollered in the bath tub and listened to his voice going all around the bath room walls. That evening when he was talking, Alma Lee said she made Sonny come up even closer right by the porch to play and she sat on the steps in the shadow of the wisteria vines, listening some more. While she was down there getting Sonny to come up she had heard his voice roll out like a preacher's. He said, *"Thank God I am a white man."* When he saw her on the steps he came over and stood by her in the dark and went on talking. She didn't hear anything else he said because his leg was pressed against her shoulder and she didn't want to listen. But the sound of those other words thumped in her, like a steamboat does, *white* man, *white* man, *white* man.

I asked Alma Lee if she had seen him lately. She said no he hadn't been around for a month, now, since Miss Eloise had found out and told her to go. The cook must have spied on her and told. One day Miss Eloise had sent for her to come upstairs and had got after her, and called her a bad girl, and what a disappointment, after all she had done for her, giving her her own old shoes and dresses, and extra money sometimes. Alma Lee said she didn't know what devil got into her, but she had answered back. And Miss Eloise had told her not to be impudent. Sonny was there, and funny how a little one like that would feel ugly words like they were using, and get the sound of voices. Alma Lee said when she talked back he said, "Don't you talk to my mother like that." He took up for his mother right away. Funny, when she had put him to bed and dressed him and all—pretty cute of him taking up for his mother. She thought maybe he felt it about her being a nigger. Once Alma Lee had been in the next room and had heard him ask Miss Eloise if she would eat with a nigger and Miss Eloise had told him no and he mustn't either. Anyway, when he told her to hush like that Alma Lee said she didn't talk any more. She went out of the room and got her things and Miss Eloise paid her and she came home and hadn't seen any thing of any of them since. She had been to the Indian mound twice, but it was scary down there without anybody waiting.

I asked Alma Lee some questions and she answered them. It looked as if now she had begun she didn't care how much she talked. But she did ask me not to tell her mother. "Tell her I've got malaria," she said. "That's what I've told her. When I went to see the doctor I got some chill and fever medicine and I take it to make her believe." I asked her how she would keep it from her mother. She said she didn't know. Her neck sagged down—then. She said probably she would go away. I said I wanted to help. I felt it was a responsibility. So Alma Lee promised that she would come into Baton Rouge and see me. I told her I would send the money right away and she agreed that it was the best plan. After I made her promise that I went away.

Day before yesterday I got word from Alma Lee's mother to come down to that Red Cross camp where the family was staying. Alma Lee's mother asked me if I'd gotten any news of the girl being found by rescue parties. I told her I hadn't. She said they had left Alma Lee at the cabin with the boys. They were to pack up the things and bring them into town on the wagon. She went over and over it—telling me how well Alma Lee had packed everything, wrapping the dishes in newspapers, helping the boys and making a place for the chickens and the hog. When they had fixed everything in the wagon Alma Lee had made her brothers go ahead with the wagon. She had said she wanted to rest a while and that she would walk to town. She sat down on the doorstep of the cabin and they left her there. Alma Lee's mother and father hadn't met up with the boys until the next morning. They had spent the night in the barn of the white people they had been helping. When they went back to the place where the cabin was they couldn't get anywhere near it. It was all covered with water. But they saw the cabin. It had floated down and a big willow tree had caught in the hole in the roof of the leanto and held the cabin there. There wasn't any sign of Alma Lee.

All the time her mother was talking I kept on thinking about what Alma Lee had told me and how I was the one who'd gotten that place for her. I kept on wondering whether Alma Lee's body that had rested so heavily in the rocking chair had held her down on the step of the cabin when she had really meant every minute to get up and go, or if she had stayed there, wanting the flood to come and take her.

I told Alma Lee's mother I'd look everywhere and see if I could find any trace of her. But I don't think it will do any good. I think Alma Lee must have gotten caught in the willows. Or maybe the river took her on down to the delta. I don't know. But I think I won't go to see Alma Lee's mother any more. There doesn't seem to be any use.

ESCAPE :: A STORY

ALICE PASSANO HANCOCK

WHEN he was a little chap of six or so, he had gone into his mother's room every morning to watch her do her hair. His mother stood before the long glass by the south window in her petticoat and a camisole laced with orchid ribbons. Her hair was black and hung straight and fine almost to her knees. When she ran the comb through it, the teeth left little paths, dividing the hairs the way a ship cuts the water with its sharp narrow prow. His mother combed her hair languidly, lifting her bare arms high above her head. When she raised her arms he could see the intimate white skin of the undersurface faintly threaded with blue veins. At the armpit there was a patch of curling black hair, crisp as fine wire.

Henry sat in the window with his knees hunched up under his chin watching the movement of the comb as it slid downward through the smooth hair, watching the rise and fall of his mother's breasts beneath the thin silk of her camisole. She turned, smiling at him from between lifted arms.

"If I were you, I'd run outdoors and play. Where's Freddie? You and Freddie haven't played together for ever so long."

"I don't, want to," said Henry. "I like it better here." He crawled down from the window ledge and stood close against his mother's side. "I like it better here," he repeated softly.

***

When he was eight years old his cousin Eve had come to visit them. Cousin Eve had been married to Cousin Jack, but now Cousin Jack was married to someone else and Cousin Eve was visiting the family until she got settled. Getting settled meant getting a husband, father said.

She wore black satin dresses and gray stockings pulled tight over her fat calves. Above the low cut V of her dress, bits of pink ribbon were continually popping into sight and being thrust back again.

She and Mother talked a great deal while Henry played around in the room pretending to be busy but always watching Cousin Eve. He was a puny, undersized child, with little crisp bones that could have been snapped between a thumb and finger. His hair, which was as fine and soft as mole's fur, grew up from his forehead in a twisted cowlick.

Once when Mother was out of the room, Cousin Eve had called him to her, and pressing him close against her body, had kissed him on the mouth. Through the thin stuff of his little blouse he could feel the warmth and softness of her breasts. Her mouth was wet against his. When she released him, he stumbled over to the window and stood staring out across the roof tops to where the factory chimneys were thrust against the sky, like great black cigars, smoking furiously. He felt queer and sick and happy inside, and he felt ashamed. But he wished Cousin Eve would do it again. Women were different from men. Softer. He liked women better.

The next day Cousin Eve went away. That was the last time he ever saw her.

$$* * *$$

It was vacation time. Miss Fowler had gone, and the school books were locked up out of the way behind the glass doors of the bookcase. Long idle days with nothing to do. Long days lying on his stomach before the bedroom window, looking at a print of a Virgin Mary with the child Jesus which hung above his head, and drawing pictures on a big yellow tablet. He had a copy of a Zorn etching which he had torn from a magazine. He kept it hidden at the bottom of his playbox, only bringing it out when he was alone.

Once his mother came silently into the room and found him intent on a drawing.

"Let's see your picture, Henry." she said. Henry turned a slow dull red and put both hands over his drawing. But when she pulled them away, she saw only a series of long curving lines like little flat, bare hills traced against the background of yellow paper.

"Silly," she laughed, and rumpled his hair between her fingers.

After that, Henry kept his drawings hidden in the playbox with the Zorn etching.

He lay in bed listening to the swirl of wind as it whipped the rain against the windows. He lay flat on his back with his arms rigid along his sides, his toes curled under with the intensity of his willing. If he relaxed only an instant it would come back, rolling over him like the ninth great wave, carrying him away past all decency, all hope. He concentrated furiously on sheep. Sheep jumping over an eternal stile. But the other pictures would crowd in, blotting out the silly bleating animals. He yielded suddenly, with a whimper of shame, burying his hot cheek in the pillow. And the wave covered him, submerged him, dragged him down—down—

* * *

Henry was going away to school. The doctor recommended it. "Football, out-of-door life, discipline, that's what he needs."

"Yes," said Henry's father. He turned toward Henry who was sitting by the open window with his back to the light.

"Wait for me outside, son." he said.

Henry went through the narrow hall and stood at the top of the steps, jerking his shoulder a little and twisting the corner of his mouth between his teeth. In a few moments his father joined him.

"The doctor thinks you'd like it at Dunham," he said as they turned up the avenue.

"All right," Henry answered quietly. But inside it was as though little hands were clutching at his stomach, making him sick.

When he heard the chapel clock strike four, Henry rose and buttoned the book he had been reading out of sight beneath his Norfolk jacket. Already it was growing dark in the shadow of the trees along the river's edge. He started back toward the dormitory, cutting across the playground. When he was close to the building Butch Mattheson spied him and came running toward him, arms and legs flying.

"Well, here's our Hennery. Wait, Hennery, darling."

Some of the other boys stopped their games and came running too. This was going to be sport. Butch caught Henry by the shoulder and swung him around.

"Well, dearie, where have you been all afternoon? Mamma's been anxious."

He gave him a shake and roared with laugher. The book stowed away beneath Henry's jacket slipped down and fell on the grass, the leaves fluttering open. Butch picked it up. "Little Rollo's picture book," he said. He flipped the pages over, then stopped abruptly and examined the book with interest.

"So," he said at last. "That's the sort of a kid you are. Well, I'll be damned!" He spat out a word that made Henry recoil with shame.

The Headmaster, crossing the playground to his office, saw the little group of boys and joined them.

"What's the matter?" he questioned sharply. "What's that you have, Mattheson?"

Butch thrust the book into his hand. The Head glanced at it and then at the group of silent boys.

"Where did this come from?" he asked.

Butch jerked his thumb toward Henry. "Him."

"Come to my office in the morning, Evans." said the Head, and swung off toward the building.

The next morning Henry was closeted with the Head for two hours. When at last he emerged he went straight to his room and shut himself in. Then he stood a long while by the window staring down into the empty playground, his hand fumbling with the curtain cord.

In the morning his father came to take him home. That was the end of his school career.

***

It was during his seventeenth year that his Uncle George came East on a visit. Uncle George owned a cattle ranch in Montana, in the Butte country. This was the first time he had been East for over ten years.

He told the family long stories about Montana. Miles and miles of bare, brown hills rolling up to the horizon. Strange flattened buttes outlined against the sky. Henry listened avidly. He liked the stories of cowboys riding alone across the prairie. He pictured them with brown throats, singing against the wind, sleeping under the stars with a saddle for a pillow, untroubled by dreams. He asked Uncle George many questions, leaning forward eagerly, his cheeks faintly touched with color.

Uncle George and his father had been shut in the library all evening. When Henry passed the door he could hear the low murmur of their voices. He wondered what they were talking about and asked his mother, but she only went on taking quick short stitches in the scarf she was embroidering and did not answer him. Finally the door opened and the men came out. Father crossed over to the reading light and picked up the evening paper, Uncle George stood with his back to the fire, grinning down at Henry.

"How'd you like to go back West with me?" he asked.

Henry started, and his mother cried "No-no-no-!" very quickly and spread her sewing out over her knees like a little white flag of truce.

His father stirred and put down his paper. "Seems to me that's for the boy to decide," he said slowly.

Henry felt a faint stirring of excitement. ... Bare, brown hills rolling up into the horizon; the strange flattened outline of buttes against the sky. ... He had read in books of men going West—wicked men—and it changed them completely. Something happened to them out there that made them different. Perhaps. ...

"Better come along, kid," said Uncle George.

"All right," he answered. His voice came from far down in his throat as though it were someone else speaking.

"Good idea, Henry," said his father. He took a cigar from his pocket and carefully, musingly, bit off the end and threw it into the grate. Then he sat chewing the unlighted cigar, saying nothing.

***

A dozen times a day during the trip West, Henry longed for the clean coolness of his bedroom at home. The heat in the long narrow pullman was grilling. When he put his hand down on the window ledge it stuck to the hot varnish. At night, lying behind the green curtains of his, berth, he twisted restlessly, feeling beneath his cheek the scratch of cinders. Even the stars looked hot, like bonfires seen at a great distance.

They alighted late one afternoon at a small town called Cedarcrest. Two cottonwoods, gritty with dirt, grew by the station. There was not another tree in sight. The town was hideous. In the glaring afternoon sunlight, the houses sagged crazily like children's drawings.

One of the men from the ranch was waiting for them with a wagon. Uncle George climbed in front, Henry got in back with the luggage. They drove out of the little town and along a road that wound between bare hills covered with sage brush. The dust rose about the wagon, sifting over their bodies like flour. Henry could feel a thin fine coating of grit upon his teeth and in the corners of his eyes. Bare hills rolled away to the horizon. Now and then a gopher with a striped back and a stiff awkward tail like a spoon handle darted across the road. There was no other sign of life. Not even a bird fluttered out of the bush at the side of the trail. God, it was hot! The whole world was slowly burning up.

Above the rattle of the wagon and the padding of the horses' hoofs, rose the voices of Uncle George and Bill. Henry caught fragments of their conversation.

"Not so good—not so good. It takes a man with guts to stand this life."

A moment of silence broken only by the jingle of harness and the steady creaking of the wagon springs. Then Bill—"Any good looking skirts where you was?"

"Fair," said Uncle George, and spat from between his teeth.

"Wait 'til you see the big Swede at Hatfield's." Bill chuckled. "She's some stepper!" He gave Uncle George a poke with his elbow and roared with laughter. "Ain't tried my band on her yet. But I'm goin' to some day. You betcha."

Henry leaned forward, alert. What were they saying? A big Swede—a stepper? A stepper was a—He wished the wagon wouldn't rattle so—

Toward evening, when the shadows of the buttes were growing long, they sighted from the top of a little hill a low ranch house sprawled along the bank of a dried-up stream.

"That's Hatfield's place," said Uncle George. "We'll stop there over night. Its a good five hours further to the ranch. By golly, you look all in, Henry."

Mrs. Hatfield, a little woman in a faded percale apron, came to the door to meet them. Henry climbed out of the wagon and staggered up to the porch where Uncle George introduced him. Mrs. Hatfield looked at him with concern.

"Poor kid," she said, "You're all wore out. You'll feel better after a wash-up and some sleep. I'll get Olga to take you to your room. She called into the dark hall, "Olga."

A big Swedish girl came through the hall and stood framed against the open door. She wore a fresh print dress that showed the splendid modelling of her throat, and her hair, like pulled taffy, was twisted about her head in two thick braids. She was a Zorn woman.

Henry followed her up the stairs and along the hall. She opened a door on the right and held it for him to enter. The shades were drawn in the bedroom and it looked cool. The counterpane on the bed gleamed like a patch of snow against the darkness.

Henry turned. Olga was staring at him with her little, deep-set eyes. He stared back, fascinated, forgetting how tired he was and how miserable. The girl's breasts moved up and down under her thin cambric frock. When she smiled, he saw that one of her teeth was missing. For some reason, this seemed inexpressibly funny and he laughed, a shallow, childish laugh.

Olga came towards him slowly. When she was quite close she put out her hand and ran it lingeringly along his arm. "You're a purty boy," she said softly. Then she turned and went out of the room. He saw her open the door across the passageway. Before she closed it she looked back and smiled at him again, a slow smile.

Henry found himself trembling with a suppressed, inner excitement. For a moment he stood quite still in the middle of the floor where she had left him; then he turned and flung himself face downward on the bed. He slept almost immediately, his face buried between his arms, one dirty shoe on the white counterpane.

*** *** ***

All through supper Henry was conscious of Olga. When she refilled his glass she pressed close against him. It made him feel queer and a little dizzy. The way he had felt long ago when Cousin Eve had kissed him. The sleep had done him good. He was rested. A little stiff perhaps—but rested.

After supper he walked up and down in the ranch yard. The men sat on the porch smoking and talking about stock. Through an open window he could watch Olga washing dishes in the kitchen. She had rolled her sleeves above the elbow and he saw the tender white flesh of her upper arm.

A little breeze came up and rustled the leaves of the cottonwoods that grew along the stream bed.

"Guess well turn in, Henry," called Uncle George.

Henry went back to the porch and followed Uncle George into the house and up the narrow stairs. The light from the candle was dim and wavering against the darkness.

*** *** ***

It seemed as though he had been lying in bed for hours, flat on his back, waiting for Uncle George to fall asleep. Uncle George turned, flinging the covers from his shoulders. "God, its hot!" After a long while he began to breathe deeply. Henry waited until he was sure, then he slipped out of bed and crept along the floor in his bare feet. At the door he hesitated, the muscles of his stomach taut with fright. But something stronger, more overwhelming, drew him forward.

The hall was black and empty. Carefully he groped his way across until his fingers touched the opposite wall. Then he felt for the door. He found it at last, and slowly, quietly turned the handle. The door yielded easily.

After the darkness of the hall—light. One candle which flickered on a table at the bedside. Olga sat on the edge of the bed in her nightdress with her hair falling in two thick braids across her shoulders. She was leaning forward a little and her gown hung open at the throat.

She did not move, only looked at Henry with her little green cat-eyes. It was as though she had expected him. Neither of them spoke. They simply stared at each other while the candle flared and threw strange glancing shadows against the walls. Then without shifting his glance, Henry began to move slowly, cautiously toward the bed.

When he reached Olga, he dropped on his knees and put both arms around her waist. Through the flimsy gown he could feel her warm damp flesh. Still neither of them spoke.

Suddenly, with a quick, abrupt movement of his body, Henry buried his head deep in the hollow between Olga's breasts. He could feel them pressing against his cheeks, smooth and warm and a little sticky. He could feel Olga's heart beating clear and strong, close to his right ear, and her big hands moving slowly, slowly, along his back.

"My purty boy," said Olga, "My purty boy—"

***

The men were off the next moring before sunrise. Uncle George, heavy-eyed with sleep, gulped down a cup of strong coffee and munched a roll. Henry lingered over his breakfast, savoring each mouthful. He was unusually hungry.

Mrs. Hatfield waved to them from the steps as they drove off; no one else was stirring. The air was clear and fresh, still cool with the dampness of early morning. The first rays of sunlight outlined the farthest butte. Black ivory against the pale sky.

Henry was amazingly, unreasonably happy. It was good to feel the wind cool against his throat and to hear the soft padding of the horses' hoofs in the dust. From a bush at the roadside, a meadow lark skimmed upward, leaving behind a thin, sweet curl of song. Henry shivered with ecstasy and began to whistle, slightly off key.

"Good Lord," said Uncle George, "The kid looks better already." He gave Henry a resounding slap on the knee, then turned back to talk to Bill.

Henry learned forward watching the sun send exploring fingers of light into the dark valley. Golly, it was a great world. He liked this country. It made him feel good. Dandy! He'd settle here forever and ever. He'd learn to ride hard and shoot straight. That's what a man should do— ride hard and shoot straight. Women? Hell! He knew all about women. They were all right in their place. But this was a man's world....

IS THIS AMERICA?

YOSSEF GAER

Orchard Street is hot!
Orchard Street is busy!
Orchard Street is wide awake!

The row of pushcarts close to the narrow sidewalks carry their permits, tacked on to the outside, and the varied stocks upon them with a flaunting pride. The passing crowd and prospective customers shuffle along in single file, their ears assailed by the loud calls from vendors shouting the virtues of their wares.

"*Now, now, now! Genuine Koptchankas! Two for a nickel!*"

"*Siveet as sugar! Sweet as honey! A nickel! Five Cents! Melons! Melons! Melons!*"

The noise of the vendors and the effluvium of smells rise and mix with the dense heat of the day.

Near one pushcart half-filled with peaches sits an old woman. Her head shakes faintly, and her weak eyes blink in a nervous manner. It is hard to tell whether troubling thoughts make her shake her head and blink that way, or whether it is old age.

"And how much are your peaches, grandmother?" asks a short stubby woman, herself old enough to be a grandmother, who stops to inspect the peaches.

"Two pennies, daughter," the old woman points to the sign tacked on to her cart. She does not move from the box she is sitting on, but watches her customer interestedly. And before the customer has time to put down near the pushcart the large paper bag overflowing with her purchases, the old fruit vendor shakes her head again, and begins in a complaining voice:

"Ai-ai-ai! Is this America? Is this justice? Not a crumb of pity has it in its heart! Not a crumb of justice! Here I go and tell them: Find me Gedalyeh Osher Berel's and he'll already help me. Do I ask any favors from them? God forbid! Only I'm getting old, too old to work. If I could only find Gedalyeh he would help me. Gedalyeh has a golden heart and he would help me! But go and find him in your America! So I ask people: Tell me, Jews, how after all am I to find this Gedalyeh? So they say: Go to the *Forwarts*, he'll find him already. You understand? I should go! Why can't they go? They are younger than I am. But no, I must go! I tell you my soul melts to see how heartless these people are!"

She stopped, breathless with the flow of her talk, then shook her head again, despairingly:

"Ai-ai-ai! Here is your America! Here is your Golden Land! Would they let an old person go like that in Lublin? God forbid! But here they say: If you look for your Gedalyeh then go to the *Forwarts!* Do you think I didn't go? With these sick feet of mine I went there. What are you squeezing the peaches for, daughter? They are fresh peaches. Sweet as sugar. They melt in the mouth like honey. And fresh! Pst! You can see they still have some green leaves on them. Do you think they gain in health if they are squeezed?"

"Who squeezes? I squeeze? I don't squeeze, only for green grass I don't need to pay money in cash! And by the dozen how much are they?"

"By the dozen? How many dozen for instance?"

"What's the difference? One dozen. Or maybe I'll take two dozen, if they are cheap."

"Two dozen I'll make it for you twenty-two pennies a dozen."

"And one dozen?"

"Noo, since I said twenty-two let it be twenty-two. But better take two dozen. Sweet as sugar. And fresh! Look, they still have some leaves. Ai-ai-ai! So I came already to the *Forwarts* there and I say to them I say: Find me Gedalyeh Osher Berel's. He has a golden heart. He wouldn't let a poor cousin fall. So he says I have to go upstairs the devil knows where on the ninth floor to find Gedalyeh! Do you hear? The impudence! I with my sick feet should go up! Ai-ai-ai! And where is respect for age? And where is justice? But what could I do? Argue with him? So I went up. So listen on purpose what can happen in your America. They drag me up and then they ask me for Gedalyeh's name. So I tell them: What should his name be? Gedalyeh! But no, they want to know what his second name is. So I tell them that my cousin has, praised be the Lord, only one name: Gedalyeh! Let them find him and ask him and they will see that I tell the truth. What then, I, a woman of praised be God seventy-six would lie to them? But no, they would not listen to me. He must have a second name, they say. And if he has no second name they wouldn't even as much as look for him. So I argue with them: Mr. Forwarts, why am I to blame if Gedalyeh has no second name? Is that why an old woman should be left to fall without help? But talk to them and talk to the wall! Either your Gedalyeh has a second name, or we don't look for him. So what should I do, I ask you? Should I lie to them and say he *has* a second name when he hasn't?"

She stopped to catch her breath again. Now she was deeply stirred with indignation:

"I tell you your America is only for thieves and liars. If you can't lie to them they wouldn't even find your cousin for you. I argue: tell him I, Beila Esther Chaim Milchiger's, your cousin Beila is looking for you— and he'll already know. But no, they say. Either a second name, or no Gedalyeh! Ai-ai-ai-! That is your America!"

By this time the customer had picked over the entire pile of peaches and segregated a heap of choice fruit.

"So you say if I take two dozen you'll let me have them for twenty cents a dozen. I really don't need so many, but to give an old woman a chance—"

"I didn't say twenty. I said that if you take three dozen I'll let you have them at twenty-one pennies a dozen. Just as they come. But not picked over. Picked over like that they are two for a nickel. And believe me they are worth it. I tell them Gedalyeh, and they ask Boybrik! They want a second name! And if I'll give them already a second name they'll want a third name! What can you do when you have to deal with murderers who haven't a crumb of pity in their hearts!"

"*Here, here, here, here! Thirty cents a pair! Silk! Pure from silk!*" shouts a husky sox vendor.

"*Look 'em over! Over here! Bathing suits a dollar! Slippers a dollar! Dresses a dollar! Look 'em over!*"

"*CO-nnie IS-land LE-mo-NADE! ICE-cold LE-mo-NADE!*"

The noise of the vendors fluctuates like the shimmering heat. Another woman stops to buy some peaches from the old woman.

"Are they good for jam, grandmother?" she asks.

"There are no better, daughter. Sweet as sugar. Ai-ai-ai! You say jam! And I think, ai-ai-ai! That is America for you! Not a crumb of pity has it in its heart! And your Reb *Forwarts* isn't any better! I go to him and tell him: Find me Gedalyeh Osher Berel's and he'll help me already! Do I ask any favors from them? God forbid! Only I'm too old to work, and if I could find my cousin Gedalyeh—"

GOD PUT ANOTHER ONE IN :: A STORY

GRACE LUMPKIN

ALL the people who lived on lower Blossom Street in Corinth, West Virginia, knew Mamie because she was the daughter of the Salvation Army Captain and they all said it was too bad about her teeth. She was a pretty girl even if she did have a sallow complexion and thin cheeks. Her eyes were blue and her hair was real gold. The kind that would shine under the electric light when she was singing with the Salvation Army Band. But it was too bad for a girl of nineteen to wear false teeth. They told Mamie's Ma that and she said it was but the doctor and the dentist both said it had to be. Mamie's Ma blamed it on the pellagra that Mamie had when she and her Pa and older brother were working in the cotton mill down south. But Mamie said her Ma would blame a little toe ache on that pellagra. She had got the disease when she was ten and working in the Olympia mills, the largest cotton mills under one roof in the world. When they were living down south there were three younger children and the older brother who died later, but now there were three more children making seven with Mamie. Pretty soon after Mamie got well of the pellagra her Pa joined the Salvation Army and he was so good at it they made him captain just before the last baby was born.

They thought it was better than the factory even though Corinth wasn't much of a city and made up mostly of coal mines and factories except across the bridge where the rich lived. There weren't many people that would come to meetings or gather round on the streets when the band sang *Love Lifted Me* or something else or when Mamie's Pa preached. Half the Italian miners couldn't speak English and those that were religious believed in the priests they had out there at the settlements.

Mamie's Ma didn't like it much that Mamie went such a lot with Rosa, because Rosa's uncle that she lived with was a miner and Italian, too, though Rosa was just half Italian—her Ma had been English and that helped some. Mamie's Ma came from English stock herself, way back, and she was proud of it. Of course Rosa was a smart girl. Mamie's Ma had seen her and Mamie working at the laundry together. They'd stand in front of the machine and before two kids could slap out "peas porridge hot, peas porridge cold" they'd snap a sheet from the rollers and fold it into shape for the wrapper. Even Mrs. Newsome who owned the laundry thought they worked together fine. The forelady told Mamie's Ma that. Mamie's Ma said yes, and Rosa was helpful round the house, too. Every Friday when she spent the night with Mamie she'd help put the kids to bed and wash the supper dishes before she and Mamie went to the Y.W.C.A. for the meeting of the Four Leaf Clover Club.

And now Mamie was saying she wouldn't go any more to the club meetings, not while her teeth were out and if Mamie didn't go then Rosa wouldn't because Rosa didn't like it much anyway, but went because Mamie did, and because after the meeting they had dates to go to the movies with Jake and Bill who were drivers for the laundry. When Mamie said they wouldn't go any more the Y.W.C.A. Industrial Secretary begged them not to leave the club because they were leaders and their leaving would break it up. Mrs. Newsome helped to support the Y.W.C.A. and the Board would say the Secretary wasn't any good even though she had worked so hard to get the Fine Finish Laundry girls interested and went once a week to eat lunch with them down in the cellar of the laundry where the girls had their meat and bread at noon time. But Mamie said she just couldn't go, not with her teeth out.

When they were away from the Secretary, Rosa asked Mamie if she was sure she wouldn't go to the Four Leaf Clover Club meetings and Mamie said no, she wouldn't, not with strangers around in the halls, and the Secretary and Miss Flora, the president of the Board, coming to meetings. "I'd feel like I was Trixie," she said. They laughed at that because Trixie was Miss Flora's old dog, a mixture of pug and bull dog and so old she didn't have any teeth. But Miss Flora loved Trixie and everywhere fat Miss Flora waddled right behind her came Trixie waddling just like Miss Flora.

Then Mamie got ashamed of laughing and said sort of reproving to Rosa, like she did sometimes, "Miss Flora is sweet to us," and Rosa said if sweet meant one of those everlasting Y.W.C.A. smiles and a pat on the head then Miss Flora was sweet. And Mamie said, "Rosa, you know you really like the Y.W.C.A." And Rosa said she did not. She said, "What do we do? Go up there and sit around like ladies and sing songs hope and one is for faith and one is for love you know—and God put another one in for luck…" She asked Mamie what could be like that one about one leaf is for sillier than that, and please not get her started on the Y.W.C.A. Mamie said that was exactly what she didn't want to do, and to talk about something else. So they did.

Mamie had to stay away from work three weeks while her teeth were being taken out. She had fever from the stuff the dentist put in her jaws and was in bed for part of the time. While she was out Rosa got fired from the laundry because without Mamie to hold her down she told Mrs. Newsome some things. Mrs. Newsome was getting after the girls because they had let the Four Leaf Clover Club break up, and Rosa told her why didn't she give them eight hours instead of ten to work and then maybe they'd have time for clubs. And Mrs. Newsome said well if she did what would they use it for—not the Y.W.C.A., but most probably the movies or maybe the Triangle.

The Triangle was a place across the River where a triangle was made by the railroad tracks and the river and on the land of the Triangle were lots of little hotels and red light houses and a public dance hall, the only one in Corinth.

When Mamie got better she went back to work, but she lagged at it and then begged the forelady to get Rosa back. So the forelady talked to Mrs. Newsome and Mrs. Newsome said take her back then, but it seemed awful to have a troublemaker like Rosa in the laundry. She was sure it was Rosa who made the girls look away from her, and whisper to each other when she came. And she did so want her girls to be happy. She thought of their happiness just like she did her own daughters' happiness. But Rosa wouldn't appreciate it. That day when she took a lovely poem and read it to the girls down in the lunch-room—a poem all about the sanctity of labor—Rosa had snickered in the most beautiful part and Mamie had snickered, too, copying Rosa. So would the forelady speak to them? The forelady promised she would.

A good while after that the Y. W.C.A. had a Board Meeting. They had the Secretary up and talked to her about the Four Leaf Clover Club. Miss Flora sat behind the table to preside and she got up and said they must keep after the girls—that they were at impressionable ages and must be prevented from going wrong. "There are girls right now over there," she said, pointing to the Jail that was across the street from the Y.W.C.A., "who would be in their own homes happy and contented if the Y.W.C.A. had got them soon enough." She said there were many pitfalls for young girls in Corinth. "I have only to mention The Triangle and you ladies will understand," she said.

They talked some about it all together until Miss Flora made them hush. Then she told the Secretary they must get the Fine Finish Girls back because just a few days before she had gone to Mrs. Newsome for some money for the Y.W.C.A. and Mrs. Newsome had said what was the Y.W.C.A. doing for her since there wasn't a club any more. So Miss Flora had an idea and that was for her and the Secretary to get Mamie to go with them to see Mrs. Newsome and get Mamie to promise her to start the club again.

When Mamie told Rosa about going, Rosa said, "Mamie, why do you want to help beg money of her?" Mamie said she thought the Y.W.C.A. did some good, and Rosa said maybe it did even if she couldn't see it, but she hated to have Mamie go begging off a rich woman who ought to be paying Mamie higher than $9.50 a week so she could pay off her dentist bill sometime before she died. She said that Mrs. Newsome lived in a big house with four layers of carpets on her floors and she could afford to pay. Rosa had seen the carpets one Saturday afternoon when Jake had taken her on the wagon and they had carried Mrs. Newsome's laundry round to the back and the cook had let her see inside the house because Mrs. Newsome and her two daughters were out.

Mamie said she didn't see any they told her goodbye, because they were going on out to Corinth Gardens to see some other rich people and Mamie went back to the laundry still with the handkerchief to her mouth.

She told Rosa about it right away, and Rosa said not to worry that she would go with Jake that afternoon to deliver and they would get the cook to let her look for the plates.

So Rosa went with Jake. The cook wasn't there, because she had every other Saturday afternoon off, but the back door was unlocked, and while Jake waited in the kitchen Rosa slipped into the hall. She was looking for the door to the library full of books that Mamie had told her about when Mrs. Newsome came down the stairs and saw her. For a minute she got scared and slipped back in a hurry to the kitchen. She told Jake and they went right out so Mrs. Newsome wouldn't see them. They were laughing because they had run so fast but when they were in the wagon driving off Rosa got sorry about not getting the teeth for Mamie. "Why didn't I walk right up to her and ask for them?" "I guess you was scared," Jake said. Rosa said she was but she was ashamed. There wasn't anything to be scared of. "Let's go back," she said. But Jake wouldn't, so Rosa had to find Mamie and tell her she didn't get the teeth.

She said that on Monday they could ask the Secretary to go after the plates, but Mamie said her Pa was mad enough already, because he was helping pay for them, and couldn't they do it right away. So they went to the minister's house next door to the Y.W.C.A. where the Secretary lived, but she had gone away with Miss Flora to a Conference at Morgantown. When they came out the men up in the jail yelled at them as usual—they always did it when the girls went to the Y.W.C.A.—and this time it made Rosa mad. She said "Damn that Y.W.C.A."—everybody called the Jail the Y.M.C.A. Mamie thought it was right bad for Rosa to curse like that, but Rosa didn't care because she was mad at everything, herself, too. "What are we going to do now?" she said. Mamie thought they'd have to wait until Monday afternoon when the Secretary would be in town again.

But Sunday morning Mamie's Pa got his dander up and went to Mrs. Newsome's right up to the front door. Nobody was at home except the cook, so he asked her to look for the plates, but she couldn't find them. The cook said the maid had cleaned up there that morning, but she was at church and she would ask her when she came back if she had found them, and would send word by her husband.

But she didn't send word. And the reason she didn't was that there was some excitement at Mrs. Newsome's. One of her daughters said she had left a box of jewelry on the table in the library on Saturday morning just before she went to Morgantown to a dance at the University. She had laid the box on the table while she put some rouge on her lips and then in the excitement she had forgotten it, because they were honking for her outside. Besides some other things the box had a diamond and platinum necklace in it that her mother had given her last Christmas. The necklace had twelve diamonds besides being made of platinum, so there was a lot of trouble over it.

Rosa and Mamie didn't know about that and they were going to ask the Secretary to go after the teeth just as soon as they could leave work on Monday. But they didn't do that because at eleven thirty, while they were at work in the laundry, a policeman came in and arrested them both. They found out about the necklace when they got to Jail. Mamie was crying but Rosa was scornful and that didn't make the police any nicer to her.

Mamie and Rosa were put on the top floor of the Jail where the women were. They could hear the men in the cells downstairs. Mamie was afraid of the women up there so she went to the window and looked through the bars at the Y.W.C.A. But Rosa stayed on her cot and sat there without looking up. The matron brought some clothes that Mamie's Ma sent so they had night gowns to wear, and the next day Rosa's uncle brought some clothes for her, and food her aunt had cooked.

While they were waiting for a trial the Secretary and Miss Flora came every day, and they got after Rosa for moping so much. Miss Flora said of course they were not guilty. Mamie said would she be likely to throw away her teeth, and where were they if she hadn't lost them at Mrs. Newsome's. Miss Flora said not to worry, that Mamie's Pa had a lawyer for them and everything would be all right. Rosa's uncle came and said that he had collected some money from the miners for the defense, but they couldn't give much because they were all out on strike. Mamie's Pa came and had them down in the Matron's office and prayed over them. Rosa wouldn't pray so he said she was a stubborn girl and he made Mamie join him in singing *Almost Persuaded* to make Rosa feel close to Jesus. When they sang one verse, Mamie cried so she couldn't do any more. The tears poured into her mouth because it was so flabby from not having any teeth she couldn't keep them out. But her Pa kept on with the verse ending up with "Oh, sinner, come."

He looked at Rosa when he sang but she wouldn't come. And he was very much troubled and sad over it. He knew God could prove that they were innocent, but if Rosa held out like that maybe God wouldn't. He felt bad toward Rosa, and Mamie was sorry, and tried to get Rosa to repent. But Rosa said "What of" and Mamie didn't know.

One day Mrs. Newsome came to the Jail and wanted to see them both down in the Matron's office. Rosa said she wasn't going—she sat on her cot, so stubborn Mamie almost got mad with her. She said all she wanted was to get out of there. "I'll do anything to get out." Rosa said she would, too, but not that. Then Mamie said she was afraid to go by herself, and she cried, so Rosa went.

Mrs. Newsome was very sweet. She shook hands with them and asked how they were. Mamie said they were all right except they couldn't sleep for the bed bugs, and some of the women having nightmares and yelling. Mrs. Newsome said she was grieved about the whole matter and if Mamie and Rosa would confess and tell where the necklace was she'd have everything hushed up because she and her daughters weren't anxious to go into court. When she said that Rosa got up and walked out past the matron and up the stairs.

Mamie cried and said they hadn't done it. It was her teeth they wanted and that was all. She knew she hadn't done it and Rosa hadn't either. Mrs. Newsome could asked Jake. Mrs. Newsome asked Mamie how she knew Rosa hadn't done it. And Mamie said she didn't know she could just feel, and please believe her. She was telling the truth, she could swear before God. Mrs. Newsome said she wanted to believe Mamie and she really thought Mamie was innocent. She said Mamie was such a good girl, the kind who would cooperate with the person she was working for, and Rosa wasn't, and more than anything else that made Mrs. Newsome think Mamie wasn't guilty and—she hated to say it—that Rosa was. And that if Mamie could swear that she hadn't taken the necklace Mrs. Newsome would believe her and withdraw the charge against her. Then

Mamie said, "And Rosa, too?" But Mrs. Newsome said no because anyway she had no confidence in Rosa and wouldn't believe her even if she swore, but Mamie was a real Christian girl—she sang with the Salvation Army and did good to the poor.

But talking about Rosa made her think of a warning she wanted to give Mamie. There were people like Rosa, she said, who were always disgruntled and unhappy. If you put them in a palace they would be complaining about something. One reason for this was that Rosa didn't have a sense of humor. That was something all real Americans had, thank God. They could see something humorous in any trouble, and it kept them sane and sweet. But foreigners were different. They took things so seriously. Mrs. Newsome said she had had her own share of troubles and afflictions. She knew what it meant to be poor. She had been a girl in a laundry just like Mamie, and had married the foreman's son who had been to college. They had come to Corinth and started a little laundry of their own with nothing but a few dollars and some credit and abounding faith in God. That was twenty years ago. She had worked in the laundry and had even helped her husband deliver the wash to the back doors of the people of Corinth. It had been a hard pull. Her husband hadn't been much of a business man and she had to urge him along all the time. But she had her duty to her children and she didn't let anything stand in the way of that duty. After her husband had died and she had gotten over that terrible sorrow she had plunged in and managed the business herself and now they had branches in two other cities.

It was because she had prayed and done her duty as every American mother and wife should that she had gotten where she was. She said her sense of humor had helped her all along the way. Whenever the women of Corinth had looked down on her, she had just laughed about it, and thought of the time when she would have money, too. She said the Bible truly said that "to him that hath shall be given" because when her business got to be successful the very women who had almost insulted her began to invite her to their houses. And her daughters went out with the most exclusive set of young people. She said of course she had told Mamie all this in confidence and she knew she wouldn't betray her confidence. Mamie said she wouldn't.

Mrs. Newsome said everybody could do what she had done if they persevered and had faith in God's mercy. But she wanted Mamie to know that she understood suffering, because she had suffered herself. But she understood the other thing too—the bitterness that Rosa had, and it never got anybody anywhere. She said she wished when Mamie got out of Jail she wouldn't have anything to do with Rosa again, because Mamie had a sweet character, it was her chief charm, and the reason people loved her. But a girl like Rosa could work on her and make her bitter, too. Mamie said she didn't think so that she and Rosa were friends and Rosa was always good to her. Mrs. Newsome said was she so sure that Rosa was her friend. Is anybody a friend who will try to make somebody like Mamie discontented and miserable? Did Rosa go to church? Mamie said she didn't know—she never saw Rosa on Sundays. Mrs. Newsome asked Mamie if Rosa helped with the Salvation Army and Mamie said no, she never did.

Then Mrs. Newsome said she must be an atheist, a person who didn't believe in God at all or in religions and was that the kind of friend to have? And was Mamie sure that Rosa didn't take the necklace? Was she there with her on Saturday afternoon? Mamie said no, but Jake was, and Mrs. Newsome said that didn't prove anything because Jake was in love with Rosa and a girl could do about anything with a man if she wanted to, especially a clever girl like Rosa. And she herself knew that Rosa was in the hall, and since she was there she might have been anywhere in the house for all they knew—and she had slunk away like she was guilty. Mamie said, yes, but . . .

"Now, about your teeth," Mrs. Newsome said. "We can probably get you some new ones right away. Wouldn't that be nice?"

Mamie said it would. Then Mrs. Newsome told Mamie she would get the District Attorney, who was a friend of hers and make it all right. "I'm going to *Try to get jobs and stick together* matters so I can take you to your father and mother tonight," she said, "so go upstairs and get ready."

When Mamie got up to the women's room Rosa was sitting on her cot. Mamie told Rosa that she was getting out and would work on the outside for her. She felt that because Mrs. Newsome had suffered she would understand that Rosa was innocent when Mamie told her all about it.

Rosa helped Mamie get her things together. It was getting darker every minute and the only light they had was a small one in the corridor so they tried to hurry. But Rosa was so heavy and slow in moving about they were not ready when the matron came. Mamie made Rosa keep one of her night gowns so she would have an extra one. When they were through Rosa went to the door to tell Mamie goodbye. Mamie put her arms around Rosa and felt her body shake with crying and when she took her arms away she saw that Rosa's mouth was swollen and red. Her arms were hanging at her sides and her back was bent over like she had smoothing irons in her hands pulling her down. The matron was very sorry for Rosa and she tried to close the steel door softly but it was heavy and slipped from her hand and clanged to behind her and Mamie jarring the steel bars all along the corridors so they gave out little sounds like dogs whimpering in their sleep.

After Mamie left the Jail Miss Flora stopped coming, but the Secretary kept on. One day Mamie came with her and the Secretary went away and left Mamie with Rosa. Mamie said her Pa wouldn't let her come before but this time she slipped off. They talked some and then they got quiet. Rosa didn't talk free like she had and Mamie was sort of strained. When they had been quiet a little Mamie said, "Rosa, you didn't do it, did you?" Rosa said "What did you say?" like she was dazed, and Mamie asked her again if she had taken the necklace. Then Rosa got up and Mamie was scared, she looked so fierce. Rosa said, "You think I took it, do you?" Mamie said no she didn't, not exactly, but they all talked like she had, even Miss Flora thought she had done it now and Jake was in the kitchen so he couldn't be sup—nobody could be sure, not even the Secretary—it was all so mixed up for Mamie. Mrs. Newsome kept asking everybody who took up for Rosa if they were in the library Saturday afternoon while Jake was in the kitchen and if they weren't how could they be sure she wasn't guilty? "Well," Rosa said, "you know me, don't you?" Mamie said yes she did, and because they were friends wouldn't Rosa tell her if she had done it. All of them, Miss Flora and Mrs. Newsome too said it would be all right if Rosa would confess. Rosa lay down on the bed and put her face in the pillow for what seemed a long time to Mamie. Then she sat up and told Mamie she thought she'd better go. Mamie said she wanted to help Rosa and she tried to take her hand, but Rosa doubled up her fists and put them in her lap and was so still Mamie was afraid to touch her. Rosa said, "Seems to me if it was you I'd say she isn't until I knew something else and I'd say it so hard they'd believe me, instead of me believing them." Then she told Mamie again to go. She said, "You'd better go before I call you Trixie." When she said that Mamie got up and went on out without stopping to say goodby or anything because she knew Rosa meant she was waddling after Miss Flora. Rosa had been so quiet all along that the women up there were scared when they heard her scream, and saw her crouch down by the cot and beat her fists on it. They got her some water, but she wouldn't take it, and was quiet again right away.

The next day was the trial. They made Mamie tell about her teeth and Jake said Rosa had been out of the kitchen just a few minutes. The maid told about how she had found the teeth mashed into the carpet when she had cleaned up Sunday morning after the party. Mrs. Newsome's daughter testified about leaving the necklace on the library table, and Mrs. Newsome told about seeing Rosa in the hall Saturday afternoon and how she had slunk away like she was guilty when she saw Mrs. Newsome.

The forelady at the Fine Finish said that Rosa was a good worker but had a grudge against Mrs. Newsome because she was rich. Then the District Attorney had two girls from the laundry and they told some things Rosa had said about Mrs. Newsome.

When that day was over Rosa was right sick. They called in a doctor and he gave her some medicine but it didn't do her any good.

The women didn't pay much attention to her because there was some excitement in the Jail all night. In the afternoon five hundred miners that were striking had marched down the river road right into Corinth trying to make people see they were in earnest about striking and the police had gone after them and knocked them down and then brought four hundred of them into the Jail. All the citizens got excited and took out their guns and stood guard all over town to protect it from the miners.

If Rosa hadn't been so worn out she would have been excited when those four hundred men were brought to the Jail. After they were put in they tried to sing but the police went in and hit some of them with their clubs—so they stopped.

The next morning the Secretary came over to see Rosa. She wanted to know if she could do anything. Rosa said no, but she was much obliged anyway.

Rosa's case came up later on that day. She had to answer some questions and the District Attorney asked her if it was true that her uncle was a striking miner and she said, yes, it was true.

When the trial ended the jury said Rosa was guilty. The Judge gave her two years which he said was a very short sentence because she was only twenty-one years old.

The day Rosa was to be taken away the Secretary came up to see her. She said she had left Mamie over at the Y.W.C.A. Rosa asked how Mamie was, and the Secretary said she was feeling fine because she had gotten her new teeth that morning—a gift from Mrs. Newsome, but she was worried about Rosa and wanted to see her. Rosa said she thought she couldn't see Mamie right at that time. Then the Secretary brought out a note from Mrs. Newsome. She read the note out loud because Rosa didn't seem to want to take it. The note said that even if the necklace, which was a gift from Mrs. Newsome to her daughter, was gone forever, Mrs. Newsome would feel kindly toward Rosa and forgive her for the sake of her own girls. She hoped Rosa would learn something from this experience and for her to remember that "blessed are the meek for they shall inherit the earth."

The Secretary asked Rosa if there was any answer and Rosa said no. So they shook hands. But when the matron had let the Secretary into the corridor and closed the door Rosa said "Wait" in a hoarse voice. The Secretary turned back and Rosa went up to the door. Seh held on to the bars and looked out between two of them. "Tell her," she said, "They're taking me up for two years—but I'm coming out, and I'm going to begin right where I left off. Tell her there's a war going on and she and me are on different sides." She was crying, so she walked away and looked out of the window to keep them from seeing. The matron took the Secretary on downstairs.

In a little while through the window Rosa saw the Secretary go out of the Jail and Mamie come to meet her down there in the middle of the street. She saw Mamie open her mouth to talk and the sun shining on her new teeth.

DID GOD MAKE BEDBUGS?

MICHAEL GOLD

It rained, we squatted dull as frogs on the steps of the rear tenement. What boredom in the backyard, we didn't know what to do with ourselves. Life seemed to flicker out on a rainy day.

The rain was warm and sticky; it spattered on the tin roofs like a gangster's blood. It filled our backyard with a smell of decay, as if someone had just dumped a ton of rotten apples.

Rain, rain! The sky was a strip of gray tin above the terraced clotheslines, on which flowery shirts and underwear flapped like flags in the rain. I looked up at them.

I heard the hum of the sewing machines in my father's little shop, a dreary sound like surf on a lonely island. A feeble baby wept, and its mother answered hoarsely. The swollen upper half of a fat woman hung from a window, above two elbows like hams. She stared for hours with dull eyes at the rain.

A decaying wooden shack occupied a fair portion of the yard; it was the common toilet. A bearded man in suspenders went in there.

There was nothing to do. Masha sang from the next tenement yard, she was a blind young prostitute girl. The deep sad Russian songs helped her pain, she was homesick for Kiev. The other girls often sang with her, many nights I was soothed to sleep by that lullaby, but now she sang alone, drearily.

Because there was nothing to do. Rain, rain, we had tired of our marbles, our jacks and playing store games.

The backyard was a curious spot. It had once been a graveyard, and some of the old American headstones had been used to pave our Jewish yard. The inscriptions were dated a hundred years ago, but we knew them all, and were tired of weaving romances around the ruins of America.

Once we had torn up a white gravestone. What an adventure. We scratched like ghouls with our hands deep into the earth until we found mouldy dirty human bones. What a thrill that was. I owned chunks of knee bone, and yellow forearms, and parts of a worm- eaten skull. I had them cached in a secret corner of my father's dark shop, wrapped in burlap with other treasured playthings.

But it would be boring to dig for bones now. And we were sick of trying to sail paper boats in the standing pool above the drain pipe. It was choked with muck, too sluggish for real boat races.

Then a cat appeared in the rain and macabre gloom of the yard. We were suddenly alert as flies.

It was an East Side gutter cat, its head was gaunt, its bones jutted sharply like parts of a strange machine. It was sick. Its belly dragged on the ground, it was sick with a new litter. It paused before a garbage can, sniffing out food.

We yelled. In slow agony, its dim eyes cast about; as if searching for a friend. The sick, starved mother-cat suspected our sudden whoops of savage joy. It leaped on a garbage can and waited. It did not hump its back, it was too weary to show anger or fear. It waited.

And then we pursued it like fiends, pelting it with offal. It scrambled hysterically up the fence, we heard it drop on heavy feet into the next yard—where other children sat in the rain.

2. TOO MANY CATS

There is nothing in this incident that ought to be recorded. There were thousands of cats on the East Side; one of the commonplace joys of childhood was to torture cats, chase them, drop them from steep roofs to see whether cats really had nine lives.

It was a world of violence and stone, there were too many cats, there were too many children.

The stink of cats filled the tenement halls. Cats fought around each garbage can in the East Side struggle for life. These cats were not the smug purring pets of the rich, but outcasts, criminals and fiends. They were hideous with scars and wounds, their fur was torn, they were smeared with unimaginable sores and filth, their eyes glared dangerously. They were so desperate they would sometimes fight a man. At night they alarmed the tenement with their weird cries like a congress of crazy witches. The obscene heartbreak of their amours ruined our sleep, made us cry and toss in cat nightmares. We tortured them, they tortured us. It was poverty.

When you opened the door of your home there was always a crazy cat or two trying to claw its way inside. They would lie for days outside the door, brooding on the smell of cooking until they went insane.

Kittens died quietly in every corner, rheumy-eyed, feeble and old before they had even begun to learn to play.

Sometimes Mommer let you pity a kitten, give it a saucer of milk which it lapped madly with its tiny tongue.

But later you had to drive it out again into the cruel street. There were too many kittens. The sorrow of kittens was too gigantic for one child's pity.

I had chased and persecuted cats with the other children; I had never had much pity; but on this rainy afternoon I pitied the poor mother-cat.

I found myself thinking: Did God make cats?

3. THE RIOT IN A CHAIDER

I was oppressed with thoughts of God then because my parents had put me in a Chaider. I went to this Jewish religious school every afternoon when the American public school let out.

There is no hell fire in the orthodox Jewish religion. Children are not taught to harrow themselves searching for sin; nor to fear the hereafter. But they must memorize a long rigmarole of Hebrew prayers.

Reb Moisha was my teacher. This man was a walking, belching symbol of the decay of orthodox Judaism, for what could such as he teach anyone? He was ignorant as a rat. He was a foulsmelling emaciated beggar who had never read anything, or seen anything, or felt anything, who knew absolutely nothing but this sterile memory course in dead Hebrew which he whipped into the heads and backsides of little boys.

He dressed always in the same long black alpaca coat, green and disgusting with its pattern of grease, snuff, old food stains and something worse; for this religious teacher had nothing but contempt for the modern device of the handkerchief. He blew his nose on the floor, then wiped it on his horrible sleeve. Pickled herring and onions were his standard food; the sirocco blast of a thousand onions poured from his beard when he bent over the Aleph-Beth with you, his face close and hot to yours.

He was cruel as a jailer. He had a sadist's delight in pinching the boys with his long pincer fingers; he was always whipping special offenders with his cat-o-nine-tails; yet he maintained no real discipline in his hellhole of Jewish piety.

I was appalled when my parents brought me there, and after paying Reb Moisha his first weekly fee of fifty cents, left me with him.

In the ratty old loft, lit by a gas jet that cast a charnelhouse flare on the strange scene, I beheld thirty boys leaping and rioting like so many tigers pent in the one cage.

Some were spinning tops; others played tag, or wrestled; a group kneeled in a corner, staring at the ground as though a corpse lay there, and screaming passionately. They were shooting craps.

One of these boys saw me. He came over, and without a word, tore the picture button of W. J. Bryan from my lapel. The boys gambled in buttons.

At a long table, hacked by many knives, Reb Moisha sat with ten surly boys, the beginner's class, and soon I was howling with them. Over and over again we howled the ancient Hebrew prayers for thunder and lightning and bread and death; meaningless sounds to us. And Reb Moisha would pinch a boy, and scream above the bedlam, "Louder, little thieves! Louder!" He forced us to howl.

There was a smell like dead dog from the broken toilet in the hall. A burlap curtain hung at one end of the hall to disguise the master's home, for he was the unlucky father of five children. His wife's harpy voice nagged them; we could smell onions frying; always onions for the master.

His face was pale, peaked, sinister, like a corpse's; it was framed in an inkblack beard; he wore a skullcap; his eyes glittered, and roved restlessly like an ogre's hungry for blood of little boys.

I did not like this place. Once he tried to whip me, and instead of the usual submission, I ran home. My mother was angry.

"You must go back," she said. "Do you want to grow up into an ignorant Goy, a Christian?"

"But why do I have to learn all those Hebrew words? They don't mean anything, Mommer!"

"They mean a lot," said my mother severely. "Those are God's words, the way He wants us to pray to Him, in Hebrew."

"Who is God?" I asked. "Why must we pray to Him?"

"He is the one who made the world," said my mother solemnly. "We must obey Him."

"Did He make *everything*?"

"Yes, everything. God made everything in this world."

This impressed me, I returned to the heder, and in the midst of the riot and screaming I would brood on my mother's God, on the strange man in the sky who must be addressed in Hebrew, that man who had created everything in the world.

4. GOD IS A JEW

My mother was very pious; her face grew solemn and mysterious when she talked about her God. Everyone argued about God. Mendel Bum, and Fyfka the Miser, and my Aunt Lena, and Jake Wolf, the saloonkeeper, and the fat janitor woman, and Mrs. Rif-kin, of the umbrella store, my mother's best friend, and Mottke Blinder, and Harry the Pimp—all were interested in God. It was an important subject, and when I discovered this, it became important for me, too.

(This Jewish God! Chief of a tribe of desert fanatics, moody tyrant, dictator, sadistic king who loved the smoke of innocent blood, of burning cities!

(You were a mighty captain on the hills of Palestine, you told the Jews they were your chosen people, you promised them the earth, you led them to victory and injustice!

(You were their strong God, and then you failed them. They became the dregs of the nations. They lived in the cellars of the world.

(But they CLUNG TO YOU! They did not reproach their Judas. They built synagogues to their pale shrunken defeated ghetto God. They were martyrs for you, Viper!)

(But that was in Europe. This is America, end of the centuries, here you are fated to perish at last!)

Meyer Sheftel, was a pale lonely young immigrant, one of my father's three workers, with a dangly head and blue protruding nearsighted eyes. He was always in a daze. He shambled about, his clothes flapping on his scrawny skeleton. He was always reading, reading. A Russian book was propped against the head of his machine, and even while he worked, he was reading.

Once, from this abstraction, he leaped up with a scream of pain. He had run the needle through his finger. A doctor was called, it was a painful operation. But Meyer, his finger bandaged, went on reading hungrily that same afternoon. It was life to him.

My father and his friends respected Meyer because he read so much. They assured each other he was very wise. What he was reading, or what he thought, no one knew. He rarely spoke; and this silence made him the more impressive.

One day a funny thing happened in the shop. Mottke popped in the door, dragging Mendel Bum by the coat. They had been arguing about God in the saloon; cross-eyed Mottke was all asweat with emotion. His face of a gentle gargoyle was purple with excitement.

"Meyer," he said, puffing indignantly, "we want you to decide a bet. You have read books, you know things. This Mendel, this bum, he says that there is no God. And I say there is. So we have bet a quarter."

The student's pale face flushed faintly. He was embarrassed because we were looking at him.

"Well," he stammered.

Mendel, that rogue, grinned and winked at my father, as if he had already won the bet.

"Well," the young student began, "I think so, that is to say: I think there is a God."

Mottke laughed, he showed his yellow stumps, then he slapped Mendel on the shoulder.

"Nu, free thinker," he crowed, "hand me over the quarter!" But Mendel went on arguing, he shrugged his shoulders.

5. A HORSE NAMED GANUF

I couldn't get the thought out of my head; it was God who made everything. A child carries such thoughts about him unconsciously, the way he carries his body; they burrow and grow inside him. He sits quietly; no one knows why; he himself doesn't know; but he is thinking. Then one day he will speak.

In the livery stable on our street there was an old truck horse I loved. Every night he came home weary from work, but they would not unhitch him at once, he would be made to wait for hours in the street by Vashka.

He was hungry, and that's why he'd steal apples or bananas from the pushcarts if the peddler was napping. He was kicked and beaten for this, but it did not break him of his bad habit. They should have fed him after a day's work, but he was always neglected, and dirty, fly-bitten, gall-ridden. He was nicknamed the Ganuf—the old Thief on our street.

I stole sugar from my home and gave it to him. I stroked his damp nose, and gray flanks, or gray tangled mane, and he shook his head, and stared at me with his large gentle eyes. He never shook his head for the other boys, they marvelled at my power over Ganuf.

He was a kind, good horse, and wise in many ways. For instance: Jim Bush abused him. Jim Bush was a fiery little Irish cripple who lived by doing odd jobs for the prostitute girls. Jim Bush was a tough guy from the waist up. His blue fireman's shirt covered massive shoulders and arms; his face was red and leathery like a middle-aged cop's; but his legs were shrivelled like a baby's.

He cracked dirty jokes with the girls, he was genial when sober, but when he was drunk he wanted to fight everyone. He would leap from his crutches at a man's throat and hang there like a bulldog, squeezing for death with his powerful hands, until beaten into unconsciousness. He always began his pugnacious debauches by abusing Ganuf the Horse.

He seemed to hate Ganuf. Why, I don't know. Maybe to show his power. He was the height of a boy of seven. He stood there, eyes bloodshot with liquor, mouth foaming, and shouted curses at the horse. Ganuf moved; Jim struck him over the nose with a crutch.

Jim grabbed the bridle; "back up!" he yelled, then he sawed the bit on poor Ganuf's tongue. Then he clutched the horse's nostrils and tried to tear them off.

The poor horse was patient. He looked down from his great height at the screaming little cripple, and seemed to understand. He would have kicked anyone else, but I think he knew Jim Bush was a cripple.

People always marvelled at this scene. I used to feel sorry for my poor horse, and imagine there were tears in his eyes.

This horse dropped at work one summer day. They loosened his harness, and slopped buckets of water over him. He managed to stand up, but was weak. He dragged the truck back to the stable. Waiting there for his supper, he fell gasping; he died on our street.

His body bloated like a balloon, and he was left there until the wagon could come to haul him to the boneyard.

When a horse lay dead in the street that way, he was seized upon to become another plaything in the queer and terrible treasury of East Side childhood.

Children gathered around Ganuf. They leaped on his swollen body, poked sticks in the vents. They pried open the eyelids, speculated on those sad, glazed big eyes. They plucked hair from the tail with which to weave good-luck rings.

The fat blue and golden flies swarmed, too, around the body of my kind old friend. They buzzed and sang with furious joy as they attacked this tremendous meal sent them by the God of Flies.

I stood there helplessly. I wanted to cry for my poor old Ganuf. Had God made Ganuf? Then why had He let Ganuf die? And had God made flies?

The millions of East Side flies, that drove us crazy in summer, and sucked at our eyelids while we slept, drowned in our glass of milk?

Why?

6. DID GOD MAKE BEDBUGS?

Did God make bedbugs? One steaming hot night, I couldn't sleep for the bedbugs. They have a peculiar nauseating smell of their own; it is the smell of poverty. They crawl slowly and pompously, bloated with blood, and the touch and smell of these parasites wakens every nerve to disgust.

(Bedbugs are what people mean when they say: Poverty. There are enough pleasant superficial liars writing in America. I will write a truthful book of Poverty; I will mention bedbugs.)

It wasn't a lack of cleanliness in our home. My mother was as clean as any German housewife; she slaved, she worked herself to the bone keeping us fresh and neat. The bedbugs were a torment to her. She doused the beds with kerosene, changed the sheets, sprayed the mattresses frantically. What was the use; nothing could help; it was Poverty; it was the Tenement.

The bedbugs lived and bred in the rotten walls of the tenement, with the rats, fleas, roaches; the whole rotten structure needed to be torn down; a kerosene bottle would not help.

It had been a frightful week of summer heat. I was sick and feverish with heat, and pitched and tossed, while the cats sobbed in the yard. The bugs finally woke me. They were everywhere. I cannot tell the despair, loathing and rage of the child in the dark tenement room, as they crawled on me, and stank.

I cried softly. My mother woke and lit the gas. She renewed her futile battle with the bedbugs. The kerosene smell choked me. My mother tried to soothe me back to sleep. But my brain raced like a sewing machine.

"Mommer," I asked, "why did God make the bedbugs?"

She laughed at her little boy's quaint idea. I was often jollied about it later, but who has yet answered this question? Was it the God of Love who put pain and poverty into the world? Why, a kind horse like my Ganuf would never have done such a thing.

THE DISTURBER

The movie was about a poor slob chauffeur who loved his master's beautiful daughter. We gasped, bawled, beat our breasts, and were surprised when we sensed one in our midst who didn't sympathize with the aspiring young hero. Following other annoyed glances my eyes fixed on a youngish chap slumped in his seat. I caught a glimpse of his face, expressionless, but queer clothes he wore intrigued us, and we were unable to pay unadulterated homage to the famous stars of the silver sheet. Yes; among us sat a person in gray blouse and pants, these unrelieved by color except for red ribbon across left chest. Eyes sunken and thoughtful, lips enigmatic and tight. "Garbage sweeper?" a buxom matron inquired. "Don't know," I snarled. "He's just pulled a hanky cleaner than mine," protested a stenog at my right. I tried, and the good people around me tried, to follow the far-trumpeted movie. Alas! this motionless fellow in shapeless clothes had captured our attention. Somebody shied spitballs at him. No movement. Now, on the screen, the hero clasped his high-born dearly beloved. We yelled, cheered, all but one who slumped still farther down in his seat and *yawned*. I was enraged. I recalled hearing at our last Rotary meeting of disaffected persons who didn't like anything truly American, taking a snobbish attitude toward native productions; we growled as the lecturer proceeded, and it sounded ominous to me. The feature came to a beautiful end; chauffeur moved into a suite in the great house, and was to be given the master's daughter in honorable marriage. Our applause was a thing never to forget, except to one person; of course the chap in gray blouse wasn't impressed one bit. "Heehee!" he *laughed*, in a coarse undignified manner. Forgetting my training as an American gentleman I shouted: "Who the hell are you?" He half rose. On his lap I glimpsed a cap with a five-point star that seemed to be burning angrily. Instinctively a woman of delicate sensibilities fainted at sight of him. In staccato, foreign-accented tones, glittering with contempt for me, he said: "I am a Bolshevik soldier."

GEORGE JARRBOE.

A 5 AND 10 CENT STORE GIRL

WILLIAM EDGE

Not far from where my buddy, Slim, and I lived in the Mission, in San Francisco, lived the widow O'Reilly. She had five children, two boys and three girls. One of the boys was about seventeen. He was a tough-looking youngster who worked in a warehouse downtown. We did not see much of him—neither did his mother—for he was a sort of semi-delinquent who came home only when it suited him. He gave his mother a dollar or two sometimes; but he took, on the whole, little responsibility for the widow and her younger children.

The widow O'Reilly was a tiny, slender, small-boned woman of perhaps forty, though I arrive at her age by the age of her children rather than by her appearance. Poverty and privation had given her a face which might have gone with a body of sixty years.

But it is Margaret, the daughter, whom I am really concerned with. Margaret was sixteen. She, too, was slender and small boned, and undernourished, but not so tiny as her mother. You would have noticed her eyes first of all, but not because they were blue and abnormally large. They were wild. They made you think of the restless, roving eyes of a caged beast. Or they made you think of fever and insanity. Shining, burning, wet, never-resting—such were her eyes. Her hair—a light brown, and her complexion fair.

Now, a girl at sixteen is, I suppose, legitimate prey for a man who was as young as I was in 1921, when all this happened. But Slim had warned me:

"It wouldn't exactly be robbing the cradle; and I daresay she would be pleased to play with you or any other acceptable young man. But

I happen to know—to feel quite sure, rather—that she is still a virgin. She is not game for your guns. You've had too many educational and cultural advantages to try any funny business with her. Pick on somebody your size from the standpoint of experience in life and training."

And since I admired Slim very much, and since Slim was nearly ten years my senior, I put Margaret out of my mind, though I couldn't see any harm in visiting and chatting with the O'Reilly's. Sometimes I had luncheon with them. It hurt my heart to see Eleanor and Mary, both under ten years of age, eating one piece of bread and one piece of bologna, and drinking one cup of warmed-up coffee for lunch. Nothing more. Day in and day out. I accepted their generous hospitality because I could help them only if I played the role of guest. Heaven knows I was poor enough myself. But the O'Reilly's were so poor that I could experience the satisfactions of a philanthropist when, invited to lunch, I brought with me a quart of milk or a bag of apricots.

Sometimes Slim and I came to see the O'Reilly's in the evening. The younger children were in bed; Margaret and her mother were usually ironing the wash they took in as their only means of support. Slim, who was a great teaser, would joke with Mrs. O'Reilly about her religious convictions.

To the poor lady Slim's banter was unfathomable.

"You know, Mrs. O'Reilly, I think wings will be very becoming to you."

"Wings?"

"Of course. You're going to be an angel when you die, aren't you?"

"Land sakes, I guess so."

"Well, you'll be wearing wings. And I was just saying, I think you'd look stunning in wings. You'll be playing a golden harp. Do you know anything about music?—I wonder what the old man looks like, up there in heaven?"

It seemed to me that Mrs. O'Reilly started at the thought that she would meet her husband again.

Slim would continue. "It takes a long time to learn how to play a harp. Wonder how long it took your husband. Dead five years. Five years.

I suppose he's getting to be pretty good by now. Some of those young angels have no ear at all for music. They're an awful nuisance."

And so on, for an hour or more, while the widow and her daughter ironed and ironed and ironed. Sometimes Mrs. O'Reilly would stop to interpolate minor objections, objections which Slim would brush aside—frequently accusing her indignantly of disloyalty to God, the Father, the Son, the Holy Ghost and the Church. Slim, incidentally, had been educated in a Jesuit school, something which gave him a tremendous advantage in such matters over any mere atheist.

The children were usually in bed but still awake when we left. Ironing, washing, sleeping, cooking, eating, visiting—all were done in the same room. It was my custom sometimes, just before leaving, to tickle one of the children. Slim would tickle another, and the delighted squealings showed that our attentions were very welcome.

One night Margaret was in bed when I arrived alone to have a little chat with the good widow. Upon leaving I gave one of the children my customary rough housing when the inspiration came to me to tickle Margaret. I went to her bed, pulled off the covers, and began to tickle her. Hearty laughs from the widow encouraged me, and delicious, frightened looks from Margaret's wild eyes goaded me on. She struggled against me as the babies could not struggle. She pulled down her nightgown quickly, and I felt her flying hair in my face.

Still the widow laughed as if it were all an innocent joke. But my blood was surging. With an effort of will I stopped; and, to seem casual, I tickled one of the younger children before leaving.

I saw Margaret several times after that, and it seemed to me that she averted those restless eyes when I was near. Soon after this I left San Francisco for good. There is a slender aftermath to all this.

A year after leaving San Francisco I received a letter, something like the one printed below, from Margaret. I have lost the letter, but I have re-read it often enough in the last six years to give a tolerably authentic reproduction.

Do not laugh at the letter. Think, rather, of the tragedy in it. A five and ten cent store girl. The miserable education which her letter reveals. The casual marriage she seems to be contemplating—at seventeen.

Dear Blondey Slim said if I wood rite the letter he woud give me a envlop with you're naim and address so hear goes. I am working in the 5 and ten cent store and I am going to marry Herbert Quinn soon only dont tell anybody because its a seecrit.

How are you, anyways? I'm real well now. If you want to write me hear is where I work—Market Street because if you writ home Eleanor will tease me she always says I'm in love with you anyhow. Ha! ha! Well I gess this is ennough for today.

Yours truly,

Margaret O'Reilly.

THE RIGHT TO DEATH

MIRIAM ALLEN DeFORD

MY FRIEND was dying. For seven months I had taken her daily to a chamber of horrors where her fatal wound was probed, where useless serum was shot into her, where she wept and argued and refused another operation. At three or four o'clock in the morning she would call me up. I would stumble out of bed, in my suburban home across the bay, and listen half asleep to the telephone.

"I can't stand it. I can't lie down, I can't sit, I can't stand up, I can't walk. What shall I do?"

"How can I help you?" I would cry in despair. "Why don't you call your doctor?"

A moan would answer me.

She was living on four grains of morphine a day. In between she sniffed chloroform, enough to drown the pain. She would sob:

"I have clothes laid away in the second drawer of the bureau. Dress me in them and have me cremated."

As patiently as a detective I tried to get from her her mother's maiden name, the place of her birth—the things the death notice and the certificate would require.

It is no fun to watch anybody die.

One day she said to me:

"Will you kill me? There is plenty of chloroform. I tried, but I only burnt my face, and I couldn't go on with it. Please kill me. I'll lie quietly and let you put the sponge over my mouth and nose."

I thought of the apartment house janitor who would testify that I had been the last to call on her, and how afterwards they had found her dead. I thought that after all she was not very dear to me; she was only the teacher in my aunt's school whom I had known since I was a child. I could not do it.

Three months later I shipped her back to her brother in Cincinnati, and a month later she died, in atrocious agony.

If I had loved her I could have done it, as the woman in Paris poisoned her lover who was dying of an incurable disease. Why is it that one cannot kill the person one does not either hate or love?

The bootlegger told me two stories. One was of a man I had known. He used to hang around the speakeasy. We called him Slim. Once he cooked us a dinner, a southern dinner of Virginia ham and corn bread. He was slowly dying of cancer of the stomach.

"Slim wanted me to kill him," the bootlegger said. "One night when I asked him to have a drink he said no, he couldn't stand it. Then he was quiet for a while, and all of a sudden he said:

" 'Is that stuff of yours poison?'

" 'Not that I know of,' I told him. 'I've drunk a lot of it, and I'm not dead yet.'

" 'If it was poison,' Slim said, 'I'd drink it until I couldn't hold any more, and then I'd go upstairs and die.'

" 'Slim,' I told him, 'If it was poison I'd stake you to a gallon, and I'd feed it to you till you dropped.'

" 'You've got a gun,' Slim said. 'Will you shoot me?'

"But I couldn't do it. We passed it off for a joke."

Slim drifted away into a hospital, and after a while he died there.

The bootlegger is an old railroad man. The war lost him his job, and when he came home from saving the world for democracy, he opened a bootleg joint.

"Once," he told me, "I was brakeman on a road between Washington and North Dakota. There was a little town in Montana called Horton. It was nothing but a row of shacks in the mud aside of the railroad tracks, and every shack was a saloon or a gambling joint or a 'house.' 'Rails' weren't welcome there; they'd run us out of the town more than once.

"We stopped there one night to take on water. The tank leaked and there were lots of high weeds growing under it. While we were waiting we saw two men come down and throw something in the weeds.

"I had a young fellow working with me, a young hick from Missouri. We went over and looked, and what they had thrown there was a man. He was bent double, holding on to his belly.

"We turned the lantern on him, and he looked up at us. He was bleeding on the weeds—not much, just a trickle.

"He said, 'I'm going to die. Will one of you fellows kill me?' " " 'What happened?' I asked him.

" 'I was playing and I was three hundred dollars to the good. They got mad and they shot me.'

"He lifted up his shirt above his pants and there seven holes in his stomach.

" 'I know one of you's got a gun,' he said. 'Won't you kill me?'

"We put him in a flat car and we carried him to the next town. The nearest doctor was a hundred and fifty miles away. The Missouri boy and I talked it over. I had a gun all right—had it in my pocket. The fellow kept moaning. I went up and talked to him again.

" 'Where are you from?' I asked him.

" 'New York state,' he answered. But he wouldn't tell us the town, or what his name was.

"We stopped again to water—we had to stop every half hour in those days, with the small tanks we had. The Missouri hick and I took him out and laid him on the grass. Then we went aside and talked it over. The boy from Missouri wanted to kill him. He had a pickaxe, and he said he would hit the guy in the head with the handle and put him out of his misery. I could have shot him easy. I knew if we didn't, he would live four or five hours and then die.

" 'We can't do it,' I said. 'Those guys in Horton are after us rails anyway. If they found this fellow with a bullet through his head they'd say we did the whole thing, and maybe get us for it. We don't dare.'

"The fellow was wriggling around there on the grass and moaning. 'I'll give you a hundred dollars to kill me,' he said. He took the money out of his pocket and held it out to us.

" 'I don't want your money,' the Missouri hick told him. 'I'll do it just to help you.'

"He started toward him with the pickaxe, but I pulled him on board and the train started.

"Two days later we came by that way again. Somebody was just burying the fellow. He must have lived several hours."

That was the bootlegger's second story, and I thought of my friend. Why can't we kill anybody we neither love nor hate?

Twice in the past few years fathers have killed children who were, in one case imbecilic, in the other hopelessly crippled. They were both acquitted.

But that is a common duty we human beings owe each other. Doctors always deny that they give overdoses of narcotics to patients who are going to die anyway. But unless they are monsters they must do so sometimes. An old woman I knew was dying of a tumor. She was over eighty, and it was useless to operate. She was in dreadful pain. The doctor simply kept her under morphine until she slept herself out of life. Yet a dozen years ago when a physician in Chicago was called upon to deliver a baby born without a posterior opening for its alimentary canal—a freak doomed to a miserable death—and he refused to operate, but simply let it die, he was tried for murder. Why? Why does anyone allow the idiots and monstrosities to live? Why are there two pairs of twins, at least, alive in America today, joined by their spinal columns, unable to separate, destined to abnormal lives, to wretchedness camouflaged with publicity? Why are we so afraid of death, kindliest of solutions to unanswerable problems?

There should be trained anaesthetists, called in when a child is born who cannot possibly live a normal existence, when a human being is so afflicted that a painful death is inevitable. Then the wise and kindly anesthetist should bring out his means of relief, and end this misery at once. But we make a fetich of mere living, however horrible and ignoble, and we condemn people to a life worse, far worse than death.

When my friend went back to Cincinnati there was a campaign on against dope addicts. Her brother, shocked by her allowance of four grains of morphine a day, reported her to the police. She was taken in her stretcher to jail and thrown into a cell. The next day the judge dismissed the case, and she was taken back to her brother's house to die.

But as she lay in the cell, hearing the shrieks of addicts "kicking it off," tortured by her disease, in agony of body and soul, I wonder if she thought bitterly of me, and of my refusal to end her pain quickly and without a pang.

I am sorry the theological taboos of civilized society forbade me to perform that act of human decency and kindness.

SOLDIER OF CHRIST

CHARLES YALE HARRISON

I

He was a Methodist lay preacher; when the circuit minister couldn't make the rounds he acted as the man of God. He came from somewhere in the backblocks of northern Ontario. A thin, nervous little fellow of forty or so, slightly bald in front and a pimply face. We first became aware of him in the Peel Street barracks in Montreal where he enlisted. Anderson was his name.

It was after midnight on pay-day. The boys were beginning to dribble in after a night's carousal "down the line." Most of them smelled of booze and women. A few jaundiced electric lights burned here and there in the barn-like bunk room. Anderson in his heavy regulation gray woolen underwear sagging at the seat, stood at the edge of his bunk.

He waited cautiously for a lull in the rowdy, drunken conversation and then: "Some of you men'd put your bodies where I wouldn't put my swagger stick." His voice sounded like an insistent piccolo above braying trombones.

Cries and hoarse shouts came from the yellow-black recesses of the room:

"Shut up."

"It's good for pimples."

"Pipe down, sky pilot."

The shouting died away and Anderson continued in his squeaky voice: "Well, anyway, God didn't make your bodies for that." The last word with fervor.

II

He was a great favorite, of course, with the Y. M. C. A., secretary and some of the officers; the men detested him.

The night we entrained for Halifax the whole outfit was blind drunk. Anderson alone was sober. The battalion was to march down to the Windsor Station at eight o'clock. At four in the afternoon the evening papers appeared on the streets:

.. MONTREAL'S HEROES OFF FOR HALIFAX TONIGHT

* * *

Royal Regiment To Get Rousing Send-off at Eight tonight.

* * *

Men Eager For Fight

It took an hour to line the men up for parade outside the barracks. The boys sprawled drunk on the cots and brawls were the order of the day. Kids of sixteen lay puking over the sides of their bunks.

"Quick march!" The band struck up "Tipperary" and the staggering column started down the street. Under his ninety-pound pack Anderson marched sober and erect. At the comer of Peel and St. Catherine streets thousands of people cheered and waved handkerchiefs. Flowers were tossed into the swaying ranks. Sleek men standing on the steps of the Windsor Hotel threw packages of cigarettes into the twisted column. Drunken, spiked heels crushed roses and Camels. Befurred women laughed and cried in patriotic hysteria. A banner strung across the street read: For King and Country.

Anderson marched by my side. I heard his excited, piping voice above the thunderous farewell. "The finest people ... see ... this Christian city ... sinners ... drunken ... the Lord will ..." The bloodthirsty ovation blotted out his words completely.

On the train the boys were green under the gills. White faced men reeled to the toilets. The floor of the car was slimy and wet.

III

We were very apt at learning the smutty marching songs. Gallows-humor, I think the Germans called it. The boys sang with a terrifying eagerness for the comic.

> Mad'mselle from Armentieres, parlay voo
> Oh, mad'mselle from Armentieres, parlay voo
> Mad'mselle from Armentieres,
> Hadn't been ... .ed in forty years,
> Hincky dincky parlay voo.

Anderson complained to the chaplain. "Suppose we were bombed or something. Imagine going to meet your God with a dirty song on your lips." He was frightened. Then men roared their marching songs, shouting and singing down the terror that gripped each heart.

> Oh madame have you a daughter fine,
> Fit for a soldier up the line—
> Hincky dincky parlay voo.

IV

Bethune was a haven for the Canadians. It was fifteen miles behind the Canadian front and could only be reached by naval artillery. Just outside the town stood a coal mine largely owned by German shareholders. This fortunate circumstance kept the German gunners from shelling the town although the surrounding territory was pock-marked with shell holes.

There were showerbaths in the mine buildings and here we bathed our lousy and scratched bodies after three months in the line. But water was scarce even here. Fifteen seconds under the shower then out and soap yourself; fifteen seconds under again for rinsing. Then into clean underwear with lice as large as rice seeds lurking in wait in the seams and crotch. The mortal enemies of the soldier: lice and officers.

Bethune was a haven of rest for trench-weary soldiers. Bethune had a shower bath; it also had an official brothel. Then there were innumerable estaminets, poker joints, crown-and-anchor gambling places and French war widows who made a living by selling huge platters of eggs and chips, six eggs and a mountain of browned potatoes, for five francs. But the official house of "joy" in Bethune was the big attraction.

V

The house had six filles de joie on duty all the time. Three for privates and three for officers. The officers even had a separate entrance. It was said that inside the hostesses did not recognize this distinction of military rank but jumped into a breach as the press of business demanded. When our battalion of seven hundred odd men was paid off, there was a line-up stretching for five blocks from the privates' entrance. The younger soldiers would grumble impatiently but the older men waited stolidly.

When it was still light enough to see, the men in line joked with each other and passersby. "You gotta wait in line for everything in war time." But as night deepened the queue became a long silent line of avid men who stared hungrily as the brightly-lit ever-opening door spewed forth khaki-clad figures which hurried off into the dark.

No one ever know how Anderson solved his sex problems. One day he confided to me that he saw the battalion chaplain sneaking into the officers' entrance. The telling of it gave him a vague sort of satisfaction, I thought.

VI

Passchendaele was a corpse-infested hole. For months heavy artillery pounded the ridge sector, pulverizing the earth so that when the November rains came the area was a sea of thin mud about four feet deep in parts. They built "duck-boards" on a roadbed of sandbags up to the front lines. One road up for supplies and the other down for walking wounded. Men coming down from the front, weakened from the loss of blood, staggered off the boards and drowned. Nobody knew what we'd do in case Heinie came for us over the ridge and forced a retreat; swim, the men guessed.

Into this nightmare of shells and mud and stinking corpses they sent our battalion—and Anderson. The outfit crept towards the front one black night. Green Verey flares sizzled up into torrents of rain lighting the way for us and reflecting deathly green in the sea of black mud. In the distance we heard the shrieks of wounded artillery horses.

We were a machine gun section. When we found our positions Anderson stretched out his rubber sheet and sighted his gun according to orders. We expected to go over the top just before dawn. How we were to plow through the mud God only knew. Shortly after midnight our lines were raked by a murderous artillery fire. The sky reflected the firework display of the heavy guns down below. The concussion made one's ears bleed. In a little while lines of silhouettes appeared against the night sky. They were coming!

In our trenches all was confusion and terror. On all sides machine guns went into action. Gaps began to appear in the lines of the black figures. They fell over like targets in a Coney Island shooting gallery. But the lines kept coming.

Our gun glowed red with heat. Anderson kept feeding fresh belts of ammunition to the gun which quivered and leaped like a living thing in torment. He was sweeping the battle area with a monotonous sweep. A flare lit up the scene and I saw him looking up to me, his lips moving. It was impossible to hear for the terrific noise. I put my ear to his mouth to hear what he was saying. I thought he might be wanting something.

He was praying! "Oh Lord and Savior Jesus Christ, look down upon me. ..."

***

A few hours later we went over the top.

The official communique the next day read: "Advances at Passchendaele made at great cost. Ratio of casualties to gains high. Advances were insufficient for ultimate purpose."

Ultimate purpose. ...

A SILK WEAVER'S SON

MARTIN RUSSAK

Winters were a long torment of wet shoes, frozen extremities, and eternal coughing. The house stood exposed and thin-walled, inhaling currents of frigidity, and assailed by an incessant wind. We slept all in one bed and had hot irons for our feet. Only the school and the mill gave security against the cold. At home the bedroom door was closed until bedtime and life was restricted to the kitchen and the neighborhood of the stove.

All life was severely restricted in winter. Life, revolving relentlessly about the centripetal mills, moved from the first to the last frost in a radius shortened to the length of a weaver's shuttle or the spoke of a winder's spindle. Harsh, imperative, overwhelming grew the power of the mills. A man or woman who came late by four or five minutes found an unyielding door shut against him and a new worker in his place when he returned at noon. The whip cracked; the lash bit; and under the redoubled cracking of the whip men were terrified out of manhood.

Outside the wind blew incessantly, sharply and bitterly edged with ice. The frost came; the great frost; the old maple groaned aloud; traffic ceased in the street; below the city lay bleak and frozen. The snow came, descending upon the city, upon everything; and rising out of that white beauty in the first sunshine of early morning, the high chimneys seemed to have attained a frank and absolute purity of blackness

A scuttle of coal was winter's symbol of life. My mother made the fire when she came home from the mills. She had to get down on her knees to light it from underneath, and the act was like a gesture of prayer.

My father sometimes took me on expeditions for coal. We got out the sled, coasted down the hill, and dragged back a sackful of the precious stuff. On fine evenings, with a firmly packed snow underfoot and a moon above that made the world a glittering expanse of green silver, we would boisterously resume our coasting. There under the moon one became conscious of young German and Italian workers, neighbors whose existence was a discovery.

A friend or comrade would come to use our bathtub. Ours was the only bathtub among our people in the hill section. A vigorous discussion would invariably commence between my father and his visitor—a stream of language unbroken while the visitor backed, gesturing, into the bathroom, and adding a few last indispensable gestures through a suddenly re-opened door, until the host stood shouting through the glass panels and the other answered in a muffled voice amid splashing water.

In deep darkness, before dawn, the morning whistles blew for work. In darkness, after day, the evening whistles blew for release. In winter time I never saw my parents in the light of day.

REVOLT

Came the time of struggle and revolt, when the workers matched their strength against the strength of the mills, with the winning of a share of their lives in the balance. A strike mood fluttered like a crimson banner in the air. Old men told thrilling tales of struggle, tales garnered from the rich book of every-worker's memory. Young men raised furious heads from their toil. The whip no longer intimidated them. It impassioned them with revolt.

It was late summer of 1912. The mills were going full blast. All day great clouds of smoke blew out of the chimneys and smudged the sky above the town. At night the smoke was visible only under a clear moon. But in the evening, after work, little knots of men stood about on street corners. I could see them under the hill, I passed them across the river by the crowded saloons, where my grandfather took me and stuffed me with pretzels while he drank with big, loud-voiced strangers. When we walked home I clung a little frightened to his large warm palm. His breath was so strong that I was almost intoxicated by it, and he did not answer many important questions I asked him. One night he stopped on the bridge and, shaking his fist over the rail, hurled marvelous imprecations at the silent mills, vast shadowy cliffs walling in the tumult of swift water.

'We'll show you yet, you monsters, you blood-suckers!" he shouted.

My father was calmer, more calculating. As the time of struggle drew near he became less an individual. He gauged forces and measured the perspectives of victory.

"There couldn't be a better time for a strike," he said to my mother across the supper table; "the bosses have big orders and can't stand a shut-down of the mills."

"We must strike," she answered; "we're starving in the mills and we may as well starve at home."

Meetings took place almost nightly in the house on the hill. The strike was well organized and fell suddenly. The workers emptied all the mills, emptied the air of smoke, emptied the factory neighborhoods of factory din. But the streets resounded with the tramping of police. The whip had become a club.

After a brief struggle the masters gave in. They could not afford the idleness of workers who had nothing to lose by idleness. The masters lured my father and his fellow-workers back into the mills, yielding all demands, and after filling their needs of production they closed the mills against these upstart toilers who had dared grasp at a ray of sunshine. It was the great lockout. It was the winter of horror. The mills opened again only for those who would go back under the dictation of the mills. How great are hunger and despair! How mighty are the mills that wield such weapons! Men were broken, more terribly than ever before, upon the iron wheels of industry. 1913 was at hand.

1913

1913 is a beautiful name. 1913 is a symbol of pride and love. 1913 is a torch of direction and encouragement. In the late afternoons of work, when the day fails and we turn on the fore and aft lights of our looms, and the weariness of the grinding hours seems impossible to bear, the thought of 1913 often comes to cheer us and to give us determination.

.. The old weavers who fought the Great Strike of 1913 are our legend-ary heroes. Big Bill Haywood is our one great epic figure. The irascible,

the inaccessible Italian workers are everywhere respected for their leading role in 1913. It is precisely so. The proletariat in the City of Silk was
molded into a conscious class in the furnace of 1913. The tradition of 1913
binds all groups of Paterson workers together. In the hush of noon-hour,
when the looms are at rest and weavers come out into the aisles, we young
fellows had rather listen to an old-timer's memories of 1913 than talk
across a winding-frame to the prettiest girl in the shop.

I remember first of all the wonderful presence and friendship of my
father that gave a holiday air to every day. He took me to picket lines and
to strike meetings. We escaped unhurt from the great meeting in Prince
Street, where an assemblage of thousands was assaulted by mounted
police. Never were there such picket lines. People rushed to the patrol
wagons, eager to get in first, fearful of being left out. Who could keep
track of all the arrests? At first it was glorious if your father was arrested;
you were lionized by all the boys. Then the thing became too common,
hardly a boy whose father had not been wounded or thrown, into jail.

When all the halls were closed and we were not allowed to meet anywhere in town, our meetings took place in Haledon Woods. It was a huge
picnic. Great crowds fraternized on the hillside and gathered around
the farmhouse where, from a second-story porch, our leaders spoke—
Elizabeth Flynn, Carlo Tresca, Gene Debs, and the others.

. .We boys climbed into the trees for vantage points. Our cheers we
reserved for Bill Haywood. Not a man in the crowd was bigger than he.
He filled the little porch; behind his white shirt with the rolled-up sleeves
the green dress of Elizabeth Flynn disappeared; shaking a terrible fist
against the sky, he spoke; and his speech was a clarion call. The crowd
roared in answer; a thousand fists were raised against the sky; and a great
wave of revolt surged from that hillside down upon the smokeless chimneys in the valley.

A fever of ardor and exaltation swept through the town. They had
closed the mills, they had come out of their separate slums, they breathed
the blue air of morning and the golden air of afternoon, they tasted freedom, and the taste was sweet though there was no bread to eat it with.
Dim-eyed, slow-witted thousands; they had been kept apart, hating
each other; now they were one, Italians and Syrians, Jews and Polocks,

Germans and Yankees. The proletariat that had not been aware of its own existence, discovered itself. You found yourself the brother of thousands, children of one parentage: sweat and blood.

Ah, the mighty masters of life! Theirs is the kingdom and the power. Hunger and want, the long and hard clubs of the police, were foes too strong for those angry masses of resourceless workers. Hunger and want crushing the revolt of workers! It was merely for the alleviation of hunger and want meekly endured, for the alleviation of intolerable toil, that the struggle was waged. An insuperable wall confronted those brave men and women; against that wall they beat their heads in desperation; their heads were broken; the wall remained.

The summer wore away amid scenes of downfall and desolation. The bread lines grew long and grim. With a thousand other children I was sent to New York to be cared for wherever possible. The Great Strike drew on to its fatal conclusion. We came back to silent parents and to tragic homes. 1913 was at an end.

But 1913 was an arrow of fear driven into the hearts of the masters. The whip trembled. Within the next few years the ten-hour day became an eight-hour day. But I have lived through the time when the eight-hour day became a twelve-hour day.

THE RIVER

The City Hall is a granite building with a beautiful tall tower. In front of the City Hall stands a statue of Alexander Hamilton, historic founder of the city of Paterson.

.. It was the Falls at this point of the River that lured Hamilton, toward the close of the eighteenth century, to come here in his silken hose and upholstered carriage and to endow factories on the site of old Godwin's pioneer fording-post. The Passaic River; the Passaic Falls.

The River comes to us out of the mountains of the west, flowing with a gentle motion around beautiful wooded hills and through beautiful fields of corn and rye, hay and oats. Men, women, and children work in those fields, plowing, cultivating, tending crops of delicate vegetables. Cows come down to drink and stand knee-deep in the water. Then the River grows wider; for miles its banks are over-arched by green loveliness of willow, hickory, oak. A region of sunshine and still water, with bunga-lows on the riverside under the trees, with people canoeing, with laughter echoing in the mild air.

Soon a ribbon of asphalt appears and follows the stream. It is the road; ponderous trucks and swift autos roll on it all day long. Now the River is brown, wide, and deep; it has lost its air of laziness; it has many bridges behind it; it flows with easy but impressive power. Here scattered factories, rectangular masses of sooty brick and an upward chimney, begin to appear.

The River enters the town with a prodigious leap over a precipice of trap-rock. There is a glorious splash, a flinging of spray that falls back to earth like a heavy rain, and enough foam is churned out to last for two miles of tumultuous swiftness ...

From the bottom of the Falls to the point where the town is left behind, the River flows through factories. On either bank, rising directly from the stream, is a wall of sooty brick, each section of wall with its sootier upward chimney. Before the River leaves the town it must pass under nine bridges.

The dye shops are all along the River. They empty their refuse, streams of yellow, black, green, red liquid, into the River. Before the River has left the town it is a sewer of powerful odor and varied hue.

The River is black by day and blacker at night. In the daytime its blackness is smitten by golden quiverings of sunlight, in the nighttime by yellow quiverings of street-lamps.

. .No one notices the River. Trucks and autos rattle over the nine bridges all day long. Crowds of people file over the nine bridges going to work and coming home. No one stops for a moment except to spit into the stream.

But the workers who work in the old factories along the banks love the River. For them the River is a vision of marvelous beauty. At noon-time they eat their sandwiches on the windowsills and gaze down at the River with wonder and love. They never tire of watching this strange flow of water that comes from afar and ceaselessly hurries by them, flecked with foam, and bound for the open sea. They study all its fluctuations, all its changes of color, its floods and hurtling fragments of ice in spring, and grow sad to see it wither away in the heats of summer. In winter they peer through grimy window panes to glimpse the fall of white snow into black water. They love this stream that rushes so hopefully into the invisible distance, they feel a kinship with its abandon, its foaming recklessness, its passage onward, ever onward, by day and by night, time without end.

The River enters the town flowing directly north. Halfway through, it makes a complete turn and quits the town flowing directly south. The town stands on this great bend, embraced by the encircling arm of the River.

ART YOUNG'S CONFESSION

September 1st: As I begin these notes, I am where I ought to be in the summer, at my home among the stone-fenced hills of Connecticut. I will be 60 years of age January next.

Three things are worshipful—the Sun, giver of life; a Human Being who believes something worth while and will die for it if need be; and Art, the recreator of life.

I walked to the village today and noted a gentle rise of my spirits as I watched the butterflies careen through the fields of goldenrod.

September 2nd: I look out over the hills this beautiful forenoon. It ought to be a day care free. Nevertheless, a taint of anxiety is in my mind. The rural postman has not brought the right letter. One with a check in it. The thought of expenses and inadequate income persists. This is the blot that is ever before the beauty of the world in the lives of most of us; anxiety that disturbs the harmony with our inner selves over money matters. There is a divine discontent that a humble man of understanding accepts gracefully, but this dollar discontent, this adjustment to a commercial age, is what prevents the artist-soul in all people from expanding.

September 18th: To call one a propagandist is generally to dismiss him from the sacred realm of art. The favorite cry of critics, "Oh, he is a propagandist, not an artist." These propagandists against propaganda amuse me. Propaganda is a kind of enthusiasm for or against something that you think ought to be spread—that is, propagated. Your propaganda may be wrong or not worth while from another's viewpoint, but that is a personal matter.

Duty, sacrifice, beauty, bravery, death and eternity—all allowable subjects for poets and dramatists—out of which they can fashion works of art. When others do not believe in your enthusiasm your work runs the risk of being condemned as propaganda. There never was a real work of art in which it is not plain that the author wants you to share his loves and sympathies and his ideas of right and wrong.

September 21th: Had I been ambitious to be a politician, I would have qualified in one way, so well and instinctively that I might have gone far. I like to kiss babies. Not being a politician I just pat their cheeks. To get that responsive smile gives me delight. In the old days, when a candidate had a habit of shaking hands and kissing babies, it was taken as a pretty good sign that once in office he would be a man of the people. But it did not always turn out that way.

September 28th: I saw some maiden flowers growing in a community of grass and old weeds.

One day I watched a bee that was buzzing around the outskirts of this community, peddling pollen.

One of the flowers may have waved to the bee; anyway, he called on her and stayed for quite some time.

Immediately, it was whispered about through the grass and old weeds that another flower had been "ruined."

October 11th: A strange thing about my early youth is that I refused to tell anybody how much I was affected by the beauty or ugliness of things. I saw beautiful village girls, who had married farmer boys, in a few years turn into hags, and I have wanted to cry out against this humping of feminine backs, wrinkling of necks and whiskering of faces. But no one else seemed to care. I looked upon myself as a lonely minority and helpless. And yet, queer paradox, I always had a liking for those who were ill-treated by circumstances. It was the unpopular girl that I often sought at the town parties. Not with uplifting sympathy—but feeling that I might discover a rare individuality and beauty overlooked by others—and I did.

October 27th: When anyone tells me he hates a particular race of people, I can work up a little hate myself—not for the racé—but for the one who is talking.

October 31st: When I studied in Paris I had an ambition to be a painter.

I knew it was a long road to accomplishment, and how would I live in the meantime? I saw this to be the problem of most young painters;

they were painting with one hand and reaching for a beefsteak with the other. It was all I could do to get sustenance while working at marketable drawings. Paintings would be still less marketable.

One has to catch a train in this kind of a civilization. You can't be careless or gay, you must crowd in and go somewhere, or get left on the desert of your dreams.

November 3rd: That boy, John Reed, interested me when first I looked at him. He had finished at Harvard and was entering the newspaper and magazine field in New York. At the Dutch Treat Club, of which I was one of the original members (but resigned during the war), he entered into the spirit of our annual frolics. Once he wrote the libretto for an opera and carried off the honors of the evening. We called him Jack. If ever a boy had the spirit of daring and doing it was Jack. Once he thought he had discovered a girl with a marvelous voice. He rented a hall and invited his friends to hear her. No one in the entire hall except Jack thought she had a voice of superior quality.

When he began to get actively interested in the radical movement, it was a matter of regret on the part of some of the "quality" boys who had known him at Harvard. One of them was heard to say, "Too bad about Jack. He is writing this humanity stuff when he could be writing good light opera." During a big silk workers' strike in New Jersey, Jack was one of the moving spirits to mobilize the strikers for a pageant in Madison Square Garden. Here, he and some of the I. W. W. leaders staged the strike scenes at the factory with the strikers themselves on the stage. I saw Jack impetuously waving a baton as he tried to lead a polyglot chorus of hundreds of workers of many nationalities into a vociferous rendering of the "International." He disregarded failure. His fun was doing. He seemed to enjoy being with the group of artists and writers of *The Masses*. In 1915 he went to Mexico and traveled with Villa's peon army and saw war for the first time. Then he accepted the assignment as European correspondent of the *Metropolitan Magazine* and saw most of the battle-fronts of Europe. He was always coming or going. He would enter a room, hitching up his trousers, rough and ready—a kind of grown-up Gavroche, with big eyes, and he-man shoulders—which he would shrug with an amusing coyness. He was a master reporter of strikes and conventions or whatever interested him. I traveled with him to illustrate the Republican and Democratic National Conventions of 1916 for the *Metropolitan Magazine*, the former in Chicago, the latter in St. Louis. A few years later we went to Chicago to report the trial of the I. W. W. leaders. At this time he was continually hounded by detectives. Suspected of being a Russian propagandist, in Cleveland, where he had a lecture date, his suitcase was seized, taken to police headquarters and searched for bombs, seditious literature and other odds and ends for overthrowing governments. He narrowly escaped arrest after the lecture (which was "patriotic") by a strategic move through a basement exit. Boylike, he seemed to enjoy outwitting government officials. He had no regard for regularity; he would write all night, and was careless of his health, especially in the matter of food. He lived just as intensely with one kidney as before. He was coming out of Russia when he was arrested in Finland by a White Guard government, and put in a dungeon, where for almost three months he lived on raw fish. Finally released and unable to get passports for America he was soon back in Russia again to continue help in the reconstruction that followed the "Ten Days That Shook the World"—(the title of one of his books). But Jack could no longer stand the strain of the full front to all the hardships that he encountered—that dread disease, typhus, got him. He died in Moscow and was buried by the Russian Soviet government outside the Kremlin walls with all the honors of a hero, which he was.

November 8th: If marriages were more generally mixed as to nationalities, such as Africans with the Eskimos, the

Chinese with the Turks, the Swedes with the Indians and so on, it would make for a better understanding between the peoples of the earth, and would eventually improve the human race.

I am writing this partly in a mood for jesting, but I will hazard the guess that there is something biologically sound in the idea.

March 1st: Judged by that standard of success which most of the American people accept and believe, I would be classed among the failures. Now past sixty, with an obvious talent and reasonably industrious in doing the work I like, yet never in my life very far from bankruptcy. If I should happen to be a money success when I am old—and the years ahead of me very few—the fact remains the same; in the common vernacular,

I lacked brains to get on and clean up; throughout all the years of an average life-time. I belong with the failures—with the man who is sitting at home tonight after his day's work who knows that his wife, his relatives and friends think; "he is a failure." I'm with this man and the whole army of splendid men and women who wear the ragged badge of defeat. I know that some people are successful who deserve to be, but I am with the unadaptable, the out-of-luck, the weary with the money-struggle. I am with them but not sadly because in my vision of a new world there is going to be a different definition of success.

ARTLESS ART

UPTON SINCLAIR

rt Young wrote a piece about me in the NEW MASSES, paying me some compliments; and now if I pay compliments to him, the suspicious reader will say, "Aha! You scratch my back and I'll scratch yours!" That wouldn't do any good to either Art or me, so I have to figure out some way to write an unfavorable review of Art's autobiography, so that the reader may see that I am a stern and incorruptible critic.

Here goes:

In the first place, this book is entirely lacking in dignity. The artist-author puts a picture of himself on the jacket, showing a stout old man with a large paunch, and a cigar in his mouth, and his legs crossed, which my mother taught me is bad form. He is riding in an old barouche, or victoria, behind an old horse; and when you read the book you find it isn't even true, because he admits that he never has ridden in that vehicle, which he bought from a broken-down cabbie for fifteen dollars; he has spent many times that amount keeping the thing in storage, hoping that some day he would get an old horse and a chance to ride. This, as you can easily see, is mere vanity and waste of time, and what right has a man who spends his money that way to complain because he is poor in his old age? He is setting a very bad example to young persons, who have such a fine chance to get rich, now that Hoover is safely elected and we are going to get eight more years of prosperity.

Moreover, this is a very unpatriotic book. The writer was indicted for sedition in war-time, and he has no shame to express, but on the contrary tries to make a joke out of the whole thing, by drawing a picture of himself expressing contempt of court by falling asleep while on trial. It seems to me that this kind of laughing at authority is the surest way to break it down, and so I shall send a copy of the book to my friend Superintendent of Police Crowley of Boston, with the idea that he will cause the book to be banned, and thus let the rest of the country know that it is a dangerous book, which should be kept out of all Sunday school libraries. I am also going to send a copy to the police authorities of Japan, who have recently cut out a part of *The Jungle*, and to the Minister of Education of Italy, who has ordered all my books out of the libraries.

Moreover, it is a very carelessly written book. It rambles all over the place, and you are as like as not to find yourself being told about butterflies by the wayside, or dead leaves falling from a tree in autumn, right when you have got interested in being told what President Harding said about having a sense of form, and wanting to be a sculptor, which is really educational. This book is just an old man rambling along, talking about anything that comes into his head, and making jokes and foolishness; I can't see much sense in printing a book like that, which is of no interest to anybody in the world except children, and artists, and rebels, and disturbers of the public thought, and idle and unpatriotic persons who do not appreciate or deserve the eight years more of prosperity which Mr. Hoover is going to give to everybody who works hard and keeps his eye on the main chance.

There now, I have been a stern and incorruptible critic. I hope you will forgive me if I add that in spite of all its faults, I read the book all the way through. There must be something wrong with me, in spite of my best efforts to be a really good American, as my parents brought me up.

RAINY DAYS IN LENINGRAD

JOHN DOS PASSOS

1. Finland Station

The train ran into the station and stopped;—an empty station without bustle: broad clean asphalt platforms, grey ironwork, a few porters and railroad officials standing around. Very quickly the American conducted tours were absorbed and disappeared bag and baggage. I waited on the empty platform for a man who was doing something about a trunk. This was where Lenin, back from hiding in the marshes had landed and made his first speeches during the Russian October eleven years ago. How could it be so quiet? I'd half expected to catch in the grey walls some faint reverberation of trampling footsteps, of machineguns stuttering voices yelling All Power to the Soviets. Could it have been only eleven years ago?

At length we get into a much too small cab driven by a huge bearded extortioner out of the chorus of Boris Godunov, and start joggling slowly along the too wide streets under a low grey sky. In every direction stretch immense neoclassic facades, white columns, dull red, blue or yellow stucco walls, battered, silent, majestic, and all like the Finland station, swept free, empty. How could it be so quiet when only eleven years ago ... ?

2. Hermitage

We ducked out of the chilly rain under a porch held up by tired looking stone women that I suppose must have meant something noble and artistic to somebody sometime, and through swinging doors into the vestibule of the museum. That vestibule full of people standing round waiting to check their coats and goloshes was a tower of Babel. A party of

Americans was being conducted up the stairs, a few German students in windjackets and shorts stood round, a horde of dark people from southeast Russia were speaking Tatar, there were pale blueeyed soldiers from somewhere in the north. A young man standing next to me asked me something and I tried him on English thinking he was a Chinaman. He turned out to be a Kirgiz.

We walked round together, and as he was as pleased to be talking to two men from America as we were to be talking to a Kirgiz, we none of us saw any of the pictures.

He was a metalworker, an unskilled laborer. He'd been in Leningrad a year just making enough to live. He and his brother had left the tent of their fathers on the Kirgiz steppes and their herd of shaggy-maned ponies, because they wanted to find out about the world and the revolution. His brother was a party member and was studying at the university for eastern peoples. No, he himself wasn't a communist. Well, mostly because he had not seen enough yet, he had not made up his mind as to whether they were right or not. He didn't know. He was too young yet. He'd have to see the world and draw his own conclusions. Criticize? Yes the workers in his factory said about what they pleased ... of course if someone made a habit of talking directly against the Party, the G. P. U. might bring pressure to bear. He wasn't sure. As for him, it wouldn't convince him that the Party was right if they locked him up, he thought they understood that. He had to see the world and find out for himself.

And his people, the nomad tribes of the great steppes of Central Asia, stock-raisers still living in the age of Abraham, Isaac and Jacob? The ideas of the revolution were just beginning to reach them, through schools, through young men like himself who went to work in the Russian cities. They talked about the revolution in their tents at night, 'round their smoky fires. The old people still clung devoutly to Mohamet's law, but the young men were like him, they wanted to know what was right, what was good for the world. Perhaps five per cent. of them were Communists or Comsomols. Many of the rest of them, like him, wanted to see for themselves.

We talked about books. He said he was reading Gorki and until he had read everything Gorki had ever written he wouldn't have time for any other books. It was only since the revolution that there had been books among the Kirgiz.

What about the position of women? At home it was very complicated, it was all a matter of money or cattle, getting a wife, neither party was free; but here among the Leningrad factory workers you could do pretty much as you pleased with your individual life, if a fellow and a girl liked each other well enough they lived together, and then if they got very fond of each other, or if she was going to have a baby they registered the marriage. The only place the police stepped in was if either party failed to chip in supporting the child.

But what about America? We must tell him everything about America, whether you could get work, how much pay you got, what the schools were like, whether life was good there, what kind of marriage we had, whether the workers had power, how mighty was capitalism.

Yes he wanted to go to America, he must see as much as he could of the world, so that he could make up his mind.

3. Smolny

We had just come out from the bare stone corridors of Smolny Institute, huge austerely proportioned building that stood serenely athwart the grey drizzly afternoon; we had seen the little room where Lenin had lived and worked from the time the Bolsheviki seized power in the name of the peasants and workers until the government was moved to Moscow, a bare room with a few chairs and a table and a little cot behind a partition, we walked down the road and out through the gate in a sort of trance. Eleven years ago … and now Smolny was history, like the music of Bach, like Mount Vernon, like the pyramids. I wondered which was more actual, the Smolny I turned 'round to take a last look at in the endless grey northern drizzling afternoon, or the Smolny that had been created for me by the hot slugs from the linotype of Jack Reed's sinewy writing. We wanted to find a place to drink tea and asked two youngsters who had also turned 'round to look back at Smolny.

The question of tea was lost for a long while in the questions about America they peppered us with. They were communists, students at the university at Odessa in Leningrad on an excursion run by Narkompros.

Smolny for them was the beginning of everything. They were too young to have much memory of the old Russia of the Czar when Smolny had been a ladies seminary for daughters of the nobility. To them the October days seemed as long ago as the fall of the Bastille. They had finished their two years in the red army and were studying to be teachers. It took a definite effort for them to imagine how things must be in the capitalist world outside. Our routine questions about freedom of opinion and the economic position of the peasants didn't interest them. It wasn't that they didn't care about these things, it was that their approach was from an entirely different side. For us October, Smolny, Lenin were in the future; for them they were the basis of all habits, ideas, schemes of life. It was as hard for them to imagine a time when Marxism had not been a rule of conduct as it would be for an American high school kid to doubt the desirability of the open shop or the Monroe doctrine.

"Why," they kept asking us, "why can't they understand what we are trying to do, why can't the workers in America understand that we are building socialism, why can't the workers in England realize that we are working for them as much as for ourselves?" Though we found the tea and sat drinking it a long while the question never got answered.

4. Proletari

In the restaurant run by the cooperative "Proletari" you could get a dinner consisting of a vast bowl of cabbage soup with meat in it and a plate of meat with vegetables for forty kopeks (20 cents). The waitress was a large melancholy woman who spoke French. Her husband had been a chef in aristocratic families and restaurants; she had lived in France. She was not enthusiastic about the way things were going, life was raw and grey and there were no more little elegances to make things plausible. You didn't have to work so hard, as a worker, she admitted, she had all the privileges, but the revolution had shattered all her dreams. She and her husband had been saving up, they wanted to open a small restaurant all their own, to cater to a purely distinguished clientele, strictly French cuisine, everything cooked with butter.... They would have made it a success, she knew, they would have made money, and have had a little house in European style. She'd never liked to live slapdash the way the

Russians do, she was at heart a European. There were tears in her eyes when she took away the plates. When she came back with stewed fruit and tea, she said: "I don't want you to think I'm against the revolution. It was necessary, but it's very hard."

5. Peter the Great

The man who was taking us round town that evening was the son of a rich man. He had joined the red guards and fought with them all through the October days. Later he had been head of a division in the Red Army through the civil war. He had gotten into trouble somehow, been expelled from the communist party and spent a year in jail. People told me afterwards that he wrote first rate poetry. He called himself, half jokingly, a counter-revolutionary. He spoke English.

He showed us the great square where the monument to the October dead was and told us how it had been made on one of Lenin's Saturday Afternoons, when bunches of soldiers and factory workers would tackle some particularly unsightly corner of the city and dig it up into a park. He told us about the enthusiasms and comradeliness of those days. He showed us the streets where he had fought eleven years ago, the place where they'd held the barricade against a desperate attack from the cadets, squares where the red guards had camped for the night, houses they had taken shelter in. Maybe he almost wished things still were as they had been eleven, eight, six years ago, when it was still possible to kill and be killed for the revolution, and politics was as simple as the mechanism of a machine gun.

We came out on the bank of the Neva. It was about twelve. You could still see things dimly in a faint milky twilight. The stately palaces along the Neva, the spires of the Peter and Paul fortress, the wide bridges, the clear grey swift flowing river must have looked about the same as they had looked to Pushkin a hundred years ago. We walked down the embankment till we came to a small park. A young man and a girl sat on a bench talking low. At the end of the park on a base of granite rock was a statue, a huge black mass rearing into the pale night, a man on a prancing horse. The man who had been showing us around pointed to it: "There's my favorite Russian in history," he said, "Peter the Great, who brought order out of chaos, the first Bolshevik."

6. Peterhof

When we got off the Ford bus at Peterhof a drunken man who said he was a chauffeur offered to show us the way to the palaces of the Empress Catharine. He tried to talk sensibly, there were things he wanted to know about Detroit, about the Taylor plan, but he was too drunk and had to submit to being led away by a little boy, probably his son, who tagged along at his heels. We walked off through dripping gardens full of fountains, eternally autumnal like some place in a story by Hans Anderson, along the edge of the grey sea and the grey sky of the Baltic. At the end of every vista in one way was the sea, at the other a spouting fountain. Then we came to eighteenth century palaces in red brick. Inside you had to put on slippers over your shoes and walk through acre after acre of state apartments carefully preserved by history-loving employees of the department of education. After a mile and a half of royal furniture I balked and we managed to get out through a side door.

Then we walked for a long time down a muddy country road and fell in with a man who suggested we go to see the local rest house run by the Leningrad Trade Unions Council. It was in an immense gawky fake gothic building that had been the royal stables. In two directions enormous parks formed a backyard for the Leningrad workers. One of the doctors in charge showed us around and set us up to an uncommonly good dinner. He was so wrapped up in his work he could talk of nothing else. He wasn't a party member, but he had no private practice, he never had time. As far as I could see he barely had time to eat and sleep, working as he did in several hospitals, inspecting this huge rest house and several subsidiary smaller houses, lecturing on hygiene and popular medicine, attending to people who were in need of special diet and treatment during their stay in the rest house. The house that held three thousand, a combination of sanatorium and summer hotel, was run by the Leningrad Council of Trade Unions. The aim was to have enough such houses to accomodate all the members of all the unions represented in the council for two weeks free every summer. At present there weren't enough, but there would be soon. During those two weeks the people running the place had to see that the workers had plenty of means other than alcohol for having a good time, give them a short course in the care of their own bodies and of those of their wives and children, provide lectures and shows and give each person a thorough physical examination. With the children it wasn't so hard, but to undo the evils of a lifetime of poverty and bad living in two weeks was a pretty desperate task.

Another night we ate dinner with him again and visited various subsidiary rest houses and saw the show gotten up by one two weeks' batch as it was leaving, to entertain the newcomers. There were musical numbers and recitations and a little farce about a mixup among people in the doctor's waiting room, and a physical culture expert made a speech suggesting that people ought to sleep with their windows open. This was too much for the audience that had eighteenth-century ideas about the dangers of the night air, and he was howled off the platform. Then the doctor explained his aims and methods of work and was received with cheers for he was evidently very popular.

When we walked down to the station to catch the last train back to Leningrad, the responsible director of the institution walked part way with us. He was a big quiet faced man with grey hair who had been a baker before the revolution. He was the actual executive and organizer of the entire place. He walked with big strides beside us, asking almost timidly what we thought of it, whether it was clean, whether we thought the food was good, whether we thought the people looked as if they were having a good time. Then he asked us to excuse him as there was still work to do (he worked eighteen hours a day), embraced the man with me who was a Russian, shook hands with me and left us.

A WRITER'S APOLOGIA

JACK WOODFORD

My ancestors were among the first gangs of religious fanatics, malcontents and ne'er-do-wells to come over from England. Some of them fought in all of our holy wars. Seven that I know of were customary colonels in the Civil War. One had bits of himself shot off in the late Wilson fiasco—and is now starving with the rest of the banged-up patriots, who were dragged whimpering from good jobs to make the world safe for American Dollar Diplomacy and English Imperialism. Another was recently ordered out with the Marines, to put down sales resistance upon the part of a South American republic and learn 'em that God is Love, and America God's Country—with the aid of such evangelical organons as machine guns, poison gas and æroplanes with which to drop bombs upon their women and children.

I am the black sheep of the family, "irreligious and unAmerican," because I have never killed for Apis, or spent enough time cheating and haggling to become objectively "successful."

***

Being a writer of some experience, most of it pretty sad, I know that anything flowing from the Castalian fountain must be pretty liberally treated with chlorine before being served upon McCall Street.

The costive *res publica*, disintegrating before our eyes, smelling to the skies of corruption, materialism, ignorance, lechery and a perversion of values which amounts to a complete triumph of the meretricious, in every department of our national life, may be kidded, in a half humorous vein, but never pictured precisely as it is: a conscienceless oligarchy, ruled by thieving politicians who bleed us and then, through publicity addressed to the mob (and paid for by Big Business) bring the greater part of us stupidly to the polls at election time to perpetuate them.

Book publishers place no rigorous taboos upon political and economic "controversial subjects" but authors avoid them more and more, as they get richer and richer, and become almost indistinguishable from the dollar-rooting swine whom they fawn before in their books, and in their social contacts.

***

Today public utility magnates and oil mongers, both before and after they have blandly confessed to corrupting Congress and the Cabinet, mingle with reasonably honest people and move about in society with the utmost bravura—as though they were as good as anyone else!

Certainly it is bad anough that Americans should be dedicated almost entirely to pouncing upon cash, but it is doubly lamentable that, becoming hardened, even our men of letters recognize no distinction between merchants and those who create beauty.

Even were one to confine oneself to ordinary matters, it would still be impossible for a novelist, writing and publishing in the United States, to make his characters real.

***

If any American novelist were to paint life as Zeuxis did grapes, he would be pecked at by a swarm of vultures so numerous as to shut off the sun and drown out completely, with the flapping of their wings, the feeble objections of those few who still rally weakly to the defense of the truth teller.

***

The American novelist writes, primarily, to make money; because, in America, a man without money is in as perilous a position before his hanseatic peers as a murderess, who has no sex appeal, in an American court of justice.

* * *

I am fully aware of writing as though the novel were the only literary vehicle in America today. It is. Poetry has shriveled up and swooned pinkly, not to say wetly.

As for the short story form, nobody with the slightest vestige of self-respect would write for publication a short story which he knows is to be used merely as a bait to attract the attention of morons to the illuminated business cards of wights wanting to market mild antiseptics as cures for bad breath and baldness, teachers desiring to impart French in ten lessons, and the fifty or sixty motor car manufacturers, each of whom make the "One Best Motor Car In Any Price Class."

Those who simulate literary criticism, in the pay of newspapers and magazines having book publishers' advertising accounts to solicit, are too much absorbed with the greasy side of their bread to bother about being inconveniently honest. Not that these gutless prægustators are downright dishonest; they are merely "contacted," being the quarry of a powerful lobby that makes Good Fellows of ninety percent of them, willy nilly. Pope, in his *Dunciad* described the condition well enough, as it existed in his time:

> *"Blockheads with reason wicked wits abhor,*
> *But fool with fool is barb'rous civil war.*
> *Embrace, embrace, my sons! be foes no more!*
> *Nor glad vile poets with true critics' gore."*

Hence, we have the growing group of reviewing pediatricians who never definitely find a book good, bad or indifferent, but content themselves with putting their names at the top of review columns and writing below essays touching upon the complex and vaguely highfalutin idiosyncracies of the man whose name is at the top of the column.

This contemporary coterie have succeeded in setting up the dicta that a critic who frankly kicks hell out of a rotten book is a crude fellow having no rightful place among the male Eleanor Price Posts who dictate the correct manipulation to be accorded book criques.

With the exception of a handful of sticklers, such as Upton Sinclair, who are thought not quite nice by their gigman colleagues, no one in these states feels it worthwhile to call attention to the low condition to which our letters have fallen.

***

Of course, many an American Literary Guy longs to write cleanly and wholesomely (in the true, not the American connotation of the words)—but timidity prohibits: our wives would give us hell and the members of the bridge club, however much they would sympathize with us if we got jailed for having traffic with contraband liquor, or falsifying our income tax reports, would frown social excommunication upon us if we got locked up on behalf of our more complex ideals, however praiseworthy the same.

So, most of us content ourselves with vehemently declaring that we don't even want to write honestly—lots of us, after a time, begin to believe it.

After all, in a country where it matters not at all what one *is*, and what one *has* is all that counts, why not don the red kimono, put an automatic piano in the study to provide the proper atmosphere, spring to our typewriters when our publishers call out "Gentlemen calling; ladies in the parlor please!" and when Upton Sinclair calls us prostitutes, let Mencken answer, unchallenged, in the pages of his publication (now well filled with advertising matter) "Prostitutes, certainly—but they are content."

In another generation even the inhibited desire to be men will have disappeared in the United States, the flame of art will have been completely stamped out, and we shall become a loathsome fascisti.

FANTASY: 1929

HERMAN SPECTOR

I t was a National Safety Week, sponsored by the Society for Prevention
of Cruelty to Poets. Religion was in a bad way: the church funds were
being defecated. Signs in all the cars of every train in each subway-line
read as usual:

> Spitting is Prohibited,
> being a Crime, or $500,
> or BOTH!

There were newspapers, and where there were newspapers, there were
journalists. Seven pimply virgins had committed crimes in a single
week: the situation was Enormous. Two famous novelists, (married to
each other), said that the main issue of the forthcoming election was
prohibition. A professional jew had written a novel advertised to be "As
TENSE and PATHETIC as an Erotic Dream. Freud was overwhelmed
with remorse. A notorious broadway playwright announced that the
communists had no money and no influence, whereupon five bookre-
viewers cheered. "Nation's Business" promised an american mussolini,
and Dorothy Parker rhymed "zowie" with "-andhow." A manifesto
depreciating the purity of public comfort stations was issued and signed
by Wyndham Lewis, F. P. A., Wood Krutch, and Charley Chaplin.
Highschool girls began to find Mencken an awful bore, realizing the infinitely greater wisdom of Valentino, who died on time. This kind of rep-
etitious cynical bilge was probably discovered and patented in the times
of Gilbert Seldes, god rest his weary soul, and later adapted and used with

phenomenal success by Variety, Vanity Fair, The New Yorker, and The Commercial World.

... The lights glow tenderly on fifth avenue, they sweat on broadway, they sneer and smirk on riverside drive. There are persons who prefer to read Books and go about thinking Art. Homosexuality attracts them; they are Liberal that way; they live in the Village for a thrill. Others drugged in a routine of work, productive or assinine, go to hear a blackface jew comic at the Hippodrome, with a glib tongue, enunciate nothing painfully. In the public libraries there are crowds of people trying to forget that they need a job, money, happiness; they have been taught to laugh at communists. Hunchback literati, sincere or careerist, they go from the Automat to Zero's Tub, talking Art: they have been taught to sneer at communists. A columnist in the World jocosely explains that animal good-health is making of him a "philistine" (hee,hee!)—having had a fairly adequate meal at the Algonquin, he observes that the rebels are envious. A reader replies: I spit upon your stale cautious phrases, you puerile academician, you ... He weeps into the wastebasket, rebukes the correspondent for lacking a sense of humor. Ohhh-h-h! the jazzmusic cries, dress-models think the Boss is the nicest kind of man since he predicts greater prosperity for All, and a kid of 16 with gloating hopeful eyes works 13 hours a day for advancement: he has been taught to despise communists. If at first he dont succeed, he has been taught to try, try again. Thus doth virtue triumph, say the teachers of the land, who are virtuous, crabbed, and Loyal. And near times square a moving lighted sign announces: "Prince Matchiabelli Smokes Our Cigarettes!" ... Suddenly: "And Who the Hell Are You?" it asks. The logic is indisputable. A white-haired philanthropist stands in the center of columbus circle and shouts to an audience of fairies, disappointed soda-jerkers, tired harlots from new england, crummy bums: "God is Love and money is Money; so don't confuse the two, or rather, the three!" The louder he shouts, the wider their mouths. It is late, late as hell; they are missing precious sleep; the white-haired philanthropist sleeps all day long; my, what pleasure he takes in trying to make these people as miserable as possible; he is not long for this earth; thank God. These thoughts, and others even less pertinent, assail them as they wait and listen undecidedly, but for a God which is Love but not

MONEY they have nothing but scorn. Listless, they leave one by one; until at last, alone in the center of columbus circle, the spick, philanthropist, suddenly ceasing to smile, stumbles from the platform. ... In central park the lamps are languid, dazed with the slow death of night, its last lingering caress ... turning over and over, the sleeping phantom form of a lover, the park, involute paths and bends. ... Once, in a dream, a man approached another man along a solemn silent street at night, and guided him up tenement steps to a room where a pink girl lay; pacific, placid, toothpick-chewing. He looked, and lo, it was good, and as it sayeth in the Bible, he went in and was surfeited. He walked outside; the streets were still, and pools of phlegm shone under lights; the stone was smooth, hard, 2 a. m., and no-one moved. Coldly the wind came, filled his nose, bitterly blowing: he drank and he sobbed and he stifled a yawn. ... Rumor later reaching him to the effect that the panderer was her illegitimate son; he recalled with a shudder the ratty softspoken guy, the sad look in his eye. And her name was Mary. ... So reads the sunday-morning paper, and it shows how an gorilla or orang-outang; it do not think; but We, We are M-E-N; we Think. Therefore we also see the estimable Mr. Brisbane, he writes a cartoon showing how some peop-le, they are Drunkards, and enjoy them-selves; but Good people, they do not Enjoy themselves; they work for a Boss. Moral: Think, think; if at first you don't succeed, don't Drink yourself to Death or play Roulette at Mounty Carlo; but try, try again. And so, blithely remarked F. P. A. and Heywood Broun, two of our leading liberals, and So to Bed, each by each, and nicey nicey dreams. ...

IN A RUSSIAN TRAIN

HALLIE FLANAGAN

"You can't know Russia unless you travel 'hard,' my friends tell me—and are inconsistently distressed because I buy a third class ticket from Moscow to Leningrad. After a day of Russian farewells, compounded of tears, kisses on either cheek, gifts, philosophizing on life, death, meeting, parting, sorrow and joy, I am sealed into a narrow cell with two planks facing each other and two planks which let down for upper berths. The compartment is conspicuously sanitary, though I find it a trifle depressing to reflect that the strong medical odor which takes the place of air is due to the government edict that carriages occupied by 'hard' passengers must be daily scrubbed out with antiseptics. My travelling companions prove to be three: a woman from the provinces in layers of shawls and mysterious head-wrappings; an imposing Soviet officer with service stripes and gleaming cavalry boots; and a blue bloused worker with a basket of apples, which he consumes in number truly awe inspiring.

The advantage of traveling 'hard' is at once apparent. I have voluntarily become one of them and they accept me as such, plying me with friendly questions. The Soviet officer speaks a little English, the woman speaks German, the tovarish speaks not a word, but presses apples upon us with great cordiality until he presently retires to an upper plank and to unabashed and audible slumber.

We talk as if lack of a common language is in no way a barrier, as, indeed, it is not the greatest barrier. The woman has been visiting her son in Moscow; she dislikes what she saw there and is at no pains to conceal it. Once her son was a wealthy man, his wife had fine clothes, they did nothing all day but ride about to great dinners given by their rich friends; now they are all poor, they must work, and live crowded together, and wear coarse clothes such as formerly their servants wore. The good days for Russia are over, she declares, and the least said about the present state of affairs, the better. The representative of the criticized government listens with apparent amusement, though of course, I have no way of ascertaining whether he later shot her in the back, as, according to the *London Daily Mail*, he assuredly would have done.

The interest of the officer seems to be at present, dramatic rather than political. He is writing a play which is to be a satire on war, performed without words, entirely by military formations, which are to result, logically enough but rather startingly, in the destruction of everybody, including the onlookers.

The woman from the provinces finds his drama sleep inducing and asks whether she may retire. She fears to sleep below because she has a horror of the upper plank collapsing, as, she assures me with dramatic gesture, it often does. I eye her vast girth apprehensively as, creaking and puffing, she disappears from view. The Soviet army now gravely removes its boots, first gallantly insisting that I make a mattress of the voluminous army coat. The light is snapped out, the compartment is lit by faint moonlight, and I lie reflecting upon the curiousness of life. Here am I, eating the apples of one comrade, sleeping upon the coat of another, and in momentary danger of being completely annihilated by the collapse of a third. Tovarish, indeed! I am at last becoming a part of Russia.

These sentimental reflections are shattered by a terrific jolt and crash, and the train stops dead. There is a long pause, as of bewilderment on the part of the train officials. The pause prolongs itself to such alarming proportions that I recall the sentence in the Soviet guide: "If any train in the U.S.S.R. reaches its destination five days (or was it fifty?) later than due, the money of the passengers will be partially refunded." Gradually, one by one, the trainmen spill out. They walk back and forth, stamping on the snow, blowing on their fingers. They discuss the situation mournfully, gathering in groups, gesticulating toward the train. From the uncurtained window I can see that we are in the middle of a snowfield, and here, it appears, we are to stay. The trainmen seem to have given it up as a bad job: they retreat, build a fire in the snow, and sit around it, indulging in black bread, yellow bottles, and an avalanche of talk.

At first I am indignant. In any other country in the world, I think in irritation, something would be done about the train balking like a donkey. A telegram would be sent, a committee would be appointed, the train would be taken apart and put together again, a new train would be made—*something* would be done. But since it is Russia, though the thermometer is bursting, they will sit down and talk it over.

Gradually I sink into a sort of Russian-ness, born of moonlight on snow, and the rise and fall of Slavic voices. After all, what is time? What matter whether we reach our destination tomorrow? Time is nothing ... time is nothing ... annoying if one is keeping an engagement, but glorious if one is shaping a new world. What is a decade, more or less, to a Georgian who traces his lineage historically to Noah and mythologically to Jason and Medea? We, who are slaves of time, who think in terms of schedules, desk calendars, extra fare trains, come into a land which thinks in terms of centuries. Show us everything you have done in ten years, we demand. The Russian smiles, patiently: yes, but what is a span of ten years? merely a passing expression on the face of history. How many schools, factories, diet kitchens, tramcars in Moscow? Not enough, the Russian answers, and not good enough, but let us show you the plans of those we are to build in 1940. Nonsense, we cry, these people are not efficient, they will never get anywhere. By this we mean that they will not get where we are. Nor will they, nor, inconceivable as it may seem to us, do they wish to.

"Astrological mentality" Junius Wood calls it. Their eyes are on a star and they stumble through the dark and the dirt to get to it ... But as for us, we cannot stop to build fires in the snow to ponder over what is wrong with the train, to ask whither we are bound ...

After several hours it happens, as it occasionally does, that an idea is born of talk. Someone crawls under the train and tickles it with a stick and immediately all is well. The train resumes its nonchalant course into the unknown.

REVOLT AMONG
AMERICAN INTELLECTUALS

V. F. CALVERTON

American intellectuals, on the whole, are so superficial that their revolt is seldom revolutionary. Whether there is "something in our climate which belittles every animal, human and brute," as Alexander Hamilton contended in a moment of explosive despair, and which expresses itself in de Tocqueville's observation, "that in no country in the civilized world is less attention paid to philosophy than in the United States," can be answered by a consideration of the American intellectual, and the gesturing antics of his existence. The difference between American intellectuals and European is at once conspicuous by its profundity. This difference runs into every field and is characteristic of the intellectual radical as well as reactionary. One is almost tempted to say that there is among intellectuals a European and an American outlook. Or at least whenever one discovers in America that rarity which we shall call a deep-thinking, radical intellectual we have a tendency to say that his attitude is European.

The superficiality of the American intellectual, of course, is not a sporadic or capricious thing, but is rooted deep in the currents of American life. It is a reflection, in the clearest sense, of American economic and social existence. The cultural background of the European intellectual, radical as well as conservative, has always been richer than that of the American. In America the criss-cross of several types, none as deep rooted as the European, and in many instances amounting to nothing more than slavish imitations of their earlier origins, has resulted in a product that is uniform chiefly in its affinity for the mediocre. The cultured intellectuals in the North, with but an exception here and there, never became serious rivals of their English contemporaries. For a long period they made open obeisance to their English dictators of taste and convention, and even admitted their imitation as a virtue. In the South all that was rich in the aristocratic culture of Europe soon petered out, in the 19th century, under the influence of slavery, into vain artifice and affectation. On the frontier, where currents were set into motion that shook the entire nation, invading the White House, and in a way giving caste to a national culture that lingers with singular emphasis even today, an exaltation of the practical and utilitarian became the prevailing attitude. Booklearning was scorned, and intellectual attainment was outlawed by the frontiersman. The cultural traditions of New England, or of Europe, were sneered at by the exponents of this new philosophy. Bret Harte, Joaquin Miller, and Artemus Ward embodied its sentiment in prose, poetry and humor, and in such a farce as *Innocents Abroad* we have a vivid expression of its mocking contempt for European culture and tradition.

Out of such a milieu, a profound intelligentzia could scarcely arise and flourish. Everything discouraged it. America was too much with us. There was no room for it on the frontier, no need for it in the South, and no reason for it in the North with England so near. On the frontier an intellectual was a pariah, in the South an anomaly, and in the North an imitator of his English forefathers. Gradually as the English influence weakened in the North, a sentimental puritanism, dwarfed and distorted by the environment of the new world, remained; but steadily, as even this puritanism started to wane, the frontier attitude and spirit in the form of Whitman and our own contemporaries began to pervade our entire literary outlook and tendency. The result has been tragically obvious. We have never had, never been able to have, a real intelligentzia. The only significant philosophers we have ever had have been practical. Whether it is the pragmatism of James, or the instrumentalism of Dewey, its practical motivation has never been obscured. When it has not been so, the philosophers have remained isolated and uninfluential. Our artists too, with but rare exceptions, have represented little deviation. Their practicality has been manifest in their bourgeois didacticism and puritanic timidities and trepidations.

The American intellectual thus has become ingrown rather than expansive. He has been as afraid of adventurousness in the intellectual life as the pioneer was unafraid of adventurousness in the practical life. He has been superficial in his approach to things because the life about him demanded that superficiality for his survival. The deeper, more embracing problems of life than the merely obvious and practical have rarely engaged his attention. What American critic would ever have undertaken the magnificent and sweeping analyses and interpretations of Taine, St. Beuve, Brunetiere; or Pisarev, Bielinsky, Chernishevsky, Plechanov; or Buskin, Arnold, Carlyle, Wyndham Lewis; or Grillparzer, Lessing, Hebbel, Hesse, or Hoffmannsthal; or Gentile or Croce; or Azorin. Unamuno and Madaniaga? There is no audience in America for such work, no incentive for its creation. What American radicals would have ventured such a work as Dietzgen's *Positive Outcome of Philosophy*; Bogdanov's *Empirio-Monism*; Lenin's *Empirio-Criticism*; Kautsky's *Foundations of Christianity*; Sorel's *Reflections on Violence*; Bonger's *Economic Conditions and Criminality*, or Friedrich Adler's defense of Avenarius? What radicals in America are interested in those problems? Or in sex, what radicals would have hazarded, in such an immense way, Bebel's *Woman*, Engel's *Evolution of the Family*, or Kollontai's *Communism and the Family?* Or what liberals, occupied in the same field, would have attempted Ellis' *Studies in Sex*, Briffault's *Mothers*, or Hobhouse's *Morals in Evolution?* Only those with what we shall have to call, however vaguely, a European outlook would ever dream of such endeavors. The American outlook creates little men with small vision. There is no incentive or inspiration for the creation of big men with large vision. How well all this is borne out by our intellectuals today. They are all in revolt but are never revolutionary—or perhaps we should say, hardly ever. They are in revolt against a hundred things, but seldom against anything fundamental. They are muddled and confused, and their energies are lost in a frustrating chaos. They have no sense of coordination, no vision of things beyond the specific. They are afraid of theories, and in terror of dogma. They live within their little worlds like merchants of the intellectual life.

One can fully appreciate the attitude only when one sees how it has gripped almost everything upon American soil. At a meeting of a number of American intellectuals, editors, critics, professors, and what not, I recall certain individuals, well-known to the American reading public, asserting in a kind of uncanny unison—

"We don't care about your theories—tell us what to do and we'll do it." In other words be pragmatic, be up and doing, active, utilitarian, eager with practical initiative. Don't worry about the philosophy behind it, don't concern yourself with the deeper problems of existence, don't reflect, but *do*. The result has been that American intellectuals have never reflected, have never perturbed themselves with radical categories, but with the attitude of a frontiersman have managed to do rather than to probe. And the result has been that what they have done merits very little probing at all.

Let us glance at the work of a few American intellectuals in order to see the emptiness and superficiality of their revolt. One cannot deny that the American intellectuals are in protest against the prevailing civilization. In the 19th century this was not so. There was then, in large part, an acquiescence that was disturbed only at time of crisis. Since the days of Frank Norris and David Graham Phillips, with the decline of the influence of Howells, insurrection has become common. The insurrection, however has often been isolated and esoteric. Mr. Dreiser, for instance, is certainly in revolt against many of the forms of capitalism, and against the system of society itself, and yet his revolt finds expression in nothing more definite and revolutionary than a cynical despair. His appreciations of Soviet Russia reveal a superficiality of outlook that is almost pathetic. They are scarcely more profound than the observations of Ivy Lee. Sherwood Anderson is frank in his condemnations of contemporary society, but in his attack there is a medieval atavism that is touchingly sentimental in its hopelessness. He would have us return to the days of the artisan, deny machinery, and create a utopia of hands. A sweet dream this, but fantastic and futile. Its stultification, however, is to be found in his recent endorsement of Al Smith. Floyd Dell with a genius for style that is all too rare in America, alienates himself further and further from everything radical, and spends his time upon fiction that has neither deep meaning nor challenging significance. With an essentially fine understanding of the philosophic aspects of radical reconstruction, he nevertheless surrenders to the American urge for commercial creation. W. E. Woodward, who has been slashing into American life in *Bunk* and *Lottery*, suddenly discovers that one can now be respectable and be a socialist. He addresses a letter to his friends, urging them to vote for Norman Thomas and the cause of clean politics. One would think that all socialism meant in these days, to judge by our intellectuals, was exterminating the corruption in the capitalist parties. There was one time when socialism was associated with "Gum-shoe Pete" and the proletariat; but today, argues Mr. Woodward, socialism has been so refined that one no longer has to elbow proletarians in order to be a comrade. A fine picture this, of what socialism has become with the American intellectuals! A fine picture of their depth, and their vision of what radicalism embodies and signifies!

It is in the work of such American intellectuals as Waldo Frank, Van Wyck Brooks, and Lewis Mumford that the sharp disparity between revolt and revolution is most tragically apparent. While the reaction of Mencken against the older literature never rose above a spirited and vigorous protest, the reaction of these men has always risen to an eloquent and moving revolt. They always promised more than Mencken. Not that Mencken was not, and to an extent still is a greater *force*, and despite his vaudevillian superficialities often an inspiring force, but that Mencken never pretended to the seriousness and profundity that has always marked their approach. Mencken, in every respect, has represented America; his writing is Americanese; even his Nietzscheanism has been American in character and outlook. He has been the Mark Twain of American criticism. These men, however, have aspired toward a European outlook. They have striven to rise above America in order to understand it. Their efforts, fine as they have promised, unfortunately, have largely resulted in defeat and contradiction. While each has pursued a somewhat different method, there has been an underlying similarity about their general ideas and deductions. Waldo Frank has, perhaps, struggled for the largest vision of them all. In *Our America*, applying the thesis of Jung, he essayed an interpretation of America and the shallowness of its culture that was charged with an amazing earnestness and intelligence. In places his words were a cry and a challenge. His attack upon Emerson was signal. Repelled by the coldness of New England culture, Emerson failed to apply his genius to the realities of life, and escaped by making "a transcending leap away from all that was mortal-human." This is brilliant and perspicacious observation. His analysis of Poe pursued the same logic. In order to "escape," Poe "landed in a macabre region of synthetic horrors." In *America's Coming of Age* Van Wyck Brooks advanced an interpretation of American authors and American culture that was very similar in conclusion if not in approach. His comments upon Poe will illustrate a similarity of conclusion that is immediately striking.

"Poe having nothing in common with the world that produced him, constructed a little parallel world of his own, withered at the core, a silent comment. It is this that makes him so sterile and so inhuman."

And of Hawthorne he said:

"He models in mists, presents cloud pageants and creates a world within a world ... He was himself a phantom in a phantom world."

Correct observations, penetrating insights, fine illations.

But now let us see what has happened to these observations, insights and illations—to Mr. Frank and Mr. Brooks. Slowly but steadily Mr. Frank and Mr. Brooks have become the very souls that they decried in Emerson, Poe, and Hawthorne. Has America been too much for them? In recent years Mr. Frank has turned to a mysticism that is almost religious in its aspects, and argued that with the dissolution of western culture there has "come the apposite introduction into Europe of Hindu religious ideas," which he praises as having "always been based upon a deeper unity." Opposing now the scientific approach, which to a considerable extent he had adopted in *Our America*, and losing sight of the real world with which he was so concerned in this earlier work, he has now become anxious to "prepare the intellect to receive mystery," and vigorously contends that "the man who receives mystery in his mind is already part of the truth." From these few citations it is not difficult to note that Mr. Frank's indictment of Emerson, that Emerson escaped the realities of life by making "a transcending leap away from all that was mortal-human" is an equally fine indictment of himself. That anyone can be aware of, and in grips, with, the realities of our age, with their economic compulsions, and psychological propulsions, and advocate the mysticism of Mr. Frank is illogical and absurd. Mr. Frank has, like Emerson and Poe, moved on to another world. In *Virgin Spain* he has addressed his mystical attitude to historical fact. The result is a work of ardent prose, swarming with rich, voluptuous metaphors and comparisons, but without sound substance or logic. His picture is that of a people pasted on a painted canvas. We see the people, but all the while we know that they are unalive and immobile. If Mr. Frank has not escaped into a "region of synthetic horrors" he has escaped into a land of unreal mystery and dream.

In his recent articles in *The New Republic*, dedicated to a Rediscovery of America, the rediscovery, however enriched by a warm, poetic prose, is a rediscovery of Mr. Frank's own soul rather than that of America. It is somewhat the same story with Mr. Van Wyck Brooks. Conspicuous in the days of Seven Arts, active again later on *The Freeman*, devoting himself to genuine attack and challenge, Mr. Brooks in recent years has turned to different themes, and isolated himself from the very factors and forces that constitute the active realities of life.

In Lewis Mumford we have an intellectual who has not yet surren-dered to either isolation or mysticism. His *Golden Day* is a very creditable continuation of the theme of *Our America* and *America's Coming of Age.* Mr. Mumford writes with verve and skill, and lends to his style a pol-ished wit that lightens and livens the severest scrutiny and analysis. His approach is candid, and his conclusions are courageous. Nevertheless, his revolt never becomes revolutionary. *The Golden Day*, for Mr. Mumford is the day of Emerson, Thoreau, Fuller and Whitman. Unquestionably it was an important period in American literature. That its literature was a great literature can easily be disputed. In that it expresses the height of the individualistic trend, however, it may be called golden, yet not with-out an enthusiasm that is anachronistic in essence.

It is Thoreau's dream—"of what it means to live a whole human life" that enchants Mr. Mumford. These men and women of the mid-nine-teenth century, in the opinion of Mr. Mumford, inspired "that complete culture (which) leads to the nurture of the good life (that), permits the fullest use, or sublimation, of man's natural functions and activities." Mr. Mumford's attitude, at least in its glorification of this period, is unconcealingly individualistic. Emerson's cry—

"Nothing is at last sacred except the integrity of your own mind... What have I to do with the sacredness of traditions, if I live wholly from within... No law can be sacred to me but that of my own nature," and then his later assertion:

"Is not a man better than a town? Ask nothing of men, and in the endless mutation, thou only firm column must presently appear the upholder of all that surrounds thee," are both excellently illustrative of the individualistic attitude that dominated this period of American life and literature. The whole Transcendentalist movement, the entire sweep of mysticism that pervaded the philosophy of Emerson and intruded into the early pages of the Dial, the concept of the Over-soul, derivative of Novalis and Swedenborg, the feminism of Margaret Fuller, the hermitage of Thoreau, all were expressive of this vast movement of individualism that had overtaken the modern world and was consuming America. The inspiration of the frontier still remained. The attitude was ubiquitous. At Brook Farm it was manifest, and even into the little colony of the Fruitlands, famous for the Alcotts, the spirit swept. Poe, with his morbid eccentricities and aloofness from the political scene, no more escaped it than Thoreau. In Emerson's words, which we quoted before: "A man is greater than a town," its philosophy is crystallized. It was a philosophy that fastened its faith in the individual. Thoreau's hegira to Walden is a concrete example of one form of its defiance.

The vision of that period is not our vision. Our direction is social. Our ambition is cooperative. That there were courage and fervor, spirit and defiance in the attitude of these nineteenth century leaders, is undeniable. We do not begrudge, but rather admire their challenge. Yet it is a challenge that today is obsolete. Our criticism of Mr. Mumford's striking analysis is not that he has failed to portray the individualism of the epoch, but that he maintains that "from their example we can more readily find our own foundations, and make our own particular point of departure." "For us who share their vision"—"they dream Thoreau's dream!"

Brave as is Mr. Mumford's revolt, it still is not revolutionary. We can no longer see in Emerson's vision an incentive for a new world. Emerson's vision and the vision of a new social world are in irreconcilable conflict. Mr. Mumford has confused his categories, and in his fine enthusiasm failed to appreciate the inevitable direction of the change that has come upon us. He has not yet learned to direct his revolt into revolutionary channels.

And to all this failure of the American intellectuals, there is the incessant cry—it is the conditions in America. And while we may admit this, we must further realize that it is not until we as radicals change these conditions, or rather act as a changing influence upon deeper-lying changes that are actively at work today, that we can ever develop greater thinkers, deeper radicals, finer artists, superior critics, and a more splendid vision.

FLIVVER TRAMPS

PAUL PETERS

Scarface Al Capone came to Los Angeles last winter and made himself at home. The newspapers broke the news to the police. The police didn't know what to do about it at first! but when public opinion became too hot, they suggested politely that Scarface might move to Tiajuana and enjoy the races. Scarface thought it over. In due time he moved.

Me the police treated differently. But then I was only a working stiff without friends or money or a job; whereas Scarface is a crack gunman and knows the most distinguished crooks of the nation and has cleaned up a cold million on moonshine. You can see that the police would treat us differently.

They kept me in jail all night. "Choose between 90 days in jail or leaving town in 24 hours," said the judge. So I left town. They are not lenient with you for the crime of poverty in Los Angeles. You fare better if you're a gunman.

I left the city as a poor man travels, on the highway. Zoom, roared the cars as they passed me by in streaks of gloss and nickle. Up the coast, over the mountains, through the valley—467 miles to San Francisco. I had gone ten. My feet were sore. Sweat oozed out of my hat. Dust formed mud with sweat and caked my weary body. I knew there were breadlines in San Francisco, so acute was unemployment. Imagine what chance I had of finding a job, a stranger, travel-stained, almost broke. But that did not trouble anybody in Los Angeles. The main thing was to get rid of jobless men like me. Our presence annoyed the tourists. Where we went or what the next town did to us, how in hell was that any of Los Angeles' business? San Francisco could pass the buck to Portland, Portland to Seattle.....

Before and behind me the road was dotted with plodding black figures. I was one of an army. Glum, bitter, I fell in line.

For hours I stood on that corner, waving at cars, shouting, whistling. Not one slowed up. I would gaze for a moment into a pair of cold, set eyes: then I was swallowed up in dust and the stink of gasoline fumes. The women were the worst. They would glare at you as if you were a lump of meat. How they loathed you out of their plate-glass rolling palaces, out of their silks and their cool complexions. "Get out of my sight," said their look. "Go bury yourself. You are foul to my eyes. You make us feel *uncomfortable*. You are a mangy cur. You should be carted to a pound and chloroformed."

A light delivery truck drew up at the curb and a small-town face leaned out. "Hey you! You can't wave at cars like that in this town. Get the hell out of here."

"Who says so?" I retorted.

"I'm the constable here. Now get out, damn quick, or we know what to do with tramps like you."

I walked a square and sat down on the curb. I had a mad desire to jump on running boards, to pound my fist on sneering noses, to scream obscene curses. "Isn't it enough that you drive us out of your cities, you pigs! Must you choke us off your highways too? You fat nickle-plated swine!"

Then the flivver tramps came along, a man, a woman, and three small children. Their rickety old Ford was held together with rope and wire. It bulged and spilled over with blankets, washboards, washtubs full of clothes, paper packages, boxes of tinpans and cups, rusty tools, worthless tires. A junkshop on wheels.

"Hop in," cried a friendly voice. "Where you goin'?"

"Frisco."

"Us too." We chugged out into the black, arid highway.

I travelled with the flivver tramps four days. We were sorely cramped. Most of the time I held one of the kids on my lap. All of them were wet and dirty and they stank. I didn't mind, I knew it costs money to be clean on the road, and the flivver tramps were poor, desperately poor. They had been on the road eleven months. Starting from Indiana, they had drifted down to Tennessee, through Arkansas into Texas, then west across the Mojave desert and up the coast. You had only to look at the kids and see that often they had hungered.

We did not take life too seriously. We sang, we told jokes, we swiped fruit from orchards, I spun yarns for the kids. But we made rotten time. We were always running out of gasoline. Every fifteen miles we had a blow-out or a break-down. Then the man and I would march to the nearest town, borrow tools on a deposit and pick up cast-off parts from garage scrap heaps. We made some money too, haywiring broken parts in gib cars stalled along the road, siphoning out a gallon of gas for them—when we weren't begging for some ourselves. You soon learn to overlook the unction with which tourists and drummers slip a dollar or two into your hand.

The Old Man, as his wife called him (though he surely wasn't over 32,) had been a mechanic in a garage in Muncie. One day a car slipped off a jack and shoved his ribs half through his lungs. They patched up his ribs more or less, but his lungs were never the same. When months later he crawled out of bed, all his starch was gone. His hair had grown gray. His eyes had become watery. His face had assumed an absent sort of smile. He tried for a time to get a clinch on his old job, but he didn't have the strength any more, the job shook him off. He tried other jobs, but jobs were hard to get, harder to keep. Who wants the starchless leftover of a man with pussy lungs? He gave up trying. He packed his family into an old car and became a drifter, working a week here and there, camping out, eating or fasting: a flivver tramp, sweet and simple—and whipped to a pulp.

It was the Old Woman from whom I got most of this, though she did not talk much. At twilight, when the kids became sleepy and cross, we would turn into a tourist camp in a clump of trees down a hollow, and rent a shack for a dollar. Then I would help the Old Woman strip the car of tinpans and blankets, haul wood for the fire, carry water, boil it, prepare the grub. Grub consisted mainly of dandelion greens, potatoes, bread, chicory, maybe an orange for the kids. I paid them a quarter a meal. If we had a day rich in stalled cars the Old Man and I would hike into the village and haggle with the Chinese grocer over half a dozen eggs or a can of pork and beans. On the way back, through the highland night, he would gab in a quiet, drawling, incoherent way: the war, the life on the road, the guy stalled near Albuquerque who handed him a twenty dollar bill, the new start he was going to make in Frisco. Man, this time luck was going to come his way. Luck was always just around the corner, always just out of reach. But Frisco, Frisco would be different. In Frisco he was going to grab luck by the "britches."

I used to listen to him silently, plodding wind-burned and tired at his side, sick at heart with pity. I used to think: "Yah, a fine system. You smash a man up. You tear the heart and guts out of him. Then you turn him out on the road like a broken old nag. A hell of a fine system."

After supper we pulled off the top layers of clothes from the kids and laid them, already half asleep, in a row across the bed. Then while she slopped up the tin plates, the Old Woman would talk a little. I had to piece her story together, filling in the gaps myself. There was no bitterness in her. She was a large strong woman, serene and stolid. Her hair was coarse and wind-blown, her face rough-skinned, her hands red and heavy. She made you think of one of those motionless peasant women of Millet. But sometimes she would break into a slow furious fire; and then suddenly you knew that under the placidity of her face were fears, grudges, anger, revolt. The Old Man was whipped, but the Old Woman still had fight.

"I guess he won't never settle down," she told me once when the Old Man left the shack. "First in Memphis, then it was Little Rock, then El Paso, then Los Angeles. Now he keeps sayin' Frisco, Frisco. But he ain't a-goin' to stay there neither. I ain't a-blamin' him. It don't make no difference for me. But the kids, that ain't no way to raise kids. It aint right for the kids."

They would squeeze into bed with all their clothes on, beside the kids. I slept outside, jack-knifed in the rear seat of the car.

The last night was so cold and foggy that I had to rent a separate shack. I heaped the stove with wood till its belly was blistered red and the pipe spat sparks. Then I huddled under newspapers on the bare yellowed mattress.

I sat up with a jerk out of a half-sleep. I could hear the doorknob gritting; the hinges squealed faintly; then the door was closed again. Some one was standing in the room. After a moment of bewilderment and fear, I saw that it was the Old Woman. She took a step toward the bed, and I got up.

"The Old Man sent me over," she said slowly. "He thought mebbe you'd want a bed-mate."

Still dazed, I answered: "Sure. There's lots of room over here. Send him over."

She seemed to hesitate. I can still remember her face, broad and red in the glow of the stove. But now she was smiling faintly; and in her smile there was both shame and pain.

"No, you don't understand," she answered simply. "The Old Man thought mebbe I could earn a couple of dollars by stayin' with you a while, as a bed-mate. We aint got no more money."

I had about four dollars in my pocket. I counted out two and pressed them into her hand. I couldn't look at her face. I could only see her hands holding the money out stiff before her.

For hours I crouched over the stove, cold and despondent.

All the next day, driving down the peninsula into Frisco, the Old Man gabbed at me in his incoherent way. The Old Woman did not talk at all. We avoided each other's eyes. Sometimes I felt that she was studying my face. Once our eyes met, and in hers shone an intense sort of dumb animal kindness for me. We both smiled sheepishly and looked away.

Now we were rolling through the outskirts of the city. Big, flashy motorcars whizzed by. "God, aint that swell," cried the Old Man, laughing like a child. "Cheer up, Old Woman. This hyer 's where we stop—in the Golden West."

It was night when we drew up on a bright corner of Market Street. They didn't know where to spend the night, and I could help them no longer. I said goodbye and followed down a side-street in search of a flophouse.

Night fog swirled around me. The Golden West, I thought bitterly . . . .

A DAY IN THE LIFE OF AN AGITATOR

CARLO TRESCA

I started the day with a firm resolution to get Andreichin out on bail. We were leading the Mesaba Range strike of iron miners in Minnesota. Andreichin was pining away in the county jail of Grand Rapids, Michigan, and we needed him badly in Hibbing, Minnesota. The young man was absolutely indispensable. He was the only one who could speak a Slav language, arid the strikers were either Italians or Slavonians. In fact, there were ten thousand Slavonian ore diggers who had gone out on strike, and none of us could say a word to them outside of Andreichin. To a large extent the fate of the strike depended upon our success in securing his release.

It was a beautiful August morning and the hills of that section of Minnesota were in a haze. The sun was shining and the prospects of the strike seemed to be bright. In Hibbing we had comparative freedom, and contact with the stalwart fighters always was a source of inspiration for me. That morning I was inspired with a bright idea. In a flash I decided to take the bull by the horns: to go to the City Judge and ask him to release the seven hundred dollar bond he had imposed on Andreichin. Jauntily I walked into the chamber that was full of deputy sheriffs and strange looking mine guards. His Honor was sitting on the bench. I approached him, and upon his asking, "What do you want?" I told him that we needed Andreichin in the interests of peace. "The Slavonians," I said, "are very restless, the situation is serious. Andreichin's imprisonment in Grand Rapids has only increased the tension." If the Judge were to release the seven hundred dollars I would go, I said, there and bring him back. I knew the proposition was a bold one, but, ... the Judge looked squarely into my face and then turned his gaze to the mine guards and deputy sheriffs. In a low tone he told me; "Well, I guess we'll have to do it, but don't let them know what it's all about. Come later, I will fetch the money for you."

One hour later I had the seven hundred dollars. In a few more hours I had collected three hundred more and was on my way to Grand Rapids.

1. G—D—AGITATOR!

Our delegation consisted of three: a local lawyer by the name of White, myself, and the chauffeur, who was a friend of the strikers and the owner of an Italian grocery store in Virginia, Minnesota.

It was about one o'clock in the afternoon when we left Hibbing and three hours later we entered the County Court building in Grand Rapids. Our way led us to the District Attorney's office where we found one clerk. The clerk politely replied that the District Attorney would be back in a few minutes and asked us to take seats. Soon the telephone rang and there was a short conversation between the clerk and somebody on the other end of the wire. I cannot explain why that conversation stirred me. Is it because the tense situation made me supersensitive? Is it because I was in fear of danger, or did I actually overhear something? At any rate, I felt that there was danger in the air. This sense of lurking danger was nothing new to me. I had experienced it hundreds of times in similar situations. I leaned over to White and told him: "This clerk has received orders to arrest me." To which White replied: "Nonsense. They cannot do anything to you here." My assurance, however, was so great that I offered immediate proof. Whispering to White, "Watch," I took my hat and started toward the door. The clerk immediately jumped up and told me: "Mr. Tresca the Sheriff wants to talk to you." That was sufficient proof of the danger. But such is human nature that I almost triumphantly turned my face to White as if saying: "I told you so."

Just then the District Attorney stepped into the office. He was a young, nice looking American type, very polite, very correct, very officious. Mr. White introduced me to him. He shook hands with me. "Glad," he said, "to see the dangerous leader of the strike." We sat down and had a nice chat. He expressed surprise at my insinuation that I was about to be arrested. He was all courtesy and decorum. Presently, however, while this polite conversation was going on, we heard a noise outside like the tramping of soldiers' feet. Turning to the door we beheld a dramatic scene. The Sheriff in shirtsleeves with a belt of cartridges around his belly, with one gun on his hip, ferocious looking, stepped into the office with two husky deputy sheriffs at his heels. The man was red in the face, and without introduction began to shout: "You goddam agitator, what did you come here for?" I replied: "For business." To which the deputy sheriff in a still more rasping voice said, "And it's my business to run you out of this County as quick as I can." Facing me at close range, he peremptorily ordered: "Give me that gun."

Tense as the situation was, I didn't fail to realize the comic side of it. I did not reply. The man approached me very closely, shouting into my face: "Give up that gun." I said, "Why don't you take it?" The Sheriff hurled at me a number of very ingenious insults, and only after giving vent to his temper did he order a deputy sheriff to search me. Of course, no gun was found on my person. This only increased the Sheriff's ire. I looked at the District Attorney. I was really interested to watch his reactions. He finally interfered. He took the Sheriff by the arm, led him to another room where they had a brief consultation. Presently the young, polite fellow returned and informed me, first, that I had no business to come to his County; second, that White had nothing to do with the case; third, that he would not let me see Andreichin, and fourth, that I must get out of Grand Rapids and back to Hibbing as fast as I could. I tried to protest. In fact, I exchanged a few very sharp and unpleasant words with the Sheriff, but I decided to go back promptly. There had been three mass meetings organized in Hibbing for that night, and I couldn't really stay away. In turning toward the door I said goodbye to the District Attorney in a courteous way, to which that polite and charming young officer replied, "Get the hell out of here, you S. O. B." This was about too much for me, I stopped, looked squarely into his eyes and told him, "Look here, you are many and I am alone. You are armed and I am unarmed." But before I finished, I felt the muzzle of the Sheriff's gun at my back and the Sheriff was shouting, "Get out. Get out." There was nothing to do but leave.

II. THE LYNCHING PARTY

There begins now our journey back to Hibbing—a trip I'll never forget as long as I live. It was more than a trip. It was a procession. Our little truck was followed by two other cars with the Sheriff in one and a number of armed men in the other. At a distance of three blocks from the Court House three more cars appeared from a side street, filled with men holding rifles in their hands. The three cars joined the procession. Soon we had left Grand Rapids and the country stretched on either side of us. We were alone,—three men followed by five cars filled with armed, hostile keepers of the Law.

In a few minutes we were approaching the mining town of Mishaevaka. Mr. White again seized my arm and nervously pointed at something ahead. There, at the entrance to the town, two columns of men many of them armed with rifles were lined on either side of the street, watching in silent gloom. White said to me: "This is a lynching party for you." The only thing I could say was: "The sooner, the better."

There was no misjudging the character of the groups that awaited us. My chauffeur-friend became very excited. Mr. White was becoming whiter and whiter. Both were speechless. I saw that it was upon me to take the initiative. I said to White: "Let me get out of the car and walk back of it very slowly, while the chauffeur and you remain in your seats. Let's go through the crowd facing them calmly. Never mind what happens to me. Take care of yourself. If this is a lynching party, let me be the victim. If we escape, then we'll get into the car after the danger is over."

Thus our strange procession entered the space between two lines of enraged, armed men. We heard curses on either side. "Damned agitator." "Sucker". "Damned foreigner." "Get the hell out of here." Fists were being clenched; distorted faces emitted words of insult; some of the men in the lines were about to throw themselves on us, but I soon discovered one element in the picture which made me breathe more easily. Behind the lines of armed men I noticed groups of miners in threatening postures. I heard shouts from the distance: "Courage, Tresca! We won't let 'em hurt you. Hurray for the strike!" I presume that this and our composed demeanor held the crowd in leash.

Amidst the storm of shouts, threatening gestures, curses and general bedlam, we proceeded to the end of the town. The imminent danger was over. We soon reached the county limit. By this time I was back in our truck. The Sheriff stood up in his car surrounded by the four other cars and gave us the last warning: "Remember forever that this place is not fit for you. When you come again I will kill you. Go, and keep going." I certainly did keep going for more than an hour until we reached Hibbing late in the evening with my mission unaccomplished.

III. EXTRA! EXTRA!

I was almost ready to say: "This is the end of a perfect day," when I realized that the end of the day was not yet. Passing through Main Street, opposite the office of the local paper, we saw boys rushing with shouts of "Extra! Extra!" There it was, printed with fresh black ink: "Clash in Biwabick. Deputy Sheriff Murdered." Biwabick was another mining town where the strike was on. The murder of a deputy sheriff was not to be disregarded. There seemed to be more trouble ahead.

While I was reading the paper, a crowd of strikers and sympathizers surrounded me, only to confirm the alarming news. Three strikers had been killed, they told me, and the situation was very bad. I hastily took leave of Mr. White and rushed to the local strike headquarters, only to find the place deserted, closed and dark. I had the creeping feeling of impending danger. I couldn't rest. I had to go to Virginia which was the headquarters of the strike committee and also my own headquarters. I asked the chauffeur to drive there. The poor soul replied: "I'll be damned if I do. For God's sake, let's stay here; I'm afraid." I didn't blame the man, but I had to go and was about to take the trolley car. The faithful soul didn't let me go alone, however, "I don't care what happens," he said, "I must go with you." And so we started out for Virginia, the very same evening.

What a deserted city! What gloom! What an eyrie feeling! All stores closed. Headquarters deserted. Dark. Nobody walking in the streets. I was looking around for any one of the Committee. Could find none. Nothing remained for me to do but to go to that little Italian house where I used to spend my nights. It was a modest one story frame structure owned by one of the strikers. I used to sleep there because I felt protected: eight young, strong Italian strikers always slept with me in the same house, all armed with guns and ready for action. They did not sleep all the time, either: they kept vigil in turn. I found them on the spot.

My first question was about Frank Little, who was among the leaders of the strike. I was particularly concerned about Frank because I knew he did not feel well; besides, he was practically alone since the strikers were either Italians, Slavonians or Finns with hardly a native American among them. To my consternation I learned that he had gone to sleep in a hotel, contrary to the advice of my Italian friends. Under given conditions this was a foolhardy step, to say the least. The only thing I could do was to go to his hotel and beg him to go hiding. I explained to him that, owing to the Biwabick situation, there was every likelihood that we would be arrested; that the only thing to do was to stay away. Frank, half asleep, muttered: "You are seeing red, Carlo! You mustn't get excited." When I insisted he said: "Oh, go to sleep. Let me alone." I: "They will come, Frank, and take you." He: "Aw, let 'em come. What do I care?" It was rather amusing to see this fighter displaying such a degree of equanimity. He turned his back to me and fell asleep. Still, I did not want to leave him alone, I sent my Italian body guards back and took a room in the same hotel, keeping only one man with me, the I.W.W. organizer, Gildea, a native American.

IV.—GUNS AT NIGHT

It was about four o'clock in the morning when I heard loud knocks at my door and harsh voices shouting: "Get out there." I jumped out of bed asking who it was. Through the window that opened onto the corridor (the room was dark while the corridor was lighted), I saw two search-lights playing and the muzzles of two guns pointed into my room. It was a very interesting play of silhouettes against the opaque glass. I cannot say that I felt very comfortable, yet I knew that I had to be firm. I said: "I won't open before I am told who it is." To which a still harsher voice shouted: "You are wanted by the sheriff." When I asked about a warrant, the strange voice replied: "We don't need no warrants for fellows like you." Whereupon I said: "If that's the case, you might as well break the door at your own risk."

And thus we stood in the room, Gildea and I, without lighting the lights, ready to meet the assailants in case they should break the door. It was the part of wisdom to stay inside from the window, through which the guns were stretching their threatening muzzles. Soon new voices were added to those outside. There was a tramping of feet, a hubbub of conversation and a woman's voice screaming at a high pitch: "For heaven's stake, Mr. Tresca, come out and spare us the trouble, or else our hotel will suffer damage." To which I replied with all the gallantry I could muster: "Well, Madam, I never fail with ladies. If you tell me who is there, and tell me the truth, I will open the door." There was some whispering and shuffling behind the door, then the lady imparted to me the cheerful news that there were outside of the door eighteen plain clothes men with a chief. The information made it advisable for me to surrender. I said: "Well, Madam, if you tell me to open the door, I obey."

In the County jail where we were temporarily interned, we found Sam Scarlett, an I.W.W. organizer and Frank Little, without a coat, but in a very cheerful mood. "You see," Frank said, "they did spoil my good sleep, those rascals." Before long detectives and policemen invaded the jail, handcuffed all four of us and took us out without telling us where we were going. As I looked around, I realized that we were being escorted by a large number of policemen and deputy sheriffs, armed with rifles.

V. CHARGED WITH MURDER

There was little time for meditation, however. It was not long before we reached the little railway station where we found a special train, consisting of an engine and one car. We were ordered fo enter the car where we found four men, three of them handcuffed to each other by the wrists, while the fourth was lying on a bench badly wounded in the legs. All of them were without coats; their shirts were badly torn and bespattered with blood; the head of one was all bandaged. Nor were the strikers alone. There were other deputy sheriffs there and the whole thing bore the marks of something very mysterious.

As soon as we entered the coach, our handcuffs were removed and we were seated, each on a bench with two detectives on each side,

It was all very queer. I was used to all the vicissitudes of labor struggles, but this journey in the early morning in a special train was something new. I asked my "companions": "Where are we going?" The reply was: "I don't know; I don't care to tell you. But be sure you won't see Virginia any longer."

As the train sped on through meadows sprinkled with dew, among clumps of trees swaying in the light morning breeze, under a clear sky that looked bathed after the night's gloom, the tension relaxed. We began to talk to each other. The guards relented, and we soon learned what happened in Biwabick. Four deputy sheriffs had gone to the house of a striker by the name of Philip Masonovich with a warrant for the arrest of one of the boarders. The men of the Law were very rough and they beat up Philip's wife. There were three Montenegran workers boarding in the house. The fellows were former soldiers who had participated in many a war in the Balkans. They were courageous fellows. They could not allow the deputy sheriffs to continue their dastardly acts. So they dashed against the four deputy sheriffs, took away their guns, killed one and severely wounded another. There was a real battle between deputy sheriffs and the strikers, and they were all arrested. These were the four men that we found in the railway car. They were all being conveyed to Duluth to be imprisoned on a charge of murder in the first degree. As to Little, Gildea, Scarlett and myself, we were also charged with murder as *accessories before the fact*. This is why we were in the car. We were being accused of a murder that took place in our absence in a different town. We were being attached artificially to the murder case in order to eliminate us from the strike picture.

It was about ten o'clock in the morning when we finally landed in the Duluth jail and I could tell myself that one day of my life had been completed. 'Twas a crowded day, indeed.

IT SOUNDS FUNNY NOW

KENNETH FEARING

They picked me up about seven o'clock on Monday night, I and the two fellows that was with me. The dicks didn't say what they wanted us for, they just took us down to the station and ran us in, booked for vagrancy. That didn't look so hot, of course, but it didn't look so bad either. I had some jack in my pants, proving I wasn't no vag, so I figured at the worst they'd fine me and throw me out of town. And then, Holy Christ, it turned out what they wanted us for was some job in a restaurant. There was a wop restaurant where these two birds used to hang out, with the rest of their gang, and somebody broke in there Sunday night and cracked the safe. The wop had it on his brain the job was pulled by somebody in this gang, which was probably true, and the dicks were just as positive. Well, I heard them talking about it but I still wasn't worried much, because I wasn't really a part of this mob, I'd just gone around to the restaurant three or four times with these other two fellows to eat. But they were there all the time.

And then, Holy Christ, the wop showed up at the station that night and he couldn't remember these other two birds at all, but he put the finger on me. So there I was, between the guts and the sweat. And the dicks didn't waste no time, they started to work out on me right away. They took me into the back room as soon as the wop was gone. I remember, hell, it sounds funny now,

I was walking out of the room, and one of the dicks caught me on the back of the neck, a sweet one.

"Well, come on, good-looking," he yells, and wham! I nearly did a nose dive into that back room. Right then I started to get worried.

They shoved me down in a chair and the dicks, there was four of them, stood around in a circle, one of them sitting in a chair facing me. And there was a little guy at a desk over to one side.

"Well, how about it?" One of the dicks started off with some crack like that.

"How about what?" I said.

"Listen, Jack," that dick must have been at least seven feet tall, "I hope you don't think you're tough? We like tough mugs. Don't we, Mike?" Oh, Jesus, you should've heard the chorus! They'd rather have a tough mug to play with than drink beer. There was grins on their pans a mile wide. "Now listen, Jack," he got sort of confidential and friendly. "We don't want to shellac you unless you're so dumb there's nothing else to do. But if you think you're tough, just say so, and we'll show you different."

"No," I said, "I don't think I'm tough."

"Then that's all right," said the dick. "Show us you're a right guy and we'll be easy on you. See?"

"Sure," I said, "I ain't tough."

"All right, then," said the dick. "Now, how about it?"

"How about what?" I said. Of all the dumb remarks, that was about the dumbest I could've pulled. But I couldn't think of nothing else, at the time, it just popped out. The dick in front of me pulled out his night-stick and banged me on the knee, a sweet one. I put out my hand, sort of rubbing the knee, and he cracked down on my hand so hard I thought it was broke, sure as hell, and I nearly passed out.

"How about that restaurant job?" says one of the dicks.

"What restaurant job?" I says.

"Say, you," says the dick, and he sounded sore as hell, "didn't I tell you what'd happen if you tried to get hard?"

"I ain't hard," I says, "But I don't know what you're talking about. You pulled me in here, I got the once-over by some wop out front, but I ain't even heard the charges."

"Read this dumb yap the charge," says the dick to the clerk, and he sounded kind of restless and impatient. "Maybe he ain't sure which job of his we got on him." So the little guy at the desk leaned forward and read from a paper.

"You, Thomas Halprin—" and then there was a lot of words winding up with I was charged with having burglariously, or whatever you call it, broke into this wop's restaurant and cracked his box for about two hundred bucks.

"Who," I says, when the bird finished, "me?" I know it must've sounded dumb and funny as hell, but I couldn't help it. I was still trying to figure out what it was all about. Well, I was looking at the clerk when I said that, and the dick on the other side of me clipped me a nice one on the jaw.

"Yes, you," he says. "That means you. Nobody else."

I turned around and started to try to explain something, and a guy on the other side slammed me on the other side of the jaw. "How about it?" he says, and the dick in front was rapping me over the knee with that hunk of gas-pipe and every now and then just to join the chorus he'd yell, "Come on, you, how about it?"

"Listen," I said, "I don't know anything about it. I wasn't no-wheres near that restaurant on Sunday night." Believe me, I was between the guts and the sweat. I was trying to do some fast thinking, but I didn't have no chance, and anyway, my head was spinning like a top.

"Where was you Sunday night?" They finally got down to that.

"At the hotel," I says, "the Davis." And I give them the name of the hotel I stayed at while I was in K. C. and said I was in bed all night.

"The hell you were!" says one of the dicks. "The clerk says you didn't even come in Sunday night. Where was you?"

For about five minutes after that dumb crack of mine the air was full of nothing but elbows and jacks and thumbs, with them dicks yelling where was I Sunday night. With me trying to think of where to say I was. See, I couldn't say where I really was without getting a friend of mine and his girl into trouble. I remembered I stayed with them all Sunday night, and if I used that alibi everything would be jake for me, but it'd get this friend of mine into a hell of a jam. And I certainly skidded when I said I'd been at the hotel in bed, because as soon as they pulled me in they'd gone up there and talked to the night-clerk and searched my room. They didn't find nothing in the room, of course, but the clerk told them my key'd been in the rack all Sunday night. So that made it twice as bad, that slip of mine. The dicks was twice as positive I'd pulled the job. And I couldn't really explain.

I know it sounds funny as hell, now, but it wasn't so funny then. Of all the dumb remarks to make, I finally said I was out all Sunday night walking around, looking for a job. It certainly sounded phoney, looking for a job on Sunday night, but that was the best I could think of under the circumstances and I stuck to that. I don't remember all the rest of what happened at that first ball-game, but they finally had enough and two guys dragged me downstairs and threw me in the can. I had plenty to think about that night, but I wasn't in the mood for thinking. It was cold as hell down in that basement, I hadn't had nothing to eat since Monday noon, and my jaw was broke, I thought sure, to say nothing of my arms being about twisted off me. And there didn't look like any prospects of anything but a nice five year stretch at least on this phoney charge they thought they had me on, me without enough jack to beat the rap, no matter how bum it was. So I had a swell night. It's hard to explain the feeling, and it probably sounds funny, but when they get you like that you find out the meaning of fear. You're alone, you know, with no chance to get out. You could be bumped off in there and nobody be the wiser or give a damn, just a line somewhere, "Thomas Halprin, held on a charge of vagrancy, fell from a cell-bunk and died of a fractured skull." You know, you see it in the papers every day. You don't know what fear is until you've been in a jam like that.

You can feel every damn thing in the world against you, like a bunch of loaded rods pressed into your guts and the guys holding them itching to start blasting just for the fun of it. What the hell are you, anyway? Nothing. So I spent a swell night nursing that jaw and reflecting, as they say, on the errors of my ways. Which was mostly, the way I figured it, the error of not being in that hotel room of mine on Sunday night. Holy Christ, it must sound dumb and funny. But that's the way it was.

Every now and then, until pretty late that night, they'd drag in another guy the dicks'd been sapping up on upstairs. If I looked like any of them guys did I must've looked like something the cat dragged around a long time before he found a place to bury it. And I guess I looked the same, all right. My shirt had some blood on it and my clothes, it was a new suit I bought that morning, was tore in a couple places. But I remember they brought in a guy about forty years old and put him in a cell next to mine, and I got talking to him, about what sort of an alibi I should fix to get out of this place. This guy was a paroled prisoner himself, he'd only been out three or four months after a ten year stretch, and him and his gang got pulled in for swiping a load of furs. That was the charge. They'd caught them with the truckload, going somewheres, and can you imagine their dumb alibi? They'd found the truck, that's all. They'd just happened to be walking down the road and they found it. Well, anyway, I explained my case to this bird, I had to laugh, I could see he didn't believe it, he thought I really had pulled the job, but he said, stick to my alibi.

"Which'd you rather have," he says, "getting beat up four or five times, or ten years in the can? You don't know what they got on you. Maybe they got something, but probably they ain't got all they want, otherwise why would they bother to give you the works? Stick to your alibi, because that can't make you no worse off and there's a chance it'll spring you."

Well, that was good news, that I was liable to be sapped up a few more times. I'd thought I was all through with that and there was nothing more except to say good-morning judge. So that was something else to look forward to. And next morning, Holy Christ, every time I heard keys rattling or a door slam I was ready to kiss myself good-bye. There wasn't nothing to do except sit around and wait, of course. Along about noon the old guy in the cell next to mine threw an entertainment of his own. He waited till the prison doctor come around, with an attendant, and started to throw a fit, yelling his head off. All the guys hollered for the doc to come and find out what was the matter with this bird and shut him off. So the doc asked him if he was in pain, and the mug said Oh, hell, he was dying with pain. They made up their minds it must be appendicitis, and I guess in another minute they would have yanked it out on the spot, but the old bird finally stops moaning long enough to say to the doc, "I know what's the matter with me, doctor." They asked him what, and he said, in a kind of dying voice that sounded funny as hell, "I am the victim of a drug habit, doctor." But it didn't work, of course, because it made the doc sore. In another minute that old boy was the victim of a special party he wasn't expecting, besides the drug habit. And after that there wasn't nothing to do but go right on waiting.

Finally it got so bad I begun wishing they'd come around and drag me out for anything, even another picnic upstairs in the back room. And them station-house screws didn't make it better, they're like nobody else in the world. They're the lowest bunch of rats in the world, I guess. At noon one of them came up to the door and said how would I like some beef stew and java, for instance. So naturally I hopped up to the bars, with my mouth open and my tongue hanging out. I suppose they got to pull stunts like that to pass the time away. It was water and some stale bread. And another one come around, and when I asked him what're the chances of my having a hearing or crashing out, he says some friends of mine was upstairs now arranging bail. I knew he was lying, of course, because I didn't have no friends in K. C., I hadn't been there long enough. But you know how it is, a guy believes what he wants to believe, and for a while, I know it sounds funny, I halfway thought it was straight. But after a couple hours more I realized it was bologney, and then it was twice as bad as before.

Nothing happened until the next morning, Wednesday that was, and then they put me in the show-up. That was jake, of course, nothing to it, and of course there wasn't nobody put the finger on me for any other jobs. But after that there was another baseball game in that old back room. I was the ball, and believe me, them dicks knocked about a hundred home-runs. They was a different lot from the other mob, and they went over my alibi with a microscope. A microscope and a couple of pick-axes, I should say. I was out walking around all Sunday night, was I? Well, who did I meet could identify me, where'd I walk, where was some of them places I went looking for a job, and so on. I was in a tough spot and the way they asked them questions didn't help me to answer them. Take anybody under even ordinary conditions and ask him exactly what he done night before last, and see if he's got any prize answers on the tip of his tongue. Well, I suppose some of my remarks must've sounded funny as hell. And of course I didn't meet nobody, and I'd keep forgetting what streets I'd been on, although I'd put in my spare hours downstairs memoring the route for a swell walking marathon. I'd laugh if anybody ever tried to ramble over them streets and boulevards I laid out, and do it in one night. It'd probably take a week straight on a bicycle.

But I didn't say nothing I didn't have to, and finally they'd simply beat the tar out of me until I couldn't of said nothing even if I tried. I wasn't more than half there by the time they was through with their setting-up exercises and I don't really remember the rest of it until I sort of come to late that afternoon, and I was back on the old homestead downstairs.

So that was all there was to it. I guess the wop must've changed his story or decided not to bother with it, or something. I guess the dicks finally realized they was on the wrong track, or maybe they still thought I pulled the job but they didn't have enough on me. Next morning, Thursday, I heard them keys rattling and the door opened and I thought here goes for another ten-round battle of the century. But the screw brought me over to another part of the basement, instead of upstairs.

"All right," he says, "get in there, you vag."

Holy Christ, it was the vag tank, and I hopped into it like it was paradise. That's what it looked like to me at the time. And a little later that morning they brought me upstairs and I got fined five bucks and they turned me loose. They let the other two fellows that was with me when they picked us up go, too. We went outside, and it was snowing like hell, but it would've looked good to me if it was raining paving-blocks.

We went down the street and there was a couple of dicks waiting for us on the corner. It seems one of the fellows with me, a big guy, got real hard when they was sapping up on him, he must've kicked the dicks in the shins a couple of times, and they was anxious to polish him off some more. They invited all three of us out to the edge of town somewheres, if we thought we wasn't satisfied, or had a grudge, or something. But we told them to go peddle their papers somewheres else, and then they said they give us twelve hours to get out of town. If we was seen around K. C. after that, they said, we hadn't seen nothing compared to what would happen if they caught us then.

Well, these two fellows just grinned and started off for someplace where they could get some junk and marijuana. But I had enough of K. C. so I went back to the hotel and checked out. I happened to have about a hundred fifty bucks left, with some new clothes I bought Monday morning, and I decided to go to Chi. All in all, I got out of that pretty lucky. I had a tooth knocked out, that was all. Of course I wouldn't of had even that if I could've used my real alibi, being with them three fellows, they was pals of mine, on Sunday night. But that would've got them into a sweet jam and I couldn't use it. And besides, I'd had a little trouble else-wheres, in Texas and California, and while I was in the can in K. C. I was all the time afraid they might find out about it and then it would've been good-bye, no matter how bum their rap was about the wop restaurant. So I was really pretty lucky, all in all.

HUMANISM: LITERARY FASCISM

V. F. CALVERTON

The sudden interest in humanism that has sprung up in the last few years, and in particular in the last year, carries with it the burden of a vast prophecy. It is more than a fad, this humanism of our moderns. It is a new declaration of faith—nothing more and nothing less. In America it marks the end of the period of flippancy and cynicism, the passing of the decade of the sneer. It spells the passing of Mr. Mencken, who was the infatuation of our college-boys since the War, and the rise of Mr. Babbitt and Mr. Eliot, who have become the mixed inspirations of our college-boys of today. Anyone who has been near or within our American colleges in recent months knows how complete this change has been. Five years ago the name of Mencken was on the lips of every sophomore. Today it is *humanism* which has become the new inspiration. While business men, clergymen, and lawyers, still read the *American Mercury*, our youth has already begun to speak of *the late Mr. Mencken*.

Now there is something very significant in this change, something that serves as an excellent index to what is happening in our social world today. In the ten years that have just passed, youth accepted and defended the Menckenian boast of believing in nothing. Today it must believe in something. Religion has already begun to return in numerous forms. In both England and France many of the leading intellectuals have accepted the old faiths. T. S. Eliot and Jean Cocteau are familiar examples of that reversion. C. E. M. Joad tells us that we must create a new religion to satisfy modern man's quest for faith. Herbert Read would have us believe in a sense of glory as a means of escape. Romain Rolland would have us turn to Asia for our new inspiration. And in America, the professors, who after having been trampled on for a decade are once more in the saddle, would have us believe in *humanism* as the best way out.

Now the question we must immediately ask is: best way out of what? The answer is simple. The best way out of the bankruptcy of the old values. If there is anything that all this cry for new faiths represents, it is the disintegration of the middle-class logic of life. Middle-class values are no longer believed in today. The morality of the middle-class has completely decayed. The old faith in religion that the middle-class once had, which even exploited hell as a source of moral efficiency, has waned. The belief in democracy, which rose as part of the middle-class challenge of the feudal order, has lost its force. And modern humanism—or the new humanism—is nothing more than a philosophy to make the intellectuals comfortable in an altogether uncomfortable intellectual world. Its whole inspiration is one of intellectual escape.

The new humanism represents two significant tendencies: first, the tendency to exalt individualism in the philosophic sense of the word, and secondly, the tendency to attack science as the final source of authority in the intellectual world. In the instance of the first tendency, one can find many contradictions—verbal contradictions at basis, however—among the leading humanists of today; in the case of the second, there are no contradictions at all. In its attempt to reduce everything to law, science has tended to minimize the importance of the individual and to magnify the importance of forces—forces outside of man rather than within him. Modern machinery has standardized production to such a point, that the part that the individual plays in it has become increasingly microscopical.

To give up that individualism is to move in the direction of collectivism, which, because of its association with communism and all that the middle-class intellectuals fought and loathed, is the thing above all to be avoided. Mr. Mencken, like most of our contemporary liberals, has been extolling individualism and at the same time advocating our modern methods of production and our modern methods of science. Such logic is shallow and anachronistic. The humanists, in their philosophy at least, whatever we may think of them as individual philosophers, have been too clever to fall into that contradiction. They not only exalt individualism as a philosophy, but they also oppose the methods of science and the nature of a social order which tend to destroy individualism as a factor. It is easy to attack their absurd opposition to science—we shall waste no space on that aspect of their argument—but it must not be denied that they have hit upon the only reliable weapon a modernist can employ to combat the growing collectivistic logic of our age. In advocating philosophy, or religion, as do T. S. Eliot and others, instead of science, the humanists have saved themselves from the naive contradiction of the liberal. Philosophy or religion as the new humanists conceive of it has more in it of solace for the exaltation of the freedom of the individual than has science. And what is more, it offers a new battlecry against the whole spirit of the modern age. (It can very easily be made to fall in accord with all the anti-Soviet propaganda that is rife today in reference to the attitude of the Soviet Union toward religion.)

Now what is most interesting about the new humanism from a radical point of view is that it will eventually force the intellectuals into choosing between two crossroads in their logic. To defend individualism one can no longer use the method of science or the touchstone of external reality. One must develop a philosophy of escape, a metaphysics or religion that depends upon an inner, mystic reality, such as Babbitt's idea of "intuition" or "inner force," if one is to invent any consecutive consistency of logic. If humanism as a philosophic doctrine spreads, as I think it will among those reactionaries who seek this form of escape it will be because it offers a *Weltanschauung* that is complete instead of fragmentary in its conception. It will not be long, with this new development, before the intellectuals will have to be either consistent individualists or consistent collectivists—which will ultimately mean consistent communists.

The new humanism has an historical connection with the old humanism that has not been perceived by most of our contemporary critics. On the whole, the anti-humanists, who have raised such a cry over the rise of humanism, have done little to clarify the logic. They have attacked the humanists on those points which are the least significant in the humanist credo. And they have done this with such dismaying consistency because their attack is the attack of the liberal. They have assailed the humanist criticism of science, but have said nothing of the humanist exaltation of individualism as a philosophic doctrine. They have said nothing in condemnation of this because they are believers in individualism themselves.

Humanism in its original form arose as an outgrowth of the doctrine of individualism in the early days of the Renaissance. It represented then a defense of the *human* point of view in opposition to the supernatural. The church stressed supernatural values; the humanists stressed human ones. It is significant to remember that this early humanism grew out of the *commercial revolution*, when the material factors in a swiftly-changing world prepared the way for individualistic advance. It had a genuine part to play then in support of the new philosophy of life that was later to emerge from the Renaissance. The new humanism today, however, is still defending individualism in a world that is totally out of accord with it.

Since it is impossible in an essay of this brief nature to take up all the numerous arguments of the various humanists,* it is best that we focus our attention upon the logic of their leader, Irving Babbitt. Mr. Babbitt has been advocating humanism for several decades now. It was no doubt as a direct result of Babbitt's teaching that T. S. Eliot became a humanist. Mr. Babbitt, representing a Boston Back Bay outlook upon the universe, can well afford to preserve an inner calm and a self-imposed discipline in his interpretations of human life and individual behavior. In Mr. Babbitt's own arguments we can immediately discover the reactionary character of the new humanist logic!

"The humanitarian is not, I pointed out, primarily concerned, like *the humanist*, with the individual and his inner life, but with the welfare and progress of mankind in the lump."—*(Democracy and Leadership)*

He is interested not in social reform but in self-reform. As a consequence, he is interested in religion (in the way he defines it) and not in social revolution:

"According to Mr. Lloyd George, the future will be even more exclusively taken up than is the present with the economic problem, especially with the relations between capital and labor. In that case, one is tempted to reply, the future will be very superficial. When studied with any degree of

---

* See: Norman Foerster: *Humanism and America (a Symposium). Farrar & Rinehart,* $3.50.

thoroughness, the economic problem will be found to run into the political problem, the political problem in turn into the philosophical problem, and the philosophical problem itself to be almost indissolubly bound up at last with the religious problem."—(*Democracy and Leadership*)

While Mr. Babbitt will not agree with Mr. T. S. Eliot that "humanism without religion ... is sterile," he admits that, in the last analysis, he ranges himself "unhesitatingly on the side of the supernaturalists."—(*Humanism in America*).

Beneath all this argument, however, there lives the venomous spirit of social reaction. Quoting Burke as an example, Babbitt claims that whatever has been excellent in our civilization has depended upon two principles: "the spirit of a gentleman and the spirit of religion."—(*The Forum*), This emphasis upon "the spirit of a gentleman" is linked up hand in hand with the rest of the humanist philosophy. Like golf, this humanism is a "gentleman's" game—fit game for the would-be gentlemen's sons who crowd into our universities each year. In Babbitt's *Democracy and Leadership* which was the book that started so much of the present humanist-controversy, the reactionary social doctrine that lies behind the whole humanist philosophy is viciously conspicuous. The laborer he contends "is not using his relief from drudgery to enjoy leisure in the Aristotelian sense." Mr. Babbitt can well afford to say that—living the life of a gentleman in a leading American university of our day. It is equally easy for him to suggest, in good humanist style, that it is more important to start "with loyalty to one's self" than with "an expansive eagerness to do something for humanity." And equally consistent for him to observe that "if the laborer wishes to add to these comforts or even to keep them, he should not listen to the agitator who seeks to stir up his envy of every form of superiority."

While humanism may dodge many verbal issues, it does not evade the social one. It is reactionary to the core, and makes no effort to deny it. Mr. Babbitt announces it without equivocation. "The choice to which the modern man will finally be reduced," he writes in *Democracy and Leadership*, "is that of being a Bolshevist or a Jesuit. In that case (assuming that by Jesuit is meant the ultra-mundane Catholic) there does not seem to be much room for hesitation. Ultra-mundane Catholicism does not, like Bolshevism, strike at the very root of civilization. In fact, under certain conditions that are already partly in sight, the Catholic Church may perhaps be the only institution left in the occident that can be counted on to uphold civilized standards."

In the final analysis, therefore, the new humanists are the intellectual fascists of the present (and the forthcoming) generation. Babbitt at least faces the issues with an honesty that is not characteristic of most of his followers, or, for that matter, of most of his critics, and since Norman Foerster says, in the introduction to his symposium on *Humanism in America*, that "Irving Babbitt has done more than anyone else to formulate the concept of humanism, ... and is at the centre of the humanistic movement," it is in no sense unfair to Humanism to criticise its doctrines through the medium of Babbitt himself. Babbitt is, in every way, the fit leader for the intellectual fascism that humanism represents. Here are his words to his followers:

"Circumstances may arise when we may esteem ourselves fortunate if we get the American equivalent of a Mussolini; he may he needed to save us from the American equivalent of a Lenin."

What do the anti-humanists have to say about this? Why are they so silent about this aspect of humanist doctrine? Because most of them at heart are but intellectual fascists of another stripe. Humanism is not to be fought as a literary disease; it must be fought as a philosophy of *social* reaction.

SISTER JOHNSON'S STORY

LANGSTON HUGHES

(As told on the front porch at Aunt Hager's house on a summer evening in a Kansas town)

The old sister took a long draw on her corn-cob pipe and a fiery red spot glowed in its bowl. While Willie-Mae and Sandy stopped playing and sat down on the porch, she began a tale they had all heard at least a dozen times.

"I's tole you 'bout it befo', ain't I?" asked Sister Johnson.

"Not me," lied Jimboy, who was anxious to keep her going.

"No, you haven't," Harriett assured her.

"Well, it were like dis," and the story unwound itself, the preliminary details telling how, as a young freed-girl after the Civil War, Sister Johnson went into service for a white planter's family in a Mississippi town near Vicksburg. While attached to this family she married Tom Johnson, then a fieldhand, and raised five children of her own during the years that followed, besides caring for three boys belonging to her white mistress, nursing them at her black breasts, and sometimes leaving her own young ones in the cabin to come and stay with her white charges when they were ill. These called her Mammy, too, and when they were men and married she still went to see them, and occasionally worked for their families.

"Now, we niggers all lived at de edge o' town in what de whites called Crowville, an' most of us owned little houses an' farms, an' we did right well raisin' cotton an' sweet taters an' all. Now, dat's where de trouble started! We was doin' too well, an' de white folks said so! But we ain't paid 'em no 'tention, jest thought dey was talkin' fer de past time of it … Well, we all started fixin' up our houses an' paintin' our fences an' Crowville looked kinder decent-like when de white folks gin to 'mark, so's we servants could hear 'em, 'bout niggers livin' in painted houses an' dressin' fine like we was somebody! … Well, dat went on fer some time wid de whites talkin' an' de coloreds doin' better'n better year by year, sellin' mo' cotton every day an' gittin' nice furniture an' buyin' pianers, till by an' by a prosp'rous nigger named John Lowdins up an' bought one o' dese here new autimobiles—an' dat settled it! … A white man in town one Sat'day night tole John to git out o' dat damn car cause a nigger ain't got no business wid a autimobile no how! An' John say, 'I ain't gonna git out!' Den de white man, what's been drinkin', jump on de runnin' bo'ad an bust John in de mouth fer talkin' back to him—he a white man, an' Lowdins nothin' but a nigger. 'De very idee!' he say and hit John in de face six or seven times. Den John drawed his gun! One! two! t'ree! he fiah, hit dis ole redneck cracker in de shoulder, but he ain't dead! Ain't nothin' meant to kill a cracker what's drunk. But John think he done kilt this white man an' so he left him kickin' in de street while he runs that car o' his'n lickety-split out o' town, goes to Vicksburg an' catches de river boat …

Well, sir! Dat night Crowville's plumb full o' white folks wid dogs an' guns an' lanterns, shoutin' an' yellin' an' scarin' de wits out o' us coloreds an' wakin' us up way late in de night-time lookin' fer John, an' dey don't find him … Den dey say dey gwine teach dem Crowville niggers a lesson, all of 'em, paintin' dey houses an' buyin' cars an' livin' like white folks, so dey comes to our do's an' tells us to leave our houses—git de hell out in de fields cause dey don't want to kill nobody there dis evenin'! … Well, sir! Niggers in nightgowns, an' underwear, an' shimmies, half naked an' barefooted was runnin' ever which way in de dark, scratchin' up dey legs in de briah patches, failin' on dey faces, scared to death! Po' ole Pheeny what ain't moved from her bed wid de paralytics fo' six years, dey made her daughters carry her out screamin' an' wall-eyed an' set her in de middle o' de cotton patch. An' Brian what was sleepin' naked jumps up an' grabs his wife's apron and runs like a rabbit wid not another blessed thing on! Chiliens squallin' ever where, an' mens a pleadin' an' a cussin', an' womens cryin' Lawd a Mercy wid de whites o' dey eyes show-in'! … Den looked like to me 'bout five hundred white mens took torches an' started burnin' wid fiah ever last house, an' hen-house, an' shack, an' barn, an' privy, an' shed, an' cow-slant in de place! An' all de niggers, when de fiah blaze up, was moanin' in de fields, callin' on de Lawd fer help! An' de fiah light up de whole country clean back to de woods! You could smell fiah, an' you could see it red, an' taste de smoke, an' feel it stingin' yo eyes. An' you could hear de bo'ads a failin' an' de glass a poppin', an' po' animals roastin' an' fryin an' a tearin' at dey halters. An' one cow run out, fiah all ovah, wid her milk streamin' down. An' de smoke roll up, de cotton fields were red ... an' dey ain't been no mo' Crowville after dat night. No, sir! De white folks ain't left nothin' fer de niggers, not nary bo'ad standin' one 'bove another, not even a dog-house ... When it were done—nothin' but ashes! ... De white mens was ever where wid guns, scarin' de po' blacks an' keepin' 'em oif, an' one of 'em say, T got good mind to try yo' all's hide, see is it bullet proof—gittin' so prosp'rous, paintin' yo' houses an' runnin' ovah white folks wid yo' damn gasoline buggies! Well, after dis you'll damn sight have to bend yo' backs an' work a little!' ... Dat's what de white man say ... But we didn't— not yit! Cause ever last nigger moved from there dat Sunday mawnin'. It were right funny to see ole folks what ain't never been out o' de backwoods pickin' up dey feet an' goin'. Ma Bailey say, 'De Lawd done let me live eighty years in one place, but ma next eighty'll be spent in St. Louis.' An' she started out walkin' wid neither bag nor baggage ... An' me an' Tom took Willie-Mae an' went to Cairo, an' Tom started railroad workin' wid a gang, then we come on up here, been five summers ago dis August. We ain't had not even a rag o' clothes when we left Crowville—so don't tell me 'bout white folks bein' good, cause I knows 'em ... Yes, indeedy, I really knows 'em! ... They made us leave our home."

The old woman knocked her pipe against the edge of the porch, emptying its dead ashes into the yard, and for a moment no one spoke.

***

"I know white folks." Jimboy said. "I lived in the South."

"I ain't never been South" said Harriett hoarsely, "but I know 'em right here ... and I hate 'em!"

"De Lawd hears you," muttered Hager.

"I don't care if he does hear me, mama! You and Annjee are too easy. You just take whatever white folks give you—*coon* to your face and *nigger* behind your backs—and don't say nothing. You run to some white person's back door for every job you get, and then they pay you one dollar for five dollars worth of work, and fire you whenever they get ready."

'They do that all right," said Jimboy. "They don't mind firin' you. Wasn't I layin' brick on the Daily Leader Building and the white union men started sayin' they couldn't work with me because I wasn't in the union? So the boss come up and paid me off. 'Good man, too,' he says

to me, 'but I can't buck the union.' So I said I'd join, but I knew they wouldn't let me before I went to the office. Anyhow, I tried. I told the guys there I was a bricklayer and asked 'em how I was gonna work if I couldn't be in the union. And the fellow who had the cards, secretary I guess he was, says kinder sharp, like he didn't want to be bothered, 'That's your lookout, big boy, not mine.' So you see how much the union cares if a black man works or not."

"Aint Tom had de same trouble?" affirmed Sister Johnson. "Got put off de job m'on once on 'count o' de white unions."

"O, they've got us cornered, all right," said Jimboy. "The white folks are like farmers that own all the cows and let the nigger take care of 'em. Then they make you pay a sweet price for skimmed milk and keep the cream for themselves—but I reckon cream's too rich for rusty-need niggers anyhow!"

They laughed.

"That's a good one!" said Harriett. "You know old man Wright what owns the flour mill and the new hotel—how he made his start off colored women working in his canning factory? Well, he built that Orphan Home for Colored and gave it to the city last year, he had the whole place made just about the size of the dining room at his own house. They got the little niggers in

that asylum cooped up like chickens. And the reason he built it was to get the colored babies out of the city home with its nice playgrounds, because he thinks the two races oughtn't to mix! But he don't care how hard he works his colored help in that canning factory of his, does he?

Wasn't I there thirteen hours a day in tomato season? Nine cents an hour and five cents overtime after ten hours—and you better work overtime if you want to keep the job! ... As for the races mixing—ask some of those high yellow women who work there. They know a mighty lot about the races mixing!"

"Most of 'em lives in de Bottoms where de sportin' houses are," said Hager. "It's a shame de way de white mens keeps them sinful places goin'."

"It ain't Christian, is it?" mocked Harriett ... "White folks!" ... And she shrugged her shoulders scornfully. Many disagreeable things had happened to this young girl through white folks. Her first unpleasantly lasting impression of the pale world had come when, at the age of five, she had gone alone one day to play in a friendly white family's yard. Some mischievous small boys there, for the fun of it, had taken hold of her short kinky braids and pulled them, dancing round and round her and yelling, "Blackie! Blackie! Blackie!" while she screamed and tried to run away. But they held her, and pulled her hair terribly, and her friends laughed because she *was* black and *did* look funny. So from that time on Harriett had been uncomfortable in the presence of whiteness, and that early hurt had grown with each new incident into a rancor that she could not hide and a dislike that had become pain.

Now, because she could sing and dance and was always amusing, many of the white girls in high school were her friends. But when the three-thirty bell rang and it was time to go home Harriett knew their polite "Goodbye" was really a kind way of saying, "We can't be seen on the streets with a colored girl." To loiter with these same young ladies had been all right during their grade school years when they were all younger, but now they had begun to feel the eyes of young white boys staring from the windows of pool halls, or from the tennis courts near the park—so it was not proper to be seen with Harriett.

But a very unexpected stab at the girl's pride had come only a few weeks ago when she had gone with her classmates, on tickets issued by the school, to see an educational film of the under-sea world at the Palace Theatre on Main Street. It was a special performance given for the students and each class had had seats allotted to them beforehand, so Harriett sat with her class and had begun to enjoy immensely the strange wonders of the ocean depths when an usher touched her on the shoulder.

"The last three rows on the left are for colored," the girl in the uniform said.

"I ... But ... But I'm with my class," Harriett stammered. "We're all supposed to sit here."

"I can't help it," insisted the usher, pointing toward the rear of the theatre while her voice carried everywhere. "Them's the house rules. No argument now—you'll have to move."

So Harriett rose and stumbled up the dark aisle and out into the sunlight, her slender body hot with embarrassment and rage. The teacher saw her leave the theatre without a word of protest, and none of her white class mates defended her for being black. They didn't care.

"All white people are alike, in school and out," Harriett concluded bitterly, as she told of her experiences to the folks sitting with her on the porch in the dark.

Once when she had worked for a Mrs. Leonard Baker on Martin Avenue she accidentally broke a precious cut glass pitcher used to serve some out-of-town guests. And when she tried to apologize for the accident, Mrs. Baker screamed in a rage, "Shut up, you impudent little black wench! Talking back to me after breaking up my dishes. All you darkies are alike—careless sluts—and I wouldn't have a one of you in my house if I could get anybody else to work for me without paying a fortune. You're all impossible!"

"So that's the way white people feel," Harriett said to Aunt Hager and Sister Johnson and Jimboy, while the two children listened. "They wouldn't have a single one of us around if they could help it. It don't matter to them if we're shut out of a job. It don't matter to them if niggers have only the back row at the movies. It don't matter to them when they hurt our feelings without caring, and treat us like slaves down South, and like beggars up North. No, it don't matter to them ... White folks run the world, and the only thing colored folks are expected to do is work and grin and take off their hats as though it don't matter ... O, I hate 'em!" Harriett cried so fiercely that Sandy was afraid. "I hate white folks!" she said to everybody on the porch in the darkness. "You can pray for 'em if you want to, mama, but I hate 'em! ... I hate white folks! ... I hate 'em all!"

MEN WANTED

ROBERT CRUDEN

Two lines of men were to be seen on Mill Road that January night. One, a ceaseless, hurrying stream which poured from autos, street-cars, busses on to the road, from the road to the bridge which spans it and thence into the plant of the Rivers Motor Company. This was the midnight shift going on. The other line, a little further down, was stationary, a long, irregular line of men who eyed enviously the hurrying, nervous workers—these were the unemployed. When the day shift had come off at four they had already begun gathering—a few gaunt individuals clustered around the wooden shack which served as a hiring office. Now it was after eleven and hundreds were in line. Before morning thousands would be there.

They were a motley crowd which greeted the workers so silently each morning. Clad only in suit and work-shirt they cowered and shivered in the wind. Their faces were blue with cold; their eyes keen with hunger. Only the Negroes looked warm—they had ragged sweaters on their heads, sacking on their feet and pieces of old quilt wrapped around their shoulders.

But now it was dark. The men could be seen only when the wind blew the flames from the coke-ovens across the road. Now they were in darkness; now they were tossed into red relief. It was cold on the line, but further on the men could see where the blast furnaces burned the sky, coloring it to a misty red glow, a glow which never changed, never faded. At times, through the wind and the hollow clanking of train bells they could hear the steady hum of the machine shop and the motor building. Away in the distance they could discern the faint aura of light which marked the gigantic sign, *Rivers Motor Company.*

Eighth in line was Jim Brogan. Jim had come out at six the same morning but had found thousands ahead of him—he would not have been able to get near the office. He turned back to snatch a few hours' sleep in preparation for his all-night vigil. But he couldn't sleep. While he lay in bed his head felt as though hammers were pounding his brain. What if he should get a job? He dared not hope. Yet the tumult in him would not down—all the frozen hope of eight months' idleness was breaking up, surging and cracking through his body. Would he be hired? Again he would reach over and read the headline, "Rivers to Hire 30,000 Men." Thirty thousand! Why, there could not be that many unemployed in the whole country! He laughed and cried alternately.

In the living room Marie was putting little James to sleep—but even the youngster was affected by hope. He howled and gurgled at intervals—but sleep he would not! And Marie! No sharp words today! No slapping of the child! She was singing today, singing as she had sung in those first few months of their marriage, singing as she had sung before unemployment had crept like a cold gray sea between them. Jim laughed and stretched himself, feeling his muscles in an ecstasy of joy.... he would be hired!

But what if you don't get hired? a sinister suggestion whispered to him. He drove it from him, saying to himself with gritted teeth, "I will be hired! I will be hired!" Things could not get worse. Good God! He had to get hired! He must be hired! Then he scanned the headline, "Rivers to Hire 30,000 Men." Of course he would be hired!

But out on the line, with a thousand jobless behind him and a black, cold sky above him, Jim lost confidence. He was eighth in line, sure, but didn't the men say that just that morning the clerks had picked out every twentieth man, regardless of how long he had been in line? What if that should happen today? The thought clutched him so that he gasped for breath. His legs felt weak. He was cold and hungry and tired. He clutched tightly at the nickel in his pocket. Should he go and get coffee? But that would mean giving up his place in line. No; he would stay the night through with his sandwiches of bread and corned beef. Where did Marie get the money for the corned beef? What did Marie have to eat that night? Jim wondered.

A voice broke in on his thought, "Got a match, bud?" He shook his head.

A Story of Detroit

"Don'cha smoke?" the man asked when he got a match.

"Sure."

"Then have one on me."

Jim took the cigarette gratefully. He had not smoked since the baby had fallen sick six months previously. The doctor had recommended oranges! Jim laughed bitterly as he remembered it. He puffed at the cigarette, feeling better as it warmed his mouth. He noticed his companion. The latter was a small man who had once been fat. His face was unshaven and blue with cold. His eyes seemed to glitter in the darkness. His suit, old and frayed at the edges, and his blue cotton shirt were little protection against the wind.

"Gawd, I wisht I had a coat," he said. He took a last puff at his cigarette and flung the glowing stub away. "'I pawned my coat," he continued as he met Jim's questioning glance. "I had to Damn it, I didn't have a penny left when I was outa work four months an' I hadda hock everythin' ".

He paused, took another cigarette from his pocket and lit it from Jim's stub, "I use't t' work here" he remarked, nodding in the direction of the motor building.

"Yeah?" asked Jim, interested.

"Sure. I worked over there in the motor building on a drill press. They raised production three days runnin' an' I said, ' Steve Miller ain't no slave, whatever else he may be' an' I quit. That was three years ago."

"It ain't no use quittin' no more," Jim said, "They're all the same now. Fellows that I know say this plant ain't no worse than the rest now."

"Yeah, things ain't never goin' t' be as good as they use't' be. I remember when the guys in Lawrence Body made fifteen bucks a day and didn't have to tear their head off to get it. Well, I was workin' there before I was laid off. Do you know how much I was makin'? Five bucks a day, an' I had to go like hell to get that."

"I know. I worked on the trim line there. You ain't married, are you?" Jim asked as he took another cigarette.

"Naw," Steve replied, "An' it's damn good thing I ain't. God knows when I'll get a job again. I don't."

By this time the midnight shift had gone on. The last remnants of the afternoon shift were going home, a straggling procession which trudged stolidly past, bent before the wind. Now and then their faces could be seen in the blaze of the coke-ovens—theirs were faces lined and dirty and tired, masks of utter weariness. Jim sighed. Down the line a man was saying, "An' then she came down to the employment office an' gave 'em hell because her man was 'too tired to make babies.' What do you think o' that-"

Silence on the line. The only sound was that of the wind, growing sharper as the night went on. At intervals, out of the darkness, came the clangor of train bells. That was all. The last worker had gone home; the last street car had already rumbled into the night. The only humans left were those huddled together along the great storm fence and 30,000 who toiled feverishly in the plant.

Who on the line did not envy the toilers? Workers from Tennessee, Arkansas, Missouri; from Dakota, Iowa, Idaho; workers from Texas, Arizona, New Mexico; men from the Mesaba Range and miners from Ohio and Pennsylvania; Negroes from Alabama, Georgia, Carolina; workers from Poland and Russia; ship workers from the Clyde and diggers of coal from the Ruhr—they were all there in their motley thousands, drawn by the headline, "Rivers to Hire 30,000 Men."

One o'clock. Steve had fallen silent. Jim was left to himself. 420 minutes to think before the office opened. ...

Two o'clock. Jim was half-asleep, slouched against the fence. Pictures, memories flitted through his brain—a grotesque pageant. The layoff eight months ago. Its laughing acceptance by Marie—it was the first layoff in their marriage. Little James had been ten months old then. How happy Marie and he had been in their happiness! How sweet it had been! It could not have been *real*—this was reality, this cold, dragging unemployment which fastened on your happiness until it fell in the embers of its own fire. Jim's heart pounded as he felt this, pounded a mad, insurgent beat of revolt. ... 360 minutes in which to think. ...

How happy they had been when James was born! With what pride and love had Jim planned the future of his son—he would go to high school, to college, even; he would make the name of Brogan famous in the world. And the tenderness of Marie; her loving caresses; the peal of her laughter—and then the layoff…and Marie had laughed no more…300 minutes…

For eight months now, day after day, he had gone from plant to plant in an unending quest of work. The answer was always the same—a shake of the head. What money they had, went. He had had to cut out car-fare—it cost at least 12 cents a day. Now he walked. He had walked six miles to the Rivers plant that afternoon.

Then James had fallen sick. The doctor would not come when he heard that Jim was out of work. Jim burned again as he remembered his passionate anger when he heard of it—how he ran to the doctor's house and hammered on the door, shouting until the place was in an uproar. Meanwhile, Marie had scraped money together from the neighbors and they got another doctor. He said the child was undernourished and had a "touch of TB". He recommended a diet of oranges for the child! James had never gotten well again. How could they give him oranges?

It was after four when Jim came to with a start. His feet were numb, so cold that he did not feel their coldness. He shivered and stretched his aching arms. As he opened his lunch Steve looked around but said nothing. He looked worn out and hungry.

"Here," said Jim as he forced a sandwich on him.

"Well,…. I guess I will. It's a goddam shame, though."

They bit into the bread, chewing it voraciously, feeling better for the bread and companionship. Men on either side of them looked longingly, but said nothing.

Out from the line, in the road, some Negroes who had just rolled up in an old, battered Rivers, started a fire. Soon it was blazing merrily, shooting up myriad sparks in the winter morning. The Negroes surrounding it were happy, laughing and shouting for the men in line to join them. A few of the men stepped out, hardly able to walk, so cold were they. They stood around the fire with outstretched hands, silent. Then one of the Negroes pulled out a big lunch and began to eat. He saw the eyes of the men on him and passed it around. It looked like a picnic there in the snow, with the fire crackling and blazing and the men eating, but only the Negroes laughed. They had arrived from Alabama the day before and expected to get hired at eight o'clock!

"Dis fact'ry done treat us jes' lak white men," one of them rejoiced.

"You're damned right it does," rejoined a worker with meaningful sarcasm.

This fire was the signal for others. Up and down the line fires were lit; bands of young workers searched for wood to keep them going. The men became more cheerful. They began to talk. Now and then a ripple of laughter passed along the line. The depression was gone; the helplessness of the individual vanished. The men felt stronger, powerful. Surely the day would bring them a job—!

It still lacked an hour of opening time when the police arrived. All night long the men had endured the snow and the wind; for months they had suffered in silence; in these last few precious hours they had hoped ... and now, like a blight, came the police. A murmur swept among the men, a murmur which rolled in suppressed undertones like the wind in trees before a storm.

Down came the motor-cycle police, sounding their sirens, straight into the fires. The men scattered; the police stamped out the dying embers. Yells, catcalls, oaths, derision greeted them as they did the work. With clubs drawn the foot police marched up and down the line, forcing the men into single file—when they were slow to move a whack with a club made them hasten.

A cop passed passed where Jim was talking to Steve. He looked at Steve, who was slightly out of line, and then jerked him out. Steve yelled.

"Get to the end of the line, you wop!" the cop shouted.

"I won't. I been here since five last night. I won't!" Steve wrenched himself free and rushed into line before Jim. "Ain't I been here all night?" he cried.

"Sure, he's been here right along," Jim spoke up.

"Oh, yeah!" the cop snarled, "An' who the hell ast you?" He grabbed his club more firmly and pulled Steve out of line again. Steve screamed as the club crashed on his head. Before Jim knew it his companion was on the ground, blood trickling from behind his ear.

Jim was enveloped in a terrible silence. He could hear nothing; he saw nothing save the face of the cop which loomed up out of a haze. He trembled. His hands were hot as he clenched them. It seemed to him that years passed while he stood there in that silence face to face with the policeman. Then anger swept over him in a sudden flood. He stepped forward—and as he did so the whole line moved forward, a mass that burst like an avalanche. The police fled, blasting their whistles. Service men of the plant ran to the gates with drawn revolvers—but the men rushed on. They were bound for the main gate.

Down went the storm-fence; the hiring office was crushed to matchwood as the thousands charged on. The road was packed with running men whose shouts and cries penetrated even the factory, scaring superintendents, filling the workers with wonder.

Jim was in the vanguard. Like the others he just sped on, bent on vengeance, knowing not where he was bound, knowing not what he would do. All that he saw as he ran was Steve, prostrate on the ground, blood streaming from his battered head.

And then the rush stopped. In a moment the men stopped, quivered, and then turned to press back against the thousands behind them. From a dozen different places fire hoses opened their icy blows on the men. Jim went down, hit in the face. He lay there, stunned, while his nose spurted blood. He was drenched. Then, through the shouting he heard the howl of a police wagon. He jumped to his feet and ran.

From behind him he heard cries and screams as the police attacked. Fear possessed him. By now he had caught up with the men but now they were turning and fleeing in all directions in a frenzy of fear. He fought his way through them to the main body still running down the Mill Road. He stumbled and cut his face on the storm fence. He looked and saw that he had fallen over a man impaled on the spikes of the fallen fence. Jim felt sick—his breath came in short, stabbing gasps; his heart beat like the rattle of an automatic press. He thought he would collapse under the weight of his drenched overcoat.

Now the crowd burst out again in a mad rush forward when screams from the rear told of the arrival of the police reserves. Jim tore off his coat as he ran, knocking down men who got in his way, falling over men who had collapsed in the excitement, himself bruised as he ran on with the men, ploughing forward in his mad desire to escape. On sped the men, past the power house, past the last gate, over the railroad into the town. ... They were safe ...

A long thin line of twos and threes trudged along the road to Detroit. Jim was walking with a man who was still wet with the water. The man's face was scarlet; his eyes bloodshot. He kept whispering to himself as he marched nervously on. Then he spoke to Jim, and in his voice was the misery of months of hunger.

"I wisht I had a gun!"

Jim set his teeth and kept silence.

HIGH BRIDGE

JACK CONROY

Indiana was a blur of green fields and sudden filling stations set in tree-arched villages, white houses and careful picket fences. Fleeing from a New Sodom, crammed with closed factories and desperate jobless workers, we never looked behind.

Finally Ed said: "Christ! It's no use tryin' to run on the rim without any gas and without money to buy any; it's no use trying to patch tires that look like a crazy quilt already and as holy as a swiss cheese. We simply gotta mooch, steal, get a job or something before we can go any further," so we pushed the lifeless Chevrolet from the slab, and started to hoof back to a little place we just passed through.

"Any work around here?" we asked a residenter dozing beside a greasing-rack.

"Hell, no! I never *did* see things so tight. This place is dead, stranger, and you better not stop here for work. Dozen men for every job—You can't buy a job ... I ain't had a day since ...."

We left him muttering. A fellow with an Illinois license drove up to the pump just as we repeated the question to the servant of Standard Oil (Indiana).

"I need a couple experienced steel men—riveter and bucker-up," the motorist said, sizing us up. "I'm on a bridge job fifty miles west."

"Why, that's lucky!" I said. "I was born with a rivet hammer in my hand and my partner's a bucker."

"Where *did* you ever handle a rivet hammer?" His blustering tone was a belligerent challenge.

"In Pittsburgh. Pittsburgh-Des Moines Steel." I had actually piloted a screaming steel saw there at one time, and my ears ring yet.

"Well, I'll give you a trial, anyway."

With gas and re-patched tires we limped along and came to the high bridge etched against the sunset, spanning a muddy river. We slept jack-knifed in the car as usual, and in the morning reported stiffly for work.

"You've worked high, of course," the boss answered himself. "Don't get dizzy."

"Sure!" I was lying. Height terrifies me; I'm a fellow that was born to have one leg on the ground all the time; but how we needed that job! Oh, how we needed it!

I lifted the air hammer, assuming an air of familiarity, and cautiously pressed the trigger. The plunger shot out and banged a laborer on the shin. He cursed me fervently.

"Hey, be careful, you!" bawled the boss. "Is that the way you handled a hammer in Pittsburgh? Want to break a leg for somebody?"

I learned to stand the hammer loosely on a plank and tap away like an energetic woodpecker beside my foot. Some men never get used to climbing, never learn to forget the ground and remember not to look down. I'm one of them. The river spun like a pin-wheel with the bridge in the center, fields swung madly in a blur of color. I felt myself slipping but my head cleared just in time. I pulled the heavy hose and hammer along; scooted fearfully along the eye-beams. The old hands were scornfully nonchalant; walked cat-like across narrow girders without holding.

Try it if you think it's easy, you who have been thrilled by the shoot-the-chutes at Coney. Wind plays a high bridge like a harp; the structure sways to a weird rhythm. To nervous feet a hundred feet in the air, steel is like the glass mountain in the fairy tale.

From a platform far below a bored rivet heater tossed fiery rivets to Ed, who was supposed to catch them in a large cone with handle attached, but more often he missed and they fell hissing in the river, followed by a shower of sparks like the tail of a comet. Ed clung affectionately to a girder, and would not sway to and fro to stop the rivets.

"Not so hot, kid," I encouraged, but he finally caught one, only to find the holes out of alignment. It was necessary to punch them into line, and by that time the rivet was changing from red to purplish, and grey scales were flaking off. It's hard enough to buck a hot rivet but a beginner is out of luck trying to buck a half-cold one. It backed up, though Ed jammed the bucking bar against his chest and hung on bravely with elbows and knees. You can't hold a rivet hammer straight, I found. You must weave it in a circular fashion to make a good head. The vibration shook Ed like an ague, but still there was half an inch play and the head was a misshapen blob.

"That won't do," the foreman reproved, passing us on his way down. "You got to have a snug fit and a perfect head. Get your crack chisel and cut that out."

About an hour of this, and a stiff breeze rose off the river. My cap blew off, and instinctively I wheeled to grabbed it, slipped and fell. I clutched wildly but only tore off my two finger nails to the quick as my hands slipped off. Nothing could stop me. It seemed like the bottom dropped out of my belly. But a girder caught me and I hung limply balanced like a bag of bran, my breath forced out in an explosive yell. The pneumatic hammer had plunged to the end of the hose, snapped the coupling, and disappeared in the river. Among the gusset-rods, the hose writhed and hissed like an angry snake. Weakly I clung, and Ed, his face blanched, began to climb gingerly down toward the good old solid ground.

"Come down, you farmer! O you awkward son of a bitch!" the boss roared from below. One of the old hands helped me down.

"Steel men! Steel men, hah?" the boss sputtered, "A hammer lost! Get out of here! Don't *ever* say you can work high again, you dumb bastards ... you! ... you! .... "

Ed clipped him neatly on the chin and he went down like the Titanic. We left him sprawling on the bridge floor and started to run for the car. Nobody offered to follow us.

"He needn't worry," I rasped painfully, my windpipe yet in a knot. My guts still hurt, and the blue ridge has never faded away altogether. "He needn't worry. Catch me off the ground working again! ... "

"Well," Ed cheered philosophically," we got five gallons of gas, and the tires may hold up fifty more miles. I was afraid he'd make us work out the price of the hammer."

REPARATIONS

SCOTT NEARING

I.

The sound of hob-nailed shoes on the frosty pavements breaks the winter morning silence. It is six o'clock. I leave my room and walk through the blue darkness of German city streets.

I cross under the railroad tracks and pass a butcher-shop and a bake-shop where workers wives are already buying their day's provisions. At a distant corner under a street lamp moves a procession of dim figures. They emerge from the shadow, flit through the circle of light and then disappear into the shadow again. I join this procession of workers.

Across the dimly lighted street there is a woman with a child. She is poorly protected against the penetrating cold; over her head is a scarf and her hands are bare. The child is more warmly clothed. He is about two years old, and his little legs move reluctantly at half-past six of a cold winter morning. I leave the stream of workers and walk slowly along behind the mother and child.

For a time the two go on together; the high childish voice sounding incessantly, the mother answering in monosyllables. The child stops beside a lamp-post; the woman who is several steps in advance, turns and calls. There is a discussion. Again reluctantly the child goes on with his mother. Time after time this procedure is repeated as the two make their way through the gloom.

At length they turn into a lighted entrance over which there is a sign: Day Nursery. I stand in the shadow and watch. Woman after woman leaves the line of hurrying workers, and goes into the day nursery with her child. Some of the children are as old as five or six. Some are infants in baby carriages.

I step into the circle of light thrown from the doorway and look at my watch. It is twenty minutes of seven.

Another block—the factory. A Siemens factory, one of a chain belonging to the great German industrial Siemens concern.

Towards the open gateway is pouring a steady tide of workers, men and women. Some come on bicycle. Most walk; their hobnailed boots clattering and echoing through the street. They loom out of the semi-darkness, pour into the factory maw and are swallowed up, while their places on the street are taken by other hurrying forms.

At five to seven the crowd is thinner. Here and there a few stragglers are making a rush for the gate. Lights flash up in the factory windows. A bell rings. Belts begin to move, pulleys whir. There is a buzz of machinery. It is seven o'clock. More than three thousand men, women and children are at work.

II.

The Siemens interests have issued an annual statement. Their total sales between 1929 and 1930 have fallen 6 percent—from 850 to 800 million marks, but there have been important retrenchments that have resulted in an increase of net earnings. The usual dividends have been paid.

How were these retrenchments made possible? The report does not give all of the details, but with a 6 percent decrease in total business there has been an 18 percent reduction in the number of workers. A regular phase of Siemens policy is to increase output while they decrease workers. In 1924-25, the Dawes Plan year, the Siemens interests employed 112 thousand workers and did a total annual business of 500 million marks. 1929-30 the number of workers employed was 113 thousand while the business done was 800 million marks. Thus for each worker the increase in business done was about 60 percent.

The Siemens interests have employed another means of retrenchment. On November 1st of 1930 they cut wages 2 percent. On February 1st 1931, they again cut wages—5 percent. The workers are producing more but they are getting less.

REPARATIONS

Another item in the Siemens Report, of particular interest to workers outside Germany, deals with exports. During this last year of hard times and world economic crisis, while the total amount of Siemens business decreased 6 percent, the exports of their products rose more than 8 percent. Wage-cutting and speedup in Germany are having their effects on international markets. Siemens are underselling their competitors in the world struggle for imperial wealth and power.

III.

Allied Imperialists drew up a Treaty in 1918-1919 based on the slogan: "Germany must pay!" Ever since the Treaty was signed, one of the chief tasks before French, British, and other imperialist statesmen has been the collection of reparations.

The huge burden loaded by the Allies upon Germany could not be paid in money nor could it be paid in goods collected at one time. It could be met only if Germany sold more goods than she bought, year after year, for half a century. To sell these goods in the world market, the masters of Germany must lower their costs of production, either by increased exploitation of the workers, or by reducing the profits of the German exploiters.

Since both German economy and the German state machinery are in the hands of the exploiters, it is obvious that they would do their best to avoid meeting reparations payments out of their own pockets, and to load the burden on the workers. Even though the German exploiters should wish to meet the demands of the Allies by reducing their profits, they could not do so.

Under a system of capitalist economy, if profits are reduced in one country, the capital from that country will flow to neighboring countries where profits are higher, thus making capital so scarce at home that the interest rate must rise and restore profits to their former level. German exploiters cannot be made to pay. The cost of reparations must therefore be met by wage-cuts, speed-up, and lowered living standards for the workers. And these lowered workingclass standards in Germany must drive down the workingclass standards in the capitalist countries with which German exploiters are in competition.

This process is very apparent all over Germany. Not only in the Siemens plants but in the entire German industry, wages are being cut, workers are being speeded-up, increasing quantities of goods are being exported and relatively high profits are being paid.

And so reparations demands are being met not by the exploiters of Germany, but by the German masses. During the Revolution of 1918 the German workers failed to wipe out the capitalist imperialism and join the workers of the Soviet Union in their program of Socialist construction. Today they are paying the penalty—carrying on their backs the burden of reparations.

Berlin, Germany.

LYNCHING IN THE QUIET MANNER

JOSEPHINE HERBST

The new trial for the eight Negro boys at Scottsboro, Alabama, condemned to die on July 10th, has at this writing been denied. It has now been appealed to the state supreme court. The Jackson County papers are upset at the publicity thrown on this case. They would like everything to run in a nice quiet gentlemanly way. Those well meaning people who wish to depend on "legality" to save these boys, are, whether they are aware of it or not, hand and glove with Jackson County. The South has always been strong for lynching in the quiet manner, without even the confusion of the law. Now that the law is brought in, they would like to see it oiled so that the boys could be shot through to the chair without disturbing anyone's feelings. If you read the transcript of the first trial and particularly the Judge's admonition that there is to be no demonstration, you will be impressed with the legality. It was, from Jackson County's point of view, perfectly legal. Quiet in the courtroom, and outside a brass band playing Dixie to the cheers of thousands in celebration of the verdict of guilty. The trouble with legality is that it has a hundred different interpretations. Legality alone has never been known to accomplish much. Without social pressure it can run in grooves hundreds of years old. Law is supposed to represent the mores of a group and it lags behind several hundred years and is never brought out of its rut without social pressure. The particular handling of the Scottsboro case is a remnant of legal slavery. The Negro has never really emerged from slavery. Conditions of tenant farming, vagrancy laws, chain gangs have conspired to keep him in his place. If legality is going to be his last appeal, he might as well give up.

Legally, the Negro is penalized all over this country, north and south. He can't beat the law game when it is interpreted by white men still dominated by a slave owner's code. The Negro may run a better chance in the north but only because the north never depended on the Negro for its big labor supply. The Negro wasn't as necessary in the north when there was a steady stream from Europe of Wops, Bohunks, Micks and Polacks. The south has never got over the Civil War. Down there you may still hear youngsters talk about the war and wonder what war. Why, the Civil War. They are still fighting it. In the mind of the South, the Negro has never got past his Civil War status. The first laws concerning the Negro were made when slavery was introduced in this country and those laws, in different forms, still exist. They are still there to guarantee Negro labor in the south.

Jackson County is stepping lightly in this case. They expect, if given time, things will quiet down. Then the legal machinery can roll on quietly to their satisfaction. But they are fooled. The longer it is postponed the louder will be the protest.

Left to legality, the superstition of rape would finish off these boys in the chair. The testimony of the alleged victim, Victoria Price, conflicts with itself. Her version of the affair is a gaudy one. A knife was at her throat and twelve Negroes all brandishing knives and guns leaped over the side of the gondola at her. Although her mouth is smothered by a hand or arm and she is almost beside herself she manages to keep track of the boys and to identify them in the order they vanquished her. Out of the corner of an eye she also takes in the customers of Ruby Bates, her fellow traveler. Such an all seeing eye dumbfounds one. It isn't to be believed. And it confutes itself the next day when she admits she cannot identify the boys in the order of their attack. She isn't even sure of Ruby's customers. Her ears have sharpened, however, because on the first trial she hears one shot; on the second, seven. She betrays herself with slips of the tongue. Denying that she ever saw the white boys in. the gondola before, and ever spoke to them, she yet calls one of them by name. "Thurman" she says, "saw the Negro grab me as he went over the side of the car." It is for these women, established as prostitutes, who were not overpowered or hysterical, according to the doctor's report, but merely talkative, that eight Negro boys were legally condemned to die.

The Nation comes more or less halfheartedly to the defense of the case. It wants a gentlemanly defense. If this were a "just" world there would be a good deal to say for that. Depending on legal machinery is continuing to trust where trust is no longer justified. It was all very legal in the Sacco and Vanzetti case. Whatever reprieves Mooney has won were got by working class protest and a wave of public sentiment that started in time to save him at least from the chair. It is too late to be polite in cases of this kind. The law is not abstract, impartially arbitrating between conflicting social classes; it is a tool in the hands of those who govern.

The N.A.A.C.P. (National Association for the Advancement of Colored People) have complicated matters by refusing to cooperate in the defense. Because they are largely subsidized by upper class money they pretend to smell a rat in the I.L.D. defense. They claim that the case is only being made into Communist material; and rather than pollute themselves they confuse the boys on trial and reduce the issue to one of petty squabbles. Eugene Gordon, Negro writer, comes out with a strong statement against this process. "The N.A.A.C.P. no longer exists for the advancement or the advantage of the lowly Negro."

Some say this is not a labor case, but these boys were on the move because their families were poor and they had no work. The whole race problem in the south is first of all economic. It is his position as a laborer that forces him back into the legal status of a slave. The ignorance and poverty which *The Nation* so deplores is an economic problem. It isn't a mystical one. The Negro worker is ignorant and poor because it has seemed to be an economic advantage to keep him that way.

Mrs. Wright, mother of two of the boys, may be poor, and she may even be ignorant but character and fortitude she certainly has. Her husband has been dead for seven years. She leaves the house every morning at quarter past five and gets home at half past seven. For this, she gets $6 a week. It was lately raised from $5. She is very tired when she gets home and doesn't cook much, just opens a can of something. It isn't so healthy but there is very little money. Carfare costs so much. This winter things were pretty bad. The boys couldn't get a thing to do. Then her daughter came home. They were on a farm and it was closed out on them. She and her husband came to live in their house. Of course, she brought along a lot of canned stuff, and that was as good as money, and she brought along her own meat. Yes, she brought a pig weighing 135 pounds and that was fine all right. But they soon ate that and he couldn't find work. Her six dollars, five at first, didn't go far. Her boy, that's Andy, he said he just wished he'd get work so she could sit her down. He says, I just wish you could sit you down. But there weren't no work and so him and Roy said they would go to Memphis and maybe find some.

That's the way the two boys left home. Then one day she was on her way to the five fifteen car and her sister that lives near the carline came out with the paper. "Where's your boys, Ada?"

"Why my boys are in Memphis," I says.

"No, Ada, your boys ain't in Memphis," and she hands me the paper. I read it and I just says, "Well, well, well." I couldn't think of another word.

Of course these boys didn't get much schooling. One went to the third grade, the other got as far as the sixth. The other eight boys have similar stories. They are, as *The Nation* says, poor and ignorant.

The Wright boys sometimes teased to go to a movie and then their mother says to them, well if you boys want to go without your supper, you can go, I can't afford supper and movies, and then the boys would go without their supper. It was either supper or movies and they didn't get to the movies often, because they were always hungry.

The legal machinery is very rusty in the south with its traditions of slavery, its superstitions and its fears. It will take more than that to save these boys. It will take what Jackson County is afraid of, working class protest, the pitiless eye of publicity, that will expose, evidence for evidence, the flimsiness of the case against them, that will not only show up the evidence but the mob psychology aroused, stimulated and constantly exploited by the governing classes of this country.

THE NEGRO'S NEW LEADERSHIP

EUGENE GORDON

Until today it has been axiomatic with the Aframerican since his socalled emancipation that no white man lives whom black men may trust as one trusts a comrade. "You can't trust no white man no time," the Negro worker said. They taught their children to say it. "It don't make no difference how much of a friend a white man makes out he is," they said; "soon's he gets what he's after he's all through with you." Thus white man in the United States, boss or worker, has been looked upon by the black worker as a double-crosser, a hypocrite, and a liar. The Negro's own duplicity when dealing with whites was excused on the grounds of justifiable retaliation. "Never give a white man no quarter," they said, "because he won't give *you* none—'ceptin' to get a stronger hold on your throat."

This doctrine of justifiable retaliation has been widely disseminated and closely adhered to. It has been bolstered up by the ruling class both of the North and of the South. The ruling class's ideology of Nordic supremacy has engendered in the white workers distrust of the Negro; in the Negro worker it has built up complexes of inferiority and defeatism. Shut out of unions affiliated with the American Federation of Labor, the black workers have been driven back upon themselves. You who have seen cattle herded into a small corral know how they swirl concentrically upon themselves until the center is a maelstrom of locked horns and legs. There seems to be no way out; there seems to be no way of disentangling themselves. The state of the Negro worker was similar to that of the cattle. There was leadership for them neither within among the blacks nor without among the whites. Even if the whites had proffered them a leadership the blacks would doubtless have scorned it.

Negro leadership immediately following the civil war was almost completely in the hands of illiterate and ignorant gospel shouters. Black ministers who dominate that field today are fully as ignorant, if somewhat more literate. Previously to his "emancipa-scious, willing and unwilling, tools of the masters, and they executed the orders their masters issued. It was a venal leadership. The direction it pointed was lost in a maze of "spiritual" superstition and capitalistic ideology; the guidance it afforded was a check upon and a preventive of revolutionary thinking and acting; the encouragement was all to the effect that the black man would continue to be an inferior until he could become a parasite like his master.

When the leadership was not immediately dictated by the white ruling class, it nevertheless reflected the ideology of that class. To work with the hands was the degradation god almighty stamped upon the slave. The well born—the gentlemen and their ladies—did not work. Therefore every "po' white" and every ambitious black who hoped some day to attain the class of the well born, to be a gentleman or a lady, shied away from working with the hands and studied like hell to "better" themselves: they became doctors, lawyers, school teachers, preachers, politicians, editors, and small business men. Their ideal was wealth and idleness, with illiterate blacks to wait on them. "Better your condition," the leadership advised; which implied: "Rise above these common blacks so you can have someone to look down on. The Negro can't have a higher class if there isn't a lower class." The leadership encouraged individualism of a roughshod and ruthless kind: scheme, connive, double-cross, crush. Climb to the top on the thick skulls of these stupid blacks who worship you because they see in you a reflection of their white masters.

This ideology was not confined to the "spiritual" leadership. It pervaded the atmosphere breathed by the professional man, business man, and politician. It stimulated the growth of the petty bourgeoisie which today is as close to the working class that supports them, in aims and in sympathy, as Seventh avenue is to Lenox. A chasm lies between the two classes, and those at the top are frenziedly digging to make the chasm wider. They have <a> is the kind that the Negro has been afflicted with. But he is beginning at last to open his eyes. He is beginning to see that these "big" Negroes are not concerned about him and his future. He is beginning to see that some white men may honestly wish to help him. He is discovering, to his dazed bewilderment, that a new leadership is beckoning to him.

When the National Association for the Advancement of Colored People was founded and it announced its program of fighting for the rights of the under-privileged, the black masses of the country thought they had at last discovered a leadership they could follow with absolute trust. But, although these workers did not know it, the NAACP was, after all, a ditch-straddling body which depended for sustenance on the whims of rich and doty liberals. The organization was no freer, therefore, to condemn the system upon which its capitalist supporters battered than the Negro preacher out of slavery was to fly in the face of conditions winch kept the "freedmen" peons. The system which in both cases brutalized the workers also fed, pampered, petted, and flattered the men it picked to mislead the workers. In its early days the NAACP frequently did things which were almost daring; but its most daring performance was simply a compromise. However, a compromise, Negro leaders in the South tell us, is better than a surrender, and the NAACP has finally admitted surrendering completely. It is no longer the National Association for the Advancement of Colored People, but the Nicest Association for the Advantage of Certain Persons. It has as much to do with the black masses of workers and share-croppers as any similar group of scented, spatted, caned, and belly-filled white parasites have to do with the white masses. It is ultra-nice, ultra-respectable, and ultra-fastidious. It has a reputation to preserve, so it cannot afford to be seen in company with dirty reds or other radicals, no matter what the common end is supposed to be.

This dainty withdrawing from an organization because it is composed of common workers has done more than any other one tendency of the NAACP to reveal its true character to the Negro masses. Observing its aloof and grudging "help," the Negro worker recalls suddenly that there has never before been a body of men who, white and black, actually *fought for* the most degraded black man in the country. The Negro masses have of late been stirred to enthusiasms by the action of the International Labor Defense, the League of Struggle for Negro Rights, and the Communist Party of America in going to the very stench-hole of

American capitalist class hatred and challenging the thugs and lynchers on their own ground. Seeing all this, the black workers remember the incident of the NAACP secretary in Texas, some years ago who, caught pussyfooting by thugs hired by Texas bosses to get him out of the state, was beaten and chased to the railroad station. They remember the letter of resignation this NAACP official wrote, in which he asserted that he saw no hope of securing the Negro's rights through the means his organizations was pursuing. They remember their feeling of despair when they read his wail of defeat; a wail which implied that if others wished to risk their hides for the sake of "common niggers," let them; he certainly didn't intend to do so any more.

Then Negro workers think of the countless times Communists have been beaten insensible for defending the Negro workers, yet have gone from the hospital right into the fight again. They remember the white men who were tried and convicted in the USSR, and remember the trial in New York of a white worker who was tried and humiliated for his jim crow attitude toward black workers. and humiliated for his jim crow attitude toward black workers. They look at the most daring experiment in American journalism, the actual printing of a Communist newspaper in Chattanooga, the heart of the lynching desert, and they are thrilled! They hear of members of the LSNR, white and black, going to eat in an "exclusive" Washington restaurant and wrecking the place when the Negroes in the party are refused service. They see the ILD and the LSNR, supported by the Communist Party, rushing defense to the nine Negro youths at Scottsboro long before any other organization in the country has condescended to glance superciliously in their direction, and they see the loyalty and the staunchness of the men and women who are giving their time and energy and money and talent—everything they have—to save these boys. Seeing and hearing all these things, the Negro worker in the United States would be a fool not to recognize the leadership that he has been waiting for since his "freedom." And the masses of blacks being *no* fools, they *have* recognized it and they have begun to accept it. The Negro workers are beginning to understand that such leadership is the only leadership for the man who works, whether he be white or black.

FAREWELL TO AMERICA

BORIS PILNYAK

From ancient ruins archaeologists sometimes unearth primitive stone images of women and marvel at their beauty, the lines of their bodies, the perfection of their appearance. But if, while the archaeologist marvels at his discovery, a tiny ant should begin to crawl across the face of the stone beauty, this ant would see something entirely different from the loveliness which thrilled the scientist. The ant would simply crawl along the stone, from crevice to crevice, from valley to valley, from mountain to mountain. The same would happen if the beautiful woman were not inanimate stone but were walking down Fifth Avenue in the flesh. A man, startled by the beauty of this woman, might stop in the street to admire her; a mosquito crawling down her cheek at this moment, would see hills of face-powder; to the insect this cheek would be the red desert of Arizona, and if by chance it should crawl into her nostril, the insect would feel as if it had fallen into the crater of a live volcano.

This lyrical introduction seeks to show that in order to appreciate beauty we must measure up to it and that everything in this world is relative.

There is a strange land where miracles happen. In this land there are at the same time icy blizzards and burning sandstorms; deserts lie next to oceans; winter and summer, spring and fall flourish simultaneously; arctic and tropical regions lie side by side. In this strange land English, French, African, German and American villages and cities stand next to each other and in the streets of the villages and cities peoples of all races and classes walk about in costumes for every season of the year. Next to a duke walks a Negro, next to a naked Indian walks a man in a fur coat; a Hindu in loin cloth talks to an American aviator.

This strange land is called Hollywood. Behind the high walls of the Hollywood film lots (the walls are carefully guarded—"industrial secrets") there are certain houses that look like barracks. Inside there are long corridors on each side of which are small rooms which look like solitary confinement cells in a prison. Each of these cells contains a chair, a table, another chair, a typewriter, and a telephone—and nothing else. In these cells, from nine in the morning until five in the evening, there sit people who do nothing; their legs are propped on the table or the window sill or slung over the back of the second chair. Sometimes several of these people get together and talk. These people with their legs in the air are writers working for the film companies of Hollywood.

The writers are collected from various parts of the country. Somewhere a young man or young woman has written a book, which has attracted attention; this young writer received a telegram: "you are to live and work in Hollywood for so many dollars for so many years, handing over all your writings to such and such a firm." Indeed, Hollywood is the land of unlimited possibilities, the firm argues; the young writer shows some talent; perhaps he will amount to something some day; it is better to buy him now than to pay him three times as much later; and it is better if he works for us rather than for our competitors.

But these writers are not invited to studios to write, to create. Each firm has its own writers and "creators" in addition to the writers in the solitary confinement cells.

A film may be born thus: special readers in the employ of a movie company read the new novels and plays and recommend those which they think are suitable for filming. Summaries of these novels and plays eventually reach the supervisors who have the power to say "O.K.!" and to set the wheels of the movie firm in motion. What appears on the screen bears only the remotest resemblance to the original novel or play.

There is another way in which a film may be born: special inventors on the staff of the film company patch together various ideas; they invent the scenes that are to appear on the screen; they describe the milieu of the action, the country and period in which it takes place; they specify what the villain shall be like. The hero and heroine, of course, are always the same; everybody knows them; they are never more than 25 years old.

These inventors convey their ideas directly to the supervisor. When a theme has been approved they begin co write the story, the treatment, the scenario and to prepare for the actual filming. Sometimes advisers are called in from the outside. Suppose a writer is familiar with the life of sailors at sea. He is asked to read certain books, to write out suggestions for improving the scenario. Fear of competing film companies surrounds the whole procedure with an almost childlike secrecy. The tentative drafts of the story are slugged with mysterious titles which are changed as frequently as the secret code of conspirators. The writer called in for advice writes. Will his name appear on the screen? Not necessarily. His suggestions or his story will be corrected by the supervisor and the director. The corrected script will go to a highly-paid well-advertised staff writer whose name has the weight of a trademark. It is this name which will appear on the screen; it will be the name of an "expert" who will take some one else's knowledge of life at sea and pour it into the standard Hollywood mould. Other experts will do the treatment, the dialogue. Thus the final product is the work of many minds, while the screen carries the name of one writer who, in some cases, may have contributed nothing but the advertising value of his name.

Editors Note:—*This year the interest in the Soviet Union is colossal. Suddenly too, the American literary world discovered Boris Pilnyak. It swept him into a Ufe he had never seen: literary teas, mass interviews, photographs, the publicity racket, Hollywood. Otto Kahn offers to introduce him to Al Capone. A movie magnate tries to tell him what is going on in the Soviet Union. Pilnyak, talented Soviet writer was a great success here. If he enjoyed it at all, he owes it to the Soviet workers: for the revolution which gave him something to say, and for the success of the Five Year Plan which made America willing to hear what he had to say. Before leaving the United States, Pilnyak left behind him the following paper containing some impressions of his stay here.*

Who is the real boss of the movies? Is it the general manager? the supervisor? the director? the stockholder? The movies are an industry, an extraordinary financial organization. Every night in the week Americans pay a voluntary tax to this industry. If you ask the captains of this industry, they will tell you that the real boss of the screen is the average

American, the hero of Sinclair Lewis' Main Street. When the supervisor puts his O.K. on a story he often professes to despise the script but excuses himself on the ground that he is compelled, for the sake of the profits which the stockholder demands, to cater to the mythical taste of the "average American."

What is interesting here, however, is not so much the technique of the film industry as other questions which it affects: art, the role of the writer, individualism. Art is creative only when it produces new forms, new ideas, new emotions: when it awakens, not when it stupefies. In order to create, a writer must believe in his work, he must believe in its necessity, in its significance. This, of course, is much more important than money. Recall how many products of genius have been turned out in garrets and in hunger. The writer must be individual and free in his work—and America is proud of its individualism ...

The writer of this article has had his taste of the movies. One day this spring I received a telegram:—so much money, so much work, to act as adviser on a Russian film; leave New York for Hollywood on such and such a date. I agreed, but although I spent a number of weeks in Hollywood, and participated in a dozen conferences, and made a number of speeches, and re-wrote other peoples scripts, I did not succeed in being an adviser on the Russian film, in the sense that my advice had little effect. I then began to understand why nearly all the writers I met in Hollywood were ironical about the film industry.

When I arrived in Hollywood I was handed the script of a Russian story. The theme, the characters, the situations were invented on the lot by people who knew nothing about Soviet Russia. I was asked (in my capacity as adviser) whether certain situations on which the entire action of the film hinged could possibly happen in contemporary Russia. I replied that such situations could not possibly happen. I was told: that is too bad, but we must somehow think up of ways and means to make these situations plausible on the screen because they would appeal to American spectators. Life in the Soviet Union was so falsified to fit a preconceived formula as to what constitutes an exciting movie. I replied: of course, it is possible to show on the screen an orange grove blooming in Greenland, but then Greenland would no longer be Greenland. Besides, I said, what was the use of paying me for advice on a Russian film if my knowledge of conditions in my country was disregarded for the sake of the alleged expectations of American movie fans? I did not know at that time that one movie firm had already produced a "Russian" film in which Siberia was decorated with eucalyptus trees...

My advice was not very useful and the film is being produced without my participation.

In spite of the prevalence of prohibition and the absence of bootleggers, Americans, by some miracle, manage to drink no less than other peoples; and writers, even when they work in monastic cells, are writers nevertheless and there is something fatal in their destiny. During a farewell party on my last night in Hollywood, a young movie writer said to me during a discussion of American individualism:

"I'll tell you about individualism: all day I sit in my cell in the writers barracks and write precisely those things which I repudiate at night when I write my novels. At home I have only a sheet of paper, a typewriter and a head which the day's work has exhausted; while the film industry has a tremendous organization, machinery, millions of dollars, and claims to have 24,000,-000 fans. My individualism butts its head in vain against this vast machine, but I must say Hollywood pays me good money and that settles the matter."

It was this aspect of American "individualism" which I saw in Hollywood...

From Hollywood I travelled to New York in a Ford. I went through quiet states, Oklahoma, Texas, Louisiana. The sun was burning, the roads were deserted. Once we approached the little town of G... on the border of Texas and Oklahoma and I beheld the incredible. Traffic was as thick as in New York. It was impossible to walk or ride through it. The cars carried license plates from many states, some even from Canada. Trucks, Packards, Fords, Chryslers, Chevrolets, Buicks were crawling, bounding, flying along the road between the towns of G... and L...

We had come across an oil rush. Whether there was really any oil there I do not know, but oil stock was already being sold, land was being bought from Negro farmers and offered at higher prices. Who knows, today you pay a dollar for a square foot of land, tomorrow it may be worth a hundred (or you may lose your investment!)

And so the automobiles were flying along the roads to buy, sell and organize; they were jammed with people anxious to become millionaires over night. Everybody was in a hurry; everybody was afraid he might be too late; everybody was bluffing everybody else.

The anxious passengers in the automobiles could see the wells which had already been sunk, the shafts rising to the hot blue sky; they could see the engineers drilling. Houses and shacks were being built rapidly along the road; trucks were rushing supplies to the new town that was to rise over night. Negroes were offering their land for sale in the streets, and some of them, with their derbies pushed back over sweating foreheads, were peddling stock to the occupants of the automobiles dreaming of millions. The grass in the fields of Negro farmers was crushed under the rubber tires of the cars. In one place workers were setting up a merry-go-round, a shooting gallery, and the other trappings of an amusement park. Bootleggers and prostitutes were plying their trades briskly. The earth was opened for gaspipes and electric wires. Men—rich and poor alike—too much in a hurry to wait for the wooden houses to be built had already set up tents in which they had settled for the time being with their wives and children.

The automobiles kept coming, jammed with people who came to make their pile. The oil town was sweltering in the early summer heat of Texas. From various tents came the shrill voice of the radio. Some of the incoming speculators had sold all their belongings back home. They had staked all their possessions in the world on this oil rush; perhaps they would come out of it penniless, perhaps rich.

They came in a terrible hurry to make money, these individualists ...

A hundred miles beyond L ... we again rode past the silence of Negro fields, Negro poverty, Negro toil.

... From ancient ruins archaeologists sometime unearth primitive stone images of women and marvel at their beauty; but if an ant should begin to crawl across the face of the stone beauty, it would see something entirely different from the loveliness which thrills the scientist; it would simply crawl along a vast expanse of stone, from crevice to crevice, from valley to valley, from mountain to mountain. From the tower of the Empire State Building one sees New York, a beautiful, striking, indescribable city, the only one of its kind in the world, extraordinary in its architecture, overwhelming in its power. To a European looking down at this city, it seems more of a dream than a reality—a dream which cannot be compared with anything except perhaps the fragment of a memory of a childhood fantasy about the biblical city of Babylon. But this mythical Babylon of childhood imagination none of us has ever seen, while here from the roof of a skyscraper we see below us in the world of reality an inhuman city, monstrous, overwhelming and beautiful.

A man standing in the tower of the Empire State is on a level with the beauty, the unique grandeur of New York. But when he walks along the streets (or rides in an automobile, it makes no difference) New York is a terrible city, the most terrible city in the world, whether one looks at it from Park Avenue or the Bowery; a city which inhales not air but gasoline; whose streets are barren, without grass or trees; a city that looms up towards the sky like an enormous smoke stack.

It is impossible for a man to live here, just as it is impossible to ride along the streets of the city in an automobile. Streets of this city are filled with the greatest number of the world's automobiles riding on top of each other.

The man who, figuratively, stands on top of the skyscraper and looks down on the metropolis where he enjoys wealth and power may indeed feel the grandeur of that individualism, of which one hears so much and which for him, at any rate, must have some meaning; but in this world, where everything is relative, what a different picture the metropolis must present to the millions of ants who crawl from crevice to crevice along its stone body.

1919 :: TWO PORTRAITS

John Dos Passos

House of Morgan

I commit my soul into the hands of my saviour, wrote John Pierpont Morgan in his will, *in full confidence that having redeemed it and washed it in his most precious bloody He will present it faultless before my heavenly father, and I intreat my children to maintain and defend at all hazards and at any cost of personal sacrifice the blessed doctrine of complete atonement for sin through the blood of Jesus Christ once offered and through that alone.*

and into the hands of the house of Morgan represented by his son

he committed

when he died in Rome in 1913

the control of the Morgan interests in New York, Paris and London, four national banks, three trust companies, three life insurance companies, ten railroad systems, three street railway companies, an express company, the International Mercantile Marine,

power,

on the cantilever principle, through interlocking directorates

over eighteen other railroads, U. S. Steel, General Electric, American Tel. and Tel, five major industries;

the interwoven cables of the Morgan Stillman Baker combination held credit up like a suspension bridge, thirteen percent of the banking resources of the world.

The first Morgan to make a pool was Joseph Morgan, a hotelkeeper in Hartford Connecticut who organized stagecoach lines and bought up

Aetna Life Insurance stock in a time of panic caused by one of the big
New York fires in the 1830;

his son Junius followed in his footsteps, first in the dry-goods business, and then as partner to George Peabody, a Massachusetts banker
who built up an enormous underwriting and mercantile business in
London and became a friend of Queen Victoria;

Junius married the daughter of John Pierpont, a Boston preacher,
poet, eccentric, and abolitionist; and their eldest son,

John Pierpont Morgan

arrived in New York to make his fortune

after being trained in England, going to school at Vevey, proving
himself a crack mathematician at the University of Gottingen,

a lanky morose young man of twenty,
just in time for the panic of '57.
(war and panics on the stock exchange, good growing weather
for the House of Morgan)

When the guns started booming at Fort Sumpter, young Morgan
turned some money over reselling condemned muskets to the U. S. army
and began to make himself felt in the gold room in downtown New York;
there was more in trading in gold than in trading in muskets; so much
for the Civil War.

During the Franco-Russian war Junius Morgan floated a huge bond
issue for the French government at Tours.

At the same time young Morgan was fighting Jay Cooke and the
German-Jew bankers in Frankfort over the funding of the American war
debt (he never did like the Germans or the Jews).

The panic of '75 ruined Jay Cooke and made J. Pierpont Morgan
the boss croupier of Wall Street; he united with the Philadelphia
Drexels and built the Drexel building where for thirty years he sat
in his glassed-in office, red-faced and insolent, writing at his desk,
smoking great black cigars, or, if important issues were involved,
playing solitaire in his inner office; he was famous for his few words.
Yes, or No, and for his way of suddenly blowing up in a visitor's face

and for the special gesture of the arm that meant, *What do I get out of it?*

In '77 Junius Morgan retired; J. Pierpont got himself made a member of the board of directors of the New York Central railroad and launched the first *Corsair.* He liked yachting and to have pretty actresses call him Commodore.

He founded the Lying-in Hospital on Stuyvesant Square, and was fond of going into St. George's church and singing a hymn all alone in the afternoon quiet.

In the panic of '93. at no inconsiderable profit to himself Morgan saved the U. S. Treasury; gold was draining out, the country was ruined, the farmers were howling for a silver standard, Grover Cleveland and his cabinet were walking up and down in the blue room at the White House without being able to come to a decision, in Congress they were making speeches while the gold reserves melted in the Subtreasuries; poor people were starving; Coxey's army was marching to Washington; for a long time Grover Cleveland couldn't bring himself to call in the representative of the Wall Street money masters; Morgan sat in his suite at the Arlington smoking cigars and quietly playing solitaire until at last the president sent for him;

he had a plan all ready for stopping the gold hemorrhage.

After that what Morgan said went; when Carnegie sold out he built the Steel Trust.

J. Pierpont Morgan was a bullnecked irascible man with small black magpie's eyes and a growth on his nose; he let his partners work themselves to death over the detailed routine of banking, and sat in his back office smoking black cigars; when there was something to be decided he said Yes or No or just turned his back and went back to his solitaire.

Every Christmas his librarian read him Dickens' *A Christmas Carol* from the original manuscript.

He was fond of canary birds and pekinese dogs and liked to take pretty actresses yachting. Each *Corsair* was a finer vessel than the last.

When he dined with King Edward he sat at His Majesty's right; he ate with the Kaiser tete a tete; he liked talking to cardinals or the pope, and never missed a conference of Episcopal bishops,

Rome was his favorite city.

He liked choice cookery and old wines and pretty women and yachting, and going over his collections, now and then picking up a jewelled snuffbox and staring at it with his magpie's eyes.

He made a collection of the autographs of the rulers of France, owned glass cases full of Babylonian tablets, seals, signets, statuettes, busts,

Gallo-Roman bronzes,

Merovingian jewels, miniatures, watches, tapestries, porcelains, cuneiform inscriptions, paintings by all the old masters, Dutch, Italian, Flemish, Spanish,

manuscripts of the gospels and the Apocalypse,

a collection of the works of Jean-Jacques Rousseau,

and the letters of Pliny the Younger.

His collectors bought anything that was expensive or rare or had the glint of empire on it, and he had it brought to him and stared back at it with his magpie's eyes. Then it was put in a glass case.

The last year of his life he went up the Nile on a dahabiyeh and spent a long time staring at the great columns of the Temple of Karnak.

The panic of 1907 and the death of Harriman, his great opponent in railroad financing, in 1909, had left him the undisputed ruler of Wall Street, most powerful private citizen in the world:

an old man tired of the purple, suffering from gout, he had deigned to go to Washington to answer the questions of the Pujo Committee during the Money Trust investigation: *Yes, I did what seemed to me to be for the best interests of the country.*

Wars and panics on the stock exchangé

Machine gunfire and arson

Starvation, lice, cholera and typhus:

Good growing weather for the House of Morgan.

Randolph Bourne

Randolph Bourne

came as an inhabitant of this earth without the pleasure of choosing his dwelling or his career.

He was a hunchback, one of a family of hunchbacks, grandson of a congregational minister, born in 1886 in Bloomfield, New Jersey; there

he attended grammar-school and highschool and at the age of seventeen
went to work as secretary to a Morristown businessman.

He worked his way through Columbia
working in a pianola record factory in Newark
working as proofreader
pianotuner
accompanist in a vocal studio in Carnegie Hall.
At Columbia he studied with John Dewey
got a travelling fellowship that took him to England
Paris Rome Berlin Copenhagen,
wrote a book on the Gary schools.
In Europe he heard music, a great deal of Wagner and Scriabine
and bought himself a black cape.
This little sparrowlike man
tiny twisted bit of flesh in a black cape
always in pain and ailing
put a pebble in his sling
and hit Goliath square in the forehead with it.
War, he wrote, *is the health of the state.*

Half musician half educational theorist (weak health and being
poor and twisted in body and on bad terms with his people hadn't
spoiled the world for Randolph Bourne; he was a happy man, loved *die
Meistersinger* and playing Bach with his long hands that stretched so
easily over the keys and pretty girls and good food and evenings of talk.
When he was dying of pneumonia a friend brought him an eggnog;
Look at the yellow, it's beautiful, he kept saying as his life ebbed into
delirium and fever. He was a happy man) Bourne seized with feverish intensity on the ideas then going around at Columbia, he picked
rosy glasses out of the turgid jumble of John Dewey's teaching through
which he saw clear and sharp

the shining capitol of reformed democracy
Wilson's New Freedom;
but he was too good a mathematician;
he had to work the equations out
with the result

that in the crazy spring of 1917 he began to get unpopular where his bread was buttered at the *New Republic;*

for New Freedom read Conscription, for Democracy, Win the War, for Reform safeguard the Morgan loans

for Progress Civilization Education Service

Buy a liberty bond

Straff the Hun

Jail the objectors.

He resigned from the *New Republic;* only the *Seven Arts* had the nerve to publish his articles against the war the backers of the *Seven Arts* took their money elsewhere; friends didn't like to be seen with Bourne, his father wrote him begging him not to disgrace the family name. The rainbowtinted future of reformed democracy went pop like a pricked soapbubble.

The liberals hurried to Washington;

some of his friends plead with him to climb up on Schoolmaster Wilson's sharabang; the war was great fought from the swivel chairs of Mr. Creel's bureau in Washington

he was cartooned, shadowed by the espionage service and the counter-espionage service; taking a walk with two girlfriends at Wood's Hole he was arrested, a trunk full of manuscript and letters was stolen from him in Connecticut (Force to the utmost, thundered Schoolmaster Wilson).

He didn't live to see the big circus of the Peace of Versailles or the purple Normalcy of the Ohio gang.

Six weeks after the armistice he died planning an essay on the Negroes and the industrial workers as foundations of future radicalism in America.

If any man has a ghost

Bourne has a ghost

a tiny twisted unscared ghost in a black cloak

hopping along the grimy old brick and brownstone streets

still left in downtown New York, crying out in a shrill soundless giggle:

War is the health of the state.

DEATH OF THE COMMUNISTS :: A STORY

WHITTAKER CHAMBERS

The Communists were introduced into the jail shortly after Thanksgiving, in the evening. Naturally, gentlemen, the clang of a metallic door, closing behind our backs (it reverberates, no matter how deadened) cannot be expected to have the same value to your ears as the even more guarded sound of the door someone throws open for you. But while, in prison, our aural discriminations are also effected for, and not by, us, we become more than commonly acute to the selected sounds that mark the wastes of silence. Therefore, I hastened to peer through the bars.

Perhaps I should interrupt myself at once and ask indulgence if I offend by the nature of what I am recounting. But I recall the wasps that used to build under my high window in summer, and how they drew their sustenance even from the bodies of base and unformed larva, which they know to numb, but do not kill until they are quite drained of life, and which contrasted with the irresistible and attenuated beauty of the banqueters, seem designed to no higher end than to perpetuate its pitilessness. May I ask you gentlemen to go to the wasp? To hold in abeyance your natural repugnance to the subject until we have drained it of its last possible drop of interest. Then—the coup de grace. But for the moment let your minds enter, like those fierce and efficient insects, into the cell of which they were the voluntary, as I the involuntary, inmates.

That is how I came to see the Communists. Not distinctly, to be sure, since the cell I occupied was in the upper tier, and they were marched too close to the cages below for me to distinguish more than that they were five, a woman and four men.

If the presence of the woman surprised me, it aroused the inmates who began to shout obscenities, and apparently to reach out to touch her, for I heard a blow delivered by a guard, and a howl of pain as an arm was retracted. Then, gentlemen, the outbreak was terminated by what I believed, and what doubtless you, too, will agree was the absurdest spectacle I had, until then, been called upon to witness. Spontaneously, as if a button had been pressed by the striking of the blow the five began to sing a, to my ears (though I make no pretense to musical appreciation) atrociously rattle-trap tune, in voices, with the exception of one man's, as painful as the song. The words, repeated to me later by a convict, were:

> *Arise, ye prisoners of starvation,*
> *Arise, ye wretched of the earth,*
> *For justice thunders condemnation;*
> *A better world's in birth.*

And so on to the end. Laughable, though I would not in any case have laughed (for the brutality of the guards was extreme, for a less justifiable reason I am afraid, than an injured esthetic), had not one of the most uncouthly villainous of the convicts, in the cell opposite, a face from which one might have expected any atrocity, observed with the utmost awe in the silence following the song—"Political prisoners!" The quasi-technical term, pronounced in that strained tone by that unspeakably debased mouth, enabled me, as you gentlemen will readily understand, to do what I did for the first time, I believe, since entering the jail—laugh out loud. But becoming instantly aware that my laughter was the sole sound among the cells, I suffered a twinge of my old fear of lunacy, always a companion with me there.

It was not until the guards had left the newcomers alone that the silence was broken by a series of questions and answers, which I will try to repeat, but for whose sequence and accuracy I cannot vouch.

Who are you?

Communists.

Why are you here?

For organizing soldiers in the fort.

Why do you want to organize soldiers?

The soldiers are workingmen in uniform. We are trying to organize them to better their conditions, and to oppose the timing war, which the capitalist class, from which come the officers, is planning to wage to destroy the Soviet Union where the working class rules. Millions more men will be killed in that war than in 1914.

Yes, another Communist voice resumed, in their terror the capitalists will even take you out of the jails, will put a new kind of uniform on you, will drill you, will give you guns and promise you that when you have destroyed the power of the working class for them they will set you free. But you have learned from your lives, or you would not be here, what they will do for you. You will know which way to turn your guns.

I am quite certain that I am not misquoting, gentlemen, for I remember that a considerable silence followed.

Then they were asked why the military authorities had not put them in the military prison.

They answered that at first they had, but later transferred them to this civil prison. They did not understand why, but thought it peculiar that the woman was left with them in a men's jail, and they were afraid for her.

At this point the woman joined the conversation, saying the their fears, like all fear, (the comparison, gentlemen is hers) were foolish, and that the explanation was quite simple. The authorities, not knowing the extent of the Communists' activities, and connections, were terrified into believing that, even incommunicado, they would find means of corrupting the soldiers, for a democratic government lives in fear of nothing so much as that its soldiers may begin to think. No woman's prison was at hand, so they had put her here pending a decision.

It took just a week gentlemen, for us to learn how totally inadequate are such minds in the apprehension of motive.

During those seven alternations of light, signifying so little to me, and hardly more to them, perhaps, I had occasion to make further, though slight, observations upon these persons from a world so different from ours, which, momentarily, nevertheless, had impinged upon my own. And yet not by chance, it seems to me Peter Thompson would maintain but as the result of a chain of causation implicit in the nature of society itself—if you will pardon the divagation.

I learned that the woman's name was Anna Lot, that the man who seemed to enjoy the most authority among them was the Peter Thompson I alluded to, and that there was one named Kubelik. The names of the other two I did not learn: they never spoke.

Gentlemen, I found astounding the directness with which, without any preliminaries, Mr. Thompson, as their spokesman, went to work to expound their doctrine to the prisoners, entirely oblivious, apparently, of any misgiving that he might not be understood. Amazing, too, was the rote of this mind, obviously untutored in any academic sense, whereby it was enabled to deliver itself of quotation after quotation from their most unquestioned pundits. But if I was nauseated at first, it was only to be astounded again by the simplicity with which the speaker, suddenly, in his own words, made tangible, made plausible, to those convicts the steps in an analysis of larceny, not as a consequence of individual viciousness, but as the result of the structure and pressure of a society in which some possess, but most do not. He made the convicts understand (I tell you gentlemen, they understood) their position, not only as individuals, but as part of a social whole, of a social process, in the light of a universal philosophic theory. You will pardon me, gentlemen, if I, too, join in your smile, for so plausible indeed did he become that I had to take myself in hand and recall that I was listening to an experienced agitator, whose substance I might dismiss, the better to free my mind for the enjoyment of an art so unfamiliar to me.

But it was from the uncommon persuasiveness the convincing speciousness of the Communist, Kubelik, apparently a little man, much less fluent than Thompson, that I became conscious of a feeling which has little to do with reason, gentlemen, and which I cite only because, to the convicts, his labored phrases seemed to strike like blows against their bars. I recall but one instance. He spoke once of his doctrine's having been invited by no one, but as a method, disclosing the reality of things. You have seen gravestones, he told their listening ears (their eyes could not see him) on which the words have been obscured by moss and dirt so that you could not read them. Well you are caged in by stones whose meaning you cannot read, though you feel its injustice. Communism is the emery that clears away the dirt and moss and lets you see the meaning of the stone imprisoning you, a meaning that is underlined with bars of steel. It was not, of course, delivered as I tell you, gentlemen, but, perhaps, even more simply, if haltingly.

I said that Kubelik was *apparently* a little man, for during the week that the Communists were among us, we never caught more than a glimpse of them: they were segregated, permitted, as far as I know, no recreation, and fed in their cells.

But on that seventh day, noticing a visible agitation among the prisoners, I inquired during the recreation period, and discovered a story going the rounds that our Communists had been held in jail only until the soldiers could be roused to violence against them. That was why the woman had been kept with them, since they wished to dispatch all together as a warning. The officers had by now succeeded in inciting the soldiers, the Communists were to be taken from their cells that night and shot under the walls.

The best-intentioned of us cannot always, as you gentlemen know, repress a smile at the obviously ingenuous, but I merely mentioned the thickness of the walls and the stoutness of steel and stones. My informants replied that the prison authorities would take care of that. Then, gentlemen I *did* smile. I asked, however, what the Communists thought about it, and was informed that they had not been told, no one in the prison possessing the requisite cruelty to warn them. Again, gentlemen, it was hard to restrain a smile: the jail harbored some of the most vicious eliminations of the social body.

But toward nightfall, the convicts must, after long cogitation, have concluded cruelty to be the better part of valor, for I suddenly heard Peter Thompson say aloud, "Comrade Lot, they are going to take us out tonight and shoot us. That is why they kept us together." From the completeness of the silence, it seemed to me that two hundred listening ears had closed upon his words, and it was in the same silence that she answered, "I knew it from the first."

It is difficult for me, at this distance, to convey to you gentlemen, or to explain, the force impelling me to break that silence of listening men, to join for the first time in a conversation in that jail, surprising myself by an interest, which must necessarily seem curious to you in these, after all, most remote people.

"Perhaps it is not true," I ventured.

The growl that issued from that murderous beast in the cell opposite, called my attention to the fist he was shaking at me for silence.

"It is true," the Communist answered. "Democracy is the most perfect form of government for capitalism because it offers the most perfect illusion of freedom. The democratic guarantees, freedom of the ballot, freedom of speech, freedom of the press and of assembly, are guarantees to nobody but the capitalist and his followers. Freedom to bargain for his job has never meant anything to the workingman but freedom to starve. But democracy is not something that cannot be overstepped. Democracy is a stage in the course of the development from capitalism to Communism. Now Democracy is going to kill us. That means it is afraid of us. That is good."

Of course, of course, you are right—obsession. But those are the only words we had occasion to exchange.

I do not believe, gentlemen, that all the men, who lay silent in their bunks, were asleep, nor can anyone longer tell how the Communists passed the remaining hours. But toward midnight, we heard a disturbance in the outer corridor. The soldiers, with two officers, passed between the cells in an entirely orderly fashion. They carried the keys, and there was no difficulty in removing the Communists, for though the latter attempted briefly to reason with the soldiers against their officers, the futility of the procedure seemed, from certain sounds, to be brought home rather urgently to them.

Then, gentlemen, will you believe it, they began again that absurd song. If I thought it ridiculous before, it seemed doubly so now, for they were in evident pain, and must have realized as vividly as did we that they were being marched to their deaths.

> Arise, ye prisoners of starvation,
> Arise, ye wretched of the earth,
> For justice thunders condemnation;
> A better world's in birth.

My fellow prisoners cowered in their bunks, feeling, I am sure, as did I, that our citadel invaded, we ourselves were none too safe. But I, having the least to fear, stepped to the bars, and was rewarded by my only glimpse of the five. Thompson, a lean, lined face, sallow, singing, head up. The one I took to be Kubelik, short, swart and stocky. The others nondescript. Except the woman. I am most partial as you gentlemen know, to attractive women, and she was, unfortunately, positively hideous. But, mercifully, she walked with her head bent, for the soldier holding her arm behind her back, had drawn it up between her shoulder blades. And, mercifully, too, they shut off the lights at that moment, an oversight or an afterthought in the excitement.

The prisoners continued to lie, if anything, more quietly in their bunks. But presently the howling assailed them from another side, this time from below the windows, grew louder, for the effectiveness of this execution as a threat, was postulated you may remember, upon its performance against the very walls of the jail. "The law's delay" for once strikingly amended by civistic promptitude. It did not, however, take place under my window, but one a little farther down, so that my ears were spared the full force of their incongruous and ceaseless singing whenever, for a moment, the shouting of the others abated.

The sudden crackle of shots I thought would end it. But, no. One voice hesitated and went on. I think it was Peter Thompson's, although because of the shattering effect of that first volley on the nerves, the dark, the tenseness of the silence in the cells, and an unnatural whining tone, which suggests that he may have been wounded, I am unable to substantiate the fact.

Tis the final conflict, let each stand in his place:
The international soviet shall be the human rrrrrrrrrr

The initial r of the word "race," which, I am given to understand is the word that the single rifle shot checked in our Communist's throat, was prolonged appropriately into a death rattle.

That is how they died, gentlemen. And to tell the truth, I had a feeling, singularly light and unsorrowful, that their deaths made no essential difference to themselves, to what they were effecting, or to that for which they stood. Indeed, I felt as I have felt only once before in my life, when I was lying on my back in a small boat, with a cool wind, but a hot sun, playing on my body, and a swell and a strong tide carrying me along with no effort on my part.

Their deaths were not horrifying. What horrified, what appalled me was, that after a brief interregnum of silence, following the end of the song, it was suddenly taken up by a lone voice in the cells which, when it had sung a bar or two, was joined by others. Ignorant alike of the words and tune, the men, who may have heard the *International* twice in all their lives, since the Communists were in the jail, began in a moaning monotone, and with voices whose rusty huskiness suggested that they could not have sung for years, barbarously to mutilate what, as I have already said, is, at best, not a good song.

> *Arise ye prisoners of starvation.*
> *Arise, ye wretched of the earth ...*

And, of course, reacting blindly, and unfamiliar with what they were attempting to sing, broke off, unfinished. After which a really deep and appropriate silence ensued.

No, gentlemen, I could not feel sorrowful at the death of the Communists. It was not the shooting, it was the outburst in the cells that was hideous. The Communists were obviously men of courage, single-minded no doubt, but capable of a kind of fanatical calm in the face of death, on the basis, however difficult for one of us to comprehend, of certain convictions arrived at by means of an intelligence no matter how limited. Were possessed, I mean to say, of intelligence, conviction, courage. Were, therefore, men, gentlemen, men. Men! Men, do your hear me, you beasts, men!

WOMEN ON THE BREADLINES

MERIDEL LESUEUR

I am sitting in the city free employment bureau. It's the woman's section. We have been sitting here now for four hours. We sit here every day, waiting for a job. There are no jobs. Most of us have had no breakfast. Some have had scant rations for over a year. Hunger makes a human being lapse into a state of lethargy, especially city hunger. Is there any place else in the world where a human being is supposed to go hungry amidst plenty without an outcry, without protest, where only the boldest steal or kill for bread, and the timid crawl the streets, hunger like the beak of a terrible bird at the vitals?

We sit looking at the floor. No one dares think of the coming winter. There are only a few more days of summer. Everyone is anxious to get work to lay up something for that long siege of bitter cold. But there is no work. Sitting in the room we all know it. That is why we don't talk much. We look at the floor dreading to see that knowledge in each other's eyes. There is a kind of humiliation in it. We look away from each other. We look at the floor. Its too terrible to see this animal terror in each other's eyes.

So we sit hour after hour, day after day, waiting for a job to come in. There are many women for a single job. A thin sharp woman sits inside the wire cage looking at a book. For four hours we have watched her looking at that book. She has a hard little eye. In the small bare room there are half a dozen women sitting on the benches waiting. Many come and go. Our faces are all familiar to each other, for we wait here everyday.

This is a domestic employment bureau. Most of the women who come here are middle aged, some have families, some have raised their families and are now alone, some have men who are out of work. Hard times and the man leaves to hunt for work. He doesn't find it. He drifts on. The woman probably doesn't hear from him for a long time. She expects it. She isn't surprised. She struggles alone to feed the many mouths. Sometimes she gets help from the charities. If she's clever she can get herself a good living from the charities, if she's naturally a lick spittle, naturally a little docile and cunning. If she's proud then she starves silently, leaving her children to find work, coming home after a day's searching to wrestle with her house, her children.

Some such story is written on the faces of all these women. There are young girls too, fresh from the country. Some are made brazen too soon by the city. There is a great exodus of girls from the farms into the city now. Thousands of farms have been vacated completely in Minnesota. The girls are trying to get work. The prettier ones can get jobs in the stores when there are any, or waiting on table but these jobs are only for the attractive and the adroit, the others, the real peasants have a more difficult time.

Bernice sits next me. She is a large Polish woman of thirty-five. She has been working in peoples' kitchens for fifteen years or more. She is large, her great body in mounds, her face brightly scrubbed. She has a peasant mind and finds it hard even yet to understand the maze of the city where trickery is worth more than brawn. Her blue eyes are not clever but slow and trusting. She suffers from loneliness and lack of talk. When you speak to her her face lifts and brightens as if you had spoken through a great darkness and she talks magically of little things, as if the weather were magic or tells some crazy tale of her adventures on the city streets, embellishing them in bright colors until they hang heavy and thick like some peasant embroidery. She loves the city anyhow. Its exciting to her, like a bazaar. She loves to go shopping and get a bargain, hunting out the places where stale bread and cakes can be had for a few cents. She likes walking the streets looking for men to take her to a picture show. Sometimes she goes to five picture shows in one day, or she sits through one the entire day until she knows all the dialogue by heart.

She came to the city a young girl from a Wisconsin farm. The first thing that happened to her a charlatan dentist took out all her good shining teeth and the fifty dollars she had saved working in a canning factory.

After that she met men in the park who told her how to look out for herself, corrupting her peasant mind, teaching her to mistrust everyone. Sometimes now she forgets to mistrust everyone and gets taken in. They taught her to get what she could for nothing, to count her change, to go back if she found herself cheated, to demand her rights.

She lives alone in little rooms. She bought seven dollars worth of second hand furniture eight years ago. She rents a room for perhaps three dollars a month in an attic, sometimes in a cold house. Once the house where she stayed was condemned and everyone else moved out and she lived there all winter alone on the top floor. She spent only twenty five dollars all winter.

She wants to get married but she sees what happens to her married friends, being left with children to support, worn out before their time. So she stays single. She is virtuous. She is slightly deaf from hanging out clothes in winter. She has done peoples washings and cooking for fifteen years and in that time she saved thirty dollars. Now she hasn't worked steady for a year and she has spent the thirty dollars. She dreamed of having a little house or a house boat perhaps with a spot of ground for a few chickens. This dream she will never realize.

She has lost all her furniture now along with the dream. A married friend whose husband is gone gives her a bed for which she pays by doing a great deal of work for the woman. She comes here every day now sitting bewildered, her pudgy hands folded in her lap. She is hungry. Her great flesh has begun to hang in folds. She has been living on crackers. Sometimes a box of crackers lasts a week. She has a friend who's a baker and he sometimes steals the stale loaves and brings them to her.

A girl we have seen every day all summer went crazy yesterday at the Y. W. She went into hysterics, stamping her feet and screaming.

She hadn't had work for eight months. "You've got to give me something," she kept saying. The woman in charge flew into a rage that probably came from days and days of suffering on her part, because she is unable to give jobs, having none. She flew into a rage at the girl and there they were facing each other in a rage both helpless, helpless. This woman told me once that she could hardly bear the suffering she saw, hardly hear it, that she couldn't eat sometimes and had nightmares at night.

So they stood there the two women in a rage, the girl weeping and the woman shouting at her. In the eight months of unemployment she had gotten ragged, and the woman was shouting that she would not send her out like that. "Why don't you shine your shoes," she kept scolding the girl, and the girl kept sobbing and sobbing because she was starving

"We can't recommend you like that," the harassed Y.W.C.A. woman said, knowing she was starving, unable to do anything. And the girls and the women sat docilely their eyes on the ground, ashamed to look at each other, ashamed of something.

Sitting here waiting for a job, the women have been talking in low voices about the girl Ellen. They talk in low voices with not too much pity for her, unable to see through the mist of their own torment. "What happened to Ellen?" one of them asks. She knows the answer already. We all know it.

A young girl who went around with Ellen tells about seeing her last evening back of a cafe down town outside the kitchen door, kicking, showing her legs so that the cook came out and gave her some food and some men gathered in the alley and threw small coin on the ground for a look at her legs. And the girl says enviously that Ellen had a swell breakfast and treated her one too, that cost two dollars.

A scrub woman whose hips are bent forward from stooping with hands gnarled like water soaked branches clicks her tongue in disgust. No one saves their money, she says, a little money and these foolish young things buy a hat, a dollar for breakfast, a bright scarf. And they do. If you've ever been without money, or food, something very strange happens when you get a bit of money, a kind of madness. You don't care. You can't remember that you had no money before, that the money will be gone. You can remember nothing but that there is the money for which you have been suffering. Now here it is. A lust takes hold of you. You see food in the windows. In imagination you eat hugely; you taste a thousand meals. You look in windows. Colours are brighter; you buy something to dress up in. An excitement takes hold of you. You know it is suicide but you can't help it. You must have food, dainty, splendid food and a bright hat so once again you feel blithe, rid of that ratty gnawing shame.

"I guess she'll go on the street now," a thin woman says faintly and no one takes the trouble to comment further. Like every commodity now the body is difficult to sell and the girls say you're lucky if you get fifty cents.

It's very difficult and humiliating to sell one's body.

Perhaps it would make it clear if one were to imagine having to go out on the street to sell, say, ones overcoat. Suppose you have to sell your coat so you can have breakfast and a place to sleep, say, for fifty cents. You decide to sell your only coat. You take it off and put it on your arm. The street, that has before been just a street, now becomes a mart, something entirely different. You must approach someone now and admit you are destitute and are now selling your clothes, your most intimate posses- sions. Everyone will watch you talking to the stranger showing him your overcoat, what a good coat it is. People will stop and watch curiously. You will be quite naked on the street. It is even harder to try and sell ones self, more humiliating. It is even humiliating to try and sell ones labour. When there is no buyer.

The thin woman opens the wire cage. There's a job for a nursemaid, she says. The old gnarled women, like old horses, know that no one will have them walk the streets with the young so they don't move. Ellen's friend gets up and goes to the window. She is unbelievably jaunty. I know she hasn't had work since last January. But she has a flare of life in her that glows like a tiny red flame and some tenacious thing, perhaps only youth, keeps it burning bright. Her legs are thin but the runs in her old stockings are neatly mended clear down her flat shank. Two bright spots of rouge conceal her palor. A narrow belt is drawn tightly around her thin waist, her long shoulders stoop and the blades show. She runs wild as a colt hunting pleasure, hunting sustenance.

Its one of the great mysteries of the city where women go when they are out of work and hungry. There are not many women in the bread line. There are no flop houses for women as there are for men, where a bed can be had for a quarter or less. You don't see women lying on the floor at the mission in the free flops. They obviously don't sleep in the jungle or under newspapers in the park. There is no law I suppose against their being in these places but the fact is they rarely are.

Yet there must be as many women out of jobs in cities and suffering extreme poverty as there are men. What happens to them? Where do they go? Try to get into the Y.W. without any money or looking down at heel. Charities take care of very few and only those that are called "deserving." The lone girl is under suspicion by the virgin women who dispense charity.

I've lived in cities for many months broke, without help, too timid to get in bread lines. I've known many women to live like this until they simply faint on the street from privations, without saying a word to anyone. A woman will shut herself up in a room until it is taken away from her, and eat a cracker a day and be as quiet as a mouse so there are no social statistics concerning her.

I don't know why it is, but a woman will do this unless she has dependents, will go for weeks verging on starvation, crawling in some hole, going through the streets ashamed, sitting in libraries, parks, going for days without speaking to a living soul like some exiled beast, keeping the runs mended in her stockings, shut up in terror in her own misery, until she becomes too super sensitive and timid to even ask for a job.

Bernice says even strange men she has met in the park have sometimes, that is in better days, given her a loan to pay her room rent. She has always paid them back.

In the afternoon the young girls, to forget the hunger and the deathly torture and fear of being jobless, try and pick up a man to take them to a ten cent show. They never go to more expensive ones, but they can always find a man willing to spend a dime to have the company of a girl for the afternoon.

Sometimes a girl facing the night without shelter will approach a man for lodging. A woman always asks a man for help. Rarely another woman. I have known girls to sleep in mens rooms for the night, on a pallet without molestation, and given breakfast in the morning.

Its no wonder these young girls refuse to marry, refuse to rear children. They are like certain savage tribes, who, when they have been conquered refuse to breed.

Not one of them but looks forward to starvation, for the coming winter. We are in a jungle and know it. We are beaten, entrapped. There is no way out. Even if there were a job, even if that thin acrid woman came and gave everyone in the room a job for a few days, a few hours, at thirty cents an hour, this would all be repeated tomorrow, the next day and the next.

Not one of these women but knows, that despite years of labour there is only starvation, humiliation in front of them.

Mrs. Grey, sitting across from me is a living spokesman for the futility of labour. She is a warning. Her hands are scarred with labour. Her body is a great puckered scar. She has given birth to six children, buried three, supported them all alive and dead, bearing them, burying them, feeding them. Bred in hunger they have been spare, susceptible to disease. For seven years she tried to save her boy's arm from amputation, diseased from tuberculosis of the bone. It is almost too suffocating to think of that long close horror of years of child bearing, child feeding, rearing, with the bare suffering of providing a meal and shelter.

Now she is fifty. Her children, economically insecure, are drifters. She never hears of them. She doesn't know if they are alive. She doesn't know if she is alive. Such subtleties of suffering are not for her. For her the brutality of hunger and cold, the bare bone of life. That is enough. These will occupy a life. Not until these are done away with can those subtle feelings that make a human being be indulged.

She is lucky to have five dollars ahead of her. That is her security. She has a tumour that she will die of. She is thin as a worn dime with her tumour sticking out of her side. She is brittle and bitter. Her face is not the face of a human being. She has born more than it is possible for a human being to bear. She is reduced to the least possible denominator of human feelings.

It is terrible to see her little blood shot eyes like a beaten nound's, fearful in terror.

We cannot meet her eyes. When she looks at any of us we look away. She is like a woman drowning and we turn away. We must ignore those eyes that are surely the eyes of a person drowning, doomed. She doesn't cry out. She goes down decently. And we all look away.

The young ones know though. I don't want to marry. I don't want any children. So they all say. No children. No marriage. They arm themselves alone, keep up alone. The man is helpless now. He cannot provide. If he propagates he cannot take care of his young. The means are not in his hands. So they live alone. Get what fun they can. The life risk is too horrible now. Defeat is too clearly written on it.

So we sit in this room like cattle, waiting for a non existent job, willing to work to the farthest atom of energy, unable to work, unable to get food and lodging, unable to bear children; here we must sit in this shame looking at the floor, worse than beasts at a slaughter.

It is appalling to think that these women sitting so listless in the room may work as hard as it is possible for a human being to work, may labour night and day, like Mrs. Gray wash street cars from midnight to dawn and offices in the early evening, scrubbing for fourteen and fifteen hours a day, sleeping only five hours or so, doing this their whole lives, and never earn one day of security, having always before them the pit of the future. The endless labour, the bending back, the water soaked hands, earning never more than a weeks wages, never having in their hands more life than that.

Its not the suffering, not birth, death, love that the young reject, but the suffering of endless labour without dream, eating the spare bread in bitterness, a slave without the security of a slave.

* * *

Editorial Note: This presentation of the plight of the unemployed woman, able as it is, and informative, is defeatest in attitude, lacking in revolutionary spirit and direction which characterize the usual contribution to *New Masses*. We feel it our duty to add, that there is a place for the unemployed woman, as well as man, in the ranks of the unemployed councils and in all branches of the organized revolutionary movement. Fight for your class, read *The Working Woman*, join the Communist Party.

PILGRIMS OF CONFUSION

ROBERT EVANS

Two worlds alternate shall be his, and he
Shall be at home in neither . . . .
A pilgrim of confusion shall he be.

JOHN ERSKINE

D uring the past year American liberal literati have rapidly shifted their interest from poetry to politics, and liberal publicists from politics to economics. The weeklies and reviews which once devoted so much space to Joyce, Proust, Valery and the new psychology, now discuss currency problems, the Five-Year Plan, revolution and counter-revolution; and it is worth noting that often the authors of these political and economic articles are men who recently wrote lyrics in the new manner of the post-war decade and swam, with or without lifebelts, up and down the wild currents of the stream of consciousness.

The first to forecast this politicalization of literature in America were leftwing critics who in the midst of the "new era" based their analysis on communist predictions of the depression, from which they deduced radical changes in the thought of the intelligentsia. Then followed the Humanists, who in literary, moral, and psuedo-philosophic language urged the fascization of American culture. And now, in the third year of the depression, the "thirties" scoff at the "twenties" as the "twenties" scoffed at the mid-victorians, and poets, philosophers and publicists rush forward daily with plans and panaceas for saving "civilization".

But the liberal intellectual is a creature caught between two worlds, an old one, which his recent experience has taught him to distrust and a new one, which his class training prevents him from fully understanding. Consequently, he fears the one and despises the other, and is "at home in neither". At best he seeks, in the realm of "pure reason", to effect a merger of the two worlds, retaining the best features of both. As a devotee of "social science" and "detached information", he reads economic reports and sees the economic crisis growing more acute from week to week. The official and unofficial surveys for the past year are enough to shoot anybody out of the stream of consciousness on to terra ferma. In this country—as in other capitalist countries—all branches of industry, agriculture and trade continue to decline, despite the cheerful predictions of businessmen and politicians. Production and prices have been steadily sliding down, a financial crisis has set in. Twelve million workers are unemployed, and capitalist society does nothing, *can* do nothing about it. The agrarian crisis has reduced the net farm income more than 70 percent as compared with 1929 and the rural areas of this country face destitution.

America, once envied by Europe as the "land of unbounded possibilities" is passing through the severest crisis in its history, a crisis that speaks loudly and plainly in the language of economics. Consider these figures: During 1931 production in the most important basic industries declined at least fifty percent below the 1929 level. Automobile production in 1931 was estimated at 2,450,-000 cars as compared with 5,358,000 in 1929. Steel ingot production during the first 11 months of 1931 was 23,000,000 tons as compared with 51,000,000 during the corresponding period of 1929. Pig iron production declined steadily during the year, and construction was only 52 percent of the 1928 level. The national income for 1931 was 32 percent below that of 1929, wage payments were 22 billion dollars below 1929. During the year 17,000 retail stores went bankrupt because in this acute crisis the masses of the American people have had to cut down their purchases.

These are normal results of capitalism, planless in production, chaotic in distribution, corrupt with social oppression, rent by violent class conflicts. Nor is the crisis confined to one country. It weighs heavily upon the entire capitalist world, intensifying the consciousness of all classes, and centering all eyes upon that other world whose economic and social progress contrasts sharply with the surrounding decay. Where the lines on the capitalist charts and graphs run steadily downward, those of the Soviet Union run steadily upward. Soviet industrial production in 1930 increased 24 percent over that of 1929; in 1931 it increased 21 percent over 1930. The Soviet Union is the one country in the world which is free of the curse of unemployment. In marked contrast with other countries, the number of persons employed is rising from year to year.

This growth in a world of stagnation and decline is no accident. The steady rise in production, labor productivity, wages, consumption, living standards, and education, the improved working conditions, the shorter hours, the elaborate system of labor protection, the profound social and cultural revolution which affects 160, 000,000 people are the direct result of an organized society in which private ownership has ben abolished, and power is vested in the hands of the workers in alliance with the peasants.

Intellectuals in other countries, impressed by the successes of the Soviet Union, grasp at every possible straw. Only a few years ago the Soviet "experiment" was a wild dream, the slogan "to overtake and surpass the advanced capitalist countries" a joke among bourgeois savants; now they are seeking to "learn"; their slogan is "to overtake and surpass" the Soviet Union. But caught in the trap of bourgeois prejudices they can think of nothing better than "planning" as the solution for the capitalist crisis. There is hardly a publicist who has not produced a "plan" for salvaging capitalism. But the very purpose of these plans dooms them to sterility. They propose superficial reforms while retaining the basic productive relations of capitalism. Yet if these basic relations exist they inevitably carry with them crises, unemployment and wars, they intensify the class antagonisms that rend capitalist society asunder; they inevitably retain exploitation for profit, wage-slavery and poverty, the oppressive power of the capitalist state and the revolutionary struggle of the workers.

The liberal mind, caught between big business and the proletariat, flounders in the face of the crucial problems which confront our epoch. The same naive faith which appealed to the "honor" of Massachusetts in the Sacco-Vanzetti case and the "law" of Alabama in the Scottsboro case, now appeals to the "intelligence" and "experience" of big business to save the capitalist system by "planning" and by "foresight". That is the universal prayer of the intelligentsia in which are commingled the voices of its abstract philosophers, popular economists and lyric poets. The philosopher Alfred North Whitehead pleads for "foresight" as the only hope for (capitalist) civilization; Stuart Chase is ready with blue-prints which will guarantee eight percent to suburban investors; the poet Allan Tate issues a manifesto declaring that "so long as we lack political leadership in its proper place, we must take it where it can be found, and the men of letters are alone sufficiently disinterested, if they were only prepared, to undertake the task." Apart from the "disinterestedness" and "preparation" of the men of letters, it may safely be said that they are a group which creates little anxiety for the class that murders miners in Kentucky and lynches Negroes in Alabama. Nor is this class likely to listen to the advice of the authors of the report on Long Range Planning published by the *New Republic* in its issue of January 13, although this advice by no means threatens the basis of capitalism, but, on the contrary, seeks to strengthen it.

What is noteworthy in these "plans", however, and in the liberal discussions about them is the frantic desire of the intelligentsia to effect reforms within the framework of the capitalist system. For this purpose, they do not even hesitate to drag in "Marxian" theories. Of course, they are too discreet as a rule to state their purpose frankly; it is masked in the barbarous jargon of the bourgeois academy; but sometimes a less discreet intellectual lets the cat out of the bag. Thus a critic of the Long Range Planning pamphlet, writing in the *New Republic* of January 27, says:

"If the writers of the plan accept the Marxian diagnosis of overproduction, then it is obvious that the measures they have proposed and the spirit in which they are asking businessmen to enter the planning organization are not calculated to make any appreciable headway against present evils.... If the problem is one that arises from a conflict of interests, as for example, international war, or the chaos of economic production according to the Marxian view, then fact-finding science is a snare and a delusion, for it tries to solve the problem of the conflict of interests by assuring us that the interests of all are identical. Whether or not the authors of the report accept the view that the conflict of individual interests is the principal cause of overproduction and unemployment, no other thesis is tenable: for not only has the Marxian analysis never been refuted, but it stands to reason that if the cause were less deep rooted than the wills of men, the remedy would long ago have been found."

The critic has obviously failed to analyse the Marxian analysis. Overproduction and unemployment are not due to the conflict of *individual* interests, but to the operations of a specific productive system, capitalism, marked by the conflict of *class* interests. The evolution of that system and the intensification of class conflict are not produced by individual wills, hence the remedy could not "long ago have been found," in the sense of being applied. The remedy was indeed found by Marx and Engels some eighty years ago, but its effective application is dependent on objective conditions, although will and conscious purpose play an important role. This is the remedy which has been applied in Russia since 1917, a remedy from which the critic in the *New Republic* seems to have learned very little. For his own "remedy" is that what "we need is not science but social statesmanship, a statesmanship which appeals to the unifying power of reason among men and which creates, on the basis of the disinterested sentiments which we all share at some moments, a physical mechanism designed to guide and restrain our ordinary interested appetites. It is obvious that such mechanism must be incorporated into the State, which is after all nothing but the developing system of the coercive guidance of individuals by society and for society". For this, it is merely necessary that the "present holders of economic privileges" shall make "sacrifices" in a "rational social manner."

It is only natural that a writer who bases himself on the "Marxian analysis" which "has never been refuted" without understanding that analysis should fall into idealism of the shallowest kind. "Social statesmanship" is a meaningless term that would not be disdained by Mussolini. The appeal to the "unifying power of reason" among the bankers and industrialists is about as effective as the appeal to the "honor" of Massachusetts or the "law" of Alabama. And there is not a racketeer, gunman, crook, businessman, general, or coal operator in the world who would deny he had "disinterested sentiments", without in the least changing his activities which are the inevitable results of his position in capitalist society. For a writer who lives in the land of Hoover and Morgan, Tom Mooney and the Scottsboro defendants to define the state as "the developing system of the coercive guidance of individuals by society and for society" would appear incredible, if we did not know that the liberal mind, steeped in idealistic prejudices, still clings to an illusion which both the bourgeoisie and the proletariat have abandoned. The two main warring social classes know that every state is a class state, and that except under communism, every society is a class society. The state is the political instrument of that class which is economically dominant. Hence it is childish, when it is not a piece of deliberate political trickery, to appeal to the capitalist state to be "just", or to modify the privileges of bankers, or in any way to act against the interests of the capitalist class.

Yet that is precisely the kind of appeal the muddled intellectual makes, and for reasons which the critic writing in the columns of the *New Republic* states frankly. "I share," he says, "with the authors of the report the concern for a peaceful solution of the social problem and the fear of revolutions to come. And I also believe with them that the best way of running industry is by utilizing the knowledge and experience of the present directors. But, unless our captains of industry are ready for a 'Fourth of September', unless they are ready to make the necessary renunciation of their privileges and pledge their services to the nation, there is nothing to do but wait and prepare on the side of labor for the readjustment of social forces. In the French Revolution the 'Fourth of September' came too late to stem the cataclysm of blood which drenched Europe for twenty-five years. Will our 'Fourth of September' also come too late? The answer lies with the captains of industry."

The lesson of the 'Fourth of September' is precisely that it is impossible to change economic and social relationships by appealing to the "unifying reason" of a ruling class, that it grants concessions *only* under pressure from the revolutionary classes, and when it learns it does so, as the critic aptly observes, "too late." The lesson of every revolution in history is that no ruling class is moved by "disinterested sentiments" to commit suicide; it does not surrender its privileges except when it is compelled to surrender its power. No governing class in history has ever abdicated until it was overthrown.

Despite the critic's "Marxian" analysis, the answer to the crisis of capitalism does *not* lie with with the captains of industry. If his "analysis" has any value at all it is that of revealing with extraordinary naivete the vacillating position of the petit-bourgeoisie between fascism and the revolution. *If* the captains of industry will apply a mythical "unifying power of reason", *if* they will surrender to their "disinterested" sentiments, *if* they will "sacrifice" a few of their privileges without altering the system of exploitation for profit, then the critic and those who share his views will support them. And since fascism and social-fascism have a remarkable way of looking like "social statesmanship", this type of intellectual is capable of supporting a fascist or social-fascist State which coerces individuals "for society", as has been the case in Italy, Germany, Great Britain, Mexico and elsewhere. But if the captains of industry will not listen to this "appeal to reason?" Then they had better beware; for although the critic "fears revolutions to come" he will "wait and prepare" on the side of labor. Is it possible, after all, that if the men of letters and the critics of planning pamphlets "prepare", that capital and labor will be able to "prepare", that capital and labor will be able to avoid the "final conflict"? Hardly. While a certain type of intellectual prays for a September 4th, the revolutionary working class prepares for a November 7th.

There are, however, more clear-headed intellectuals. Edmund Wilson for instance has apparently changed his views since he urged the intelligentsia to "take communism away from the communists." His essay in the January 27 *Nation* is a statement of beliefs which everyone ought to read.

"So far as I can see," Wilson says, "Karl Marx's predictions are in the process of coming true." And since he has understood Marx better than the *New Republic* critic, he does not appeal to the captains of industry but knows that "there is no hope for general decency and fair play except from a society where classes are abolished." Hence, when he hears the Communists today "rousing the working class on the basis of assumptions of Marx's" he says, "I pay a good deal more serious attention to them than most of my bourgeois confreres do." He places such hope as he has not in the captains of industry, for he knows that economic relations are not based on sentiments but quite the reverse. He looks to a new type in American labor.

"One finds, Wilson says, " a new kind of man today in the radical labor movements—he belongs to the younger generation and he differs perhaps from any of the young American radicals we have ever had in the past. The older men who have gravitated to the left after long experience with American labor, arid who have kept the radical movements alive through the post-war period when most people deserted them are today being reinforced by young men who start their career as convinced and cool-headed revolutionists with a clear idea of their relation to American society and of America's relation to the world. There are not many of them but they are important. They have no illusions about general prosperity based on the present economic system.... It is hard to imagine them abandoning their present principles. And as a matter of fact they are not likely to be tempted to. The longer hard times will continue, the more convinced of their position they will be, and the more young men of integrity and intelligence who come to maturity in the working-class world will take the same road as they. Such men are not democratic in the old American sense.... They look to Russia, in spite of all the differences between Russian and American conditions, as a model of what a state should be.... because it is as yet the only example of the communistic society they desire. They want, in fact, a working class dictatorship....

"And I, although I am a bourgeois myself and still live in and depend on the bourgeois world, have certain interests in common with these proletarians. I, too, admire the Russian Communist leaders, because they are men of superior brains who have triumphed over the ignorance, the stupidity and the shortsighted selfishness of the mass, who have imposed on them better methods and ideas than they could ever have arrived at by themselves. As a writer, I have a special interest in the success of the 'intellectual' kind of brains as opposed to the acquisitive kind, and my present feeling is that my satisfaction in the spectacle of the whole world fairly and sensibly run as Russia is now run, instead of by the acquisitive bankers and businessmen and the shabby politicians who now run the greater part of it, would more than compensate me for any losses that I might incur in the process. And I appeal to other theorists and artists to be careful how they play the game of the capitalists. It is bad for their theory and their art to try to adapt themselves to a system which is the enemy of theory and art. Their true solidarity lies with those elements who will remodel society by the power of imagination and thought."

There are, in this piece, many echoes of Wilson's early training. He underestimates the creative power of the masses, and conceives of the Soviet system as something "imposed" on selfish, ignorant louts by a few superior "intellectual" brains. He forgets that while the bolsheviks have led and directed the revolution, they have done so as the advance guard of the working class. If he would acquaint himself more closely with Soviet life, he would realize to what an extent its great cultural contributions are due to the creative activities of the masses, to the fruitful influence of worker and peasant correspondents, worker-inventors, and other proletarian and peasant organizations; he would know how much the scientist gains by quitting the solitude of his laboratory, the artist the isolation of his studio, the writer his lonely desk to mingle and work with the mass of the population in factory and field.

But what is most important at present in Wilson's essay is its positive element, which reveals that under the pressure of the economic crisis certain honest intellectuals have begun to see the true relationships of capitalist society, and the correct way out. It now remains for them to translate their faith into works.

THE LITERARY CLASS WAR

PHILIP RAHV

In the capitalist countries proletarian literature has as yet not reached adulthood, its most active forces being at present chiefly engaged in breaking ground for the sowing of the vital seed of Marxism. From the October Revolution it received a tremendous impetus, yet it is only with the late onrush of economic catastrophe throughout the world that it began moving towards a determined extirpation of all liberal, reformistic elements within itself. Tearing asunder the last vestigial piece of bourgeois-esthete fancy-drapery, it proclaimed its position to be that of irreconcilable class-antagonism. True, a literature of social protest against capitalism has always existed, but being based on the premises of Idealism—in the main without any overt awareness of its resultant anti-Marxist orientation—it failed to formulate a clear dialectico-materialistic world-view. Consequently such expression can be placed under the category of proletarian literature only when that concept is apprehended in extremely general terms.

The urgent task of the Marxist critic today is manifest. He must carve out a road for the proletarian writer, who, living as he does under the constant pressure of the prevailing ideas derived from the property-relationships of existing society, is faced with immense obstacles in his struggle to liberate himself from various bourgeois preconceptions which he Still unconsciously adheres to. It is the critic's task to indicate how the dynamics of dialectic materialism can vitalize the new proletarian expression, and what form their integration into the warp and woof of this expression should take. A more definite frontier between the proletarian and the bourgeois in letters should be established. This of course, necessitates a thorough critical scrutiny of bourgeois trends in this field; just as every discussion of socialism implies a corresponding discussion of capitalism, so every discussion of proletarian literature implies a corresponding discussion of bourgeois literature; the latter is the thesis, the former the antithesis, and it is the classless society of the future that will ultimately resolve the contradiction between the two by creating the economic basis for a new superstructural equilibrium.

Recognizing its present developmental stage as elementary, the critic who attempts to build a theoretical scaffolding for proletarian literature can but partially base his argument on what is actually being produced in capitalist countries at the present time. A theoretical formulation *wholly* based on actual proletarian practice would run contrary to dialectic because it would largely ignore the dynamic mobility of class-consciousness; hence, in writing of proletarian literature, the Marxist critic has his eye on the future as well as on the present, and the authenticity of his analysis cannot be invalidated by the examination of his statements in the light of present-day facts alone.

The Idea of Katharsis Revitalized:
The Greek idea of katharsis in art is one of the most fertile conceptions ever devised. However, its classic formulation by Aristotle as a process effecting a proper purgation of the emotions through pity and terror, is a static, passive conception quite in line with the needs of a slave-owning class endowed with cultural tastes and appreciative of the great art of tragedy, but unwilling to permit the even tenor of its parasitic existence to be disturbed by gruesome realities. Thus the "significant change" effected in the reader or spectator by the katharsis leaves him limp and reconciled to the "immutable laws of life." After the grand spectacle of a Sophoclean tragedy, the Greek gentleman went home to his slaves, stimulated indeed, but resigned to the whims of the gods and "human nature." This form of katharsis is merely a sort of transcendental mental laxative for a cultured leisure class.

Nevertheless, a consistent examination of the qualitative properties of artistic creation leaves one with the conviction that without katharsis that creation loses all significance, loses that high gravity which is the most characteristic function of art. Within proletarian literature one can discern the implicit form of a new katharsis, likewise a purgation of the emotions, a cleansing, but altogether of a different genus: *a cleansing through fire*. Applying the dynamic viewpoint of dialectics, a synthesizing third factor is added to the Aristotlean pity and terror—and that is militancy, combativeness. The proletarian katharsis is a release through action—something diametrically opposed to the philosophical resignation of the older idea. Audaciously breaking through the wall that separates literature from life, it impels the reader to a course of action, of militant struggle; it objectifies art to such a degree that it becomes instrumental in aiding to change the world. A proletarian drama, for instance, inspires the spectator with pity as he identifies himself with the characters on the stage; he is terror-stricken by the horror of workers' existence under capitalism; but these two emotions finally fused in the white heat of battle into a revolutionary deed, with the weapon of proletarian class-will in the hands of the masses. This is the vital katharsis by means of which the proletarian writer fecundates his art.

The impotence of bourgeois literature is best evidenced by the utter lack of katharsis within it; it is no longer capable of its traditional static signification. In its place it substitutes disgust, or simply a series of shocks attendant upon the exhibition of various *naturalia*. The literature of the bourgeoisie when it was still a revolutionary class in society, was still capable of katharsis. Now, however, in its stage of decline and imminent collapse, the signification of katharsis is manifestly impossible, for the reason that the class of which this literature is a reflection has already lost all belief in itself. Thus the novels of a writer like William Faulkner leave the reader with nothing: it is merely stylized photography, the same old treadmill of naturalism, with the wheels going around a little faster—in the thickening twilight.

Commenting on Dreiser's *American Tragedy*, Irving Babbitt writes: "He has succeeded in producing in this work something genuinely harrowing; but one is harrowed to no purpose. One has more than the full measure of tragic qualm but without the final relief and enlargement of spirit that true tragedy succeeds somehow in giving, and that without resort to explicit moralizing. It is hardly worth while to struggle through eight hundred very pedestrian pages to be left at the end with a feeling of sheer oppression." Quite true. But of course such a confirmed Brahmin and arch-defender of the status quo as Prof. Babbitt cannot be expected to think anything out to its logical conclusion. The Back Bay aristocracy does not believe in thinking things out to their logical conclusions. From Babbitt's idealistic postulates (this gentleman considers Nature as a philosopher in pursuit of an "inner check"—for the workers of course; the greed of capitalism knows no check save the organized might of the exploited masses) it follows that if Dreiser has only wished he could have significated his material: hence the bald accusation of deliberate willfulness. The fact is, however, that no katharsis can be effected by a writer who is not consciously up in arms against capitalism, who does not visualize the free, rational society of the future. When he *wrote The American Tragedy,* Dreiser was still in his phase of darkest pessimism, reducing life-phenomena to "physico-chemical terms;" this point of view is just as much a reflection of bourgeois collapse as the philosophy of Spengler, despite the fact that even then Dreiser was already pointing to the moneytheistic spirit of capitalism as the determining factor in the stultification of American life—but lacking the dialectic revolutionary solution, he was incapable of handling his material in any other way than the way he did. Literature is the integration of experience, but experience cannot be integrated when the human signification is lacking: and *capitalism and human signification don't mix.* Proletarian literature, on the other hand, supplies that want with its own form of katharsis. Every instance of a class-unconscious worker gaining class-consciousness is katharsis, every strike, every militant action, every aggression on the part of the proletariat is katharsis. Proletarian literature is replete with human signification.

In defining tragedy (and this definition is generally applicable to all works of art) Aristotle stated: "It is an action that is complete and whole, and of a certain magnitude; for there may be a whole that is wanting in magnitude." Here too we notice the constitutional weakness of bourgeois literature and the foundational conformity of proletarian literature to the classic conception of what an effective literary work should be, of course with the important modifications concomitant with the changes in economy. Joyce's *Ulysses*, for example, is marked with a certain magnitude, but only in a negative sense. It is the magnitude of death, not of life. As to the criterion of an organic whole, there is no question that it does not exist. Mrs. Bloom's long mental orgasm is quite a proper ending for such a bourgeois labyrinth as *Ulysses*. It has neither a beginning nor an end. It jumps at life like a cat at a canary, but the housewife arrives in the nick of time, and the disgruntled cat jumps out of the window and slinks down to the dungheap behind the gashouse by the bank of a slimy river, where it sinks into a fetid dream. In direct contrast to these graveyard antics, proletarian literature, by linking up the individual with the collective, achieves that genuine magnitude which follows the Marxian comprehension of the historical process as a whole.

The Highest Degree of Consciousness

The prime-phenomenon of Marxism is intense consciousness—the highest degree of social consciousness as yet attained by man. Proletarian literature, partaking of this quality, should also be tested by this touchstone. However, a literature that is a rancid hotchpotch of mystic subjective introvert speculation, arbitrary and hallucinatory, is much better suited to capitalist class purposes than one that is animated by a high degree of consciousness. The proletariat is the most advanced class in society, the class destined to bring about the survival and the further development of western culture, and since consciousness points the way to the inexorable march of this class to power, it constitutes in itself the high secret of the proletarian advance. Not so the bourgeoisie: to it consciousness, which the objective circumstances inevitably focus on the class struggle as the dominant aggregate in the social constellation, would be wholly pernicious; it is the dynamite that could blow up its most cherished illusions Consequently bourgeois literature takes refuge in a flight from consciousness, it finds a haven in the subconscious. Thus the Revolution of the Word can be explained from a Marxian standpoint. The bourgeois ideologues would like to think that they too are revolutionists, so the word-game is initiated, and we are treated to the ludicrous spectacle of grown-up people indulging in the most fatuous and infantile delusions. These experiments with word-dismembering are of no more value than the well-known experiments of children with flies, yet the bourgeois illuminati take these word-revolutionists quite seriously. In the ultimate analysis the Revolution of the Word is a pretext for indulging in psycho-pathological orgies; it represents a deep-seated craving for the prenatal stage, for non-being. The vagaries of Jolas & Co. and the necromantic method of producing literature through the immaculate conception of automatic writing are quite proper end-phenomena of a dying class, and of a crumbling hegemony.

Antithetical Psychologies:
The psychology of the proletariat is in the very nature of its class existence a psychology of production, the psychology of makers, of creators. It is a healthy psychology, in profound harmony with the rhythms of nature. After a rapid process of development we observe in the bourgeoisie of the post-war epoch the emergence of a psychology of pure consumption—particularly in America (in Europe this psychology gained ascendancy much earlier). Here we perceive how a change in the form of the property-relationships—the transition from industrial to finance capitalism—conditions the psychology of a class. Finance capitalism creates a financial aristocracy, whose psychology is that of coupon-cutters, of *rentiers*, of people totally removed from the economic life.

In his book *The Theory of the Leisure Class*, N. I. Bukharin gives an illuminating portrayal of the role which this stratum of the bourgeoisie plays in society: "We have already seen," he writes, "that the class of society here discussed is a product of the decline of the bourgeoisie. This decline is closely connected with the fact that the bourgeoisie has already lost its functions of social utility. This peculiar position of the class within the production process, or, to put it more correctly, without the production process, has led to the rise of a peculiar social type that is characterized particularly by its asociality. While the bourgeoisie as such is individualistic from its very cradle ... the individualism in the case of the *rentier* becomes more and more pronounced ... There disappears not only the interest in capitalist enterprise but any interest in the social altogether. The ideology of a stratum of this type is necessarily strongly individualistic. This individualism expresses itself with peculiar sharpness in the esthetics of this class; *any treatment of social themes appear to it eo ipso as 'inartistic,' 'coarse,' 'tendencious'* " (italics mine—P.R.)

In analyzing the bourgeoisie of his time, the American economist Thornstein Veblen concluded that theirs was a psychology of "conspicuous consumption." American critics of the left have been strongly influenced by this thesis, which is undoubtedly true of the American bourgeoisie of Veblen's time. For the present, however, I think his thesis is no longer valid. The psychology of conspicuous consumption is chiefly characteristic of the bourgeois in his prime phase, when he is still an entrepreneur; but with the transition to finance capitalism the industrial bourgeoisie, the entrepreneurs, begins to play a minor role in shaping the ideology of the class: the industrial bourgeoisie now forms the *substratum* of the capitalist class, and generally tries to ape the life-pattern of the upper stratum, the coupon-cutters. The vogue which pseudo-aristocratic manners and ideas begin to enjoy during this phase is extremely symptomatic of this shift; in short, the old straightforward vulgarity of the brutal slave-driver in direct personal control of the instruments of production is now replaced by the sophisticated vulgarity of idlers and poseurs.

In the realm of superstructure this evolution wields of course a powerful influence in determining the metamorphosis of literary ideology, both in the sphere of form and in the sphere of content. The heroes of Frank Norris' novels of industrial life are captains of industry, alive and buoyant with the optimism and vigor of a class still relatively young: they are in constant touch with the actual process of production: they are not coupon-cutters. This is no longer true of the literature produced during the period of finance capitalism. The present asociality, blind anarchic individualism, amorality, are all essential factors of the new ideology, which in its own right comprises one of those internal contradictions of capitalism that operate for its destruction. Consider this statement by T. S. Eliot: "The arts insist that a man shall dispose of all that he has, even of his family tree, and follow art alone. For they require that a man be not a member of a family or of a caste or of a party or of a coterie, but simply and solely himself..." This statement offers us a concentrated expression of the asocial psychology of pure consumption. Herein we see how the cultural representatives of the bourgeoisie irresistibly gravitate towards a complete acceptance of the ideology of that section of the dominating class which is furthest advanced on the road to extinction.

In American literature the transition from the psychology of conspicuous consumption to that of pure consumption took place during the twenties. H. L. Mencken concretely exemplifies this change. The ferocious warfare he waged against democracy, his extreme individualism, his organic inability to think in socio-economic terms—all are indications of the change. Sinclair Lewis militated against the "standardized philistinism" of George F. Babbitt and helped to bring about the individualistic philistinism of the people in *The Sun Also Rises*, George F. Babbitt is a regimented bourgeois, a garrulous booster, social with the hypocritical sociality of industrial capitalism; the protagonists in Hemingway's novel are effete hypochondriacs, cataleptic individualists—the human dust of finance capitalism. The writers of the early twenties fought for sophistication, i.e., for individualistic philistinism. (The Babbitts of the era of pure consumption are generally known as sophisticates.) Booth Tarkington could still describe the plutocrat with relish, with a certain amount of health, but the writers of the late twenties and the thirties, never. To them the plutocrat is a coarse animal; only when he spends his holidays in Southern France, patronizes the arts, and under the influence of numerous cocktails becomes capable of philosophic discourses on life, death, and the immortal soul is he worthy of respect.

Even in the commercial trash dumped by the tons on the market this transition is patent. In the thousands of novels turned out annually the heroes and heroines seem to exist in an economic vacuum—they all have money, they are all dressed up in the height of fashion, they are present at all the smart events—but where and how they amassed their fortunes is not mentioned. The assumption is that their fathers or grandfathers did well by their children, but this is not allowed to intrude into the texture of the novel.

In England the arrival of the historic moment of pure consumption for the bourgeoisie occurred much earlier, and aided by the nobility and other atavistic feudal elements its assimilation into ideology was quickly effected. Aldous Huxley typifies in himself the position of a writer who has accepted this psychology *in toto*. The characters in his novels, psychic louts most of them, are constantly peregrinating from one country-house to another, forever talking, but under no circumstances concerned with productive work. In *Antic Hay* one of them, a female adventurer, is reclining on a couch and meditating in this profound fashion: "We on the sofas, ruthless, lovely and fastidious." Huxley was ironizing in this passage, but unconsciously he was formulating his own class-position. On the sofa, febrile, inept, entangled in intellectual cobwebs, yet deeming himself exceedingly ruthless, and of course so esthetic (lovely) and sophisticated (fastidious). Nobody works except the lower classes (the servants). Mr. Huxley and his intellectual companions are all coupon-cutters, hence it is not hard to understand why he wrote *Brave New World*. The civilization of the coupon-cutters is in jeopardy, the Nirvana of pure consumption is threatened, and Mr. Huxley, like the good ideologue of his class that he is, hastens to the rescue.

The economics and sociology of the capitalists are Ptolemaic in nature. Once man regarded the earth as the fixed center of the universe, now the bourgeois regards capitalism as the fixed center of economic life for all eternity. Therefore, having accepted this position, the bourgeois littérateur feels free to relegate it to the oblivion of axiomatic truths, and begins to consider the brutalities of capitalism as eternal principles of human nature. But, just as in physics absolute distance, unrelated to some specific frame, does not exist, so in literature and all other forms of ideological expression, absolute values do not exist. Proletarian literature is enclosed within the dialectic frame of the dynamic mobility of classes. From that vantage-point it sees man and events in their round, as in a triple mirror.

Fellow-travelers and the Class Line

Since the expulsion of the economic romanticism prevailing in America till the crash in the autumn of the year 1929, American writers have increasingly shown a tendency to think in social terms, turning to the left for ideational substance. It would, however, be the sheerest wish-thinking to suppose that his can be taken at face value as an indication of a fundamental trend. It is quite certain that following the economic interests of their class, most bourgeois writers will swing towards fascism, while only a few, the most honest, the least dominated by delusions, will join the proletariat.

If it weren't for the object lesson of proletarian class-rule in Russia and the resurgence of Marxism all along the front, those writers who did take the final step would have probably sought an outlet from the confusion attendant upon the collapse of prosperity in mysticism or some type of neo-religion. It is precisely the iron dynamic of the Marxian philosophy that effected the apostasy of such writers as Edmund Wilson, Newton Arvin and Granville Hicks. I believe it is a mistake to think that it is the widespread misery and economic chaos that is the chief cause of these writers' espousal of collectivism. The widespread misery and the economic chaos merely impelled them to approach Marxism for a way out; without Marxism this misery and chaos would have simply thrown them into the arms of Mr. Eliot and M. Maritain.

With regard to fellow-travelers a lenient attitude is more or less in order. They cannot be expected to accept completely the proletarian viewpoint in one bound, but caution is necessary. If they make the Marxian world-view their own and evidence a comprehensive understanding of it, they can be counted on to integrate themselves into the proletariat. If they fail to do so, it is almost certain that sooner or later they will desert and re-join the bourgeoisie, as many socialists did during the war. The emotional, romantic approach to Communism is a paper bridge for anyone who wants to cross over into the camp of revolution. Lenin once censured Upton Sinclair for his pacifism, describing him as an "emotional Socialist without theoretical grounding." Only their ability and *willingness* to master Marxian theory will insure their loyalty. The view on the Russian Revolution they adhere to is a good test. Thus we find some fellow-travelers persisting in a pseudo-liberal attitude to the Soviet Union, perpetually deploring "the lack of freedom in Russia." Is it really so difficult to understand that the concept freedom under the capitalist regime is merely formal? "Freedom is the recognition of necessity." (Engels) Everything should of course be done to facilitate a fellow-traveler's assimilation, but once it becomes clear that his bourgeois class-roots are too strong, he should be neatly and rapidly dispatched on the road back, because he will only bring confusion into the ranks of the real militants.

In his essay *The Class Point-of-View* Lenin left us some good advice as to tactics in this respect. "The party of the proletariat," he wrote, "must learn to catch every liberal just at the moment when he is prepared to move forward an inch, and compel him to move forward a yard. If he is obstinate and won't, we shall go forward without him, and over his body."

HOMECOMING

MYRA PAGE

"Peace—Peace!" Marge and Ruth were jerked out of their sleep as a shrill voice broke in on the night's stillness. "The War's ended—Peace! Peace!" Snatching a wrapper Marge ran to the door. "Boy, here, here!" She held out her coppers for the paper.

Quaking with the chill, she sat on the edge of the bed to read the news while Ruth and Gertie, huddled up, the bedclothes pulled around their shoulders, listened with strained faces. The children on the pallet whimpered, blinking at the lights.

"Thank the Lawd it's over," Gertie murmured and dropped back on her pillow.

"Come on Ruth, let's dress 'n go outside," Marge laughed hysterically. "I'm too restless to sleep."

Lights shone dimly from the grey shacks that lined the street, doors banged as millhands joined the rapidly gathering crowd, pulling on jackets and shawls as they ran.

"Hurrah, the war's over!"

"The slaughterin' 'll stop 'n our boys come home."

"We'll have a real Christmas this year!"

Villagers pounded one another's backs, shook hands all round each time a newcomer joined them, threw caps into the air, and paraded the narrow, dirt streets singing and hurrahing until the stars paled in the greying sky and it was time for a bite to eat before going to the mill.

The super and foremen raced from one department to another, scowling angrily. "You all gone crazy? Sure the war's ended. But these here orders got to go out!"

After the super left, Miss Jones slipped over to Marge to whisper, "What you know, thar's some that ain't glad this war's over! They been makin' a pile of money, the mill has. 'N it warn't *their* sons across!" She spit viciously into a rusty pail standing nearby.

Marge caught a glimpse of Bertha's sad face as she wove in and out among the frames. Poor Bertha! Thar'd be no home-comin' for her; her man la yover thar, blown to smitherins.

"We're sailing the end of this week," Bob wrote in shaky zigzag lines, "and should be home by March." Marge sang at her machine. She had Bertha over to supper and made her a chemise for Christmas. When Bertha wept on her shoulder, "Why did the Almighty let it happen?" Marge felt guilty in her own happiness.

The mills, banks and business firms closed for half a day to greet the returning Greenville boys. Once again flags flew, khaki figures tramped, bands played martial music, flaming speeches were made. These boys, (sons of farmers, mill workers, doctors and small business men), had won the War for Democracy! They were heroes. Let them ask the best that America had to offer, nothing was too good for them!

"Bob!" Marge's vision of his thin, limping figure, his crooked smile, blurred. "You've come home."

"Lil' Marge .... Yah, I've come home."

* * *

"So Uncle Mat' broke down 'n went to spend his last days at his son's farm in Georgy? That's too bad." Bob, his second day back was still catching up on the news. " 'N what's happened to Tom?"

Immediately the entire table ceased eating, staring at him in a strange way. The two boarders, excusing themselves hastily, went outside.

"You see, Tom opposed the war," Marge began.

"Tom brung disgrace on us all, that's what!" Gertie blurted out. "Ma allays said he would. But"—her voice broke, "I never expected to have a jail bird in the family." Billy and Sam reddened, looked down at their hands.

"Doan you dare say that bout Tom!" Marge thundered. "He ain't no ordinary criminal."

"Marge, for goodness sakes, keep your voice down!" Ruth gasped.

"Wal, I ain't ashamed of Tom, if the rest of you is. He done what he thought was right. He's got convictions 'n the government put him in jail for it."

"Convictions or no convictions, he's in jail, ain't he?" Gertie demanded. " 'N if they find it out at the mill, they'll turn us offa the hill."

"Let 'em," Marge answered. "Jest let 'em. I'll give 'em a piece of my mind."

"Lotta good that'll do us," Ruth grumbled. "Marge, this time Gertie's right."

Bob shook his head. "Wal, I ain't so sure." Later he asked Marge, "Just what is it Tom believes?" They talked far into the night.

"Now the war's over, why doan they let him out? Marge questioned anxiously. "If he was a richman's son they'd not keep him locked up like that."

"If he was a rich man's son, he'd never got took up in the first place."

* * *

Bob was restless to be at work, "But wait awhile," Marge begged, "till you get rested up a mite; 'n I can feed you up on grits and gravy, 'n take that peaked look off'n you. Younr lungs 'n side ain't right yet, the doctor says."

"But honey, I can't be a-livin' offa you. You look like a rest would set you up right smart, yourself."

"I'm all right, now you're back." Her voiced dropped. "Lil' Roberty's goin' went hard with me.'

He put his arms around her. "Doan you grieve, honey. Soon as I'm well again, 'n workin' steady, we'll have another to take Roberty's place." Marge didn't answer. The old doubts assailed her, altho challenged now by a longing for motherhood which Roberta had awakened in her.

"Soon I'll be back at weavin' 'n we can start out fresh, in four rooms of our own … Gee, Marge, it's good to be back! Those fifteen months were the longest I ever spent." Only fifteen months! They looked at each other. Where were the carefree youth, the starry-eyed girl of a brief year and a half ago?

"Marge!" Gertie's whining voice sallied forth from the kitchen, "time to be a-fixin' supper."

It was evident, even to Bob, that he couldn't do a day's work at the mill. As Ruth remarked, even odd jobs around the house tired him out. What troubled Marge more than anything else wa3 that he didn't seem to improve very fast. Then, he was changed. The old Bob, with his ready laugh and boisterous confidence was gone. In his place was this quiet, brooding creature who wandered about the house as though looking for something he couldn't find.

She'd come upon him sitting with his hands hanging down between his knees, eyes staring ahead. "The war's done somethin' to him—somethin'." Coming up close behind him, she slipped her arms across his chest and pressed his head against her breast. "What's it Bob, what you a-lookin' at?" she whispered. Turning, he wormed his head against her body like a small boy. "The things I seen over thar.... Looks like I can't forget 'em."

Sometimes he would break down and sob, clinging to her, gasping out the horror of the time he'd plunged his bayonet through a fair-haired lad who'd resembled his younger brother. "His eyes haunt me. His cry rings in my ears." He told her of Will, the Mountain boy at Camp Lee who had been driven to suicide because he was hone-in' for the hills 'n didn't hanger to fight in a conflict that 'taint our war. Of bomb raids, gas attacks, of birds of prey stalking the fields.

"Honey," his grip tightened until she held her breath from the pain, "if I could jest be sure it was for somethin'. But it 'pears like over thar I lost all my belief in what we were fightin' for. I'd have come away, if I could. But thar warn't no way, 'n you had to keep killin' or get killed."

Marge, as shaken as he, tried to comfort him. "You did the best you knew how. Now it's all over 'n behind you. You're back. We got each other, 'n we gotta helpen our people here."

"Yah, us mill folks gotta fight for our rights. If I can jest get my strength back. Seems like they done for me."

"Doan say that. It takes time, but you're perkin' up a lil' every day.... When you spose we'll hear 'bout that government compensation you been writin' about?"

"Aw, the govern-ment doan care 'bout us no more, now the fightin's over!"

"But at the parade they said "

"They said! Then what for they put so much in the way between me 'n Burke 'n the others what got hurt over thar, 'n the the pay that's due us?"

"I dunno. Reckon it takes time, or somethin'."

"Somethin' is right,—somethin' we mill hands ain't got. Pull."

***

Billy and Sam were persistent in their questioning of Bob and his two buddies, Burke and Walter, "Ah, go on, tell us more about what it was like, fightin' in France. Was it sure-nough like the movies shows it—?" The family was still grouped around the cleared supper table. Various neighbors had dropped in.

Bob's fingers drummed restlessly on the red cloth. "Thar ain't nuthin' worth tellin'."

"Ah, Brother Bob," Sam wheedled, "doan act tight-mouthed. What about the night of the gas attack when you 'n Burke—"

"Do leave 'em alone," Marge urged, "can't you see they doan wanta talk?"

Walter pulled irritably at his empty right sleeve. "If you wanta be filled up to the guzzle with war stories, go in town to the American Legion. Thar's plenty boys thar who lap up this hero stuff. Us here ain't the stomach for 'em."

"They sure is modest ones," Ben Tilson's wife spoke in an admiring stage whisper.

"Naw, that ain't it, Miz Tilson," Burke gave an embarrassed cough. "Beggin' your pardon, ladies, but—" suddenly he exploded, "me'n my pals here is plum shet to hell of the war 'n war talk."

"Let's change the subject." Marge looked around uneasily.

"Tell you what," Billy, unheeding, addressed his young brother, "what you say in a coupla years we join the army? Oughta be more to it than jest workin' at the mill."

Abruptly Bob lifted his head. "All right, Billy, Sam 'n all of you, we'll tell what war's really like." He spoke sternly. "Maybe you young fools can larn some sense in time. Tho I doubt it."

Toward the end Burke described the unrest and near-mutiny in his battalion because of bug-infested rations, brutality of the officers, and senseless wasting of lives. "More'n one struttin' Napoleon near got shot down—by mistake you understand. 'N sol-' diers wisecracked between theirselfs, 'I loved this country; but let me outta this war 'n I'll never love another'.

"I was in a detail carryin' prisoners-of-war to the rear. On the way we got a lil' friendly, tho it was contrary to orders. One fella, about Ben's age an size offered me a smoke. He could speak a bit of English, too.

" 'Why you fight?' he asked me. 'You workman, me workman. Why fight?' He told me he was a textile weaver, from a place called Saxony. Jest think, a mill hand like us!" Bob marveled.

"By gorry!" Ben exclaimed, "you mean?"

"Yah," Bob nodded wearily, "it was all lies 'bout them bloody, man-eatin' Huns. I seen a lotta other prisoners, 'n once you got to study 'em, close-like, they turned out to be just common folk like us.... Now this one I was tellin' you of, he showed me a picture from round his neck of his wife 'n lil' boy." Bob gulped. " 'N he said, 'I'm glad I' a prisoner, no more fightin'.' 'N he asked me again, 'Why workmen fight each other? For their rich men! Workmen should stand together.' Then an officer come up, 'n we didn't get to talk any more. I never saw him again."

His listeners talked this over.

"When you come to think of it, what we got out of the war?" Ben ruminated. "Us here on the hill is bad off as ever, with talk of wage-cuts flyin' round."

"I tell you what we got," Walter spoke bitterly. "Bob 'n Burke got bad lungs; 'n me, I got an arm missing' outta the war. 'N thar's a new crop of millionaires outta the war. That's what we got."

"The mill-owners sure musta made money. Look at the new places they bought down in Floridy. You seen the pitchers in the papers? 'N all the new mills what went up."

"That thar war for democracy," Walter continued, "it was one rich man's war 'n poor man's fight." This saying spread from hill to hill throughout the Carolinas, Georgia, and Alabama. "Yas-sir, it was a rich man's war 'n a poor man's fight."

"The next time they wanta war," Bob frowned intently at Billy's perplexed face, "they can go fight it theirselfs."

"Democracy me shirt-tail," Burke bumped his chair against the wall, "they sure can count me out."

"John Nelson was a-tellin' me," Ben spoke cautiously, "that thar's a rich man over to Atlanta what says thar's only one more war a-comin'. That's between the poor 'n the rich. A new civil war."

"Wal," Walter also made to leave, "when it comes, I guess me 'n Burke 'n Bob 'll know on what side to fight."

Gertie threw out her hands. "You doan know what you're sayin'!" Burke stared down at her.

"Yah, when it comes, I guess we-all 'll be ready."

***

The following Saturday Marge was given her time, and Gertie also.

"Drat the bossmen's excuses, they ain't foolin' me none!" Marge pulled nervously at her sister's arm. "Jest 'cause Bob ain't strong enough to work reg'lar, they want a family in this here mill house what can supply more hands."

"That ain't all," Gertie mopped her eyes angrily. "They ain't overlooked Bob's bitter talk 'n your part in that thar walk-out last year. Now you see what trouble you all brung on us."

Marge turned away impatiently. "If our union'd lasted, they'd not be able to do this so easy!"

"That union! A fly-by-night it was, like a black crow... Now we're turned offa the hill, whar'll we go? Whar'll we go?" The older woman looked around helplessly.

"Aw Gertie, leave off. I for one am plum glad to be shet of this hill."

After a family consultation it was decided to move out of the state entirely. 'Billy had heard that wages were pretty fair at Charlotte, s on Monday the household began the trek northward.

The Winston who lived next door to their new home at Charlotte in Borders Village proved to be friendly. The first evening the entire family of eight came over for a visit, and the small dining room buzzed with mutual questioning and relating of experiences on various hills.

Suddenly Ted Winston clambered to his feet. "By gorry, I plum forgot the meetin' down at the union hall."

"Union?" Marge queried.

"Yah. Ain't you heerd about it? We got some or-gani-za-tion, with headquarters right here in Charlotte."

"Is that so!" Bob and Marge exchanged glances.

"Sure as Mike. It's some strong, too. I reckon as how forty thousand in these here two states belong. It's called the United Textile Workers of America."

"You doan tell!"

Ted Wilson hitched up his trousers preparatory to taking his leave. "When we got more time I'll tell you all about it—how we organized, 'n the union come 'n said to jine up with 'em 'n we did. This here ain't no fly-by-night, it's a real union."

"*Uh-huh*". Each syllable came out with characteristic emphasis, as only a southerner can drawl it. "I reckon," Bob and Marge agreed, "this Sadday, after work, we all'll go down to the union hall 'n sign up."

NO COLLATERAL

JOHN L. SPIVACK

Dee Jackson could never see a mule without sad memories, for upon a mule and the good Lord he had based a life-long hope, had ploughed singing to a vision of freedom, and both had failed him. For years he had saved for that mule and a plough. With these and a little seed it was possible to rent a tract of ground and pay the owner one-fourth of the crop for the use of his land, and with a season or two of good crops and high prices, there would be money enough to make a down payment on a few acres. There were niggers in Ochlockonee county who had gone from tenant farming to independence.

The day he put his mark to an agreement with Shay Pearson for the use of twenty acres, and the mule and second-hand plough were paid for, was one of rejoicing. The mule was not as young and healthy as Dee would have liked but he was the best they could afford. Louise patched their clothes by the kerosene lamp and they did with little store food that winter for so much depended upon finishing the season clear of debt.

Those were feverish days at planting time when the winter vanished in the mellow warmth of spring. When perfect stands of cotton made the long rows a vivid green, Dee ploughed the middles again to make the beds soft and with anxious care they thinned the luxuriant growths with appraising eyes. Then the blossoms appeared, flowering like good omens. The green bolls speckled, and under the burning July sun, cracked open with the smiling promise of money for their own farm. There would be almost a bale to the acre they told themselves happily.

But on the very day they went out for the first picking, it rained.

Fleecy clouds appeared in a suddenly overcast sky. Dee's face grew haggard and he clasped his hands together as in prayer. Louise looked up with a frightened air as though seeking help from the angry heavens. No one moved. And then it rained.

It seemed to them that the rain beat the fields with furious gusts of hate. Dee sank to the furrow as though the rain hammering his cotton to the ground had hammered him down, too.

And as suddenly as it had begun, the sky cleared and the sun shone hot again.

He did not stir. Louise touched him gently.

"Git up offen dat groun', Dee," she urged. "Ain' no sense carryin' on dat way."

"Oh, my good Lawd," he said dazedly. The cotton had been whipped to the ground or hung dejectedly, their whiteness stained brown from the wet leaves. The crop was ruined. They would be lucky to get a third of what it would have brought.

"Dey'll be mo' pickin's," Louise said encouragingly.

There was only one consolation: the Lord who gave him his children, a helpful wife and the strength to work must have had a good reason to do that to him. Maybe he had been so busy ploughing and chopping and dreaming that the Lord thought he was becoming too independent and took that way to remind him that He was a jealous God, or perhaps some sin long since forgot was charged against him and He had demanded a settlement. The Lord kept mighty careful accounts.

Then, in the bleak winter days, the mule became sick.

Dee slept in the barn to attend his slightest need, but nothing seemed to help. That late December night when he returned to the cabin where the lamp with its smoking chimney threw his shadow across the room, his face told the story. Louise was waiting, wrapped in a blanket and huddled in the old rocker near the stove. Twice she had been to the barn but when the mule stretched out, breathing in those painful asthmatic gasps, Dee had sent her away.

"De Lawd knows His business," she said bravely.

"Yeah." He clasped and unclasped his hands, cracking the knuckles of his bony fingers.

"Sho He knows what He's doin'." Her thick lips quivered. "He done gib you de money fo' to buy 'im an' now He takes 'im away."

The chair creaked over the loose boards in the floor.

"Sho. Lak chillun hit is. He done gib us seven and tuk fo'."

"Dey didn't hab much to eat; dat's why dey tuk sick an' died," he said resentfully.

"Talkin' dat way ain' gonter do you no good."

"You kin alius git chillun. But whey kin a nigger git a mule w'en he ain' got no money?"

Louis slid from the rocker to her knees.

"I ain' questionin' You none, Lawd," she prayed, "but did You have tuh do dis tuh us? Ain' we done eb'ryt'ing You wants done? An' now You frows us down lak dis. Caise maybe we didn't gib no money tuh de chu'ch. But Lawd, You knows we didn't hab no money."

Neighbors came with sympathy. Carts creaked to the Jackson cabin on the chilly evenings and tired blacks from surrounding farms sat before the fireplace and comforted them. Old Isaac Burr, who had ministered to the spiritual wants of Pearson niggers for a decade, came on Christmas night and told the story again of the Son of God Who came to spread the gospel of love and forgiveness; and as he talked a desperate hope awoke in Dee's breast.

"You reck'n de Lawd's too busy right now?" he asked earnestly.

"He's alius got plenty on His han's but His ears is wide open fo' anything His chillun sez tuh Him any time, anywhey in de hul worl'."

"Den lissen, Lawd!" Dee shouted, rising to his feet. "I ain' neber asked You fo' much but I'm askin' You now: gib me dat mule jes' for' one mo' season, an' I'll neber ask You fo' nothin' no mo' in dis worl'. Neber. Sen' a clap o' Yo' thunder an' raise him f'um de daid. You kin wuk all kinds o' miracles, Suh, an' dis is de las' chance I got. Lawd, doan You see dat I'll hab tuh go tuh Mist' Pearson if You doan gib me dat ol' mule back again?"

"Day's a lot o' cullud folks wukkin' fo' Mist' Pearson," the preacher said mildly. "De Lawd knows His business an' if He wants you tuh be a croppah den He's got His own good reasons fo' hit. You kin bet on dat."

Dee took the lamp in a trembling hand and with old Isaac went to the mound back of the barn, hopeful that on this night of all nights the miracle would happen: in a blinding flame of fire and a deafening clap of thunder the earth would be rent asunder and the mule would struggle to his feet ready for supper.

But there was no flame of fire nor clap of thunder. Only the lantern light and their shadows on the motionless mound, and a wind whistling.

Dee's head bowed.

"I reck'n dat settles hit, Lawd," he said dejectedly.

On the second day of the new year Dee got off a neighbor's cart in Live Oak and went hesitantly to the Southern Cotton Bank, the red brick, one story building across the square from the county court house and jail, and asked for Mr. Albert Graham, the president.

"Coming to deposit your savings, Dee?" the official greeted him jocularly.

"No, suh," he said nervously. "I done come tuh see you 'about a li'l business matter."

"Sure. Always glad to talk business with you, Dee. Come right in and set yourself down."

"I'd lak tuh len' 'bout two hundred dollars, Mist' Graham," the old man stammered.

"That could be arranged, but have you any collateral?"

Dee looked puzzled.

"Something that will make sure the bank is repaid," Graham explained.

"Sho I'll pay hit back."

"I must have something as valuable in return," the banker said kindly. "Land—or a house—"

"But I ain' got no lan'," Dee said helplessly, spreading his hands in a gesture of emptiness.

"You see, Dee," Graham pointed out regretfully, "we all know you and we know that if you have the money you will repay a loan. But now, suppose your crop is bad for a season or two—why, you'll hardly be able to pay the interest let alone the principal. Don't you see? And the bank must protect its depositors."

The Jacksons had been Ramsey niggers before the Civil War and Dee, depressed by the inevitableness of a cropper's contract, turned to Bayard Washington Ramsey as the last hope. The aristocratic white was known for his kindness, especially to descendants of his father's slaves. He lived a mile south of Live Oak in the mansion his father built before the lanky northern lawyer ruined the family's hundred and sixty thousand dollar investment in niggers, and too proud to enrich himself by Cracker tricks in dealing with blacks, had never increased the two hundred acre plantation left when the war ended and all creditors were paid.

The cook greeted Dee shrilly at the kitchen door of the Ramsey home.

"If hit ain' ol' Dee hisse'f! Whut you doin' heah?"

"I come tuh see Mist' Ramsey,' he said with a worried air.

"Whut fo'?"

"I got tuh see 'im."

"Well, you jes' set right down heah an' I'll go tell 'im."

When she returned she said, "Mist' Ramsey'll see you on de front po'ch. You go roun' dey."

The tall, white haired planter looked at him questioningly.

"You're a long way from home, Dee," he smiled. "What is it?"

"Mit' Ramsey, suh," the old man began, twisting his hat nervously, "you 'bout de only white man here 'bouts we kin come to w'en we is in trouble."

Ramsey looked gravely at him.

"An' I got mo'n a wagon load o' trouble now."

"Yes, Dee."

"Mist' Ramsey, suh—The nervous twisting of his hat became more pronounced. "My mule done laid down an' died, suh."

The white man nodded sympathetically.

"I bin a hard wukkin' nigger all my bo'n days," Dee continued, "an' I'm willin' tuh wuk de res' o' my days some mo' but I ain' got nothin' tuh wuk wid. No mule. No food. I ain' got nothin'."

Ramsey pursed his lips and stared at his fields naked in the winter's day.

"I jes' was over tuh de bank fo' tuh ask 'em tuh len' me two hunnerd dollars so's I kin git me a mule an' a lil food tuh tide us over till de nex' crop comes but Mist' Graham done said I'd hab tuh hab col—col—"

"Collateral," Ramsay said quietly.

"Yes, suh, collateral. But I ain' got no collateral. I ain' got nothin' ceptin' my two han's, an' my wife, an' David and Henrietta."

"Yes, I know.'

"An' I'll hab tuh sign wid Mist' Pearson if I cain' git no two hunnerd dollars an' if I goes tuh wuk fo' Mist' Pearson—"

"Yes, I know," Ramsey repeated.

"So I done come tuh you, suh," Dee burst forth pleadingly. "I doan want tuh be Mist' Pearson's nigger. Me, and Louise and David an' Henrietta, we'll wuk fo' you'n pay you back, suh, if you'll len' hit tuh me."

Hamsey shook his head slowly.

"I can't, Dee. I'd like to help you but I haven't money enough to start saving all the niggers in the county. I have to take care of my own niggers. If I loan you two hundred dollars and another two hundred to some other nigger caught in the Cracker buzz saw I should soon be in the same situation you are in."

Perspiration broke out in tiny beads on Dee's forehead.

"Yes, suh," he said. "Thankee, suh."

"You see, Dee," Ramsey added, putting a hand gently on the old man's shoulders, "I'm caught in their buzz saw, too."

"Yes, suh," said Dee.

Dee would have left the county but there was no place to go. There was not even a mule to pull the few sticks of furniture that were his household goods, nor food for a journey, and no matter where a penniless nigger went he would have to work for some one. In Ochlockonee county they knew him for a good nigger and would be more considerate than would strange whites in another state, so two days later Dee Jackson put his cross to the usual cropper contract.

It provided that Pearson supply him with a mule, seed, and a monthly advance of twelve dollars between February and August inclusive, in return for half his crop after all advances and interest thereon were deducted. The agreement particularly specified that should the *"said tenant fail to pay the advances made by the owner when due, the tenant agrees to surrender the possession of said premises, in which event the owner is hereby authorized to sell or dispose of all property thereon the tenant has any interest in"* and concluded with the ominous words *"and shall be so construed between the parties thereto, any law, usage or custom to the contrary notwithstanding."*

Dee could not read but he knew what it contained. Others had signed cropper agreements and were charged eighteen percent interest on advances, with the Pearson bookkeeping system, a nigger never got out of debt. And Dee knew also that the Georgia law provided that as long as he owed the planter one dollar he could not leave the Pearson farm without facing arrest and the chain gang for swindling.

So Dee Jackson became Shay Pearson's nigger.

THRU THE SWEATY EYE OF A NEEDLE

Ben Field

Hershel Feinstem, hidden in a wagon, rumbled toward the border. A soldier stuck his bayonet into the hay, and let the wagon rumble on through the night. Arrived in Bremen, Hershel found his leg swollen to a club from the jab. He lay in a hospital for several months. By that time guns were popping all over Europe. Hershel could not budge from Bremen the four years. It was in 1920 that he finally found his family in a muddy village near Warsaw. He brought them back to Germany just as the new quota law went into force. Again the wait, year after year. At last through the net alone with money borrowed from his rich cousin in America.

Up from steerage the morning the ship slipped into the great harbor limped Hershel. There in the mist the stalwart green woman with the crown full of rays like horns. He bowed before Liberty and burst into tears.

At Ellis Island his tubby cousin came to meet him. He gave him a meal and a job in the shop he had established under the name of Morton Hyams, English Custom Tailor. He promised to lend him money to bring his family across soon.

All spring and summer long it rained without stopping. Hershel felt homesick. His leg bothered him. He crouched all day near a window with bars thick as crowbars. Out in the backyard the chicory-colored earth and an occasional ragged sparrow, and rain falling like gobs from sick mouths and the sharp odor from the toilets that wouldn't work He couldn't forget his wife and children on the porch of his brother-in-law's house drinking tea in the fragrant afternoon, the nightingales crying in the wood.

His cousin laughed at him for his homesickness. His fellow tailors poked fun at him, especially Yosel Miller, a landsman. Miller was called "the flute" because he was thin and liked to sing all day through his nose over his work. He tried to get him to go with him to a house where they had nice fat Jewish girls, just like pincushions. "No, still dreaming of his cow and calves on Czar Nicholas' farm. Like the man who left his family for ten years. He meets a friend. How many children has he? Three, and the youngest is five years old. How can that be when you've been away ten years? Oh, I write letters every month."

Hershel would become red and shake with anger.

Within a year he paid his cousin all he owed him. The cousin, however, refused to keep the promise to help him bring his family over to Columbus' golden domain. Business wasn't good. He was planning to open a factory in Boston where labor was cheaper and the union didn't bother you. He borrowed instead two hundred dollars from Hershel too timid to refuse him. He would write and invite him in time to come to Boston to become one of his foremen.

Hershel hunted for another job. He tried work as a window cleaner, then as a pushcart peddler. At last he found a small store in which he did pressing, ladies' tailoring, and mending. The store was between a druggist's and a grocery with a five-pointed star which threw a shadow on the pavement like a ballet dancer.

By that time Hershel had become thin as a crane with a humped back and a bald head that looked as if the hair had been pulled out by the roots. Because of his limp and his bitter face, the children were afraid of him and called him Chicken Legs. They sang:

> "*This is the way the tailor sews.*
> *This is the way he sews and sews.*
> *He sews the whole week through*
> *And earns a penny with a hole.*"

His cousin delayed paying him back or giving him the foreman's job. Customers often failed to pay him. Another tailor, Wechsler, a Polish Jew, opened a shop across the street. He did not hear regularly from his wife and children. He had no friends to turn to. Miller the Flute used to come around occasionally, still with a smile, but a little more haggard than in the old days. He would try to poke him out of the store into the open. He would try to urge him to join the Labor Lyceum school with the torch like a brussel sprout. Hershel hitched up his shoulders indifferently, and worked harder over his needle and press.

All the pleasure he had was dreaming of the day when he would pay back his debts for the store, when he would have his whole family with him. His homesickness grew. He was always thinking of his anxious little wife, the young son, and daughter he remembered best playing with the beadle's son a few days before his departure. Later, as she was kneading dough for a cake for him, he walked into the kitchen. "I have something to scold you for, Hannele." She walked over to wash her hands in a basin. Then hands on her hips, "Now what is it, father dear?" How he had laughed. He begged them in his letters to write often, to send him their pictures. He couldn't remember their faces clearly. He took a cheap one of himself which the photographer touched because of his pallor so that he looked as if his face were smeared with jelly.

Once a week Hershel went with his savings to the bank. His personal expenses were next to nothing. He lived on bread, herring, onions, potatoes. During the rest of the week he kept his money in a teabox with a pagoda like a pile of toppling dishes. His first delivery boy got into the habit of sneaking into the only room back of the pokey store. He filed him after a violent quarrel. One night the kitten he had picked up, skinny as a finger picking phlegm frozen in the street, began spitting. Some one was rustling in the front. On the floor a little moon of light. He jumped up. A flashing shadow. He sank under a crack on the head.

When he came to, it was morning. Detectives tramped into the store and powdered the empty teabox for fingerprints. Days passed. The thugs weren't found. Mrs. Taback, the grocer's wife, advised that he give the policeman some smear. The more the better. Hershel didn't know how to go about it. At last he put a five-dollar bill into a piece of paper and chucked it as the bulled policeman with the big-barreled nose swung by. The policeman picked it up and walked off whistling.

The bandy-legged, cudgel-headed Taback was also very sympathetic. When Passover came round, he invited him to the ceremony. His father and mother had just come from the other side. They would let him know all that was going on there.

For the first time in years Hershel polished his shoes and pressed his suit. Taback sat with a red tie with a stickpin of a horsewhip on it. His fat wife shone like the sun. The two old people crouched in their chairs, slightly deaf; both had been clubbed over their heads during the pogroms. They read services from booklets issued by a bank with an eagle spread on the cover as if straining to lay an egg. Then they ate hot fish with horseradish like bloody sawdust.

The old woman talked of the horrible times they had been thru. Mrs. Taback shook her head. "Mama, don't. Eat, eat. A customer told me how during a pogrom all the Jews in the village were in a cellar. They found an old grandmother under a table stuffing a chicken's neck. 'Nu, children, we have bellies still, we must eat. If we come out alive, we'll be hungry, little hearts'."

The old man wiped his beard. "Even in Germany they are beginning pogroms with those new Jew-haters, those Hitler beasts."

Feinstein choked on the fish. He hadn't received a letter in months. The sweat broke out on his face and hands. He begged them to excuse him. He crawled out into the dark cold street. The moon was like vomit on the sea.

Mrs. Taback came in next day to find out how he was feeding. She wanted to help him. With the coming of hot weather, she told him of a good idea she had. "You look black as the earth, a consumptive, day after day, working like a horse, going out nowhere... Listen, my cousin has a big farm and hotel in the country. They need a tailor just a few hours a day. The cook is a widow without children, the wife of a painter. He climbed the ladder and fell down. The whole woman is only thirty... she is honey, milk and blood... she had a husband so long, she can not do without one... and you alone, for years without—"

Hershel held on to the wall. With a groan he grabbed his shears. Mrs. Taback backed out of the store. She fell down the steps. She slid along like a dog with an itch in her fat tail, shrieking with all her might. A crowd gathered. Taback rushed up, pounding his fists together. "I will crack you between my nails. I will—" He spat at him but the spittle fell back on his own face. The policeman with the big iron nose pushed in and warned Feinstein to keep his hands off other people's wives. Get yourself one to touch up. He would arrest him next time. Mrs. Taback was led off, shrieking, "And I invited him to eat … the pig … May the cholera take him, the cholera … "

Hershel was so upset he couldn't catch his breath. He lay down. A hot iron seemed to be going over him. He locked his shop and wandered in a daze through the streets. He came to the big park all his years in the city he hadn't visited once. He looked at the peacocks and the deer in the zoo, the grass, and he seemed to feel better. He sat on the bench. Around him mothers and their children. He crept back to his dark little room and sat, huddled all night, in a corner.

Miller the Flute showed up one day with a big brown man like a Russian bear, one eye lost in the war. He was a union organizer. They were going to form a union of the small shops against the dyeing and cleaning companies, against the racketeers who were chiseling millions of dollars out of your pockets. Was it necessary for him to show what despots the companies were? Hershel knew well enough no tailor could change his cleaner no matter how poorly dresses and suits were dyed and cleaned. All complaints were useless; the decisions of those bandits final. A tailor was assigned to a certain wholesaler and he must stick to him all the days of his life the way a man sticks to his wife. And then one tailor was charging a dollar fifty for cleaning, another a dollar, each tearing the others head off for a few bitter crumbs.

Hershel listened, but wouldn't go to the meeting. He said bitterly to Miller, "So you are a communist, another whore you've gone to."

Miller looked at him sadly. He grinned. "You worry only about your wife and children. That way you will do them harm. First a man has brothers and sisters. Fight, and you will have a safe family." He told the story of the different types of men. One who gets excited when he sees a woman a mile off, the other let him see a woman's stocking on a line and he can hardly breathe, and the third let him look merely at a lady's tailor.

Yes, he was hanging around Hershel because he was a lady's tailor. But if he wouldn't come with kisses, maybe blows would help.

One by one, the other stores in the neighborhood began closing. Hershel felt ashamed of himself. In the end, he did go to a meeting in a cold hall. The organizer sat with his paws to his nose like a bear in a cave, looking at the timid little men before him. He spoke to them fiercely, each word like a spike pounded down with his big fist. They must form a cooperative cleaning and dyeing factory. They must decide on a plan whereby a dozen retailers would no longer settle in a spot big as a hand, fiddle prices up and down, and fight each other like dogs over a lousy bone. They must boycott the bloated cleaners.

The men voted unanimously to accept the organizer's suggestions. And after the meeting a number of them filed into a lunchroom. Miller pulled Hershel in after them to have coffee and cake. "You must come out of your hole and see people. Why always hiding like a bedbug in a crack?"

On the walls of the lunchroom paintings of foreign ports and fields, windmills, a boat like a wooden Dutch shoe, a German tower. The fresh young girl, waiting on them, reminded him of his own. Hershel couldn't sit still. He left long before the others.

The deliveryman snorted when Hershel said quietly he could not give him any work. "You'll be begging to have us come inside of three days. I know you fellers. And if you think it's peaches and cream with us drivers, you're a goddamned fool." He drove off with the truck with the "Clean as a Whistle" sign, the whistle looking like a sugar scoop.

The driver was right. For one morning as Hershel crossed the street to chat with Wechsler the Polish tailor, he saw steam bunching at the door, the strike sign scraped off. Wechsler looked sheepishly away. His wife with the harelip, who had borne a child every time he had spat, sailed out. "Let the cholera take the union. My children and my old mother to starve because of those red wolves." She slammed the door in his face.

By the end of the second week most of the other tailors had opened. Miller came around furious but patient. "They'll wake up. This wasn't lost altogether. They'll wake up on the floor."

The strike hurt Feinstein more than the others because he was one of the last to open. He was terribly discouraged. He received a short letter from his wife. The money he had been sending for shipcards was all gone because of Hannele's serious illness. She was hearing terrible things of what was going on in America. She was thinking of going back to her brother in Poland.

The rich cousin hadn't returned a cent of the loan. All Hershel's letters to him remained unanswered. So one Saturday afternoon Hershel took the boat to Boston. He stood on the deck and watched the islands in the river. In front of a grim barred building a skinny man shook his fist at the people in the boat. Feinstein moved away from the well-fed men and women leaning on the rails, hooting back at the angry man on the island.

He didn't have any money for a cabin. He stayed out most of the night on deck. The moon came out. In the distance a sailing smack like a huge old man in praying shawl sank into the sea. He crouched over his pricked hands in his misery.

It took him half a day to find the suburbs. A servant admitted him. He stayed in the hall until one of the boys came in. He didn't recognize the greenhorn cousin. Too bad, papa and mama were off on a vacation in the car. Hershel stared at the fraternity pin salted down with tiny pearls. He crept out into the dark. He paced the street before the house until midnight. His hands pulsed in his helpless anger as if they were bleeding.

Back home, he thought of getting a lawyer. He thought of borrowing or selling the store, anything to raise a little money. He went noon hour to the bank where he had a month's savings. The bank with the old pictures—"Honesty is the Best Policy"; "Save for your Old Age"; "When Your Ship Comes In" with a picture of a ship with sails dollar bills; also the picture of a country home, a path like melted chocolate, and two children playing with a ball like an orange.

As he turned the corner, there a long line like a twitching worm. Bank guards in their letter carrier uniforms. Huddled frightened shopkeepers and workers. A woman wringing her hands and crying. Policemen with sticks. One graybeard whispering, "They'll give us back our money. They're Jews."

Hershel waited in line until nightfall. They were told to come next day. Next morning the bank was closed. It remained closed. There was a notice that the state had taken the bank over.

He lay in bed, reaching out like a caterpillar come to the end of a branch. To whom could he turn? He thought of Yosel Miller, but he didn't know where he lived. Sussman the druggist said he heard Yosel was at a strike in another city and some one else said he was arrested near a closed bank where he had been speaking against the robbers. And old customer, a baba, with a face like a cookapple noticed how he was suffering. She advised him to go to the synagogue, to be a good Jew for the holidays that were coming on, to see the rabbi who would help.

He went during the feast of atonement and stayed near the door of the packed badsmelling hall. The rabbi, a fat man with very short legs, talked about God, that God is a good boss, if you work for him you'll have riches, cars, good children and wives, he'll pay you with interest. But if you strike, woe is you. God is a good landlord, pay him rent, if not, he'll make you move out of his holy house into darkness, cold, and death.

During prayers for the dead, a little hungry girl whimpering near him. His Hannele was like that once. He turned to the mother with the beads like rock candy. "The living, the living, they're more important than the dead," he whispered huskily. She glared at him. "You corpse, you thin as a herring."

He walked out and waited on the corner. Why was it his business? And yet … The rabbi told him to come after the holidays.

In the rabbi's living room carpets, a flagon of wine, pictures. One of the pictures showed a room during the pogroms: windows cracked, furniture splintered, on the floor a woman with her dress torn, her bloody children swept into corners, and crouched at the door a bewildered grandmother with the book of psalms.

His head in a whirl, he mumbled his difficulties. The rabbi called in his son, a lawyer and state assemblyman. The son came in wiping his hands on a towel with a blue stripe—Pullman 1931. Well, let him come down to his office. The quota was filled. Why should he want to be running back to those crazy countries where people starve and they plague the Jews? There's one way of getting free. Just try becoming a Red, and you'll get deported … Come to the office …

Hershell rose with the rabbi's fee in his sweaty hands. The picture shrugged and flew suddenly above his head. The room burst like a bubble.

When he awoke he was on the floor. The servant girl was spurting water at him from her mouth as if he were something to be ironed. He thanked the rabbi with a fat hairless face like buttocks. He limped home. He sat on the dark doorsteps and stared at the shadow of the pump like a pen on the pavement. He couldn't eat, he couldn't sleep: No news from across the tearing shears of the water.

And now when Miller came to see him for a few minutes, Hershel was far friendlier. At least they were landsleit, and Miller was digging everywhere like a rooster and knew what was going on in the world.

"But why do you sit here and let worry suck at you like a big bedbug? Why do you sit and strain till the dung comes out of your eyes? Will you always be the kind of a man, who when the hooligan sticks his finger into your eye, you'll say, 'Excuse me because my eye is in your way?'"

Another time: "At least your own are not being killed and starved. Look at these pictures of little children and women in China in the city the Japs are bombing. And here in the mines, in the mills. Nu, can't you get angry? And if you are angry and don't do anything, a man goes crazy and eats himself up."

All this hammering knocked a sigh from Hershel. "You are right. I—I know. But I can see the quiet village in the old home and no steam sucking the heart out. And—" He waved his worn hand at the big press with its jaws open. His voice broke. "Yosel, I can't remember their faces."

Miller stared at the steam press. "A monster." He stuck a thimble on his head, picked up a long needle. "I will fight this like in the old days. Ach, Hershel, you are living in the middle ages."

Hershel fell back in his chair. Miller looked so funny using the needle like a sword. He gulped and burst out laughing. He couldn't stop. It was the first time he had laughed in America. He laughed until the tears dripped on his chest. Miller stood next to him and kept stroking his shoulder.

And so Miller had his way with him as with others. He made him read. He dragged him to meetings at homes, halls, street comers, squares. Still the unbearable ache did not leave. His brother-in-law in Poland had written he had not heard from the family also. But often at these gatherings his eyes opened to the sufferings of the millions lumped in the mass.

Accidentally Hershel saw the big demonstration that year of the workless and starving. On his way to a wholesaler to get some stuff for a skirt he came across the marchers. He followed anxiously. A whole army of foot and mounted cops were ready for them. One of the leaders came out of City Hall. The mayor had snickered, "When will the ice cream be served?" Another leader stood on the steps and shouted to the banners. The cops closed in. A horse trampled a shopgirl. She fell with a great ball of her insides beating from her mouth. Cameramen squatted around a bald elderly man with a snoot of red growing from his head. The ring of uniforms shoved the unemployed back. A few cops and detectives jumped up and took cracks at the heads. They turned around laughing. The mounted charged. Passersby mowed down. Hershel driven into a hallway. He fell against a wall, his leg going limp under him. The soldier's bayonet...

All the way home, he kept burying his face in his hands. Day after day, the picture roared thruout his brain. Miller showed up with a hand in a sling and a mask of courtplaster. He grinned at the agony streaking from Hershel's eyes. Oh, he was all right. That was only child's play compared to what was coming. They were looking for him. He stayed over and slept in the store.

But even in hiding he could not rest. He went out to the corner. Saddlebacked Wechsler, Sussman the horse-faced druggist, Taback with the whip stickpin came round him. "You have nothing to lose but dunged harness."

Taback's laugh was a belch.

Miller pointed a finger. "I like to laugh also. But this is no time for laughing. We must stop them before there will be no more laughing anywhere on this little earth. You mustn't be afraid. The blood in those bugs and leeches is what they've sucked from you."

Feinstein nodded.

"And how do you know, you crazy little wet-nosed tailor?" cried Taback.

"I have seen," he said quietly.

Taback hopped. "He has seen, Ohho through the eye of a needle."

Mrs. Wechsler passed on her way from the bakery shop, nursing a loaf of bread. From across the street the huge policeman. He knew a little

Yiddish. He said, "Hey, Yiddilach, if you want to davin, go." He pointed with his club to the synagogue in the shadows.

Mrs. Wechsler gasped as he walked off booming. She pulled her husband after her. "If you are not careful, you will be deported."

"We have as much right as him, that Cossack five dollar bill. The country is ours too." Feinstein choked on his hoarsened voice. The sweat broke out on his face. He blinked at his cracked trembling fist and dropped it swiftly in astonishment.

Miller took him by the arm. He led him back to the store.

That night they talked until late. A messenger came for Miller. He left, promising to drop in within a week or so. Feinstem rolled around in his hard bed. He fell asleep. Even his sleep was troubled. A great machine of iron blue men with their clubs stitching. The beaten girl. And in a flash her face. Hannele, Hannele ... He burst from sleep and bed. He crouched in his ragged underwear gasping. The bunched little cat stared at him with the green broken buttons of her eyes. He stood that way until morning.

And with the next evening his eyes were glazed, he was exhausted, feverish. He crept down the block to take a breath of fresh air. Sussman the druggist and his clerk and the baker were talking, some people from the tenements, former customers.

Sussman was saying he was a free-thinker, the salvation of the world was science. He had read the Bible once and remembered where Isaiah the prophet had said a war would come when all people would have to eat their dung and drink their water.

It looked as he was right with what was happening in every corner. People were sick. They needed medicines, drugs. You get up with a bad taste and the world is rotten. Go to a doctor and you see how the world changes, sweeter and fresher.

The policeman came up to see what was the matter.

Hershel could not control himself. He turned to the druggist savagely.

The policeman snorted through his big-barreled nose.

Hershel ignored him.

The policeman said, "If you want to davin, I told you fellers where to go."

Hershel kept on. "I will show you why. If—"

The policeman stroked him obscenely on his haunches with his nightstick.

Hershel turned around furiously. "You fool, you five-dollar bill."

The beefy face boiled red. He lifted his club and whacked.

With a wild cry, Hershel fell on him. He tore the club out of his hands. He hurled it into the gutter. He turned again to Sussman.

The punch lifted Hershel like the horn of an enraged bull. He tottered and fell face flat. He jerked over. His legs went as on a stiff treadle. He got on a knee and put his hand to his mouth. His fingers were bloody. He staggered up. He stared at the spots at his feet. A long pull of air filled him. His shoulders went back. He stood straight and calm.

The desperate cop was mouthing, "He tried to get my gun, the bastard, my goddamned gun."

Someone in the crowd said bastard. The women held their children. The men muttered.

Hershel said softly, "Tell Yosel, tell … He'll understand," he followed the cop.

SLOW DEATH

ERSKINE CALDWELL

All day we had been sitting in the piano box waiting for the rain to stop. Below us, twenty feet away, the muddy Savannah River oozed past, carrying to the sea the dead pines and rotted mule collars of the uplands.

Overhead, the newly completed Fifth Street Bridge kept us dry. We had stacked piles of brick-bats under the corners of the piano box to keep the floor of it dry, and the water that drained from the bridge and red clay embankment passed under us on its way to the swollen river.

Every once in a while Dave got up on his hands and knees and turned the straw over. It was banana straw, and it was soggy and foul-smelling. There was just enough room for the two of us in the crate, and if the straw were not evenly strewn, it made lumps under our backs and sides that felt as hard as bricks.

Just behind us was a family of four living in a cluster of dry goods boxes. The boxes had been joined together by means of holes cut in the sides, like those of dog houses, and the mass of packing cases provided four or five rooms. The woman had two Dominique hens. These she kept in the box with her all the time, day and night, stroking their feathers so they would lay eggs for her. There were a dozen or more other crates under the South Carolina side of the bridge; when old men and women, starved and yellow, died in one of them, their bodies were carried down to the river and lowered into the muddy water; when babies were born, people leaned over the railings above and listened to the screams of birth and threw peanut shells over the side.

At dark, the rain stopped. The sky looked as if it would not clear before morning, and we knew it would drizzle all night. Dave was restless, and he could not stay in the box any longer.

"Come on, Mike," he said. "Let's get out of here and get something to eat."

I followed him through the red mud up the side of the embankment to the pavement above. We walked through puddles of water, washing the sticky red clay from our feet.

Dave had fifty cents in his pocket and I was determined not to let him buy me anything to eat. He had baled waste paper in a basement factory off and on for two weeks; and when he worked, he made fifty cents a day. He had worked the day before in the factory, and the money had been kept all that time.

When we had crossed the river into Georgia, I turned sharply to the right and started running up the levee away from Dave. I had gone fifty yards when he caught me by the sweater and made me stop. Then he took the fist out of his pocket and showed me the fifty-cent piece.

"Don't worry about me, Dave," I told him, catching his wrist and forcing his hand back into his pocket. "I'll get by till tomorrow. I've got the promise of a half-day job, and that ought to be good for a dollar—a half, anyway. Go on and buy yourself a good meal."

"No," Dave said, jerking the fist out of his pocket. "We'll split it."

He pulled me along with him towards the city. We broke through the levee grass and went down the embankment to the pavement. There was a dull orange glow in the low sky ahead of us, and the traffic in the streets sounded like an angry mob fighting for their lives.

We walked along together, splashing through the shallow puddles of water on the pavement, going towards the city. Suddenly Dave stopped squarely in the middle of a sheet of rainwater that had not drained off.

"You're young, Mike," he said, catching my sweater and shaking it as a dog does a pillow. "I'm old, but you're young. You can find out what to do, and come back and tell me, and we'll do it."

"It'll take more than the two of us, Dave. We'll have to get a lot more on our side first."

"Don't worry about that," he said. "As soon as the people know what to do, and how to do it, we can go up and run the hell out of those fat bastards who won't give us our jobs back."

"Maybe it's not time yet, Dave."

"Not time yet! Haven't I been out of my job two years now? How much time do you want? Now's the time, before all of us starve to death and get carried feet first down to that mud-slough of a river."

Before I could say anything, he had turned around and started up the street again. I ran and caught up with him. We splashed through the puddles, dodging the deepest ones.

Dave had had a good job in a fertilizer plant in South Augusta two years before. But they turned him out one day, and they wouldn't take him back. There were seventy men in the crowd that was laid off that time. Dave would never tell me what had happened to the rest of them, but I knew what had happened to him. Afer Dave had run behind in house-rent for six or seven months, the landlord told him to move out. Dave wouldn't do it. He said he was going to stay there until he got back his job in the fertilizer plant in South Augusta. Dave stayed.

Dave stayed in the house for another four months, but long before then the window-sashes and doors of the building had been taken out and carried off by the owner. When winter came, the rain soaked the house until it was as soggy as a log of punk-wood. After that, the cold winds of January drove through the dwelling, whistling through the long wide slits like an angry man breathing through his clenched teeth. There was no wood or coal to bum in the fireplaces. There were only two quilts and a blanket for Dave and his wife and the three children. Two of the children died before January was over. In February his wife went. In March there was a special prayer service in one of the churches for Dave and his eleven-year-old daughter, but Dave said all he got out of it was a pair of khaki pants with two holes the size of dinner plates in the seat.

Dave did not know whether his daughter had died, or whether she was being taken care of by charity. The last time he had seen her was when a policeman came and took her away one morning, leaving Dave sitting in a corner of the windowless house wrapped in the two quilts and blanket.

We had reached Seventh Street by that time. The Plaza was hidden in fog, and all around it the tall buildings rose like century-old tombstones damp and gray.

"Go on and eat, Dave," I told him again. "When you get through, I'll meet you here, anr we'll walk back to the river and get in out of the cold."

"I'm not going a step till you come with me."

"But I'm not hungry, Dave. I'm going to get half a day's work tomorrow, and I'll be all right until I get paid off."

"Then I won't eat, either."

"Don't be a fool, Dave. I wouldn't lie to you. I'm not hungry."

"I'm not going to eat, then," he said again.

The night was getting colder and more raw all the time. Some drain water in the gutter at our feet lay in a long snake-like stream, and it looked as if it would freeze behind us, stinging our backs; a moment later it had shifted its course and was striking our faces.

"Hurry up, Dave," I begged him. "There's no sense in our standing here and freezing. I'll meet you in half an hour."

Dave caught my sweater and pulled me back. The roar of speeding automobiles and the crashing rumble of motor trucks made such a din in the street we had to shout to make ourselves heard.

Just as I was about to try again to make him get something to eat, I turned around and saw a black sedan coming around the comer behind us. It was coming fast, more than forty miles an hour, and it was on the inside, cutting the corner.

I pulled at Dave to get him out of the way, because his back was turned to the sedan and he could not see it.

He evidently thought I was trying to make him go to the restaurant alone, because he pulled away from me and stepped backward out of my reach. It was too late then to try to grab him and get him out of the way, and all I could do was to shout at him as loud as I could above the roar in the street. Dave must have thought that I was trying to make him go to the restaurant alone, because he stepped backward again. As he stepped backward the second time, the bumper and right front mudguard on the sedan struck him. He was knocked to the sidewalk like a duck-pin.

The man who was driving the big sedan had cut the corner by at least three feet, because the wheels had jumped the curb.

There was a queer-looking expression on Dave's face.

The driver had stopped, and he walked back to where we were. By that time people had begun to gather from all directions, and we were surrounded on all sides.

"Are you hurt, Dave"? I asked him, getting down on the sidewalk with him.

The driver had pushed through the crowd, and when I looked up, he was standing at Dave's feet looking down at us.

"Mike," Dave said, turning his face towards me, "Mike, the half is in my right-hand pants pocket."

His fingers were clutching my hand, and he held me tightly, as though afraid he would fall.

"Forget the half, Dave," I begged him. "Tell me if you're hurt. If you are, I'll get a doctor right away."

Dave opened his eyes, looking straight up at me. His shoulders moved slightly, and he held me tighter.

"There's nothing wrong with him," the driver of the sedan said, pushing the crowd away from him with his elbows. "There's nothing the matter with him. He's faking."

The man stood erect above us, looking down at Dave. His mouth was partly open, and his lips were rounded, appearing to be swollen. When he spoke, there was no motion on his lips; they looked like a bloodless growth on his mouth, curling outward.

"Mike," Dave said, "I guess I'll have to give up trying to get my job back. It's too late now; I won't have time."

The man above us was talking to several people in the crowd. His lips seemed to be too stiff to move when he spoke; they looked by that time like rolls of hardened dough.

"He's faking," he said again. "He thinks he can get some money out of me, but I'm wise to the tricks of these bums. There's nothing wrong with him. He's not hurt no more than I am."

I could hear people all around us talking. There was one fellow in the crowd behind me talking loud enough for everyone to hear. I could not see his face, but no one could have failed to hear every word he said.

"Sure; he's a bum. That's why they don't take him to the hospital. What in hell do they care about a bum? They wouldn't give him a ride to the hospital, because it might cost them something. They might get the goddam sedan bloody. They don't want bum's blood on the goddam pretty upholstery."

I unbuttoned Dave's sweater and put my hand under his shirt, trying to find out if there were any bones broken in his shoulder. Dave had closed his eyes again, but his fingers were still gripped tightly around my wrist.

"He's faking," the driver said. "These bums try all kinds of tricks to get money. There's nothing wrong with him. He's not hurt; he's faking."

The fellow behind us in the crowd was talking again.

"Why don't you take him to the hospital in your sedan, Dough-Face?"

The man looked the crowd over, but he made no reply.

I drew my hand out from under Dave's shirt and saw blood on my fingers. It had not come from his shoulder. It came from the left side of his chest where he had struck the pavement when the sedan knocked him down and rolled over him. I put my hand inside again, feeling for broken bones. Dave's body on that side was soft and wet, and I had felt his heart beating as though I had held it in the palm of my hand.

"How about taking him to the hospital?" I said to the driver looking down at us. "He's been hurt."

"That's the way these bums fake," the driver said, looking from face to face in the crowd. "There's nothing wrong with him. He's not hurt. If he was hurt, he'd yell about it. You don't hear him groaning, do you? He's just waiting for me to throw him a ten or twenty. If I did that and drove off, he'd jump up and beat it around the block before I could get out of sight. I know these bums; all they want is money. That one down there is faking just like all the rest of them do. He's no more hurt than I am."

I got up and tried to lift Dave in my arms. We could carry him to the hospital, even if the driver wouldn't take him in the sedan.

The driver was facing the crowd again, trying to convince the people that Dave was attempting to hold him up for some money.

"He's faking!" he said, shouting between his dead lips. "These bums think they can get money by jumping in front of an automobile and then yelping that they're hurt. It's a good lesson for them; maybe they'll stop it now. I'm wise to them; I know they're faking."

Dave opened his eyes and looked at me.

"Wait a minute, Mike," he said; "put me down. I want to tell you something."

I laid him on the sidewalk as carefully as I could. He lay there looking up at me, his hand gripping my wrist.

"I just want to make sure you know where the half is, Mike," he said. "The half is in my right-hand pocket, Mike."

I was about to tell him again that it was all right about the fifty cents, and to forget it, when suddenly his grip on my wrist loosened and his eyes clouded.

During all the time I knelt there holding him in my arms I was trying to think of something to say to Dave before it was too late. Before I could think of anything to tell him, the driver of the sedan elbowed closer and looked down at us.

"He's faking," he said. "The dirty bum's faking."

He elbowed his way out of the crowd and went towards his sedan. When he reached it, he shouted bock over the heads of the people:

"There's nothing wrong with him. He can't put nothing over on me. I'm wise to these dirty bums. All they want is some money, and they get well quick enough."

"Sure; he's a bum," the fellow behind me said, his voice ringing clear like a bell. "He might get some bum's blood on your goddam pretty upholstry."

Just then a policeman came running up. He pushed the crowd away and poked me with his nightstick and asked what the trouble was. Before I could tell him, he struck me on the back of the neck with the billy.

"What the hell you guys blocking the street for?"

I told him Dave was dead.

He turned around and walked half a block to a call-box and rang up the city hospital for an ambulance. By the time he had come back, the man who was driving the sedan had left.

"Why didn't you take him to the hospital in the car that knocked him down?" the policeman said, whirling his nightstick and looking down the street at a woman in front of a show-window.

"Hell, can't you see he's a bum?" the fellow behind me said. "We didn't want to get bum's blood all over the goddam pretty upholstry."

The policeman stopped and looked at the fellow and me. He took a step forward.

"On your way, bums," he said, striking us on the heads with the billy. "Clear out of here before I run you both in."

I ran back beside Dave and stood over him. The policeman jumped at me, swinging his billy and cursing. His mouth was hanging open, and his face in anger looked like an overflowing sewer.

All at once the street lights went completely black, and when I first regained consciousness, the fellow who had stayed with me was dragging me down the street towards the freight yards. As we passed under the last street light, I looked at him and saw the policeman's nightstick protruding from his coat pocket.

I SAW THE NAZIS

Edward Dahlberg

The author of this article is a well-known American novelist who was beaten up on the streets of Berlin by Nazis. He describes Germany under Hitler's reign of terror.

The average American reader of the daily newspapers knows more about actual conditions in the Reich today than most of the Germans do. In the main, the German population may be compared to civilians behind the lines who have no way of ascertaining what is happening at the front. The Germans are being virtually held incommunicado in their own country.

To say that the German press is muzzled is inaccurate. With the exception of *The Red Flag*, and possibly two or three other Communist organs, which are circulating underground, there is no opposition press. Catholic, Jewish, Liberal, Social Democratic newspapers no longer exist. Printing presses have been sabotaged, buildings demolished and in some instances the editors have been murdered. Mosse, the little Hearst of Germany, sold the *Vossiche Zeitung*, *Berliner Volkszeitung* and *Berliner Tageblatt*, three of the most important dailies to the Hitler Government.

People are even afraid to gather together in their own houses. Everyone is on-guard. Telephone conversations are completely non-political. Many have had their telephones disconnected. Since no one knows in these times whether or not the next man is a Nazi or an agent provocateur, there is not even any criticism of the present regime made by word of mouth. Dr. Curtius, a conservative and a member of the Bruening

Cabinet, and one who has always treaded on political rubber heels, sent a statement to the press that he could grant no interviews.

Many of the cafes and coffee houses, where radicals and the Berlin literati used to go, now seem drained. Or else for a time they are patronized by groups of uniformed Nazis who go there in order to drive away other patrons.

The Alexanderplatz, the workers' district, and formerly the nerve center of radical activity in Berlin, today seems subdued and deserted. Before the elections even the missions were flying the red flag, but now the Swastika banner has been hoisted up everywhere in its stead.

Publishing, too, is at a stand-still, for most of the larger houses are left. Publishers of proletarian literature have closed their doors and fled the country. Translation of foreign books has in the main, been discontinued, for the Hitler Government wishes to discourage the taste and palate for cosmopolitan ideas. Literature, with political or social implications is taboo. Apart from Nazi romances, novels whose purpose it is to increase the nationalistic sentiment of the youth in Germany at present, the publishers do not know what they can print.

It goes without saying, that if Hitler succeeds in nothing else, he will at least succeed in becoming the pallbearer of German culture. For as most of the important writers are either Communists or almost invariably anti-Hitlerite and therefore out of the country, who is there left to carry on the intellectual and artistic life of the people. Briefly, nobody with the exception of Dr. Paul Joseph Goebbels, Minister of Popular Enlightenment, whose propaganda is neither popular and certainly not enlightenment. There are of course the psychopathic and highly sadistic speeches of Captain Goering.

Hitler's power evidently does not rest in political insight nor in his program, an economic philosophy for Dienstmadchens, but in his army of Brown Shirts. With more than a million and a half of these Nazis, and not a half pint of Jewish blood to go around, at his beck and call, Chancellor Hitler has Germany under martial law. These Nazis, ranging in ages from fifteen to twenty-one, who look like undersized and malnourished post-war children, are indeed a pathetic example of Nordic superiority. Declasse workers, starved peasants, the squeezed petit-bourgeoisie, they in many ways resemble the ragtag and bobtail of the B. E. F. Many of them have bought their own brown uniforms on the instalment plan, using their dole cards, seven marks a week, for money. The students also comprise a large element of the National Socialists. Eighty percent of the students are Nazis. Wanting the return of caste and class prerogatives which the republic took away from them, they have zealously espoused Hitlerism. The position of the Nazi students has been stated by Baron Borries Von Munchausen (a very likely name) at the University of Gottingen: "The difficult economic situation has compelled many of them (that is, the students) to work together with factory workers, miners and farmhands and their experiences have shown them plainly how unclear and impractical are the ideals of the workers." ... "All this has changed since the students have learned to know the laboring classes better and especially since these classes have carried on a bitter fight against the students, whose income is far below that of their *opponents*." (Italics, mine. E. D.)

How long Adolf Hitler, a protege of the Duce and something of an operatic Attila in his own right, will remain in power, it is difficult at this moment to predict. There is already an undercurrent of dissension between the Steel Helmets and the Brown Shirts. The Steel Helmets, who make up the soldiery of the Nationalist Party at whose head is Hugenberg, are suspect in the eyes of the Nazis who look upon these War Veterans as defeatists. Besides, the Brown Shirts believe there are some Marxist taint within the rank and file of the Stahlhelm. This psychological interplay between the Nazis, those who were too young to have been in the World War, and the Steel Helmets, those who were in the war, has been interestingly set forth in Remarque's *The Road Back*.

However, a struggle between the Stahlhelm and the Brown Shirts would be most unequal, and unless the former go over to the workers, very little can be expected from this quarter.

Hitler is also receiving some support from the Junkers and heavy industry, but here the connection is much more vague and peripheral. To begin with, the Junker at present is a Hitlerite through fear rather than through conviction. Nevertheless, the Junkers, who committed themselves to support a government of lunacy rather than hazard the return of the Communists, hope to entrench themselves again and to reassume their former military prestige on the slogan: "We did not lose the War." There is no longer any talk in the Reich about the injustices of the Versailles Treaty. That is passé and synonymous with internationalism and defeatism. In this nationalistic sentiment rests the hopes of big industry, for it is inextricably bound up with large steel, coal, chemical and armament contracts.

The respectable people in Germany believe that Paul von Hindenburg may yet exhume the Weimar Constitution and that he has the power to dismiss "his" chancellor, if he wishes to. However, the story of the octagenarian president nodding his head in his sleep and Hitler taking the nod for yes pretty well exposes his position.

Hindenburg is a papier maché president. His statesmanship may be said to be static rather than kinetic. Members of the Women's Club and the reformist A. P. A. adore telling visitors how the statuesque president stood in front of an open window while the Nazis and Stahlhelm passed in complete and reverent silence below him. There he stood, erect and immobile, in his tightly-clad and suffocating uniform, performing his august duty to his fatherland and refusing to move, although the hot air from the radiator caused him extreme discomfort.

A Junker to the core, neither age nor sentimentalism explains his acceptance of Hitler and his dismissal of Bruening. Hindenburg would doubtless have acted as he did at sixty five. He acted with his eyes open, for he knew that even Bruening was contemplating some sort of legislative processes for the nationalization of industry and the expropriation of the big estates owned by the absentee landlords, the Junkers.

Although the Communists and Social Democrats are either in jail, or out of the country, or in the concentration camps for the duration of the war, as it were, the workers may be able to call a general mass strike and in this way at least put the brakes on the Hitler movement. Certainly, there doesn't seem any other source from which counter-revolution can come. There is another factor, namely, the possibilities of a rift within the rank and file of the Nazis. Whether Hitler will last out or not will depend upon his ability to feed and shelter the Brown Shirts and also upon the mount of state "socialism" he will attempt to inject into his program.

Although the Nazis hate the taboo word, *Marxismus*, they are not averse to certain kinds of plagiarized and garbled backstairs socialism for demagogic purposes. And it may be that the Brown Shirts are literalminded and may have taken too seriously the Chancellor's radio hemorrhages on Brot, Freiheit and socialism.

Meanwhile, the workers, whose trade unions have been sabotaged, whose meeting places have been engulfed with Nazis, are carrying on some underground activity. Some are inside of the Hitler ranks. A commentary upon the workers tactics and position in Germany today may be deducted from the way they cast their ballots at the last election in one district. Two fifths of the workers voted the Communist ticket, two fifths the Social Democratic one, and the remaining fifth, which voted for the Nazis are known to be either Communists or Social Democrats. Sometimes through fear, more often as a matter of tactics to enable them to remain in Berlin and fight against Hitler. Only one third of the workers have supported the Catholic Centrist Party, the other two thirds going over almost, en bloc, to the Communists and Social Democrats.

Although it must be admitted that the Hitlerites have completely terrorized the German population, and that they have given the screw an extra turn, for they are taking no chances with Communist agitators, Hitler and his sanatorium Cabinet may yet blow up the works themselves.

NEGRO NOVELISTS AND THE NEGRO MASSES

Eugene Gordon

AS A NATIONAL minority, the Negro people in the United states had their origin in the agricultural South. The institution of slavery in this country, being confined principally to the southern section as a matter of economic necessity, was the second stage in their develop-ment from a heterogeneous medley of tribal remnants into homogeneous people. They were heterogeneus to begin with because so-called Negroes came neither all from Africa nor (when they did come from Africa) from any one section of that continent. They were brought here not only from the West Coast, the Southeastern Coast, and the Upper Niger, but also from the Sahara Desert region, from Senegal, from the Lake Chad region, and from the Zambesi Delta. Captives included also men so alien to the African black as Moors from the southeastern Mediterranean coast, Malays from Madagascar, and natives of East India. This diversity in their origins accounted for the diversity in the "racial" characteristics of the plantation "blacks" even before inter-mixture between them and the whites had taken place. On the same plantations, moreover, there were often slaves who possessed not only different physical characteristics, but customs so different as to indicate sharp differences in social and eco-nomic development. There is no telling how long this physical and social disharmony would have persisted, if circumstances had not brought an end to the first stage of development of these aliens into a nation and begun their second stage.

The second stage marked off the end of their status as indentured servants; it indicated the beginning of their status as slaves. I must go somewhat into detail at this point. Negroes were not brought to the American colonies originally as slaves, but, as many of the poor whites who were coming in at that time, as indentured servants. The status of the blacks was identical with that of the white servants. This servitude to which both the poor whites and the stolen blacks were subjected was (according to the International Encyclopeadia) "a legalized status of Indian, white, and Negro servants preceding slavery," and was common throughout the English colonies. The system originated in 17th century England, when, driven to desperation by debts, men indentured (or bound by contracts) themselves indefinitely into servitude to pay their passage to this promised land of America. "The transition from servitude to slavery was effected in the case of the black man," explains the *Negro Year Book*, "when the custom established itself of holding Negroes 'servants for life.'"

It was a natural sequence of the system that those who enjoyed its benefits should come in time to lengthen the terms of their servants from an indefinite period to life. It was a logical consequence of the system that the black servants rather than the white should be those whose status became that of private property. Being an alien race, and feared because they were an alien race, the Africans were forced deeper and deeper into the morass of servitude in perpetuity. The changed status was so gradual and occurred over so long a period of time as to be almost unnoticed. It was a change that grew naturally out of the objective conditions of society: increasing necessity for cheap labor; increase in the number of laws restricting movements of slaves (as fear of them deepened); change in the sentiment of the master class from regarding the blacks as servants to regarding them as slaves. In general terms, the reason for the change of status from servant to slave was that as slaves these black aliens, whom the master class did not understand (and made no effort to understand), were more readily controlled as slaves than as servants. Before the heterogeneus mass of blacks was conscious of what was happening, generations had passed. It was already taken as a matter of course that the child should inherit the status of the mother (a custom, incidentally, which was partly responsible for the beginning of the freed-Negro class, since children born of white servant women and black slave men were not slaves). Children born in slavery thus were slaves; the institution of slavery was thus firmly established.

The birth and death of generations of blacks, who passed from the status of indentured servants to the status of slaves, effected profound changes in the mass psychology of the blacks. The factors of slavery had already so welded together these diverse peoples that long before 1863 they had been *forced* into the category of an incipient nation. Differences in physical characteristics were less sharply apparent; a common tongue (English) had been developed; they all lived compactly together under the enveloping aegis of slavery. Here lay a condition fallow for the birth of a national psychology; here lay a promising of a peculiar national culture.

If the upper classes were unconscious of what they had created when they altered the Negro's status from one of Servitute to one of slavery in perpetuity, subsequent events made them aware of it. Certainly the 25 or more insurrections of slaves,—even before the revolution against England!—was irrefutable testimony that the black had suppressed all ethnic, tribal and cultural differences among themselves and had grown to recognize the slave-holder as their common enemy. It was directly a result of the common national understanding among the slaves that plantation owners, in gradually mounting waves of terror, began to restrict the free movement of the Negroes, that they abrogated the right of slaves to assemble even for Christian service, and that they decreed it a major crime for blacks to seek an education. In Maryland, for instance, the blacks were "forbidden to assemble or attend meetings for religious purposes which were not conducted by white licensed clergymen or by some "respectable white of the neighborhood authorized by the clergyman." The slave-owners were learning already that the church was a sword that cut both ways: toward power through organization, in the hands of the slaves; toward suppressing the slaves by anesthetizing them, in the hands of the masters. Thus, real slavery heightened the second stage of the Negro's development into a homogeneous people; gave this development an impetus that ordinary servitude could never have given.

This artificially created nation, of necessity, gave birth to an unhealthy culture. Of necessity, there arose from this culture an unhealthy psychology. Developing as a nation, the Negroes were, nevertheless, a suppressed nation, more, they were a slave nation. Natural vents to national aspirations were clogged up, so that a national psychosis resulted. National aspirations could find no outlet except in futile protests: prayers and hymns to the white "God" of the master class; uprising which, betrayed by the Christians among the slaves, were turned into abortive gestures; a fierce hatred which included all whites, but a hatred which in various slaves manifested itself in various forms,—hypocritically, as loyalty or love; as cunning or deceit; in actual physical violence against any white who crossed their path. The psychology of the slave nation was, therefore, as malodorous as the culture from which it grew. The gradual transition from indentured servant into slave-in-perpetuity, the status extending to unborn generations; the ruthlessness with which tendencies toward the most innocuous social organization were crushed; the savagery with which uprisings were put down;—these factors, bearing upon the developing national culture, created in most slaves a fatalist outlook on life, in spite of their white God. They would get what was decreed for them (having a suspicious feeling that God was a sort of puppet, anyway, manipulated by the master class). It was as inevitable that this unhealthy psychology should stamp the slaves with a sense of inferiority as it was that the psychology developed in the white servants should operate in the opposite direction. The black slave, on the one hand, had "learned" that he was an inferior being; the poor white, on the other hand, forced out of his position by the black slave, nevertheless felt a superiority over all blacks. The master class wrote "scientific" and religious treatises and books to prove that both the black slave and the poor white had the correct outlook on life.

The Civil War crystallized this geographic-economic-political situation into a peculiar national situation, and from this peculiar national situation there emerged an unhealthy national culture; an unhealthy national culture which was reflected in the national psychology in the form of a peculiar national psychosis. Cursed with this psychosis (which was a result of repressed desires for national and individual actions), the developing Negro fiction writers inevitably epitomized in their characters and situations the "virtues" that slavery had taught them most passionately to desire: in general, all those things which to the slave seemed to make life on earth worthy the struggle,—wealth, and all it signified, including especially leisure, education, a sophisticated culture, and a freedom of action comparable to that of the former master. Of course there were individual writers who approached the matter of interpreting their people according to their individual outlooks on life and their individual comprehensions of the Negro's problem.

For instance, the preacher who turned novelist did not immediately abandon the churchly for a materialist approach to life. In the case of the Rev. Lorenzo D. Blackson, to cite a specific instance, religion was the force which eventually would free the blacks; he tried to prove it in *The rise and Progress of the Kingdoms of Light and Darkness; or, The Reigns of Kings Alpha and Adabon*, a fantasmagoria based upon an illiterate preacher's understanding of *Paradise Lost* (published in 1867). Blackson's "novel" is significant only in that it marks the beginning of imaginative expression in prose among the ex-slaves. Those who followed him, however, were of hardly more value to the masses of Negroes who were crying desperately for leadership. Blackson, the preacher, thought religion would open the way out. Charles W. Chestnut, the first Negro novelist to attract the attention of the white upper class, thought an Olympian detachment was essential to an interpretation of "primitive" Negro psychology; he wrote simple folk tales, after the fashion of Joel Chandler Harris and Thomas Nelson Page, maintaining his Olympian balance so well that, as a recent critic said of Chestnutt's *The Conjure Woman* "There is nothing.... to indicate that the author was colored." Chestnutt's novels and short stories of the black masses of the South were such innocuous but sentimental portrayals as the whites of the North demanded. The fact that many of these works appeared in the Atlantic Monthly (from 1887 to 1905) is not only suggestive of their content but is also evidence of their author's upper class alignment. Being as white in appearance as any "Nordic," Mr. Chestnutt held himself physically aloof (as he had a right to do, of course), from the masses of blacks, and when he wrote of them in *The Colonel's Dream*, *The Conjure Woman*, and *The House Behind the Cedars*, he wrote as a liberal who sympathized with their plight and wished them well in their struggles for "equality before the law," but who felt no common bond between them and himself. Psychologically he reflected his class, which was the class of those who, reading the Atlantic, looked upon the ex-slaves as quaint "darkies" belonging to another world. Their only contact with these Negroes came through the sentimental "interpretations" of Harris, Page, and Chestnutt. Bostonians desired no other contact. Chestnutt was their contact man, bringing the flavors and the odors of the Old South vicariously to the quivering nostrils of the Beacon Hill bourgeoisie.

Early Negro fiction writers assumed varied attitudes in their approach to the black masses, these attitudes representing in each of them his own psychological reaction to the objective conditions of his life. There are two reasons why the Negro proletariat, during the decade following emancipation, produced no writers of fiction. One reason was their depressing ignorance, a natural heritage of slavery; another reason was that they had no leisure even to try to express themselves in imaginative prose. This was a period also of the rising Negro bourgeosie, a class which chafed fretfully under the oppression of the white upper class; a Negro bourgeoisie which, stunted in its historical development, was forced by necessity to express its resentment through the best means at its command. This means was fiction, and those who employed it most successfully for their class were Charles W. Chestnutt and William E. Burghardt DuBois. Both these men belonged to the Negro upper class, and they both, therefore, dreamed of the day when the "racial" barriers separating the white bourgeoisie from the black would be demolished and destroyed. But Chestnutt's approach to the Negro masses as a novelist was purely in the tradition of the Olympians, while that of DuBois was more the approach of a sociologist than a novelist. As a creator of "pure" art, Chestnutt did not share the pangs of those whom he made suffer; he was psychologically the aristocrat. BuBois, on the other hand, although by training and temperament an aristocrat, nevertheless suffered intensely with the characters whom he created. The reason for this difference in approach of two upper-class Negro novelists lay almost wholly in their environments. Chestnutt's was a "normal" American environment; DuBois, while still very young, came face to face with what he describes as "the veil" of color. He himself describes the shock of realizing suddenly one day that he was "different" from his white playmates when a little girl called him "nigger." Here was the beginning of a new and personal psychosis superimposed upon his national psychosis. This unhealthiness has shown itself in everything that he has written. His has resentment against white peoples in general, because, he feels, they are responsible for the ignominy of the colored bourgeoisie. His two novels, *The Qwest of the Silver Fleece* and *The Dark Prin*cess," although purporting both to be concerned with the problems of the Negro masses, are actually concerned with the problems of the colored upper class. His interest in the Negro masses is obviously theoretical.

Paul Laurence Dunbar belonged to the Negro proletariat, but his aspirations, as he acquired friends among both the white and the Negro bourgeosie, were toward the upper class. That is why his earlier poems expressed faithfully the aspirations of the Negro worker, while both his later poems and his novels reflect his desire to be with the class which had adopted him. Dunbar's three novels, *The Uncalled*, *The Love of Landry*, and *The Fanatics*, deal in a most artificial manner with the trivialities of parasitic whites. In the first two there are no Negroes at all, and in the third book black workers are used only to create "atmosphere."

There were two Negro novelists of this period whose propaganda works aimed to place the Negro masses favorably before the "reading public"; but there was no such public, because the stuff was unreadable. These men were Frank J. Webb and William Wells Brown. Up to 1920 the Negro workers had not produced a writer of fiction with a proletarian-revolutionary approach to the Negro's problems.

It is significant that the present group of Negro novelists, numbering fewer than twelve, appeared at the very moment when the bourgeoisie, having reached its apogee immediately following the World War and started upon its plunge into decay, demanded a new kind of amusement, a new kind of story, a new form of entertainment. The moment bourgeois culture in the United States began to crack and crumble, the moment the sated and blasé bourgeoisie began to realize that it need look no longer for new appetizers among the dregs of the old order, they turned to the Negro. Here lying at their very back door was a vast and unexplored dark continent, they thought, and began to investigate it at its edges. The first hardy pioneer to venture into this unknown black wilderness came later to be known as the white-haired boy of Harlem Colored society. Carl Van Vechten came to the colored bourgeoisie as the final fruition of its despairing hopes, as the answer, at last, to its fervent prayers: the white aristocracy was taking notice of the colored aristocracy. Mr. Van Vechten was treated with the deference and honor due an emissary from one great people to another great people. Nothing was too good for him, whether it was their kitchen-sink gin or their women. Van Vechten tarried, for this experience among an exotic people was exilarating. He wrote. The offspring of this strange cohabitation was named *Nigger Heaven*, and the bastard made its old man rich. Van Vechten tarried yet a little longer to thrill at the genuflections while the book was being extolled, but when the hosannas died down he began to long for home, and he took the long journey back to Mt. Olympus, the long trek back to Greenwich Village. *Nigger Heaven* was an "interpretation" of the colored upper class: a vicious distortion of the lives even of these fragile parasites. But it was what they loved, because it appealed to their childish class-vanity: they felt that now they had formed an unbreakable link with aristocracy, for, like members of the aristocracy, they had been immortalized in a novel. They did not know that instead of being immortalized they had really been embalmed. Van Vechten set the pace which Negro novelists of New York tried immediately to follow.

The reaction to *Nigger Heaven* among the Negro bourgeoisie was ecstatic, because *they* had been belatedly discovered by a "white artist" and fittingly apostrophized; their reaction to Claude McKay's *Home to Harlem* was one of general nausea and pains in sections of the anatomy other than the neck. For McKay, a retired radical sojourning in the Montmartre Monttartre, wrote of the Negro worker. It did not matter to the colored aristocracy that McKay's workers were entitled to that designation only by literary courtesy; it despised these blacks of the "lower classes." What McKay really did, however, was to write an autobiographical sketch of himself, dilating upon his love life. For *Home to Harlem* was not the story of workers who worked; it was about "workers" who swaggered through Harlem's night life perfecting the art of love. It was not a novel of workers who live in hovels of tenements; who schemed to outwit the greedy landlord and his eviction agent. It was a novel of "workers" who lie concealed in the rat holes of Harlem by day, drinking until sodden, the women fighting like beasts for the possession of some man's body, the men perpetually on the verge of committing murder to possess the body of some woman.

A novel by a radical which does not touch upon the workers' struggle to survive in a capitalist society is so queer an anomaly as to be weird: that was *Home to Harlem*. But McKay was no longer active in the radical labor movement. He had served his apprenticeship under Max Eastman on the Masses, had written an indignant poem wholly lacking in working-class content, attacking lynching, had disappeared mysteriously to the Soviet Union, and had retired exhausted to the sidewalk cafes of Montmartre. His treatment of a small group of Negroes, a few of whom had returned fashionably "disillusioned" from the World War, cannot in any sense be extended as adequate treatment either of Negro workers as such or of Negro soldiers. The returning soldier, disillusioned concerning wars in general, was rather a popular hero in fiction at that time; for that very reason, a radical ought to have handled the theme differently. For disillusionment alone—simple disgust and cynicism expressing themselves in physical debaucheries—is unfit as a theme for a working-class novel. If novelist's workers *must* have illusions, then these workers, to have any value for us, must have also disillusionment evolving into sanity of mind and clarity of vision. If there be no class-conscious action following this awakening into reality, there should be, at least, a forecast of it. Straying from this rule, fiction about workers has no validity for the working class. Certainly *Home to Harlem* has none. McKay's second novel *Banjo* differed in only unimportant details from *Home to Harlem*. The retired "radical" had grown fat, and ill, and indifferent in Paris.

Since Van Vechten captured upper-class Harlem there has been a small troop of Negro novelists, all viewing this subject from approximately the same level and the same angle. We shall consider first George S. Schuyler, who used to be called a radical, but whose enemies, even, would blush at pinning such a tag on him today. Possessed of considerable talent as a newspaper man, Schuyler is nevertheless uninterested in the working class and its struggles. The masses of black toilers are, to him, a doltish lot, and he would, perhaps, like to do something about bringing them "up" to his own rarified status as a sophisticated "intellectual"; but for the present, he believes, imperialism is an excellent training course for nations like Haiti and Liberia, while, according to his pronouncement, "we cannot do away with the clergy in capitalist America or Communist Russia," because, he explains learnedly, "under any form of society the masses of people must believe, and it makes little difference whether it is belief in the miracles of Jesus Christ or the wizardry of Karl Marx." These quotations from Schuyler, who has never outgrown his adolescent cynicism, are typical of his writings, being designed to arouse a jeer from some Communist sympathizer (since the Communists themselves ignore him). To respond to such obvious bids for response would be out of place here, especially since they do not occur in his fiction but in a newspaper column; however, these quotations are indicative of Schuyler's methods, whatever he writes. The proletarians in his novel *Black No More* are an inarticulate mass of fools with eyes set upon the conjury of pseudo-science, hoping thereby to cure their fundamental economic and political ills by changing themselves into white men. Like most other Negro writers of fiction, Schuyler believes the Negro masses to be oppressed under capitalism because of their superficial racial characteristics, and, logically, Schuyler makes his workers voice Schuyler's profundities.

Four other Negro writers have dealt with the Negro worker in fiction, these being Wallace Thurman, Countee Cullen, Rudolph Fisher, and Langston Hughes, but none of them except Hughes has, evidently, heard of the class struggle. Thurman's dilettantism, revealed in his absorption in the "problems" of white and colored degenerates and common parasites; Cullen's snobbishness, betrayed in the speech and actions of his puppets,—their philosophical imbecilities; Fisher's carefree happy-go-luckies with their repartee suggestive of cheap vaudeville;—these men are obviously not to be considered for any proletarianrevolutionary treatment of the Negro worker. They are writing for the upper classes who demand the stereotype which fits most neatly into their conception of what the Negro ought to be.

Thus far, Langston Hughes, in *Not Without Laughter*, has written the only novel in which the Negro worker is pictured as seeing the way out through the class struggle; it is the only novel by a Negro which is at the same time a critique of fiction *Not Without Laughter* is lacking in many important elements, the reason being, chiefly, that Hughes at that time was lacking almost wholly in political development; but his political development since the novel was written indicates a fulfillment of the promise it contained.

The unhealthy national culture of the Negro people,—reflected in the national psychology as a peculiar national psychosis,—is gradually evolving into a sound national culture, as works other than fiction prove. As working-class Negro novelists arise, however, and organize the experience of the Negro worker imaginatively and artistically, they will turn the black masses away from the poison of bourgeois propaganda toward a healthy consideration of their own interests.

YOU CAN'T SLEEP HERE

Edward Newhouse

L ET me see now. The thing to do is to take stock. The thing to do is to get organized. Weigh possibilities.

You couldn't weigh possibilities in all that noise and light. I crossed 42nd Street and turned down Seventh Avenue. The valleys of garment skyscrapers loomed like dows of great vultures. This was really a very remarkable city. Possibly it should be a source of gratification that unemployment didn't hit me in some one-horse Arkansas burg. Everything was numbers. Seventh Avenue. 34th Street. First National Bank.

Standing on the corner of 34th Street you could see the tallest building in the world, the greatest theatrical section, the second largest railroad station and a pack of other things. The people from Arkansas would very likely be tickled silly. A sharp raindrop landed on my cheek and flowed into my mouth. I passed between the columns of the second largest station and sat down in the waiting room.

My head droned blankly. I would shortly become sleepy. What about the stocktaking, I thought, the weighing of possibilities?

People came in shaking water out of hats and umbrellas. That was one possibility less. That let out the park for the night. I had vaguely expected to sleep there.

There was little use in going over old territory. No jobs. Aquaintances couldn't do a thing. I had neither aptitude nor stomach for the smalltime rackets at which I may have been able to pick up change.

Fellows tried lots of things. They opened beer gardens or tried to sell insurance or peddled white linen caps. One guy I knew operated slot machines. He paid out seventy-five dollars per to the manufacturing company which had the monopoly and bought protection in the form of police tabs and put ten dollars worth of slugs in each and now he was raking in heavy. He had a contact with the police commissioner's son who was reputed to be the head of the works. There was no reason why I couldn't get in on something like that. I had the nerve but not the initiative. And the little matter of finances.

The man next to me had a cowhide suitcase and a Herald-Tribune. He looked like an assistant district attorney or a line coach at Yale or a secretary to a Senate lobbyist for munitions manufacturers. I looked over his shoulder to see which section he was reading and it was sonnet at the bottom of the page. He looked into my eyes steadily and reproachfully and started back. Nonsense.

I stood up impatiently and went over to a poster announcing special excursion rates.

Let me see now. Get back to earth now. I hurried across the corridor to Seventh Avenue. The rain had stopped and a clean wind from Jersey was drying the asphalt. It was strange to see the garment center deserted like that.

Back at 42nd Street I waited for midnight edition of the Times so as to be among the first to read the want ads. When it appeared I took it into the automat and spread it open on a table. The manager came toward me. He was sorry but too many people used the place as a hangout without buying anything. If it were up to him he'd invite anybody that felt like sitting down but those were the regulations. Would I please?

Allright, I said. As I went for the coffee faucet he remained at my table, looking after me. I tried to think of something absurdly facetious to say when I came back. I thought I would buy a cherry pie and insist that he share it, saying it was an old Schenectady custom. I looked at my money but all I had was a quarter and a dime so I didn't buy anything else and when I turned around he was back at the cashier's booth. And there wasn't a single likely item in the Times. There were nine items in the Help Wanted column but they called for office executives and salesmen.

I didn't want so stay there under the supervision of the snotty manager. The coffee burned my tongue but I bolted it and walked out. It drizzled again. Nothing to do but go back to Penn station.

The man with the cowhide suitcase and the sonnet was gone. There weren't more than half a dozen people on the benches. I read the sports pages and something about disarmament. A French delegate called Beaulieu said his nation was ready to disarm if the other powers were. An associate professor of economics at Northwestern was convinced that if only somehow purchasing power could be restored, an industrial revival would follow.

I also read an interview with Winthrop Rockefeller, fourth son of John D. Rockefeller, Jr. He was taking time out of his studies at Yale to make a survey of industrial relations and he was starting at the Bayonne refinery of Standard Oil.

He was majoring in history, he had never heard of Charles A. Beard or Oswald Spengler, he didn't care to express an opinion on communism but he was interested in the labor movement. In fact, they had an association at the refinery and the men paid nominal dues only but a floral wreath is sent to the home of any member that dies. Also, "we put his name on a board out in front of the building and lower the flag to half mast."

It was only half past one but I felt sleepy because I'd been up the night before. I slid to the end of the bench and dropped my head against the papers and closed my eyes.

What the hell do I want cherry pie for, you don't see Lou Gehring eating cherry pie, he's an athlete but Babe Ruth squawked and said hell that ball was away over my head git yourself a truckload of binoculars, get a load of this, I put a nickel slug in and out comes the jackpot, of course Babe Ruth has a jackpot belly and get a load of that bottle of pop flying from the bleachers to the bullpen and around to the backstop and down on my shoulder.

"Hey, lookout," I said. At the sound of my voice I opened my eyes and a guard was standing above the bench, patting my shoulder.

"What train are you waiting for?"

"It's allright," I said, "I guess I snoozed off."

"*Is* it allright? What's your train?"

"I'm not taking any train."

"What are you doing here?"

"Nothing. Sitting."

"You can't sit here, mister."

"Why not?"

"Because you can't."

"Don't sit there arguing. Go on. Sit somewhere else."

"I like it here," I said, "Get your hands off me."

He took out a whistle. "You want to get arrested? Just say the word and I'll get you arrested."

"No, I don't want to get arrested," I said.

"Go on then."

"Keep your shirt on," I said, "no matter how dirty it is."

I walked through the corridor to Seventh Avenue again. This time I walked east until Park and turned up. I thought I could detect the motion of the hands on the illuminated clock over Grand Central. I hoped they would not kick me out of the waiting room there. How foolish of me not to have said I was waiting for some train in the morning.

There were two people on the entire vast concourse of Grand Genral, a redcap and a newsboy. The restaurants and candy stand were closed and a cat sat on the information desk. I was alone on the benches.

I slept there for an half an hour, then a guard woke me. He was older than the other one and wore a different uniform.

"What train you waiting for?" he said.

I remembered I should have found out about some schedules. I said, "I was supposed to meet my sister who's coming up from Richmond but we evidently missed each other. She must have gone on to my hotel but she didn't have the right one, you see I moved yesterday, but I'm sure she'll come back here to look for me again."

My God, I thought, that was awful.

"Well, you ain't allowed to sleep here," he said.

"I'll sit then."

The clockhand moved jerkily. Reading would only have made me sleepier. It felt as though tiny strings were attached to my eyelashes with marbles fastened to the other end, pulling down. I whittled at the bowl of my pipe and cleaned my fingernails. Two men with pails came and began mopping the floor.

The guard walked up and down. I closed the blade of my knife and went into the washroom and bathed my face in cold water. When I returned the guard was talking to one of the cleaning men. I did not want to sit back on the benches.

"I'm going to look around," I said, "If a young lady with blonde hair and yellow suitcase comes, would you mind asking her to stay here until I show up?"

"I'll do that," the guard said.

Outside I did not feel like walking. There were some wheel chairs in the hallway and I fell asleep in one of them. The guard woke me.

"You can't sleep here," he said, "Better get up and start looking for your blonde sister."

PRELUDE TO A LYNCHING

Allan Taub

NINE a. m., August 1, in Tuscaloosa, Alabama. Frank B. Irwin of Birmingham, Irving Schwab of New York and myself push through the muttering crowd outside the courthouse. We catch one voice distinctly:

"There go the sons of bitches. Let's get them now!"

We push on. The court room is crowded—perhaps 400, with about 40 Negroes squeezed together in the back. All the prominent citizens of Tuscaloosa are there, including former Governor William Brandon ("Twenty-four votes for Oscar B. Underwood!"); the two local junior counsel appointed by the court, La France and McGrath, as well as the three distinguished lawyers rushed into the case just two days before—after it became known that the International Labor Defense had been retained by the mother of Dan Pippen, one of the three boys on trial for murder. These three attorneys are John McQueen, former president of the Alabama Bar Association; former Circuit Court Judge Rice, and Reuben Wright.

A strange proceeding—five defense counsel appointed by the court for an ordinary "nigger case", which usually is disposed of in one perfunctory court day. But there was a reason, expressed by Judge Foster himself to one of the I. L. D. attorneys:

"We don't want another Scottsboro case."

And now Judge Foster himself. Seventy years old, a patriarch in every detail, long silvery hair, immaculate linen suit, his voice a silken rustle, every intonation and gesture breathing purest justice tempered by mercy.

Irwin gets up and makes a militant speech. Irwin, who has been a machinist, a barber, and a pugilist in his day, asks for a postponement.

He produces the retainer, signed by Lucinda Pippen, mother of Dan, in Tuscaloosa three weeks before. He tells the serene and courteously listening court that he has been refused admission to jail to consult his client. Consequently, the defense is not prepared.

I speak next. I assure them of the hospitable welcome that awaits any attorney from a sister state who appears in a New York court to try a case. They don't mind hearing that. I then tell them something else:

"This procedure bears a remarkable resemblance to another hearing, on the morning of April 6, 1931, held in Scottsboro, Alabama, when there were also two sets of lawyers appearing for the defense—in that case, of nine Negro boys accused of rape."

That is exactly what they don't want to hear. I point out that the United States Supreme Court had ruled in the Scottsboro case that denial of counsel is denial of due process of law—a new precedent established in the highest court by the campaign of the I. L. D. I include by reiterating that the defense, due to the denial of access to the defendant, is not prepared to go on now.

Schwab draws the court's attention to the unusually crowded courtroom and the presence of armed militiamen, in town, as evidence of open hostility to the defendant, and has these conditions noted on the record.

An hour and a half is spent in arguing. The prosecution doesn't figure. The only question is: Who are the defense counsel. And on the record is the official authorization of the mother of the defendant (Dan is only 17 and his father is in jail with him) retaining the I. L. D.

The court-appointed counsel do not answer us but ask for a recess. The judge withdraws; the other counsel and the prosecutor also leave. They return, and McQueen rises to make a motion. It takes him minutes to get out three sentences or so. He is overcome with emotion. Justice is his goal, and that of his distinguished associates. As officers of the court, they are there to take the court's directions. It is a sad duty. And (with a deep sigh) he is constrained to ask that the case be continued—which is exactly what we have been fighting for.

The prosecution calls Dan Pippen to the stand and asks him who is his choice for counsel. I object: the boy is only 17 years old; he has been beaten in jail; he is in fear of personal violence. This is no time for such a procedure. The objection is politely listened to, benignly overruled, and an exception is graciously granted by Judge Foster. The boy chooses the local lawyers. La France and McGrath. His parents, placed on the stand, express the same choice. Same procedure, same objections; overruled, overruled, exceptions noted. Then the court room is cleared; a few of us remain near the bench, lawyers and deputy sheriffs.

Judge Foster is graver, kinder, if possible, than before. Justice, fair and even handed justice, is still his great desire. He will take the matter of the defendant's representation under advisement. And there, despite newspaper reports that the I. L. D. attorneys were barred from the case, the matter officially rests today. On the record, the signed retainer of the I. L. D. to defend Dan Pippen, and in connection with it, Judge Foster's announcement that he would consider. Case postponed.

Judge Foster comes down from the bench. He is extremely solicitous about our safety. The crowd outside is reported growing dangerous. Would we like an escort out of town? A note is handed to him. More alarming news about the crowd. Pistols have been seen; even a machine gun is reported. Judge Foster asks kindly:

"Do you gentlemen want protection?"

Irwin replies meaningly:

"Judge, you know this country better than we do."

The judge does. He has been mayor of Tuscaloosa, member of the legislature, an officer in the Spanish-American war, a pillar of the church. Gravely, soothingly, he assures us that not a hair of our heads shall be harmed.

A telegram is handed to him. The effect is electric, astounding. The kindliness, courtesy, serene judicial calm, disappear in a flash. The venerable Judge Foster is gone and there remains the Southern slave holder, the infuriated master brandishing a whip. His eyes glare, his face muscles twitch as he shrieks:

"God damn the son of a bitch that sent me this telegram! I'll make him answer for it. I'll go to Birmingham—I'll go to New York. I'll kill the son of a bitch!"

Distinguished counsel press around the judge, soothing, sympathizing. McQueen looks at the telegram, finds he is referred to as one of the "lynch lawyers," and nobly assures the judge that it won't make any difference to him in his conduct of the case. Brandon whispers: "I didn't think the judge even *knew* those words." Then: "This'll stir up the niggers. Too bad, too bad. We know how to handle the niggers down here."

The telegram read:

"Two hundred thousand members and affiliates International Labor Defense demand you withdraw troops in trial Pippen Clark Harden withdraw local lynch lawyers and permit defense by ILD attorneys retained by families of defendants. Will expose your illegal manoeuvres nationally as counterpart Scottsboro.

"WILLIAM L. PATTERSON

National Secretary."

The judge is escorted to a side room. Preparations go on for assuring our safe departure. Major Jemmison of the militia is summoned, and begins to make his plans. The crowd is watching all doors. Occasionally, in the empty court room, we hear a wild yell. We look out the window. The crowd is milling around; some of them are dancing in the street.

Judge Foster comes back. He is himself again, and with a courtly gesture he says:

"Gentlemen, I am sorry. I shall stand by you and see that you are protected."

He is escorted out again. It begins to look like a curiously staged show. We wait for the next appearance. Sure enough, Judge Foster comes back a third time. He is again brandishing the telegram, and letting himself go.

"God damn the son of a bitch who sent this telegram," the judge shrieks. "I'll kill the bastard."

One of the deputies speaks up. "Judge, you won't have to do it. Somebody'll do it for you."

The judge makes his exit—and reappears, again magically composed. Soft spoken, courteous, he assures us we will be protected.

The rest is the record of a long and tense day spent in getting away from the mob. We waited three hours in the court room till the crowd was thinner. We were then disguised, smuggled out the back door to the county jail thirty feet away, taken underneath the jail to another exit, put into two cars, and driven out into the country. The cars turned back to the Tuscaloosa station, despite my objections, and there for a long seven minutes we sat waiting for the train, while the crowd grew more menacing. Two members of the mob got on the train, cut the airline, and at Cottondale, 13 miles out, we came to a stop. Several hundred of the mob had arrived. We heard tramping in the corridor outside our compartment, knocks on the dooor, and whispering and muttering. The break was quickly repaired and we got to Birmingham.

This Tuscaloosa case is the first one in which the I.L.D. was definitely prevented by the authorities from aiding the defense.

The tragic result:

Two weeks later Dan Pippen and A. T. Harden were dead, shot by a carefully organized lynch party, and Clarke, the third boy, with two bullet wounds, was fighting for life in the Tuscaloosa jail.

AN EDITORIAL ANNOUNCEMENT

With this issue the *New Masses* ceases publication as a monthly magazine. Its next appearance will be as a weekly.

In a sense, this decision has been forced upon us. Events are moving too swiftly for a monthly. In the course of four weeks situations arise, develop, and are succeeded by new and more pressing problems. History is being written with breath-taking rapidity. A swifter tempo of reporting, interpretation and comment is no longer merely desirable, it is vitally necessary.

We believe that never before has there been so great a need—and so great an opportunity—for a weekly revolutionary magazine. The bitter facts of four years of crisis have blasted the illusions of vast numbers. Millions are questioning the hitherto accepted tenets of American capitalism: "Any man who wants to work, can work." "There's always room at the top." "America—the land of opportunity." "A car in every garage."

This vast silent questioning has met no adequate answer in the press—daily, weekly, or monthly. There is a widespread, and growing, demand for more complete and realistic news of what is actually happening under the NRA. Why was the United Front delegation's historic visit to President Roosevelt, to insist on labor's fundamental rights, completely ignored in all the papers except the Communist press? Why has the naked Fascist character of the Soft Coal Code with its absolute prohibition of strikes been completely concealed from the people? For four years the press of this country has carried on a unanimous conspiracy of silence and falsehood about the crisis. For four years the so-called "liberal" weeklies have wabbled on the one hand and wavered on the other, grasped at straws, "looked before and after, and pined for what is not."

AN EDITORIAL ANNOUNCEMENT

The weekly *New Masses* will meet the demand for an uncompromising revolutionary interpretation of the news. It will cover the entire American scene—economics, politics, literature and the arts.

We are organizing our forces to begin publishing the *New Masses* as a weekly not later than the first of the year. We are grouping around the magazine, and enlisting the enthusiastic support of the best writers, critics, journalists and artists in the United States. We believe the weekly *New Masses* will represent the combined efforts of the most brilliant contributors writing and drawing in this country.

The weekly *New Masses* will positively NOT be edited for a limited audience of intellectuals. It will reach out for the broadest possible circulation among all stratas of workers and professionals. Where the monthly New Masses, limited by its publication period and its narrower appeal, reached thousands, we firmly believe that the weekly will reach scores of thousands.

The price of the weekly *New Masses* will be 10 cents; a yearly subscription, $3.50. Present subscribers to the monthly will of course be carried as subscribers of the weekly. We have set a goal of 20,000 paid subscribers to be secured before the first publication date.

The promotion work for the weekly gets under way immediately. At this time readers of the *New Masses* who wish to help make the success of the weekly certain and rapid are urged to do this: Send us at once the names of as many persons as you know who you believe will be interested in the weekly *New Masses*.